THE FALSE SERPENT KING

THE WOODLAND KINGDOM SERIES

BOOK TWO

H.J. NICHOLS

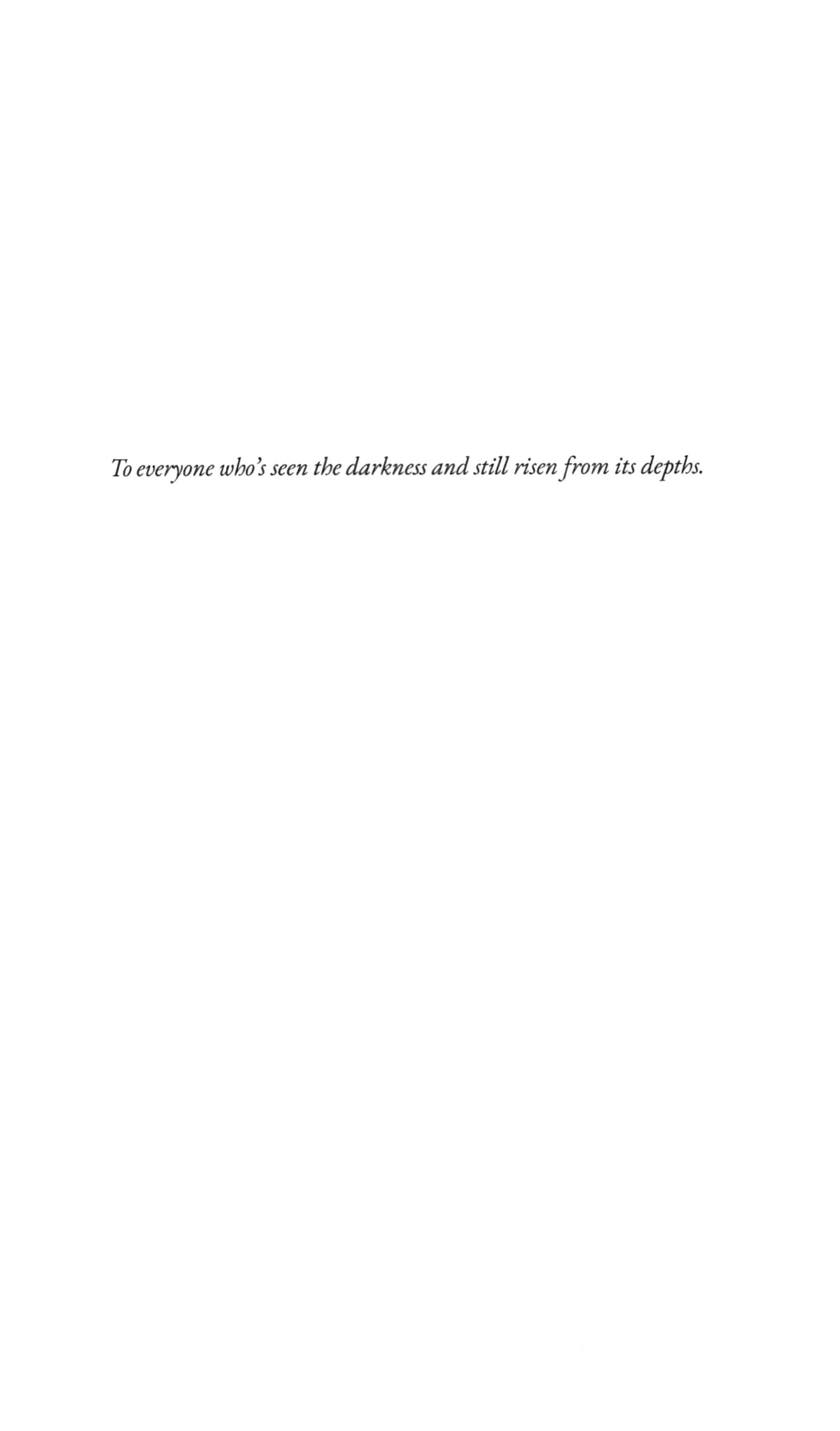

To everyone who's seen the darkness and still risen from its depths.

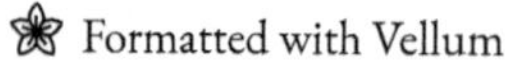 Formatted with Vellum

A NOTE FROM THE AUTHOR

The False Serpent King tackles sensitive topics, including: self-harm, suicidal ideation, suicide attempts, death, graphic violence, dubious consent, trauma, PTSD, discussion of child abuse (off-page to establish character arcs), explicit language, explicit sexual content, anxiety, and depression.

THE WOODLAND KINGDOM
THE HIGH HOUSES

House Cervidae
High King • Marik Vikander, House Serpent
High Queen • Mae Vikander

House Serpent
King Vasuki Vikander
Queen Minerva Vikander
Prince Asmo Vikander
Prince Marik Vikander (High King)

House Panthera
King Katze Kersey
Queen Issa Kersey
Princess Cassia Kersey
Prince Koa Kersey

House Ursidae
King Torben Canmore
Queen Artis Canmore
Prince Barrett Canmore

Princess Arella Canmore
Princess Eden Canmore

<u>House Canis</u>
King Conall White
Queen Sasha White
Prince August White
Princess Lola White

<u>High Fae (inactive)</u>
Princess Orla Ryley (deceased)
Princess Willa Ryley

PROLOGUE

A SLASH OF A BLADE. A burst of blood. A death sentence signed.

"With this oath, your soul will be forever mine," the devil croons to the prince.

"But why?" he whispers over the sound of his hammering heart.

The devil chuckles, low and sensual. "How do I know you'll never betray me?"

Because this is my destiny. This is who I was born to be. This is what I was created for.

The prince doesn't object. He takes the blade, and the devil drinks her fill.

PART ONE

CHAPTER 1
MAE

I HAD NEVER KNOWN the weight of true regret. Not until that night.

Sure, I've made my fair share of mistakes. A poor shoe choice on a rainy day or saying the wrong thing at the wrong time. But I had no idea regret was heavy enough to crush you into a version of yourself that you no longer recognized.

That it could push down on your chest, forcing the air from your lungs until you're hunched over and gasping. That it could sit on your shoulders and make every step forward nearly impossible. That it was heavy enough to manifest into something corporeal, capable of standing in front of you and mocking you with the truth. That it could say *You chose the wrong person. And it cost you everything.*

The starry sky shimmers through the translucent barrier that keeps the house hidden. I've been staring through it, willing the moon to move, to descend behind the trees and make room for the dawn. Like every night, it stares back at me.

Whenever I can't sleep, I sit on the cabin's porch, waiting for my skin to cool, for my heart to stop racing, for the memory of my dreams to slip away.

They don't go easily. They never do.

The moment sleep takes me, visions of my wedding fill every corner of my mind. Delicate ivory lace soaked in crimson. Marik's cruel grin and his cold, slender fingers as he reaches for the crown. Holly writhing on the floor as his flames consume her. William, and the acrid smell of burning flesh.

If those don't wake me first, Cora firing a bolt of lightning at my chest usually does the trick. Or a cambion sinking its teeth into my ankle, or Elle's neck, ripped open and gushing blood the color of the night.

I used to wake to Asmo shaking me, whispering hushed *It's okay*s as he held me in the dark. It's the only time I've let him touch me since I married his brother.

Since the day I lost my kingdom.

The wind whips past and I pull the blanket tighter around me, the worn deck boards groaning beneath me as I shift in my chair, as if they, too, are exhausted.

The front door opens. "Can't sleep?"

The question is a courtesy. Everyone knows I can't. They've all heard my screams whenever I try. Now, they're all too familiar with the creak of the floors as I shuffle from my bed, of the soft click of the front door behind me, of the rhythmic back-and-forth of the rocking chair in the dead of night.

"Me either." Ivan settles into the chair beside me, dressed in his usual all-black outfit reserved for his nightly trips into town. He rubs the white stubble lining his jaw as he leans back.

"Learn anything new?" I ask.

Every night, as soon as the moon rises, Ivan steps through the barrier that protects our sliver of safety from the outside world, and portals into town to grab the daily paper. Tonight, like every other night, he will spend hours analyzing each line, hoping to learn anything about Marik's next move.

So far, there's been nothing. It appears like everything within the kingdom is normal. Farming numbers, local events happening, updates on the weather...Even the gossip columns that Cally loved have been noticeably boring.

All the newspapers have been glaringly silent about the events of the wedding. Given the number of witnesses present, I find it nearly impossible there wouldn't be a single mention of what happened.

Cally, for one, would never be quiet about this. No, my best friend would be raising hell in the streets every day, screaming about what Marik and Cora did. My stomach clenches as I think about the only logical reasons there are for her silence. Between a cell or a grave, I'm not sure which option is better.

Yet another thing that haunts my dreams.

Ivan sets the folded *Glenn Gazette* in his lap. "Haven't looked yet." The bags under his eyes get darker every night without an update. The last month has aged him a decade.

He always joins me on the porch when he returns from town, both of us staring into the dark woods as he talks about everything and nothing, chasing the memories that haunt my dreams away with every word.

A throat clears behind me.

Asmo leans against the door frame, dressed in a plain black shirt and a pair of fraying cotton pajama pants, his midnight hair tousled and sleep still in his dark eyes. It's only been a month since the wedding, but his cheekbones are sharper than they were when we first met. A lack of food and an abundance of stress have begun to wear us all thin.

Ivan stands and tucks the newspaper under his arm. "Guess I better head inside and get started on this."

"You know, I don't have to be supervised out here," I grumble as Asmo replaces Ivan in the chair beside me. "I'm fine."

But the words taste like metal on my tongue. I'm probably the farthest I've been from *fine* in...well, ever.

Asmo is silent as he stares into the forest. Probably a good choice, as I'm sure he wants to refute my statement.

It's like this every time we're alone. Neither of us wants to acknowledge what happened between us, nor where we stand with each other. If I'm being honest, I prefer it this way. I'm only just now able to think about Marik's betrayal while keeping my pulse steady. And every time I think about my relationship with Asmo, all I can think about is Marik. How every word, every touch, was a calculated move to slither his way into my heart and onto my throne. How can I trust anyone, let alone his brother, after that?

Even so, Asmo's presence calms me in a way nothing else has been able to. He's been beside me every night since the wedding. In the days after, when I was lying on my deathbed, he only left me when necessary. He slept with his head draped across my stomach, his hand gripping mine. Every time I woke up screaming, he was there to brush my hair back, slick with sweat and tears from reliving nightmares that had come true.

Although I grumble about not needing Asmo to watch over me, I appreciate his silent, steady presence. Mostly, I appreciate his silence. Sometimes, he asks me if I want to talk. The answer is always no. When we're around the others, he's his usual snarky self. The normalcy of it has been another comfort.

"Just because my magic doesn't tell me you're lying, doesn't mean I don't know you are," Asmo says.

"Wow, that sentence was horrifying."

He snorts. "My sentence structure is the least horrifying thing about this entire shitshow, princess."

"Did Mummy and Daddy allow you to speak so poorly?" I quip in a haughty tone, hoping to direct the conversation away from me.

He doesn't bite. "You'll have to talk about it someday."

I'd rather face near death again than talk about my feelings with the male who rejected me, then had to rescue me from his brother. I've been grappling with the embarrassment of being tricked by Marik and conned by Cora for weeks now. Embarrassment, just like regret, weighs more every day.

Asmo's right—I *will* have to talk about it someday, but I'm content to wait until I'm back on the throne I never wanted.

"There's something I keep thinking about," I say.

Asmo's chair creaks as he leans back. "Hm?"

"Where do you think the witnesses from the wedding are? Everything I've seen in the papers...It's like nothing happened, right?" He nods slowly. "I don't understand how nobody's come forward. And what about the High Houses? Koa? August? Their families were there, fighting with us. Why aren't they saying anything?"

"Do we know for certain the witnesses are alive?" Asmo's voice is quiet, but it cuts through me all the same.

Although he echoes my earlier thoughts, voicing the theory feels like a loss. I refuse to give that idea any weight. Cally has to be alive. I won't think about the alternative. "I saw them leave." Their looks of terror as they fled are yet another thing I can't forget.

"Doesn't mean they left the court, princess." His voice is low. Somber.

The nickname feels patronizing this time, and I hate that I love it. It always brings me back to the first time I met him. It's so easy and familiar to fall back into this aspect of our relationship.

"You think Marik would do that?" I can't say the words. Even *thinking* that the person I chose to marry might be responsible for the deaths of innocent civilians has my lungs constricting.

Asmo shrugs, but his eyes darken. "I don't know my brother like I thought I did. After everything he's done so far...I'd say it's within the realm of possibility."

There were children there, mothers shielding their babies from the living nightmares that crawled from the hells. Shame is a constant companion when I think about my involvement in this, but it threatens to consume me now.

"Have you thought about Ivan's theory?" Asmo asks.

I've been thinking about it all day, pacing the yard in front of the cabin until the grass was flattened and the sun began to dip behind the trees.

Ivan first brought it up yesterday, all of us seated in the cramped living room after yet another day of nothing. Holly chewing slowly, her scarred face averted from the rest of us; Asmo staring at me, me trying to avoid his gaze; Luca frowning into his bowl of tinned beans, the best fare this deserted cabin has to offer.

"I believe Elle is pretending to be you on the throne," Ivan had blurted as we all ate our dinner. "She's the only one who could pull that off. With her antlers and a glamour over her hair, it could work."

I shook my head. "She wouldn't."

"No. Not voluntarily," he responded gravely.

Bile burned in the back of my throat. The thought of Marik forcing Elle to do anything... "Couldn't anyone just glamour antlers?" I asked desperately.

Asmo tossed his hand up. Antlers appeared from both sides of his head, but they looked...off. I reached for them, but my hand only grasped air. "Point made."

With another wave of his hand, the antlers disappeared. "Glamouring something like your hair or your facial appearance is easier, but to glamour something that was never there before—like antlers—is too easy to disprove. Marik would never risk it."

Now, I say, "Elle would never do it."

Asmo offers me a half-smile. "I don't think Marik will give her much of a choice, princess."

A shiver works its way down my spine. Marik is one of the best manipulators I've ever had the displeasure of meeting, second only to Cora, the witch who pretended to be my aunt for the last twenty-five years of my life. Not just any witch—the First Witch. The most powerful witch in the kingdom's history.

Now Elle is in Marik's and Cora's hands. And it's all my fault.

"I don't want to talk about this anymore," I say lamely. Shoving everything away is the only way I'm able to survive right now.

Marik played me like a fiddle. I was so fucking stupid and naïve, and it's endangered everyone I've ever cared about. Cally is gone, Elle is trapped, and I have no idea how to fix this. Every time I think about it, hot shame floods me, and my brain feels like it's seizing inside my head. So, I don't. Any time it comes up, I shut down, and shut it off.

Asmo's mouth hardens into a straight line as he stares at me silently. I can't stand the disappointment in his eyes. I turn back to the forest, the air between us filled with words left unsaid. I sink further into my chair as regret returns, even heavier than it was this morning.

CHAPTER 2
MAE

TODAY IS MARKET DAY, and I have been dressed and waiting for the sound of Asmo's door for hours. Finally, his bedroom door clicks open, then shuts. His footsteps grow softer as he nears the living room and offers someone a muffled greeting. I throw the covers back and shove my feet into boots that have seen better days.

"I have been cooped up in this Mother-forsaken house for over a month," I say as I approach the living room, foregoing any kind of salutation. I straighten and say in the queenliest voice I can muster, "I'm coming with you."

Luca freezes over his bowl of oatmeal.

Asmo looks me up and down. I tilt my head, daring him to challenge me. "And you've been half-dead for nearly half that time," he says.

"Yes, well, I'm fine now," I say, crossing my arms over my chest. "But I'm going to lose my mind if I stay here any longer."

His brows draw together and a frown flashes across his features. As if he knows that in fact, I'm not fine, and my mind is already lost.

He tosses me a canvas bag. "Fine. But if you're coming, you're going to help carry the food back."

I snatch it from the air, trying to smother the smile that threatens to take hold. I expected more of an argument.

Luca drops his dirty bowl into the basin and turns. "You think that's safe?"

Asmo shrugs and walks past me, reaching for the front door. "I think she can make her own decisions."

"She's our queen. She needs to be protected," Luca retorts.

"*She's* right here," I say, "and she's coming with you. I can protect myself. Besides, you've been going into town for weeks now and the worst thing you've seen is humans arguing over the price of eggs."

Luca huffs a sigh and shoves his feet into his boots.

"You know what, Luca? Why don't you stay here?" I ask cheerfully. "I think Asmo and I can handle the market trip ourselves."

Luca freezes, his foot halfway into one scuffed leather boot. He glares up at me, and I grin. Guilt prickles, but I need to get out of this house.

"Come on, princess," Asmo says behind me.

Luca finishes shoving his boots on, shoulders his bag, and motions toward the door. "After you, Your Highness." The title drips with condescension.

I swallow my retort. It never helps anything.

This isn't the first time Luca and I have gotten snippy with each other. None of us are used to living in a cramped, abandoned cabin in the woods, terrified that Marik or Cora will come bursting down our door one day. We're all fraying at the edges. Nobody knows what to do or how to get back to the throne. In all their years helping the High Throne, Luca and Ivan have never had to deal with a thousand-year-old witch stealing it. We spend most nights arguing over our limited options. Lately, those arguments have grown quieter, shorter. I tell myself we're not giving up.

Before we can step through the protective barrier, Asmo stops me with an arm and looks at me pointedly. "Glamour."

I throw my hand up, my magic hiding my antlers and pointed ears. Asmo and Luca do the same. They look so...normal. Shorter, rounded ears, and frankly, duller. Just like humans. Perfect for our destination.

Asmo funnels us as close to town as we dare—just far enough not to risk anyone seeing us appear out of thin air and exposing our hybrid status. The blue sky is full of white, puffy clouds, and I raise my face to the morning sun and beam. For the first time in weeks, it feels like I can breathe. I've been longing to explore the forest that surrounds the house, but I haven't wanted to risk it. Besides, it's not like anyone would have let me wander outside of the barrier.

"Let us know if you need to take a break," Luca says beside me.

"Why would I?" I ask.

"The walk is long. You're still recovering, are you not?"

He might have a point. Only two weeks ago, I was still bedridden. When I was finally able to get up, every muscle in my body ached for days. Even now, I can feel my legs growing tired. On instinct, I reach for the black mark that mars the center of my chest, the remnants of the bolt that almost took more than my kingdom. It still aches, but that, at least, lessens every day.

Holly, on the other hand, still spends most of her days in bed. Her burns are mostly healed now, but spending so much time in bed has left her weak.

"She'll be fine," Asmo says, but I can tell he's not certain.

We fall into a silence, the three of us walking single file down the path as the human town of Briar's Glen draws closer. Clean, white limestone buildings stand crowded together, thatched roofs forming a short silhouette against the blue sky. Tiny windows dot the buildings, overgrowing flower boxes nestled below.

"When we arrive, we're going straight to the market. It should be opening as we get there. We get in and we get out," Luca says.

I nod in understanding.

The town is quiet, so different from Pinebend on a sunny morning, always bustling with hybrids as soon as the sun rose. A thick lump forms in my throat as I think about the town that I called home. About mornings spent with Cally, as we did our daily inventory over shared cups of coffee in Bound, the bookstore we created together. I swallow the lump, wincing as it goes down.

The market is nearly empty, only a few people perusing the stalls and picking out the best produce. A mother and son share a pastry on a nearby bench, their rounded ears the telltale signs of their humanity. Luca mutters something about vegetables before leaving Asmo and me by a vendor selling fresh bread.

"One loaf of sourdough, please," I say to the portly woman.

Her answering smile is tired. "Three coins."

I nudge Asmo. I certainly didn't bring any money. He digs in his pockets and my mouth waters as I plop the loaf into my bag.

"We don't normally get bread," Asmo says as we walk away from the vendor.

"I know. Thank the Mother I'm here."

He shakes his head, but there's a rare smile on his face. We grab the rest of the necessities—apples, bananas, a lavender-scented bar of soap, rice, and eggs—without incident. The market gets busier as we shop, humans joining with their own bags and carts to load up and bring back to their families. Asmo pulls me to a cart overflowing with flowers— brilliant hues of light pink, pearly white, buttercup yellow, and crimson red.

The floral scent brings me back to childhood, and I can't help but smile. When I was younger, I would spend hours pretending I had my own flower shop, plucking perfect blooms and arranging bursting bouquets.

An old woman sits on a stool beside a collection of wildflowers. The sun beams down on her, highlighting her warm, brown skin and salt-and-pepper hair. She smiles in greeting, the motion pulling at wrinkles.

"These are beautiful," I say as I reach for a bouquet of light pink carnations.

She nods appreciatively. "All grown in my garden."

"I'll take a bundle." When I turn to Asmo for the coin purse, he's eyeing a small bouquet of red flowers that look like drooping hearts.

"What are these?" he asks the vendor.

"Bleeding hearts. Native to the Deer Court."

Asmo huffs a laugh under his breath. "Of course," he mutters. "These, too."

She wraps the bleeding hearts and the carnations in old newspaper and ties them together with a blue string. I tuck them into my bag. "Four coins," the woman says.

I blink. "Are you sure? Only four?"

She nods, but it's sad. Tired. "Market's turned. Most folk are sticking to the essentials. Not a lot of extra money to go around for things you can't eat or wear."

"Wh—"

"Hard times," Asmo agrees solemnly and hands over the payment. "Thank you." He grips my elbow and tugs me away. "Princess, you can't—"

"Stop. I know. You don't have to say it," I snap. Just like that, embarrassment has returned, another weight on my shoulders. Asking the locals questions only risks exposing us. I forgot where we were and who we were pretending to be. I could have ruined everything with that one question.

We find Luca leaning nonchalantly against a wall, his bag on his shoulder overflowing with fresh vegetables. A flash of relief crosses his features when he spots us. Asmo and I follow him as he sets a quick pace through the town square, which has grown even busier since this morning. We weave around men and women, muttering apologies as we go. I forgot how slow and clunky humans are.

It's been years since I left the town I grew up in and moved to Pinebend. Growing up as the only hybrid in Black Hollow was hard. Although the humans that live in the hybrid courts are friendly, the ones in my hometown were not. My antlers alone were enough to make me stand out from the other kids, but my magic was another thing. I had to make myself smaller whenever I was around my "friends," careful to avoid scaring them with the small amounts I used.

I shake my head as I think about how well Cora's plan worked. She didn't even have to do anything to stunt my magical abilities. The environment I was in took care of that. She was always there to comfort me whenever the others were too mean. She was there to be the good guy, when she was really the villain the entire time.

"Hey," Asmo calls to Luca, pulling me from memories of another town from another time. We're stopped in front of a café, the smell of freshly poured coffee and fresh pastries making my mouth water and my stomach do flips. "Let's stop here."

"We've talked about this," Luca says. "We can't—"

"We can and we are," Asmo says with finality. Even with the glamour dimming his features, he still commands power and respect. I fear Luca might explode from anger someday soon, but I find I don't care if that day is today. I haven't had a coffee in a month and it's now all I can think about.

The front door dings as we step inside. With the greatest amount of self-control I can muster, I only order one cup. They call our pretend names and we snag a table by the window.

The first sip of coffee is akin to a religious experience, even though I've never considered myself religious. At least, not like some. I worship the Mother and credit Her for our creations, as we all do. But I don't often find myself praying to Her. Although, maybe that would help get us out of this mess.

I send a quick thanks to the heavens before taking another sip.

"I know I didn't give you a choice and that me coming might have complicated things, but I really needed this," I say, breaking the silence. "Thank you."

One corner of Asmo's mouth twitches upward. A second smile in an hour. More than I've seen in the last few days.

Luca leans back in his chair, the legs scraping against the wooden floor beneath. "Sorry if I've been..."

"An asshole," Asmo responds.

Luca rubs the back of his neck. "Yeah, an asshole. This whole thing has made me a version of myself I don't like much."

I find myself empathizing with Luca, but I'm not exactly interested in letting him off the hook that easily. "Thank you for the apology," I say. I take another sip of coffee and turn back to the window. A couple walks past, hands interlocked as they stroll down the brick-paved streets. A pang of jealousy hits me as I watch them. The simplicity of it. The normalcy of it.

Moments later, another couple walks past, but their faces are pale. The man urges the woman forward, his hand resting protectively against the small of her back. He looks in the opposite direction and quickens his pace.

My heart thuds in my chest. *Relax, Mae. Maybe he saw an ex-lover, or someone else he doesn't want his partner to see.*

But then someone else starts running, coming from the same direc-

tion the man was looking back at. A woman follows him, skin flushed
and arms pumping as she passes the man.

Asmo wraps his arm around the back of my chair and leans forward,
staring out the window with rapt attention. The café door bangs open,
muting the sound of the bell ringing above, and a man stumbles in, bent
over and gasping for air.

"Everything alright?" someone asks.

He shakes his head, then looks up, face somehow pale and flushed.
"Demons."

My heart stutters. A witch could easily be confused with a demon.

Asmo goes rigid. "What do you mean?" I've heard this tone from
him before. Violence followed soon after.

The man slams the deadbolt, locking the door. "Block the doors
with whatever you can find."

"We need to leave," Asmo mutters to Luca.

A woman and her son—the same ones from the market—bang on
the door. "Please!" she cries. But the man keeps piling tables and chairs
in front of the door.

"Hey!" someone yells. "Let them in!"

"Are you crazy?" he fires back. "There are other places they can go."

Heat flushes through me, and I stalk toward him. "Let them in.
Now."

The man looks over my shoulder. "Control her, man."

Asmo's deep chuckle comes from behind me. I shove past the man
and start dismantling the barrier of chairs. He yells at me to stop, but I
ignore him and toss more chairs out of the way. That is, until his
clammy hand wraps around my wrist. He opens his mouth to say something I'm sure he would regret, but he freezes as the room darkens.

"You have two seconds to remove that hand from her." The man's chest
heaves as he stares at me, but Asmo's next words have him dropping my hand
like it's on fire. "Or I will show you exactly what it's like to face a demon."

I bare my teeth at him and he skitters off. "Anyone else?" I call to the
group of men who were content to let a woman and child be left in the
street. They all back away. I shove the last table out of the way and fling
the door open. They stumble in, tear tracks staining the boy's face.

"Thank you," the woman gasps, shutting the door firmly behind her and flipping the deadbolt.

"What's going on out there?" I ask. She shakes her head frantically, her gaze wild and unfocused. I place my hands on her shoulders and force her to look at me. "Please."

Her light blue eyes meet mine. "I don't know—I've never seen them before. But they had black..." She trails off, hand circling in the air as she searches for the right word.

"Black auras around them?" I supply.

She nods quickly. "Yes. There were these...ghost animals with them." I freeze. Cambions and osseri I know. But...ghost animals? "Dead animals, but they were alive," she clarifies. "That's the best way I know how to describe what I saw. I've never seen anything like it."

As if on cue, shadows begin to fill the street.

"Princess, away from the door, please."

I back away slowly, stopping when I bump into Asmo.

"We should never have stopped here," Luca grumbles.

"Not helpful," I fire back. "What do we do?" I ask Asmo.

He stares out the window intently, his body rigid. "Keep our cover if we can." He turns to Luca. "Get everyone into the back and hide. We can throw up a sound and protective barrier." His voice is a hurried whisper.

Luca nods and begins ushering people into the back. Without a thought, I twirl my hand and summon the protective barrier, casting it as a wall between us and the storefront. Asmo summons the sound barrier.

"You've gotten good at that," he whispers, gesturing toward the barrier that hides us from whatever is roaming the streets.

"I should hope so. I've had nothing else to do except practice my magic for the last two weeks."

In fact, that's all I've been able to do, and I've been happy to do it. In the week after Cora nearly killed me, my magic lay dormant. Asmo thinks it was because it was all going toward healing me. But it didn't take long for it to come back in a rush. Since then, it's been dying to be let out. Some days, it feels like my body is a dam holding it back. Practicing has been the only thing that has helped keep it tame.

"Shit," Asmo whispers.

I look back to the window. My stomach drops all the way to my feet. The woman was right.

Three witches stalk down the streets in all black, red leather straps tied around their wrists, some twisted version of animals trudging behind them. A grizzly bear lumbers past the window with milky eyes and a festering wound on its chest. It opens its mouth, revealing rotting teeth. A black panther with matted fur and a fatal wound in its side slinks beside the bear. But instead of red flowing from the wound, black blood has been crusted over. Like the witches, shadowy auras cling to them.

"Time to go," Luca says as he emerges from the back. "I think we can funnel away undetected."

"What if the witches return? How are they going to protect themselves?" I protest.

"Don't care," Asmo says, reaching for me and Luca. The café disappears around us, the forest of the cabin materializing in its place. With the barrier hiding the cabin, it looks just like a clearing in a forest.

"We have to go back and help those people. We're the only ones who can," I say the moment we step inside the barrier.

"You're our priority, Mae. We cannot protect everyone right now." Asmo glares at me, ready for a fight. But I don't give him one. He has a point. If we die protecting a small faction of humans before we can get Marik and Cora off the throne, even more will die.

"If the witches are already this close, it's possible they know we're here. We need to leave. Now," Luca says before storming inside the house.

Asmo helps Holly from her bedroom, a supportive arm out to steady her. My throat grows tight from seeing her still so weak. We're lucky Marik's flames didn't kill her. Even now, she spends most of her time sleeping, thanks to the medicinal sedatives we've been putting in her food and water to help her recover faster. Over the last week, her burns have turned from bright pink to nearly white.

She waves Asmo away as she trudges down the hall, but he still hovers behind her. Ivan portals us to a small cabin on the edge of another human town within the Deer Court. Luca approaches the house and peers through a grimy window before entering the front door.

The living room is covered in a thick layer of dust. The floorboards groan as we explore the tiny house that was abandoned long ago. Somehow, in all the craziness of the last hour, I managed to grab the bags of food from the market. I find a ceramic vase on a kitchen shelf and brush off the dust before plopping the bouquets of flowers inside.

I'm wiping down the counters with an old rag when Ivan walks into the cramped kitchen. "So, what happened?" he asks.

I recount our trip to Briar's Glen. "Well," he says as he leans against the counter with a sigh. "We hoped it wouldn't, but we thought it might come to this." He's right. We've been waiting for Marik and Cora to make a move, to extend their power. I just wasn't expecting them to take over a human town. With witches. And undead animals. "Have you given any more thought to my theory?"

I nod. His theory that Elle's the one on the throne. "I think it's possible. I'm not sure how else they could proceed as if everything's normal. Someone must be pretending to be me, and Elle makes the most sense." Even if it makes my heart lurch in my chest. "What do we do, Ivan?"

He shakes his head. "I'm not sure yet. Don't worry, though. We'll figure something out." But his words ring hollow.

Asmo joins me outside, sitting beside me as I hug my legs and stare out into the darkness. There's no porch or rocking chairs here. Just a blanket and the cold, hard ground. He doesn't ask to share the blanket, and I don't offer.

"What the fuck were those things?" I whisper. The memory of the undead animals and their rotting teeth hasn't left me since we left the café.

"The Cursed," Asmo responds.

"*What* were they, Asmo?" I press.

He runs a hand through his hair. "They're from a faction of the underworld. They're created by the witches, who force them to live in damnation to serve as their pets."

The underworld, also called *the hells*, is not something that's talked about in Woodland. The heavens, yes, but never the hells.

"What do you mean?"

He stretches his legs out in front of him and leans back, resting on the palms of his hands. "Please tell me you're not one of the hybrids that doesn't believe in the Sister."

"I don't," I admit.

There are some that believe in the Sister, the Mother's antithesis, and the ruler of what is below. But when you believe in the Mother, you believe that all living creations go to the heavens, as a death means that the body is restored to the earth, the only payment to ascend. You don't believe in an alternative.

But the animals from today did not ascend.

He sighs. "Okay. Well. The witches are created by the Sister. And the Cursed are one of the Sister's creations, as are the cambions and the osseri."

"How do you know that?" I ask.

He speaks of it as if it's fact, but the Sister is just a fable, a nightmare told to scare children. But so are the osseri, and those are real.

"Dark magic, which originated in the hells, was an important part of my education."

"That's how you knew about the cambions when you saved me the first time."

He nods, and we drift back into silence. I hug my knees tighter and fight a shiver as I think about that night, about how helpless I felt as the hollow-eyed girl dragged me into the woods.

Asmo once told me that he wasn't a good male, but every version I've seen of him has been just that—good. Since we've been here, all he's done is care for me. But this conversation is a reminder that there's still so much that I don't know about him. How does he know so much about dark magic? How does he know of the underworld and its creatures? How did Asmo and Marik experience the same childhood, yet turn out so differently? Or did they?

That's the question that's been lingering in the back of my mind since the wedding. Is Asmo someone I can trust?

CHAPTER 3
ELLE

It's been forty-five days. Forty-five days since I saw Willa—Cora—kill Mae.

Forty-five days since they dragged me from the throne room.

Forty-five days since they threw me in an empty room and chained me to the floor.

Four days since they broke me.

On day ten, two guards drag me to the throne room, their rough hands pinching my arms as they pull me through the door.

The throne room looks like nothing ever happened.

There's no longer a giant gaping hole in the ceiling. The massive crater in the floor is now filled and replaced with cool marble tiles, no longer the warm hardwoods that I loved. Marik sits on one of the twin thrones where Mae should be, long legs sprawled. A black metal crown of snakes wrapped around branches rests upon his raven hair. A glistening ebony chain is wrapped around his forearm, black diamonds glinting in the light as he pops plump, green grapes into his mouth.

"Hello, dear," he says, a grin on his face. It only grows when I sneer at him. "Chain her to the other throne," he commands the guards.

They abide, dumping me in the other throne of branches and berries like a sack of potatoes. The moment I'm free, I stand, ready to run. But a wall of magic forces me back down.

"You will sit and you will behave," Marik orders, his voice deep and commanding.

I glare at him from the throne. "What do you want?" Venom laces every word.

He crosses one long leg over the other. "I am offering you the chance to become High Queen."

He cannot be serious.

I remain silent.

"Okay, let's try again," he says, tilting his head. "You have two options. You can cooperate and pretend to be Mae. You can sit beside me as my wife, and we can rule the kingdom together. This is the opportunity of a *lifetime*, a chance to be the powerful queen you've always wanted to be."

My jaw remains clenched. I have never wanted that.

"Or," he says, still with that stupid grin on his chiseled face, "I force you to pretend to be Mae. And I can assure you, darling, that will not be very pleasant for you." He plunks another grape into his mouth and watches me carefully as he chews.

"Over my dead body will I pretend to be Mae," I snarl.

His smile grows, splitting his face. "That's what I thought you'd say. And I'm so glad you did."

Before I can respond, my wrists and ankles are cuffed by invisible threads of magic. My head slams back, pain flaring as it strikes the throne. A heavy, sinking sensation settles in my stomach.

Marik comes to stand before me, holding the black chain in his hands. No, not a chain—a necklace of a snake, the head biting the tip of its tail. He unclasps it and places it around my neck, the metal cold as ice. I hiss as it makes contact with my skin.

Marik stands back, surveying the necklace now resting on collar-bones that have turned too sharp. He opens his mouth, and fangs extend from his upper gumline. He uses one to prick his wrist, his face remaining apathetic, even as blood spots. He smears it on the snake's head and mutters something under his breath. At his words, a chill spreads through me. My magic disappears, leaving an empty well inside of me.

I reach, I claw, I scramble for it, but it's gone. As if it never existed. "What did you do?" I ask in horror.

Blood drips from his wrist, trailing down his forearm. "I gave you a choice, and this is what you chose. From here on, you'll only speak when you're spoken to."

I open my mouth, ready to let loose a string of foul words, but it snaps shut. Every time I try to open it, it's like my brain has lost control over my muscles. The restraints around my wrists and ankles disappear. With every ounce of power in my body, I will myself to stand.

But nothing happens.

I'm paralyzed.

My eyes are the only part of me that I can control. I stare at him, the blood in my veins a terrifying mix of the flames of anger and the icy crawl of horror. But neither of them manifest. Because my magic is gone.

He made me a prisoner inside my own body.

I'll kill him for this. I'll tear his limbs from his body, rip his precious fangs from his gums, tie him to a whipping post—

"Don't forget, *Mae.* You had a choice," he says with a smirk before turning and walking toward the exit. He pauses in the doorway. With a flick of his wrist, the lights extinguish.

And I'm stuck here.

In my own body.

In my new cage.

T he first time I hear his voice in my head is on day thirteen.

Are you ready to cooperate yet? he croons in my mind, low and sensual. It sends shivers down my spine.

Fuck you, I bite back.

His chuckle is the only answer. If I could move, I'd claw my pointed ears from my head.

I haven't moved from this damned throne in days. My muscles ache, my backside numb from sitting here. Since I'm not given leave to use the bathroom, the guards visit once per day to clean and dry my soiled clothes. I've lost any sense of shame by the fourth time. My only reprieve is when Marik loosens the hold on my face and neck to allow me to eat the meager meals they hand-feed me.

Even that is quickly taken away when I start spitting the food out. He wants me—no, *needs* me—alive.

So, day thirteen is also the day I decide I have to kill myself.

On day eighteen, Marik strolls into the throne room. He walks toward me, eyeing me up and down.

"Hello, darling," he says before coming to a stop in front of the throne. I shift my gaze to meet his, but it stops at his chest because I can't move my neck. "Here's what's going to happen," he says, clasping his pale hands together. "I am going to release you. Together, we are going to walk to your new living quarters. You will not fight me, nor will you try to escape. Nod if you understand me." My head bobs up and down, despite my inner thoughts screaming for it not to. "Right. Of course you understand, because those are my orders. Now, follow me."

Once again, my body does as he wills it. I stand and instantly stumble. My knees collide with the marble floor and pain shoots through me. My instinct is to gasp, but my jaw is locked.

Marik doesn't even look back.

My traitorous body rises and follows him from the throne room, every other step a stumble as weak legs fight to keep up.

He leads me to the foyer. Just as I think we're about to walk out the doors, he ascends the grand staircase. My thighs scream as I follow him, and I watch in dread as he walks to Mae's living quarters.

"I thought you might be more comfortable staying in your own space. It might be nice for you to sleep in a bed. You'll have regular access to food and water." He looks back at me, his face crinkling in disgust. "You've lost too much weight. Mae was thin, but not that thin."

He pauses, waiting for me to respond. I will my mouth shut.

Yes, Marik, he says in my head.

"Yes, Marik," I echo against my will. *Yes, Your Highness.* "Yes, Your Highness." This time, shame and anger burn, twin flames stoking my hatred for him.

He opens the door, but I don't move.

"Does everything have to be so difficult with you?" he grumbles.

He forces me to enter the living quarters. Everything is exactly as we left it on the morning of Mae's wedding. Dirty champagne flutes rest on the coffee table, empty bottles left discarded nearby, an ivory hairbrush in the armchair.

I grit my teeth as my body turns to face Marik.

He stands before me, posture ramrod straight. "You will be able to move freely in here. You are not to leave, nor are you to harm yourself in any way. I'll be back in a few days." He rests an ice-cold hand on my face and cups my cheek. "And remember, darling, I'm here—" he taps the necklace resting at the base of my throat, "—and here," he says, placing a gentle, cold kiss on my forehead.

The only thing I hear is the sound of my screams ringing inside my head.

M arik leaves me alone in my quarters for the next five days. I spend all five trying to break the necklace, but I can't. So, I start trying to kill myself. But every time, Marik's hold over me forces me to stop.

A knife rests in a wooden block on the kitchen counter, but my hand freezes when I reach for it. I fill the bathtub to the brim and hold myself under the water, but my body surges upward when my lungs begin to scream.

It's a mercy that I'm allowed to cry.

On day twenty-five, Marik walks through the front door, startling me from my book. I was shocked when I opened it for the first time and my hands didn't slam it shut. Apparently, I'm allowed to read. It's been a small comfort, getting lost in worlds other than my own.

I sit up straight and watch him carefully as he strolls in. The ebony crown sits on his head, complementing his all-black outfit. "Honey, I'm home," he says, dark eyes twinkling with the joke. Bile rises up my throat. "I thought you'd be happier to see me." His bottom lip sticks out in a pout. "How about a walk?"

I brace myself, expecting to feel my body rise. But it doesn't.

"Do you want to join me?" he asks, looking at me expectantly.

"Am I allowed to speak?" I ask.

He rolls his eyes. "Don't be so dramatic. Besides, I did say you could speak when spoken to, didn't I?" His tone is pleasant. I can't wait for the day I can rip his tongue out.

"My answer is no."

"Suit yourself," he says with a shrug, then leaves.

For the next nine days, he returns and asks me the same question. Every day, I say no. Until day thirty-five, when I give in and say yes. I haven't felt the sun on my skin or the wind in my hair in over a month.

Marik's brows rise infinitesimally at my acceptance of his offer, as if my response surprises him. "Let's go then."

I stand, already having grabbed a pair of shoes before his arrival. He glances down at them but doesn't say anything. He leads us down the staircase and out the front door.

The sun is absent, but the soft caress of the breeze on my skin wraps around me like a friend. My skin is pebbled with goosebumps, but I savor every second. We stroll past guards in armor as black as midnight, a far cry from the forest-green uniforms they used to wear.

"I'm going to give you another chance," Marik says. "The kingdom thinks Mae is alive. I would like to keep that illusion. It benefits me and it benefits the kingdom. They already had to go through the loss of their dear High Family, didn't they? I'd hate to break it to them that the only living relative of the great King Silas is now dead."

My heart stutters at the mention of Mae's death. No, her murder. I can't decide if I want to drop to my knees and scream, or if I want to reach for Marik's dagger and slit his throat. It doesn't matter. I wouldn't be able to do either if I tried.

"Like I said, I can make you. However, it's a lot easier for me if you just go along with it. Then I don't have to worry about dictating your every move. What do you think?" His tone is maddeningly rational, like I'm the one who's being completely unreasonable.

He's right. He can make me, and there's nothing I can do to fight him. I've been trying for thirty-five days. Whether I want to or not, he *will* put me on the throne and force me to pretend to be Mae.

I meet his gaze. "I think I'd rather die."

O n day forty-one, Marik bursts through my front door. Two guards follow him, dragging a body behind them. I shoot to my feet, but Marik throws out a hand and freezes me in my place.

The guards drag a young deer hybrid, maybe eighteen at the most. The body of a man, but facial features that haven't been hardened by the world yet. He's limp, his eyes closed. One guard holds him up while the other takes the male's right hand and holds it to the wooden fireplace mantel.

Marik strides forward, gleaming metal in his hands.

A hammer in one.

Nails in the other.

He walks up to the male and places a nail in the center of his hand. He drives it into the mantel with one swoop of the hammer.

The male jerks, his eyes flying open as a singular scream cuts through the air.

A tear slides down my cheek as Marik forces me to watch the whole thing. He hammers the male's left hand and then his feet into the ground.

Sobs wrack his body. My heart pounds against my ribcage. I reach for my magic to do *something*, but Marik's hold on me is too strong.

He turns and points the hammer at me, hatred and fury gleaming in his eyes. "You did this. *You.* I gave you every opportunity to play nice." His face is flushed, and a lock of hair slips forward, brushing against his forehead. "For every day you say no to me, I will nail another body to the walls. These people will die and I will force you to sit here and watch them. So, which is it? Are you going to do this the easy way? Or do you want to be responsible for people dying, just to spite me? Eventually, you'll hate yourself even more than you hate me."

A tear cuts down my cheek and drops to the floor.

"Well?" he growls.

I look at him, at the hammer hanging loosely at his side, the wild look in his eyes. At the monster who killed Etta, who betrayed Mae, who has imprisoned me in the only places I've ever known—my home, and my body.

I meant it when I said I'd rather die than go along with his plan. But there is no way I can live with myself if the other option is innocent people dying. I meet his gaze, every muscle quivering in anger.

"Fine. I'll do it."

CHAPTER 4
MAE

THE NEXT FEW weeks pass by in a blur, every day nearly the same—training with Asmo, pacing the strip of yard within the barrier, and wanting to pull my hair out. Asmo continues to challenge me, urging me to push my magic further. Our training sessions always leave me physically spent and mentally exhausted as my heart wars with my brain. I still can't deny the pull I feel toward him, but that one question constantly niggles in the back of my mind—*Can I trust him?*

Holly is now able to walk around the house without assistance and has begun to join me as I trample a path into the grass. It's been nice having another female around again. Even Luca's attitude has lessened since she's been more active.

She's different, a quieter version of herself, but so was I in my recovery. Most days, I still am. Almost dying has a way of turning you into a shell of yourself.

We sit in silence together on the strip of the front lawn, both of us staring at the moon. Although the view is technically different from the last house, it's still mostly the same—a dark forest filled with the sounds of birds tweeting, squirrels skittering along branches, and cicadas buzzing.

"Hey." Ivan's voice comes from behind us. "You two need to see this."

I force myself to stand, pulling the blanket tight around me, and shuffle inside. A fire crackles in the stone hearth as I lower myself into the armchair closest to it. I urge the flames higher, my skin prickling from the sudden shift in temperature. It doesn't take long for me to feel warm, but I stay with the blanket wrapped tightly around me.

Asmo watches me from the other side of the room. I look away, thinking of my first date with Marik. Of the way the flames reflected in his dark eyes, as they do with Asmo now. Despite the fire, a chill works its way up my spine.

A newspaper lays sprawled on the coffee table—Ivan's bedside table, as he likes to call it. This cabin is small, with only three bedrooms to split between the five of us. Ivan chose to sleep on the couch.

"What is it?" Luca asks from the hallway. His gray hair is tousled from sleep. Like Ivan, his wrinkles grow deeper every day.

Ivan settles onto the sofa and hunches over the newspaper. Holly studies the fire that rages in the hearth. With her burn scars, her pale flesh was made even paler. The flames reached her right cheek before they went out. The scar there glistens, then disappears from my view as she turns back and paces in the other direction.

"What's going on?" I ask.

Ivan looks up from the paper. "Apparently, the High King and Queen will be holding a tithe in a week's time."

Surely I didn't hear him right. "What?"

"All citizens of the Deer Court are expected to attend and offer some sort of payment to the High Crown," Ivan explains.

"I understand what a tithe is. But that's not something we do," I say.

"According to this," Ivan says, gesturing toward the paper, "*you* do. They didn't give a reason, just said it's now mandatory, per the High Queen."

"And if people don't pay?" I ask.

Ivan shrugs. "Doesn't say."

Fucking Marik. I turn to Asmo. "What do you think the real reason is behind this? The High Crown doesn't need any more money."

He shakes his head, frowns. "Easy way to exert his control over the kingdom. Force compliance and punish those who don't. It's just a manipulation tactic."

This is Marik's first official move. It's been weeks of waiting, and here it is. How do we respond? What do we do? Do we even do anything? It hits me. "We have to go. This is our chance to get inside the castle. To see if our theory about Elle is right."

Asmo tilts his head, chews the inside of his cheek as he considers this, the movement emphasizing his sharp cheekbones. The shadows from the fire dance along the planes of his face, and something deep inside of me stirs. Something I haven't felt in months. I look away.

Ivan has his face in his hands, massaging his temples. He looks up. "You're right. Luca and I will go."

I shake my head. "I'm coming." A part of me aches to see the castle, to walk its halls again and be back in my home.

Ivan opens his mouth, but I cut him off. "This is my kingdom, and this is my choice."

Luca leans back in the armchair, shaking his head.

Asmo pushes himself from the wall. "Let's get to planning, then."

W e spend the entire night and every waking moment over the next two days coming up with a plan to get into the tithe. We have to see Elle. The problem is Marik and Cora would spot any of us in an instant and glamours would disappear the moment someone as powerful as they are put them to the test.

"I think I know something we can do," Asmo speaks up, breaking the contemplative silence we had all been sitting in for the last fifteen minutes.

Luca stares at him expectantly from the pad of paper he had been scribbling on. Every single line has been slashed out.

"There's a dark magic spell that Marik and I used to play with when we were kids," Asmo says, glancing at me nervously and shifting in his seat.

"What a sentence," Holly mutters from her usual spot—the corner of the living room shrouded in shadows. She sits on the floor, her feet kicked out and crossed at the ankles.

"It's a blood spell," Asmo says. "It changes your appearance as long as the mark is intact. We used to transform into each other and trick our parents."

Ivan sits up in his chair. "Will it hold against any protection spells or wards embedded in the castle?" he asks.

Asmo nods curtly. I stare at his profile, but he won't look at me.

"Why didn't you mention this yesterday?" I ask sharply. We spent all day yesterday trying to figure out a way to sneak ourselves in.

He hesitates, but says, "It's not something I'm accustomed to using. It was more of Marik's interest as a kid. Plus, we're in this mess *because* of dark magic."

A memory of Marik and me sitting in bed flits into my mind, Marik telling me that Asmo was the one who used to play with dark magic. So, that's how he got around that lie.

"Yeah, well. I don't think we can afford to gloss over any tool in our toolbox," I snap, but I regret it. We're all running on fumes and acting like that isn't going to help anything. I bury my head into my hands.

"Princess, dark magic is powerful stuff. There's a reason it's been banned for centuries. *Nobody* should know how to use it," Asmo says. "It's designed to whittle away your soul with every use. But I don't think we have a choice."

I lift my head. "I won't force anybody to do it, but I agree. We've been talking about this for days and this is the best—no, the only— idea so far. It seems like our only option."

"Holly needs to stay behind," Luca says. "She's not strong enough to wield dark magic."

"I'm right here," Holly snarls at him. Gone is the sweet, innocent girl from before. Life has found a way to harden her, to sharpen her into something colder.

"He's right," Asmo says quietly. "Dark magic is hard on the body, and there's no reason you need to be wielding it."

She shoots a look at him, but nods in resignation. "Fine. I'll stay here. But I'm portaling in if you lot don't come back at the agreed-upon time."

"Portals to the castle grounds will be opened at first light and will close at sundown. They will be available in every town square," Ivan says. "Asmo, how does this dark magic spell work?"

Asmo leans forward, his weight shifting the couch. "It's one of the easiest spells in the book, so that's good news. All you have to do is think of a person as you draw the symbol. It's best to think of someone you know or look at someone right in front of you. If you try to transform your features into an idea instead of after an actual person, you'll likely end up messing something up. Marik and I used to carve the spells into our skin while we looked at each other."

"How cute," Holly mutters from the shadows.

Asmo ignores her and dips his finger into a nearby glass of water. He draws a wet symbol on the back of one of the discarded newspapers. It looks like an oval with an X in the center.

"You want us to carve that into our skin?" I ask in disbelief. I'm no stranger to taking a blade to myself, but I imagine the others are.

He grimaces, but nods. "It's painful, but it's not hard. It's like your magic recognizes what you're doing and helps you. You could always paint it on your skin with blood, but I'm worried about it flaking off. The risk is too great."

"Well, we can't exactly stare at each other and do the spell. It sounds like we need to portal to another town to get our...models," Ivan says, hesitating on the word. "I don't see another choice. Does anyone else?" he asks, looking around the room.

Everyone is silent. We know there isn't one.

Ivan nods in acceptance. "It's already late afternoon. Let's head out, find our marks, then we can come back and discuss the rest of the plan."

The portal spits us out on top of a hill. The bustling town of Roselake lies below, shoppers flitting to and from different merchant stands like tiny ants.

We begin the trek downward.

People jostle past each other on the narrow streets, everyone seemingly in a hurry to get to their destinations. The first time someone bumped into me, my pulse skyrocketed. By the fifth time, I didn't even budge.

Ivan stops in front of a rundown building, its sign crooked and aged. *The Silver Stag Tavern.* Inside, the stench of beer and stale food hits me like a wall. True to its namesake, a statue of a silver stag on its hind legs is nestled in the back corner. On the back of every chair, a silver stag head is embroidered into worn, green fabric. Although most of the tables are packed with happy hour patrons, we're able to snag a table in the back, right beside the statue. Asmo and I sit with our backs to the busy tavern while Luca and Ivan keep watchful eyes.

"Okay, Az, how are we supposed to do this discreetly?" I mutter to him.

He raises a singular brow. "Nickname basis now, princess?"

I ignore him. "Well?"

"I think taking a knife to ourselves in the middle of the day in a tavern might call a little unwanted attention. We need to follow one person, knock them out, then conduct the spell."

"That's not exactly what I had in mind, Asmo," Ivan says.

Asmo leans back in his chair and throws his arm around the back of mine. "Any other ideas?" He looks around the table expectantly. When nobody responds, he says, "I didn't think so. We need to walk out of here acting tipsy, then follow someone and attack when they're not expecting it."

Luca gives a terse nod before standing and heading to the bar. He returns with two pitchers of light beer and four glasses.

"Don't actually drink it," Asmo says quietly, looking at each of us. "Mae, use your wind to evaporate the liquid slowly while we sit here." His arm is still resting on the back of my chair and he squeezes my shoulder. "Let's look like we're having a good time, huh?"

"Since when are you so jolly?" I mutter, reaching to take a fake sip of my beer.

He leans down, bringing his lips to my ear, and whispers, "Why? Do you miss your Prince of Darkness?"

A shiver of pleasure rolls down my spine at his words, at his breath hot on my ear. I take a real sip of my beer this time. He leans back, chuckling under his breath.

It doesn't take long for the pitchers to evaporate. When they're empty, we stand and head out the front door. If we're not successful in getting the High Crown back, I think we could all join a local theater instead. We're acting like we're the best of friends, all of us laughing as we exit the tavern. We look like everyone else, blending in perfectly.

We make our way down the busy cobble street, Asmo and me in the front, Luca and Ivan following right behind. We continue walking until the crowd thins, the streets growing more deserted as we near the residential quarter. Just ahead, a deer hybrid couple walks together, the male's antlers leaning to the right as he laughs at something his partner said.

Asmo darts forward. Before the couple can turn around, Asmo is right behind them. He mutters something under his breath, and they just...fall into his arms.

"A little help here?" he says, holding the hybrids up.

Luca rushes to him, nudging his arm underneath the male's. The four of them look like friends walking home together after a long night out. Well, as long as nobody looks too closely, at the way their feet drag on the street and the way their heads loll to the side.

"You could've given us a warning that you were about to do that," I mutter as Asmo and Luca drag them into a dark alley.

Asmo pulls the knife from his pocket and hands it to me. "They won't be out for long. You have a few minutes, at most. Make the mark on your thigh. As you're carving it, call upon your magic and whisper, 'As are you, as am I.' Quick."

I pull my skirt up and grab the knife from him. "Circle with an X?" I ask, looking at Asmo, but he's staring at my exposed skin.

He nods slowly, then rips his gaze from my thigh. "Look at her first, princess. Commit her face to memory. Ivan, stare at your mark. Imagine being him. Take the knife as soon as Mae is done, then make the same symbol."

I steal one more glance at the unconscious female in Asmo's arms and place the knife to my skin. The blade is cool and it stings as I press down, but the feeling is familiar. Comforting.

It's been so long since I gave into the urge to harm myself. Despite feeling like I'm drowning nearly every moment of the day, Asmo's presence every night keeps me from giving in. The urge grows less with every day, and there's a sense of victory in that.

"As are you, as am I," I whisper, gritting my teeth against the pain. Asmo was right—the knife moves on its own, gliding through my pale flesh like butter. Blood spurts in its wake, but it doesn't run down my leg. It evaporates, forming ruby droplets in the air above my thigh. When the mark is complete, the blood twirls upward before vanishing into the air.

"Good," Asmo says before taking the knife from me and handing it to Ivan, barking at him to hurry.

I glance down at my clothing, but it's the same. My hands look... smaller, more delicate. A pink birthmark graces my right thumb.

Ivan carves the mark into his skin and whispers the words silently. The transformation is eerie. His features slowly change to match the unconscious male's in Asmo's arms. Once the transformation is complete, Asmo grabs our hands and hurries us out of the alley, Ivan and Luca right behind us.

I twist around, but Asmo pulls me along. "Will they be okay?"

"They'll be fine," he says tersely. "Pull your hood over your head." I do as he says. A ripple of fear runs through me at how risky this all is. And we still have to do it for him and Luca.

"What's the plan, Az?" Ivan's new voice asks behind us. Apparently, he's on nickname basis with the Serpent Prince, too.

Asmo turns down another alley. Two more female deer hybrids walk just ahead of us, their steps wobbly. I groan at the thought of taking advantage of two drunk females.

Before I can object, he strikes again. But this time, he flings a hand out, turning the ground underneath the hybrids' feet to quicksand. Their conversation is cut off as they panic, arms flailing and legs pumping as they try to escape. Asmo rushes to them and whispers something in their ears. They fall into his arms.

"Mae, keep watch," he commands.

Luca glances at the fallen females, eyes wide. "You expect me to take the body of a female?"

"Oh, for fuck's sake," Asmo mutters and carves the mark into his chiseled stomach, then hands the knife to Luca as his features change. His build shrinks considerably, his once-fitted clothes now baggy on his new frame, black hair replaced by brunette hair that brushes against his shoulders.

Luca grabs the knife, muttering curse words under his breath before he completes the spell. When it's done, he's approximately eight inches shorter and at least fifty pounds lighter.

Asmo takes off. We all keep our heads down as we follow him and make our way back to the portal location. My nerves are shot by the time we reach the top of the hill. I don't breathe comfortably until we're back at our temporary home, its worn exterior and smoking chimney stack a comforting sight.

The front door opens and Holly steps out. She eyes us dubiously.

"It's us," Luca's now melodic voice says, then adds, "It worked. It's me, Luca."

Holly studies us for another moment, then bursts into laughter. I still at the sound. It's the first time I've heard her laugh in weeks. I look at Asmo in surprise. Our gazes meet and send a spark through me. His now-blue eyes are crinkled, and he looks...lighter. Maybe we all do, now that we finally have a plan, and some kind of tool to help. Even if that tool is dark magic.

He turns back to Holly, who's testing the strength of the disguise as she pokes and prods at Ivan. Even Luca's antlers have disappeared, something glamours can't hide properly. We spend the rest of the evening in these bodies, getting used to them and to each other. By the end of the night, my head has begun to throb and I'm eager for sleep.

Of course, it doesn't come easy. I'm used to tossing and turning every night as memories of the past play like a loop in my head. But tonight, I can't stop thinking about seeing Marik tomorrow. Will he see right through our disguises, and see us, too?

CHAPTER 5
MAE

THE NEXT MORNING, Ivan wakes us all before sunrise. We review the plan several times, nitpicking every detail and working out every possible risk for the third time.

We dress plainly to blend in with the crowd. I'm pulling my boots on when my bedroom door cracks open. A female stands in the doorway, and it takes me a second to remember who it is. Her blue eyes study me in only the way that Asmo's black and fern-green eyes ever have.

"I'm almost ready," I say, expecting him to leave at that, but he doesn't. "What?"

"Mae," Asmo's now-feminine voice says quietly.

Glancing up, I see worry lining her—his?—features.

"What's wrong?"

"If anything happens today, please just get out. Don't worry about the rest of us. We can handle it." Every word drips with consequence.

I roll my eyes. "I'm not going to just leave you," I scoff.

"Promise me," he says. It's odd, hearing Asmo's attitude and commanding voice coming from a much shorter, much prettier, much less threatening version of him. I can't help it, but a corner of my mouth twitches.

"What?" he huffs.

"It's just funny hearing you be you, but in a *very* different body," I say.

He quirks a thin eyebrow. "Are you saying you miss my body?"

Warmth floods my cheeks. "You're putting words in my mouth."

"We could still have fun in these bodies," he says suggestively.

My jaw drops. "Get out," I say as I fire a pillow at him.

He catches it with a smile before it falls, his affect turning serious once more. "Promise me, Mae."

Again, I'm reminded of his goodness, of the way he has tried to protect me at every turn, even if it was from himself. Of how he sacrificed his future for me, of how he speaks of sacrificing himself again for me if things go wrong today. My skin feels too tight. "Fine. I promise. Now leave."

We all grill each other once more on our backstories before forming a portal to the castle, barely full coin purses jostling in our pockets. Asmo and I step from the portal and run straight into Luca and Ivan.

"Sorry," I mumble into Ivan's back.

They shuffle out of the way, but there isn't much space for them to move. The portal location is packed with civilians, everyone waiting to enter the official castle grounds.

"Busy," I murmur to no one in particular.

Ivan glances back at me and says, "They're searching everyone before they enter the grounds. At least, that's what I've heard. Probably making sure nobody enters with any weapons."

Asmo tenses beside me and I think of the blood mark on my thigh.

The line moves slowly, but we eventually reach the entry point. I don't recognize the guards conducting the searches, but I don't miss the black uniforms and serpentine broaches pinned to their chests. House Serpent guards.

My chest tightens as I'm reminded of William. He didn't deserve to die. Nobody that's been involved in this has. Etta, Adelaide, my father. The list cannot grow any longer.

The searches are cursory, just brief pat-downs. The guard's hands roam a second too long over my backside, but we make it through the checkpoint quickly. We follow the crowd as it heads toward the castle, Ivan and Luca leading our little group of imposters.

The first time I stepped onto the castle grounds, my magic sang in my blood. The forest itself felt like magic. I remember walking down this exact path next to the stag on my coronation day and hearing the excitement in the crowd. Now, it feels dark and foreboding. The sky is gray and full of clouds, not a drop of sunshine to be seen. The trees are bare, dead leaves littering the ground, as if they, too, have abandoned this place. A chill permeates the air, and I pull my scarf tighter to stave off the sharp wind rustling through the trees.

Guards order everyone into a single-file line at the foot of the path that winds around the mountain. Asmo shifts to stand behind me.

"Do you think we have enough today? You know it's been a rough month," a female voice whispers behind me. I squeeze the small bag of gold coins in my pocket, my own offering meek but substantial enough to pass.

After what feels like hours of standing and shuffling upward, we reach the top of the mountain. The castle doors come into view, people slowly moving through them one at a time. Memories of stepping through those grand doors with Elle and Holly flit through my mind. Another pang of loss hits me like a shot in the dark.

Guards pace back and forth, keeping watchful eyes on everyone. I try my best not to look like I'm hiding from their gaze, but also not willfully meeting them, as if trying to prove I have nothing to hide.

My stomach is in knots by the time we finally enter the front doors. The castle looks the same, but, like the forest, the atmosphere is noticeably different. These halls used to be filled with court members casually chatting as they went to and from their destinations. Now, they're empty, save for the heavy presence of guards. There's no casual conversation, no laughter. Just omnipotent silence.

"One person at a time. When you're called into the throne room, you will kneel before the High King and the High Queen and make your offering," the guard in front of us says monotonously, like he's said this hundreds of times today.

"Sir, excuse me," a hybrid male in front of us calls out. "My family. Are we allowed to go in together?"

"One person at a time," the guard says sharply.

"But my daughter...She's four. We only brought one offering for us as a family."

"One person at a time," the guard repeats, his tone final. He walks away, leaving the male wringing his hands together.

I glance back at Asmo. His jaw works, but he shakes his head once. *Leave it alone.* I turn back toward the family, the mother kneeling before her daughter as she whispers hurried instructions. The father pulls his coin purse out and splits the coins in half, offering a handful of coins to his wife and a handful to his daughter, leaving him with nothing.

I check to make sure the guards aren't looking before I cut Ivan and Luca in line to get to the family. Luca tries to pull me back, but I shrug him off. I pull my bag of coins out and offer a small handful to the male, holding the coins out silently. He looks at me, bewildered.

"Take it," I whisper. "Hurry."

He shakes his head, eyes wide and panicked.

I huff a sigh of impatience. "Give your daughter a few coins," I whisper briskly. "They won't be expecting much from her. Split the rest between you and your wife." He still doesn't take the coins, so I shove them into his pocket and sneak back to my original spot in line.

"That was grossly idiotic," Asmo whispers harshly into my ear.

I don't respond. It was. The guards could have spotted me, and I might have ruined this entire mission. But I'm still the High Queen and I know my husband. If he has any chance to humiliate or punish someone, he's going to take it. I can at least save this one family from him.

Asmo reaches from behind me and shoves his hand into my pocket. The jingle of loose coins has me turning to him, a protest on the tip of my tongue, but he silences me with a look.

"Next!" the guard at the throne room door announces, waving the mother forward. Her daughter is called, then the father. I can only hope I gave them enough.

Ivan, then Luca follow soon after.

"Next!" the guard calls, signaling me forward.

I grip the coins in my coat pocket and step forward. He ushers me inside, and I'm hit with a sick sense of something so familiar, yet so different. It feels like I've opened my favorite book, expecting to read my favorite story—yet, the words are written in a different language.

I raise my gaze to the twin thrones. A king and a queen sit beside each other. Marik sits on one throne of berries and branches, his tall frame slumped as if he has better things to do.

My breath catches as my gaze falls to the female beside him.

It's me.

CHAPTER 6
ELLE

"Don't be so dramatic," Marik drawls beside me. "The girl will be fine."

My jaw is clenched so tightly, I think I might crack a tooth. "You didn't have to do that. She's a *child*," I spit at him.

There have been two others since the little girl, but I can't get her panicked expression out of my mind. Her face when she realized she was going to the dungeons made me want to cry. There was no reason for it, other than cruelty.

"Call the next one in," he orders the guard, ignoring me.

A slender female deer hybrid walks into the throne room, her gaze focused on the pristine marble flooring as she approaches. Waves of anxiety roll off her. Marik must sense it, too. He perks up as she walks closer.

This tithe was his idea. He ignored me when I told him that the High House has never enacted a tithe. Actually, he made me stop talking completely by forcing my mouth to slam shut.

The female bows at the designated location, then lifts her head. Her gaze lands on Marik, then me, her eyes widening a fraction.

"State your name," Marik orders.

"Maisie Gibbs," she says, her voice sounding small. Scared.

Warning bells go off in my head. This is the third person in a row that has blatantly lied about their name. Some people have given half-truths when asked why they couldn't spare more gold, but until the last three hybrids, nobody has blatantly lied, let alone about their name.

I sit up straighter, watching the female carefully.

"State your occupation," he orders.

"I'm a gardener," she squeaks. It's a lie.

Marik nods, as if this occupation is perfectly acceptable to him. "And what do you have to contribute to your court today?"

She pulls out a gently used coin purse and empties it into her hand. Six gold coins.

Marik gives one more nod, then flicks his head toward the exit. "Place it in the cauldron on your way out."

She glances at me once more, her gaze fierce. I force myself to look away, terrified that Marik will notice my interest in her and send her to the dungeons to spite me.

"Next," he calls to the guard.

Another deer hybrid walks into the room, her blue eyes instantly finding Marik. You'd have to be blind to miss the anger brimming in them.

Marik sits up straighter and leans forward on the throne. Fuck.

She bows respectfully, then waits for us to speak first.

"State your name," Marik says.

"Eliza Rainey, Your Highness." Another liar. Unlike the last female, her voice is confident, her chin held high.

"State your occupation."

"Teacher." Lie.

I watch her carefully, but there are no outward signs of deception. No fidgeting, no avoiding eye contact. In fact, her gaze hasn't left Marik's. She seems at ease.

"What age do you teach, Miss Rainey?" Marik asks her. Double fuck. The last time he asked follow-up questions, he sent that little girl to the dungeons.

Eliza doesn't miss a beat. "Young children, Your Highness," she says, a hint of a smile on her face as she tells the lie.

"And does teaching pay well, Miss Rainey?" Marik asks, slender fingers drumming on the armrest of the throne.

"No, Your Highness." She pulls out a coin purse, two gold coins glinting in the palm of her hand. Her first truth, albeit an easy one to get around.

Marik stops drumming his fingers. He places both elbows on the armrests and brings his hands together, bridging his fingers. He rests his chin on steepled hands and leans forward. "Are you aware of the penalties for an inadequate contribution?"

She doesn't back down. Not even by an inch. "No, Your Highness." Truth.

"Well, it's not so bad. You get to sleep here for a night or two!" he exclaims, a cruel grin splitting his face.

Eliza still doesn't look nervous. *Who is she?*

"I don't th—" I start to say before my jaw slams shut.

You're right. You don't think, Marik's voice spits into my thoughts.

"How about this, Eliza," Marik says, "since you think we don't pay you enough, I'll let you keep your coins."

"Th—thank you, Your Grace," she stutters, the first and only outward sign of her nerves.

Marik extends his hand and motions with it. I know that terrible wave of his hand. My heart drops when I see the two guards coming from behind her. Their hands close around her slender arms. She jumps at the contact, fear now in her expression. Her crazed eyes go to me in a silent plea.

But there's nothing I can do. I'm a prisoner, too.

She protests as they drag her from the throne room.

Eliza Rainey is the tenth person that Marik has sent to the dungeons today.

CHAPTER 7

MAE

I KNOW something's wrong when I see the hybrid couple walk down the path before Asmo. He should have come out before them. He should be here by now.

"Let's go," Luca says, turning in the direction of the portal location.

I don't move. "No. We can't leave him," I say, my gaze fixed on the door to the castle.

Luca huffs a sigh. "We don't have time to argue this. If they caught on to him, we need to go. Now."

I turn and stare at him. "I'm not leaving yet," I say through clenched teeth.

Ivan places a gentle hand on my shoulder. "Luca is right. We have to go. We're not prepared for a rescue mission. We have no clue if they know who he is or if they're coming for us next. We can't risk staying here any longer."

He's right.

"Let's just wait. One more minute. Please." I hate that I'm asking for permission, that I sound like I'm begging, that the thought of Asmo being taken has my chest constricting this much.

Luca draws his mouth into a straight line and casts another sidelong glance at the castle doors. I count to sixty in my head, but the doors remain shut. Fuck. Without another word, I swallow my fear and the way my brain is screaming at me to stay put. Luca and Ivan flank my sides as I head back toward the portal location.

The walk back is swift but silent, tension radiating from Ivan and Luca as we walk. The fear of Marik's guards coming to grab us before we can make it back is palpable. The knot in my chest doesn't abate when we're back at the cabin. It only strengthens with the knowledge that Asmo is no longer with us. That he's now with the enemy.

Holly's confusion is evident the moment she opens the door, her features twisted and brow furrowed. "What—where's...who's missing?" she asks, frantically looking behind us for any sign of the final member of our group.

Luca slashes the sigil. "Asmo," he says, his voice back to normal.

I stalk past Holly and into the cabin. Ivan calls my name, but I ignore it. I don't think I could speak if I tried. My thoughts are spinning and my jaw is locked, too many thoughts and screams threatening to spill.

I shut myself in the tiny bathroom and sit on the stone floor, the cool surface welcome against skin that feels hot and tingly. I lay down and curl into a ball, hugging my knees to my chest and trying to control my breathing. But it's coming too fast, and my lungs feel too small, and my skin feels like it's buzzing in the wrong way.

My hands ball into fists as the tears come.

There is too much against us, and not enough of us. With Asmo, it felt like we had a chance of figuring this out, but without him...It's just too much.

My breathing slows as I focus on the feel of the floor beneath me—a trick Willa once taught me to lessen my anxiety. I refuse to think of her as Cora, to taint whatever positive memories are left.

Focusing too much on what went wrong won't help me. At least, not right now. The urge to self-harm is overwhelming, but I shove the thought away, focusing again on the feel of the stones beneath me. When my breathing is regulated and I no longer feel like crawling out of my skin, I push myself to my feet. I nearly scream when I look in the mirror and see the unfamiliar face looking back at me.

I need to get out of this body. I grab Ivan's razor blade from the pedestal and yank my pants down, exposing the dark mark. Before I can think too much about how good it would feel to draw the blade further than necessary, I mar the sigil and toss it back onto the counter. The blood evaporates in a shimmer of black before disappearing into the air. I feel lighter with the sigil gone, the dark magic no longer etched into my skin.

But then I remember that Asmo didn't come back with us.

A heavy knock pounds on the door. "Mae. We need to talk." Ivan.

I yank open the door and slink past him. He looks like himself again. Holly sits on the sofa, wringing her fingers.

"We have to go back," I demand.

Luca shakes his head in one firm motion. "Absolutely not."

"He would go back for any of us," I fire back.

"It doesn't matter. We need to give it a couple of days and see what happens. We can't go barging in there. Have you forgotten it's just us?" Ivan says softly. "We don't have an army of people to back us up."

My shoulders slump. Ivan is right. It doesn't matter that I'm still the High Queen. It's only the four of us. There's nothing we can do right now.

⁂

That night, I toss and turn and beg for sleep, thinking about Asmo in Marik's and Cora's hands. Whenever I close my eyes, images of Asmo writhing on the ground in black flames fill my mind. I swallow a scream and wrench back the covers.

Ivan is already sitting outside on one of the dining chairs that we dragged onto our sad excuse of a front porch. I settle into the other chair and he tosses me a thick blanket. I wrap it around and cocoon myself in it.

"Have I ever told you how I came to be in your father's service?" he asks me, foregoing any kind of greeting.

I shake my head, still not trusting myself to speak. Still not trusting that a scream won't come out instead.

"Your father and I knew each other as boys. He lived in the castle with your grandparents. I lived in one of the nearby villages, and I stumbled across him one day in the woods on the edge of the grounds."

He pauses, a warm smile spreading across his face. He sits back in his chair, the wood creaking as his weight shifts. I swear it creaks a little less every night.

"He was stuck in a damned tree," he says with a quiet chuckle. "He saw me and started calling out for me to help him. Now, I was a snot-nosed kid back in those days. I walked right up to the tree and said, 'What idiot in the Deer Court would try to climb a tree?' His face turned red as a tomato and he said—and I'll never forget this—'I'm Prince Silas, I'll have you know. Help me down at once!'"

One corner of my mouth tilts upward at the image of Ivan speaking back to a High Prince. To my father.

He freezes when he sees my smile, but thankfully, continues with the story. "I stared up at him and I said, 'And how am I supposed to help you?' The next thing I know, your father jumps from the tree and starts screaming. He had broken his damned ankle." His chuckle is warm and quiet, the kind that comes with a memory of a time long gone. "We became fast friends after that."

He turns his head to stare at the dark tree line, his smile fading. "One night, many years later, we were out at a tavern. Your father was rowdy then. He lost his sense of pretense when he was High King, but as High Prince? He was kind, yes, but let's just say he knew exactly who he was.

"Back then, there was tension between the Fae Court and the High Houses. I don't know what your father did, but he ended up pissing off some High Fae males. They followed us out of the tavern, yelling horrible things our way.

"They didn't pick the fight with your father, though. They picked it with me. Your father knew the basics of combat, but he was no warrior. He put up as much of a fight as he could to defend me, but there wasn't much we could do against two fully grown High Fae."

He takes a long sip of water, still staring at the forest. The moon has begun its slow descent.

"They took a blade and sawed my antlers from my head."

I close my eyes and hiss a deep breath, the winter air like shards of ice against my lungs. The pain...Bile rises, but I force it back down.

His breath is shaky as he continues. "Thankfully, I passed out. I don't remember it happening. Your father never forgave himself. After that, we started training together, promising each other that it would never happen again. We would never be weak again. He offered me the position of his second-in-command the day he took his oath."

"Ivan—" I start, but he holds up a hand.

"It was a long time ago," he says. His voice is tired in a way I've never heard from him before. I wonder how much strength it takes to smile after something like that. "In a way, it made me better. I haven't felt weak like that in a long time. But right now, I feel powerless."

I nod. I know exactly what he means. I wish I didn't.

Two days pass, then three. Three days of pacing and staring out the windows, looking for any sign of Asmo walking toward the cabin. The second night he's gone, I ended up falling asleep outside wrapped in two blankets, Ivan watching over me under the starlit night.

Now, I toss the newspaper back onto the coffee table, sending a lone pen skittering over the edge. The newspapers have been utterly useless. I had foolishly been hoping that there would be something about the prisoners Marik took during the tithe. As if he would allow something like that to be printed.

"What if we reach out to the other courts?" I ask to the remaining members of my court. "Maybe they know something."

Luca massages his temples. "We don't know if they're in league with Marik. I would highly advise against that plan." His tone is dry and laced with annoyance.

Ivan gives me a pitiful smile. "He's right, Mae. Plus, it would give up the only advantage we have—that Marik and Cora don't know we're alive."

"It's been three days of nothing," I groan, my head in my hands. "We can't just sit here."

"We have no other choice," Luca snaps. I don't blame him; we've had the same conversation nearly a dozen times. Me, wanting to take action, although I have no idea what that would look like. Luca and Ivan, shutting the idea down instantly. Holly, sitting and watching both sides silently.

Until now.

"Mae," she says softly. "Have you considered that maybe Asmo told Marik it was really him? And that they've been working together?"

I turn to her, and the fire in the old stone hearth sputters out. "Would you like to rethink that question?"

She momentarily drops her gaze at the cold fury in my voice. "I'm sorry, but Marik is a skilled liar and manipulator. Asmo is his brother, his *twin* brother. You don't think that maybe they were working together this whole time?"

Luca and Ivan share a look. As if they've had this conversation before. As if I'm not the only one who's questioned Asmo's trustworthiness.

"Asmo wouldn't betray us," I say through gritted teeth, looking around the room at each of them.

"How do you know that?" Holly asks.

I will myself to take a deep breath and I feel the temperature in the room return to normal. "I know it here," I say, holding my fisted hand to my chest. "He wouldn't do that to us." I can't explain how, but I know it in the very matter of my bones. Despite my earlier anxieties about Asmo, I find every word to be true. I just *know*. I refuse to believe that the way he held me in the dark was a lie.

But Holly has a point—one that has niggled at me in the last few weeks. I was so easily fooled by Marik and Cora. I had no idea the games they were playing. Asmo is Marik's brother.

Have I been a fool this whole time to trust Asmo? To let him into the Herd? Should I have just cast him aside the moment I woke up from whatever hell I had been floating in?

"We can't stay here any longer," Luca says.

My stomach sinks. "But what if he comes back?"

"Yeah, what if he comes back *with Marik*?" Luca hisses. "Don't be stupid. We can't stay here."

I glare at him and he straightens. He draws a breath and holds it before releasing it slowly. "Forgive me, Your Highness."

I clench my teeth, then force myself to unclench them in a monumental effort. "It's fine. You're right. We can't risk it."

I stand slowly and head to my room to pack my belongings.

My body feels heavy. My heart feels heavy. My brain feels heavy.

Elle is gone.

Asmo is gone.

My entire life is gone.

I have no idea where Cally is, if she's even safe. The male that feels like another part of me might have betrayed me.

I stuff my clothes into the duffel bag that now serves as my wardrobe. Three shirts, three pairs of pants, three pairs of underwear, three pairs of socks, three sleeping shirts. I'm lucky. The others have even less.

I cross the hall to Asmo's room. The door pushes open, revealing the tidy primary bedroom. The full-sized bed is made, sheets tucked neatly under the mattress, pillows perfectly centered against the headboard.

An empty glass sits on the side table. I imagine Asmo setting it down quietly in the middle of the night. I could never hear him in here. He was always so careful to avoid disrupting us. He never said it, but I know he felt out of place amongst us.

The side table drawer is empty. I'm not sure what I'm hoping to find. Maybe some confession of his guilt or innocence, but there's nothing.

The dresser drawers are filled with clothing, some of Asmo's and some of the former owner's. We kept the spare clothing just in case we needed them.

His sock drawer is meticulous, each one matched together in neat rolls. I can instantly tell his socks apart from the previous owner's. Asmo's are black and made of expensive wool, while the previous owner's are worn and made of once-white cotton that has since faded to gray.

I hold a pair of Asmo's socks in my hands, startling when I feel something hard lodged inside. I hastily unroll the pair. A wine cork comes tumbling out.

I let loose a giggle of relief. I can't explain why, but I bundle the socks back up, tuck the wine cork back inside, and stuff them into my bag.

Holly, Luca, and Ivan are waiting in the living room, their bags slung over their shoulders. "Ready?" Holly asks.

I nod. "Where—"

BANG. BANG. BANG.

CHAPTER 8

ELLE

AFTER THE TITHE, I'm sent back to my—Mae's—living quarters. Guards are stationed on the inside and the outside of the only door, preventing anyone from entering. Or me from exiting. It's better than the bare room I was locked in before, but it's still a cell.

"I'd like to go to the dungeons," I tell the guard stationed at the door. Like every other time, he ignores me.

The only way that I can leave is if Marik summons me or gives me permission, which has only happened a handful of times.

Thankfully, I don't have to wait too long before Marik decides to grace me with his presence. He's dressed in his usual uniform of black, the crown of twisted metal branches perfectly placed atop his head. It's supposed to be his version of the berry crown, but the black metal reminds me of his flames.

He looks devastatingly handsome.

It's a shame he's the fucking devil.

"I'd like to go to the dungeons," I repeat once he's inside the door.

"No," he says dismissively. "We have a meeting."

I freeze. A meeting? So far, I have yet to see Cora, or any visitors he's been leaving me to go see. He's been careful not to say anything around me that might give me some clue about the state of the kingdom. The only exception has been the tithe. But it's not like he could do that without me. The citizens would have asked questions if Mae hadn't been there.

"With whom?"

He leans against the foyer wall, surveying his nails. "It doesn't matter. Go get ready," he says, not even sparing a glance at me.

I plant my feet. "*Who*, Marik?"

He huffs a sigh of impatience as he picks something from his nail bed. "Cora. Get ready."

My body moves without my permission, taking me to the bathroom. It's pointless trying to fight it anymore, so I don't. No matter how hard I scream internally, nothing ever happens. I have no control, and I'm beginning to hate myself for it. Logically, I know this is Marik's fault. But I can't help but blame myself for not being strong enough to fight it.

I watch my hand open the bathroom drawer to find the blade tucked under the washcloths. "As are you, as am I," my lips murmur as I etch the mark into my forearm.

The first time Marik forced me to do this, my magic revolted in my skin. Ivan warned me of the signs of dark magic, and this reeked of it. As does the necklace that's shackled around my throat. They both go against everything the Mother intended when she blessed us with magic. Black magic seeks to harm, to control, to manipulate. All must offer a sacrifice to wield it—and that sacrifice is often blood. And there is always a greater cost.

Being controlled by dark magic to do more dark magic...I wanted to shred my soul from my body. But now? I've done it so many times that it just feels like getting dressed. And that horrifies me even more.

With the sigil etched in my skin, Mae looks back at me in the mirror. She was always so beautiful.

I detest the sight of her. Because it's not her. It's me trapped in her body.

I walk from the bathroom on my own, a small victory. Marik still stands by the front door, picking lint from his black coat.

He looks up when he hears my footsteps. "My wife," he says with a shit-eating, pearly-white grin that makes my skin crawl. He holds his arm out to me, but before he can force me to loop my arm in his, I move forward and force myself to do it.

I've come to realize that it's easier for me to just go along with Marik. No matter how hard I fight it, he can still force me to do whatever he wants. And as much as I hate to admit it, doing it myself is the only way I can have any semblance of control. Even if it's still not my choice. But I try to tell myself it is. Sometimes it works. Mostly, it doesn't.

His arm is cold against mine. Colder still is the smile on his face as he pulls me from the wing and into the nearly empty castle.

Marik's guards refuse to look at me whenever we pass. He leads us to a private office on the backside of the castle. Two guards stand silently, one on each side of the door, faces sober and impassive. Marik's hand brushes against the small of my back as he opens the door and ushers me inside the room. It makes me move faster.

Light filters through the floor-to-ceiling window along the back wall, landing on Cora's silhouette. She turns as we enter.

Eyes white as bone land on me. A chill spreads through me. I want to run. Far.

Two armchairs sit side-by-side in front of her desk. Marik takes a seat on the right, his lanky frame somehow dwarfed by the oversized chair. He gestures to the chair beside him.

"Sit," he commands, but his invisible touch is absent. I play nice and do it anyway.

"Hello, Elle," Cora says coolly, her gaze piercing my very soul.

My entire body is rigid with fear and loathing. "Fuck you," I spit.

She sighs and leans back in her chair. The sunlight dances along her glossy black hair, and it feels odd that the sun would deign to shine upon her. "Didn't anybody teach you how to treat your elders?"

Anger is a constant companion. I hold on to it with every ounce of strength I can muster. It's so much better than the empty void of depression. "Fuck. You."

Her eyes narrow to slits.

"Ignore her," Marik says coolly. "Let's discuss."

"You think it's a good idea to have her in this meeting?" Cora asks, gaze still fixed on me.

"I can control her."

My body tenses at his response, my fingers gripping the worn armrest.

"You'd better hold the leash tight," she says with a grin.

Stop reacting, Marik's voice says in my head. *That's what she's looking for.*

I blink in stunned silence. Did he just...give me advice?

"Give me the updates," he says, ignoring her comment.

She looks like she wants to say more about me and the collar around my neck, but she turns to him instead. "Witches have been placed near every major city and human town. House Ursidae has been a problem. They refuse to let Annika and Mina stay on their grounds. Houses Panthera and Canis have been compliant, though."

Marik nods as he takes this in.

Witches in every city...in every court...around humans...

Cora continues, "Casualties have been minimal, so far. There has been some pushback from the citizens regarding the assimilation of the witches, but they've been dealt with."

"Wh—" My mouth slams shut.

Cora looks at me, her eyes twinkling. "Cat got your tongue?"

I glare at her.

"I told you I could control her," Marik says. "Continue."

Her jaw ticks at the order, but she complies. "Like I said, pushback has been minor, but something needs to be done about Ursidae."

"I'll handle it. Make sure you control your witches, Cora. We don't want the citizens getting hurt or to begin protesting this. And be careful with the humans. If harm comes to them, the hybrids will not respond well. Our grip on the kingdom is already tenuous."

Her gaze sharpens, eyes somehow getting lighter as the dark aura around her strengthens.

"Watch how you speak to me, boy. Did you forget who's running things here? I'm working with you to be polite. I can raze this court and all its land to the ground."

Marik's hand grips his knee, but his face remains impassive as he says, "It would not be in your interest if you want a people to rule.

Remember what happened with the Fae? She wasn't too happy with you, was she? Let's not forget who's in control."

I blink as I try to piece together what he's saying. I had assumed Cora was responsible for the fall of the Fae, but I have no clue what he's talking about...*Who* wasn't too happy with Cora after that? Who is in control?

They stare at each other for another moment. Would it be too much to hope that they'll just wipe each other out right now? But Cora's black aura dims and she relaxes her shoulders. "How was the tithe?" she asks.

Marik's foot twitches on the ground next to mine. I want to stomp on it. Or better yet, nail it to the ground.

"Fine. Most citizens came. Those that didn't were found and arrested."

She studies something on the desk in front of her—a report of some kind, I think—her pointer finger tracing the border. "You placed ten in the dungeons?"

He nods in confirmation.

"Good," she says, circling something on the report. I squint, hoping to glean any information that I can, but it's no use. The print is too small for me to read from here.

"Can I see them?" I ask, surprised that Marik let me get the question out.

Marik glances at me. "I don't—" he starts, but Cora holds her hand up, silencing him in one motion.

It appears I'm not the only one with a leash, I fire at him before I can think better of it.

"Actually, I think that would be wise. Marik, you're the one who put them there. Let them see their High Queen showing them some compassion. We need to release them in the next couple of days anyways. Let them tell their stories. Let them spread the fear of what happens when you don't listen to the High Crown, then let them tell the story of their High Queen visiting them. Show them we are a firm, but empathetic Crown."

Marik nods. "I'll take her down there today."

She waves him off. "Let her go by herself. If you have such control over her, it shouldn't be a problem. Right?" she asks, her eyes twinkling again. "In fact, let her go now. It's high time we caught up on personal matters, wouldn't you say?"

She stares at him, a new look in her eyes. The same look from the night Marik was crowned High King.

Hunger. Desire.

Gross.

I stand and turn toward the door. They don't take their eyes off each other.

"Guard!" Marik calls, eyes locked on Cora. "Escort her to the dungeons. Don't want the little fawn getting lost, do we?"

Internally, I scoff. This castle is my home. I know every nook and cranny. Even though I've only visited the dungeons a handful of times, I know how to get there.

The guard opens the door to the office, and I lead us to the bowels of the small mountain that we call home. The dungeon's entryway is hidden in the back of the castle, disguised in a stone wall. The door creaks open as I place my hand to it, the magic recognizing my touch.

The descent is dark, every step downward steep and treacherous as the light recedes, but we make it to the bottom of the stairs without incident. Despite the chill outside, the air down here is sticky with humidity. The cloying scents of urine and body odor hit me, and my stomach quivers.

I extend my hand to summon a ball of light, but the guard stops me.

"No magic," he says gruffly.

"Why?"

"King's orders. No magic from you."

King's orders, my ass. He stole the throne. He's a false king at best.

I bite back the words. "What would you have me use, then? I can hardly see down here."

He removes a lantern from the wall and lights it with the telltale black flame of House Serpent. I all but snatch it from him. Even though we rarely held prisoners here before, the lanterns were always kept lit. Now, it only illuminates the path ahead by a few feet.

A shudder works its way through me as I pass cells of prisoners, all of them dressed in dirty, fraying formalwear. Wedding guests.

"Help, please," someone cries.

"Quiet!" the guard snaps.

I wince and cast my gaze downward. There is nothing I can do. This must be the real reason Cora wanted me to come down here. To see who else is trapped in this castle. They watch me pass them with intense, hate-filled stares. If only they knew I was in a cage of my own.

The little girl is asleep in the corner of a cell, an empty plate of food and a container of water by the cell door. Like dogs in cages. Even so, some relief comes from knowing nobody is starving or dying of thirst in our dungeons for not paying their taxes. Or attending a wedding.

She doesn't stir as I come to a stop in front of the cell. The rhythmic sound of deep breathing comes from the corner. In the cell beside her, a female deer hybrid sits against the wall, shrouded in shadows.

"Eliza, right?" I ask quietly, hoping not to wake the sleeping girl. She dips her chin in silent confirmation. I survey her cell, but don't find an empty plate or water. "Where's your water?"

She tilts her head toward the cell next to her. The girl's cell. It's then I notice a second plate beside her sleeping frame.

"Thank you," I say. "For watching over her. I'm sorry you're down here," I say, but I regret it when I remember the necklace around my throat that connects my every move to Marik.

"Can you get me out?" Eliza asks. Her voice is soft, timid.

"I—I'll need to speak with my husband," I say, trying not to choke on the words.

She tilts her head. "Are you okay?"

The question unnerves me. She should be looking at me the way the other prisoners are, with hatred brimming underneath the surface. But instead, she looks at me with curiosity.

I ignore her question. "I came down here to see if the girl is okay," I say. "Are you?"

She shrugs, leans back against the stone wall. "It could be worse."

"Yeah, it could be," I agree. The last time I was here, it was well-lit. I'm lucky that Cora has kept her dark creatures out of here. I shiver as I imagine cambions lurking in the shadows. "Where do you live, Eliza?"

"Hollowfield."

It's a lie, and a good one at that. Comprised of humans and hybrids,

Hollowfield is large enough to go unnoticed in. The perfect town to say if you don't want someone to corroborate the truth.

"That's not too far from here. You said you're a teacher, right?"

She nods, but nonverbal lies always slip past my net. Even if she had answered, it would have been a truth. She *did* say she was a teacher. Lying is an art and so is learning to detect it. I need to be smarter with my questions, but it's hard to think with the dark sigil embedded in my skin and this collar like an anvil around my throat. I want to beat my head against the cell bars.

"What age did you say, again?" I ask. I glance at my nails, trying to act casual.

"Young children. Five and six."

Her head is tilted back, still resting against the stone wall behind her, but her gaze hasn't left mine. There's not a shred of fear to be found for someone lying to the High Queen. Mother, the cocky gaze, the confidence...It seems so familiar. "That must be nice. Rewarding, even. Do you have any children of your own?"

"No, Your Highness."

Truth.

"Maybe someday then," I say wistfully. "Are you originally from Hollowfield?"

She refuses to break her stare. She even leans forward, the dirt beneath her shifting with the movement. "No, Your Highness. I'm originally from the City of Sand."

Truth. Although citizens live freely across the kingdom, most tend to live in or near their primary courts. But a deer hybrid originally from House Serpent's court? Alarm bells chime.

"What made you come here?" I ask.

"To see you," she says simply, pleasantly.

My heart begins to beat faster at the truth in her words. I breathe in through my nose and force the air back out in a controlled exhale. I don't know what could set Marik off to peer through my mind, but I need to do whatever I can to prevent that from happening.

Right now, I know something isn't right. And I need to get out of here before I accidentally clue Marik into it.

"I'll check on some more water for you," I mumble, then head back to the guards and out of the dungeon, leaving the liar behind.

I spend the rest of the evening trying to recall everything Eliza said in the throne room and in the dungeons. But the same questions continue to resurface—*Who is she, and why is she lying?*

Not that it should matter. Not really. Why should I care, when I should be focusing my energy on finding a way out of here? But I finally have something else to focus on, other than my own shitty situation.

So, the next day, I find myself descending the dark stairs once more after Marik gave me his "permission" to visit the dungeons again. The little girl is still sound asleep, her small frame tucked into a tight ball against the back wall of the cell. Eliza is in the same position as she was yesterday—seated on the floor, legs tucked to her chest, hands and chin resting on her knees. Her eyes follow me as I stop in front of her cell.

"I see you got some more water," I say quietly.

She clears her throat before speaking. "Yes. Thank you, Your Highness."

I look around for a plate, but the floor of her cell is empty, save for the bowl of water. "Have they brought you food?" She tilts her head toward the sleeping girl in the neighboring cell, toward the plate that sits discarded on the floor beside her. "Thank you, again. How is she doing?"

"She cries herself to sleep." Truth.

My chest tightens. All I want is to scoop the girl into my arms and return her to her family. Her parents are probably sick with worry.

"Eliza, about yesterday," I say, changing the subject. I don't know how much time I'll get down here. The guards could walk past at any moment, or Mother forbid, Marik. "What did you mean when you said you came here to see me?" The question gnawed at me all night as I tossed and turned.

She tilts her head. "I came here to see you, Your Highness."

Mae always hated being called Your Highness. "Please, call me... Mae." The request tastes like metal on my tongue.

Eliza raises a single eyebrow. "You want me to call you Mae?"

I nod and force myself to swallow. "What did you mean yesterday?" I ask again.

Her eyebrow drops and she goes still. "I meant what I said. That I came here to see you." Truth.

I step forward, wrapping a hand around steel. "That's the third time you've said that. What do you mean? You moved to the Deer Court to see me? I've only been on the throne for a few months now."

"Yes," she says, but it's a half-truth. Instead of something snagging on my net, it merely brushes against it.

I place my other hand on the bars of the cell. What I really want to do is open the cell door and wring the truth from her. "Is your real name Eliza?"

"Yes." Liar.

I don't know who this female is, but I know she's from House Serpent and she's lying about something. My stomach drops. What if she's a spy for Marik? What if this was all a test? What if she's reporting my interest back to him, and that's why he even let me come down here? I place my hands to my sides.

"Well, it was a pleasure to meet you, Eliza," I say with a half-smile. I straighten and walk away, trying desperately to stifle the panic, to calm my heartrate.

"Mae," Eliza calls. The name sends a shock through my system. I turn. Eliza stands at the edge of the cell, fingers wrapped around the bars as she stares at me. "I like your necklace."

"Thank you," I say, touching the cool black metal on my collarbone. "It was a wedding gift from my husband."

Her features shift, turning into something darker. "It's beautiful."

I offer her a tight smile before turning and walking away, her lies echoing through my mind. The mud under my shoes squelches as I walk back to the stairs, and I let my dress trail along the ground. Marik will likely frown when he sees the mess I've made. Perfect. I veer from the path and walk through a puddle, dragging the cream train through its sludge.

"Please," a voice whimpers. "Help us."

I chance a glance down the tunnel. No guards in sight.

The cell is dark, but there's enough light for me to see that it's crammed with emaciated bodies all wearing tattered formal clothing now covered in dirt and mud and what I'm assuming, based on the smell, is likely waste. The contents of my meager lunch churn in my stomach.

"Your Highness, please," a young woman dressed in a gown that was once the color of the sky begs, forearms straining as she grips the cell bars. "There is a girl on the brink of death. Please, show some mercy." Her voice wavers at the end, and her desperation makes me equal parts horrified, sad, and furious.

It kills me to be so trapped. So unable to help. "I—"

The woman jerks her head to the left. A guard lumbers down the walkway, torch of black flames illuminating his dark armor.

"Your Highness, it's time," he orders.

I nod to the woman in silent promise, but I have no idea how I can help when everything I'm doing is being watched. When I'm a prisoner, too.

"Champagne? Wine?" Marik asks across the formal dining table. He's enjoying a nice, thick steak while I choke down bread.

Last week, he began demanding that I join him for dinner. The first few nights, my body was forced to dress itself and walk down the stairs to sit with him at the large oak table. I was just grateful he didn't make me use the sigil.

The last few nights, I've taken myself. I hate it, but it's easier. I waste so much time fighting it, and all it manages to do is leave me exhausted and hopeless.

"No."

No, thank you, his voice commands inside my mind.

"No, thank you," I say mid-chew, stale bread in my mouth.

He eyes me with disgust, then takes a sip from his own glass of red wine. "You're the High Queen, Elle. You should enjoy a glass of wine every now and then."

I am no High Queen. I am your prisoner. I flex my jaw and swallow the retort. It's what he wants, I've learned. He likes the fight. Instead, I ask, "What do you plan to do with the prisoners?"

He glances down at his plate and saws a piece of steak with his fork and knife. His crown rests beside him on the table. How I long to shatter it into a million pieces and make him choke on every single one.

He stabs the steak with his fork and brings it to his mouth. He pauses mid-air, and a drop of blood falls back onto the plate. "What would you have me do with them?"

I blink. I wasn't expecting that response. "Release them."

He plops the bite in his mouth and chews in contemplative silence, then goes back to sawing his meal with his knife once more. It scrapes against the ivory plate, and I wince.

"And why should I?"

I rip a piece of bread off as I consider how to respond. The question is maddeningly simple, the answer even more so. Obvious, even. At least, it is for a good person. But Marik isn't good. He is evil. Corrupt. Despicable.

"You were once a decent male," I say, appealing to the male I once knew. Or at least, the one I thought I knew. Maybe this is who he's been all along, hiding, waiting to strike. A fucking snake, through and through.

He purses his lips, shrugs his shoulders. "That was a long time ago."

I resist the urge to bang my fist on the table, opting instead to dig my fingernails into my thigh. As much as I long to yell all sorts of foul obscenities at him, I remain silent. This is not the time to bite.

I go back to my bread, ripping another piece off, and plopping it into my mouth. I nearly choke when he speaks again. "Would it make you happy if I did?" he asks, glancing up from his meal.

I hesitate. If I say yes, will he say no to spite me? If I say no, will he honor my request to let them go anyway? I take a swig of my water and decide to take a chance on the male I once knew. "Yes."

"Why?"

"They're innocent. They did nothing."

He stares at me, unblinking. Finally, he nods. "I'll release them tomorrow."

My mouth goes dry at the truth in his words. "Really?" I ask.

He grunts in confirmation, then goes back to his dinner. "Thank you," I whisper. Neither of us speaks again for the rest of the night.

M arik follows through on his promise. Which means I was able to follow through on mine to the woman in the cell.

I visit the dungeons the next day to make sure. All traces of the prisoners are gone, even the little girl and the liar. Every cell is empty. No more sounds of soft crying, of people rustling in their sleep. Just the steady drip of water falling to the muddy floor in the darkness.

I breathe a sigh of relief, but it's short-lived. My questions about Eliza Rainey were never answered. Who was she? Why was there a Serpent hybrid in our dungeons pretending to be someone she wasn't? Was it all a test, orchestrated by Marik? Is that why he agreed to release the prisoners?

Or am I overthinking everything?

I shake my head. *No.*

But why else would he release the prisoners?

CHAPTER 9
MAE

Everyone freezes.

The knocks are jarring, each one loud and forceful enough to make the door shake with every *bang*.

Ivan walks to me slowly, one finger pressed against his lips. Luca positions himself in front of the door, hands extended and ready to summon his magic. Holly is frozen, looking from Luca to Ivan to me.

BANGBANGBANG.

Ivan throws his hands up and walks toward the front door on feet now silenced by his sound barrier. From my position in the hallway, I can see a glimpse of the bedroom window overlooking the front yard. I take a slight step backward, steeling myself for whatever—or whoever— it is that's outside. That's found us.

Marik? Cora? An army?

But there's nothing. No guards are stationed in the front yard, no osseri or cambions or Cursed waiting to shred us apart.

It's empty.

BANGBANGBANG.

I step closer to the window, every footstep as light as I can make it, but not quiet enough. Ivan whirls toward me, mouth forming what I assume is a curse when he sees the direction I'm heading. He waves at me, mouth moving behind the barrier, likely yelling at me to get away from the window.

I ignore him and tip-toe closer. He hurries toward me and lunges, reaching for my hand.

But he's too late.

I see who's outside.

I push Ivan away from me and sprint toward the front door. Luca steps in my path, but I shove him out of the way and yank the door open.

Asmo. And Cally, limp in his arms.

Her chest rises and falls, but her eyelids are closed and entirely too still.

Asmo looks exhausted, nearly swaying on his feet. Dark stubble lines his chiseled jaw. His black hair, normally perfectly styled, falls just past his pointed ears in an unbrushed mess. Even though he seems ready to collapse, he looks fine. Unharmed.

Cally, on the other hand...My heart squeezes in my chest. Her cheekbones are sharp as shards of glass, eyes sunken into her skull. Her chestnut curls lay flat against one side of her head, matted and covered in gravel and dirt. The corset of her berry-red bridesmaid dress is crusted in dried blood, fresh blood leaking from a pulsing wound on her stomach.

The smell of rot, of death, radiates from her. She is too thin, too lifeless. Tears well in my eyes, but I wipe them away.

"Bring her inside," Ivan says, gentle but firm. She doesn't stir as he takes her from Asmo. I choke back more tears. She is so still.

Ivan helped all of us recover in the aftermath of the wedding. But he is not a true healer. And if Cally requires more than what Ivan can provide, we might be in trouble.

Ivan shuffles down the hallway, Cally's head bobbing in his arms.

"Put her in my room," Asmo says behind me.

Ivan lays her on Asmo's bed, and tears well again. If I didn't see the rise and fall of her chest, I would have assumed her dead. How much time does she have before that becomes our reality?

Ivan gets to work, hands roaming over Cally. He stops when he gets to the blood on her dress, and glances back at me. "I'm going to cut her dress to get to this wound. You might want to step out."

I plant my feet. "I'm not going anywhere."

She is laying here because of me. Whatever was done to her was because of me, and I will not shy away from the consequences.

But then Ivan peels the dress back and my stomach threatens to empty itself all over the floor.

The wound is raised, a lump of infection, with edges that are beginning to blacken. Blood and pus create a sickening pink that seeps from it. The veins surrounding the wound are bright pink streaks, disappearing behind the rest of the dress.

My stomach protests again. I clap my hand over my mouth and shove past Asmo, and stumble back outside. I pull fresh air into my lungs and fight the nausea.

Soft footsteps come from behind me, stopping only inches way.

"She'll be okay," Asmo whispers.

I take another deep breath, and a tear spills down my cheek. It breaks the damn. I cover my face as they come. Asmo pulls me to him and squeezes me against his chest.

Cally is alive. Cally is alive. Cally. Is. Alive.

And Asmo—Asmo is back. With me—not with his brother. Even so, another part of me is sending off warning bells. Three days is a long time to be gone, and I have no idea what happened during that time. I pull back, and my heart skips a beat as I look at him through my tears.

"Miss me?" Asmo asks, one corner of his mouth tugging upward into a crooked smile.

I shove him. Anger feels so, so much better than whatever I'm currently feeling. And besides, anger has always felt appropriate when dealing with Asmo. It's our game. "Where the fuck have you been?"

"Stop." The bravado falls. His smile slips, my fleeting anger along with it. "Just come back here." I stare at him, my brain at war with my heart. Holly's words ring in my head, while my heart rails against my ribcage, as if it yearns to be closer to him. "Please," he adds. Before my brain can talk me out of it, I take a single step toward him. It's all he needs.

He pulls me back to him, and this embrace feels different than the last. This feels like two lovers holding each other in the middle of a storm. His fingertips dig into me like he's afraid he'll let go. Or like someone will take me from him. He strokes my hair while his heart beats against my cheek.

When Holly suggested that Asmo left on his own and betrayed us... That was something that I was unable to accept. But in the back of my mind, the idea lingered. I would be a fool to completely ignore any possibility. Despite my hesitation and the continued decisions we've both made not to be together, something continues to pull us back to each other. The chemistry between us is undeniable, but so is the friction.

"Mae." His breath is a whisper.

I peer up at him. His dark eyes search my amber, full of pain and longing, and I'm sure mine mirror his. It's how I feel every time I look at him. A throat clears behind us. I break the eye contact and step away, even though every part of me wants to cling to him.

"Welcome back," Ivan says cautiously as we move inside. He sits on the couch, hands clasped tightly in his lap.

"How is she?" I ask.

Ivan's expression softens. "She's alive, but her wound is severe. I cleaned it as best as I could and gave her some of the medicinal sedatives to make sure she stays asleep. She needs to rest," he says with a pointed look.

I was prepared to insist on seeing her, on sitting by her side, but I deflate—part resignation and part exhaustion. "Sure, of course."

"Sit," Luca commands, gaze fixed on Asmo. I barely contain my flinch at his harsh tone, so at odds with the somber reality of Cally laying on death's door down the hall.

"Luca—" I start.

He shakes his head furiously. "No. We have no idea where he's been, what he's been doing, or what information he's been spreading."

"It's okay. I'm a big boy," Asmo says behind me, his hand grazing the small of my back as he steps around me. Back to his usual self, then. But I saw the mask slip.

I hold my hands up. "Fine," I say as I all but collapse onto the couch next to Holly.

Asmo sits in the armchair across from us, leaning forward and resting his elbows on his knees. An errant lock of hair falls forward and brushes against his forehead. His usual carefree demeanor is gone. He wrings his hands together, squeezing his knuckles, the only outward sign that he's nervous.

Luca stands behind one of the worn armchairs, gaze stony as he stares at Asmo.

Asmo doesn't wait for any questions. "Marik locked me in the dungeons for three days. That is where I've been. You can ask Cally to corroborate." He looks at each of us as he speaks, eyes wide and imploring. His gaze lingers on Ivan and Luca as he waits for a response. They don't give one. They stare at him, arms crossed, not a hint of empathy or sympathy. "I don't know why, but something set Marik off with my story. He asked me if I felt that teachers made enough money. I answered honestly and said no. He told me I could keep my money and repay him by sleeping in the dungeons."

"Just his way of exerting control," I mutter.

"Did they know it was you?" Holly asks, then goes back to biting her nails. Her only indicator that she's as nervous as I am.

Asmo shakes his head. "No, I don't think so."

"You don't *think* so?" I ask, sitting forward.

He scrapes his hand through his hair. "No, I don't think Marik knew it was me. I didn't see him at all after the tithe. But I saw Elle."

Luca, previously shifting on his feet, freezes. "Is she okay?"

Asmo hesitates. "Physically...yes, she's fine."

"What the fuck does that mean, Asmo?" I ask, annoyed by the tidbits of information he's giving us.

He sighs and runs a hand through his hair—another nervous tell—and that one lock of hair falls back in line with the rest. "She came down as you, Mae. We were right. She's pretending to be you."

"How are you so sure?" I ask.

He puts his head in his hands, rubbing furiously at his temples. He glances up and says, "It wasn't a glamour. I think they're using the same dark magic we used to get inside the castle."

I wince. Wearing the spell felt like wearing a blanket. The longer I wore it, the heavier it became. "She has to perform that spell every day?"

He nods. "There's something else. She was wearing a necklace that seemed familiar. I think it's a Serpent heirloom."

"Okay, a gift from Marik?" Holly frowns. "So what?"

He shakes his head hurriedly and rubs his temples again. "No, no, I think...I think I've seen it before in my parents' home. They have a private room with rows of jewelry. I swear I've seen that specific necklace in a glass display case that my mother kept locked."

"So *what*?" Holly repeats, staring at him.

He sighs impatiently, as if we're supposed to know the significance of the necklace. "Our mother used to warn us away from playing with her jewelry. She said that some of it was bad. I think that she spelled them with dark magic. I think that's how Marik's keeping Elle in line."

I still. "What do you mean?" My voice is a whisper.

His eyes find mine, pity now lining them. From anyone else, that look would piss me off. But pity coming from Asmo makes my blood run cold. "If what I'm thinking is true, then Marik is using that necklace to control Elle."

I close my eyes, thinking of Marik being in control of anyone. I only saw Marik's true self for a moment after we said our vows. He set William *on fire*. What is he like with Elle, when they're alone? What happens when nobody is around to step in? What happens when his victim is powerless? A shiver runs down my spine.

"Think about it," Asmo continues. "Elle was never afraid to say what was on her mind before. But she seemed skittish. Afraid. And I would bet everything that it was because of that necklace."

Luca begins to pace in the small living room.

"What can we do?" Ivan asks.

Asmo shakes his head. "I don't know. I've been thinking about it since I saw it. All I know is if we have any chance of rescuing her, we have to find out how to remove that necklace. Otherwise, any attempts we make will be useless."

"Wait—how did you get Cally out?" I ask.

Asmo hesitates, but he says, "Someone had been begging Elle for help when she came down. They said there was a woman in her cell that was near death. But I knew Elle wouldn't be able to do anything. I was considering bringing the woman back, anyway. Maybe dumping her at an apothecary. But when I finally got to her, I saw it was Cally. I used my shadow sword to get out of my cell, then I funneled us out."

"Your shadow sword?" I ask.

"Remember when I saved you from the cambion the first time?" he responds. "It's a sword made of shadows that can be used from a distance."

Ah, yes. When the cambion's head went flying from its body.

Ivan straightens. "The cells mute your magic and the dungeons are warded. There's no way you could have used your magic, let alone funnel out."

Every muscle in my body freezes. I detected no deception from Asmo at all. If he lied, he just got around it perfectly. I check that my nets are intact. "Tell me a lie."

Asmo furrows his brow. "What?"

"Now. Anything," I demand.

He locks his eyes on mine and says, "My name is Mae. I'm the High Queen."

The net tugs. Okay, so I haven't suddenly lost the ability to detect lies.

"How did you escape the dungeons with Cally?" I repeat.

He drops his gaze and wrings his hands together in his lap. "Before we went in, I carved another mark on myself that makes me immune to wards or anything that mutes your magic."

Warning bells, once again, go off. But there's not a hint of deception in his answer. Just how much does he know about dark magic? What else is he hiding?

"That is not possible," Luca growls. "The wards are imbued with ancient magic. There is nothing that can get around them."

Asmo's gaze sears into Luca. "But there is. Because I did."

Truth, again.

"How do we get the necklace off?" Holly asks, her chewed fingernails hidden in a tight fist on her thigh.

Asmo shakes his head. "I'm nearly positive it requires venom. That was always my mother's favorite trick for activating dark magic."

Holly stares at Asmo with disgust, and I feel too hot and too cold, and like I might burst out of my chest if I don't get up. I stand and head to the kitchen, the only place I can get space without leaving the room. I grab a glass and fill it with water from the pitcher.

"Anything else?" Luca demands.

Asmo twists to face me, his chiseled jaw looking even sharper than usual. "The wedding guests…They're all in the prison."

It's a small relief that they're still alive, but if they're in the same condition as Cally, they may not be for long. "Are they okay?" I ask.

He rubs the back of his neck. "They're alive. They're being fed. But it's not an existence." *That evil bastard.* "They stared at you—Elle—with resentment. They think you're the one doing this."

My teeth grind together. Well played, Marik.

"Elle's alive, though," Holly says with the first bit of optimism from any of us in days.

Asmo nods. "I don't know why, or what it means, but she seemed to be really interested in me. There were other prisoners down there with me, but she only asked *me* questions."

I grab an apple and head back into the living room. Asmo's gaze drifts to it. I toss it to him, and he snatches it from the air before giving me a thankful nod.

"What kinds of questions?" Ivan asks.

"She asked me my name and occupation mostly," Asmo answers before taking a huge bite from the apple with a satisfying crunch. He closes his eyes as he chews.

"She knew you were lying," I say as I plop back onto the couch beside Holly.

His eyes fly open mid-chew.

"Elle and I are able to detect lies," I explain. "No clue why, but that's one of the powers we hold. I don't know how, but Marik got around it with me. Elle would have known you were lying the moment you said your name. Did she ask these questions in front of Marik?"

He shakes his head.

"Good. That's good," Ivan says.

"Asmo," I say, holding my chin high and bracing myself for what I'm about to ask him. "Did you give anybody any information about us?"

Holly shifts nervously on the couch beside me.

Asmo's gaze is unflinching. "No. I would never." Truth.

"Okay," I say calmly, even though my body threatens to collapse from the intensity of his gaze and the sheer relief that comes with his answer.

"Did you get any other helpful information? What's going on in the castle? What's their security like?" Luca asks.

Asmo swallows a bite of the apple he was chewing. "It's...somber there. They've gotten rid of anybody that was there before and replaced them with Serpent guards. They keep at least two guards on Elle at all times. The castle is locked down, and they're not letting anybody inside. That's all I was able to get. They kept me locked in the dungeon the whole time."

"Did you see Cora? Or any witches?" I ask.

Asmo shakes his head.

Holly puts her head in her hands and groans. "How are we going to get Elle out of there?"

"I don't know," I say, feeling utterly doomed. Asmo getting Cally out was one thing, but sneaking into the castle and getting Elle out will be an entirely different mission.

"We have to get her, Mae," Holly says.

"I know," I whisper.

But I have no idea how to do it.

CHAPTER 10
MAE

I END up going to bed earlier than everyone, citing a headache. Really, I need to stop thinking about Elle and all the ways we've failed her.

Cally is fast asleep when I check on her, chest rising and falling in an easy rhythm. She lays sprawled across Asmo's bed, the sheets shoved to the side. She wears some combination of Asmo's and Luca's clothes, the blood-crusted ballgown discarded in the corner of the room.

I watch her for several moments before turning back to my own bedroom. It only takes a few minutes to realize sleep won't be coming for me tonight. I lay there for as long as I can stand, then shrug my coat on.

Ivan is asleep on the sofa when I pad down the hall, his snores emanating throughout the cozy living room. The bitter night air greets me like an old friend as I step outside.

I nearly jump from my skin when I see Asmo sitting in Ivan's usual chair.

"Miss me?" he repeats the question from earlier, but without his usual cockiness. It just comes off as sad this time.

"What are you doing out here?" I rub my arms as I try to stave off the permeating cold.

"Couldn't sleep. Thought I'd give staring at the forest a try. Seems to work for you," he says with a shrug.

I grab a green and black flannel throw blanket from the pile stacked against the wall.

"Yes, well, part of why I love coming out here is the silence," I say, glaring at him as I wrap the blanket around me and settle into the chair beside him.

Asmo follows my every movement, like a predator tracking its prey. "I'll shut up then. Whatever the princess wants."

A warmth takes hold in my chest. I missed hearing the nickname. "Thank you," I say, tucking my knees to my chest.

The silence only lasts for a few moments before he breaks it again. "I can see why you like it out here so much. The forest is calming. The sound of the wind. The birds, the owls. It's peaceful."

I nod, trying to discourage conversation. I'm so tired.

"Mae," he whispers. The warmth in my chest vanishes as I take in his slumped posture, his usual cocky smile gone. He looks sad. Small. A version of himself I'm not familiar with. One that I'm certain no one is familiar with.

I've seen Asmo furious, annoyed, lustful, surprised—but never defeated. He's always seemed so strong, so unbreakable to me. But now he's staring at me like he's a broken version of himself, and like I have the power to put him back together again.

"What are we doing?" he whispers.

A gentle breeze floats past, his question hanging in the air.

"I don't know," I whisper back. "I don't know how to get it back. I don't know how to fix this, save Cally, save Elle, save the kingdom. I don't know."

I don't know how to save us.

I don't know how to save myself.

"We have to figure something out. We can't just sit here."

Anger sparks inside of me at his response. I welcome it, grabbing hold of it in an instant. Anger is a fire I can breathe life into. I glare at him. And damn it, if I don't see a corner of his mouth twitch.

"You think I don't know that? All I do is think about what to do and how hopeless it all feels. Six months ago, my biggest problem was making sure bookshelves were stocked and figuring out what I was going to make for dinner. I don't know how or why *I'm* responsible for saving a kingdom. I don't know why anybody put *me* in charge of this. I don't know what the fuck I'm doing, and now Elle is a prisoner and people are dead and I don't know what to *do*," I snap.

He nods slowly, like he's scared to push me. And just like that, the fire has been extinguished. That's not the part he's supposed to play. He's supposed to snap back at me, not be broken beside me.

"I'm just one person." My voice comes out soft.

"No," he says forcefully. "Don't do that. You're not just *one person*. You're one of the most powerful hybrids in the kingdom. You're the High Queen. You took an oath, a vow to protect this kingdom. And just because it got a little hard, that doesn't mean you just get to quit."

I put my head in my hands. "I'm not quitting, I'm just...I don't know what to do," I groan.

He closes the distance between us and grips the wooden armrests. "So, think. All you do is sit here and stare at nothing. *Think.*"

I throw my hands in the air. "Oh, if only it were that easy to figure out a way to stop Marik, and oh—don't forget—the most powerful witch in our history!"

He leans back into his chair and rolls his eyes. "Who gives a shit about easy? Do you think I'd be here, with you, if I was looking for the easy way? It would have been easy for me to just join my family in over-throwing the kingdom. But I didn't. I chose what's right. I chose you."

His response hits me like a ton of bricks. He chose me. While I chose his brother. And made the biggest mistake of my life. We've been dancing around this conversation since the wedding, neither of us brave enough to cross the line. Neither of us brave enough to admit what we're thinking to one another. I've been treading this line for weeks, scared of who he really is and how he might hold the power to hurt me again.

And right now, I find I just don't give a fuck. The weight on my shoulders grows stronger every day. If I don't do something about it, it will bury me. "I'm sorry I didn't choose you."

His eyes soften briefly before hardening again. "That's not what I meant, Mae." He runs his hands through his wavy hair, mussing it up even more. "Besides, you did. I said no."

"I could have fought harder for you," I counter. He doesn't respond. The air between us is thick with regret for the things we did and didn't do. "I'm sorry you had to choose between me and your family," I whisper.

He shrugs. "I've always hated them."

"Really? Even Marik?"

He shifts in his chair. "My parents? Yes, absolutely." He pauses. When he looks at me, his eyes are full of pity again. I look at the floor. "I'm sorry he did that to you, Mae. For what it's worth, I didn't see it coming," he whispers.

Me either. "Do you hate Marik?" I close my eyes, bracing myself for the blow of Asmo revealing himself to me.

Even the forest has gone silent. He takes three breaths, every exhale long. "I don't know," he admits. "A part of me—a huge part of me—does. For what he did to you. To Etta, and to William. But he is my brother, and the way we were raised was...I blame my parents."

I chance a glance at him, but he's lost in whatever memories he's recalling. He grips the armrests, pale knuckles bathed in moonlight. "Marik has always been ambitious. I just never thought...He was always the better one of us. He was always sweeter, more patient, kinder. Maybe that's why he did it. He always wanted to make my parents happy. I never cared about that. But Marik? He always blamed himself for the way they treated us. Maybe this was his way of making them proud."

"A pretty fucked up way," I mutter.

His answering nod is heavy. "I don't know what to do either," he admits.

I turn to him and raise my eyebrows in mock surprise. "Wow, I didn't know you were capable of admitting defeat so easily."

He rolls his eyes. "I'm not admitting defeat. Not even close. I just don't know how we can fix this. We need help."

My eyes widen.

We need help.

"There's no way the other High Houses are happy with what's happening right now. We need to speak with them."

He hesitates. "I don't think they know the truth. My guess is they believe you're on the throne and that you're responsible for the current state of the kingdom."

I shake my head, refusing to accept that. "No. They were there that day. They helped us fight. I don't understand how *that* hasn't gotten out to the public."

His mouth twists into a grimace. "If I were in Marik's shoes, I would do everything in my power to convince the Houses that Elle—or whoever it is—really is you, and that you're in agreement with everything."

"They'd never believe that, though. I know Barrett, August, and Koa."

He frowns. "You have to remember who we are, princess. Who we were raised to be. We are ruthless, but we will yield to remain in power. The High Houses have been in power for a thousand years. We have always listened to the High Family, whether we agree or disagree. The High Crown is too powerful to ignore. And if I know my brother, he's likely using other means and manipulation tactics to convince the High Families to fall in line."

I stare into the dark forest. A hawk silently cuts through the night air.

How are we supposed to fight this?

I look at Asmo. He stares at me with those damned soft eyes again, as if he's waiting for me to break down. He leans forward, reaching for me with one hand. "Come here," he says softly.

"No." I turn away from him, back to the forest, eager for anything to distract me from the pity in his eyes.

"Damnit, Mae. Let me be there for you," he growls.

I hesitate, considering giving in. But I shake my head. "No. This is my responsibility to bear, not yours. I'm fine. I'll figure this out. I'm not the fragile princess you met six months ago."

Despite my words, tears prick at the corners of my eyes again.

He stands abruptly and crosses the space between us, scooping me into his arms before he sits back in his chair. I squirm, trying to push him away, but he holds me too tightly. I stop fighting almost instantly, the feeling of being in his arms too strong to give up.

"I know you're not. You never were." His chest rumbles against my cheek. "We'll figure it out."

I close my eyes, and let myself believe him. We'll figure it out. *We.*

"How did you find us?" I ask. It's something I was thinking about while lying in bed. Somehow, nobody thought to ask him that question when he returned. I guess the bigger question was *Did he betray us?*

"Hm?" he mumbles, his breath tickling the top of my head.

I check my nets again and ask, "We moved safe houses. How did you find us?"

It's possible I'm imagining the way his pulse ticks up. "I'd find you anywhere, princess. You know that." I twist and try to get some more distance from him, but he holds me close. "Stop. Please. Just trust me."

I swallow a frustrated sigh. He's right. His words are his truth, whatever they mean. After all, he was the one who knew I was in trouble on the shower floor. He was the one who knew something was wrong. He was the one who found me when the cambion was dragging me into the woods. When the osseris—Marik—had me in its grip.

"Would you go back? To your House, if you could?" I ask, changing the subject. I peer up at him, at the moon glistening in the black pools of his eyes, at the long lashes that flutter as he avoids my gaze.

His jaw flexes once, twice. "Yes."

His answer isn't surprising. He denied me because he wanted to remain in his court.

I don't ask any more questions. There will be time for that later, time to figure out all that comes next. For now, I let him hold me until my eyes drift closed, listening to the quiet sounds of the forest and the beat of his heart against my cheek.

CHAPTER 11
MAE

I WAKE in my own bed, the soft touch of the pillow far different than the warmth of Asmo's chest. The distant sounds of rustling in the kitchen and the smell of eggs have me throwing back the covers. I stop at Asmo's door and peek my head in. Cally still lies on the bed, face pale and limbs sprawled. Sweat dampens her forehead, despite the lack of blankets covering her.

Holly hovers a skillet of eggs over dark flames in the kitchen while Luca gathers plates from the cabinet. She offers me a smile, then dips her head toward the living room, where Ivan and Asmo are whispering furiously to one another. They glance up as I enter. Asmo's eyes soften as they land on me, and I resist the urge to smooth my hair.

Ivan clears his throat and forces a smile, but it's weak. "Morning, Your Highness."

I skip the pleasantries. "What's wrong?"

Sure enough, Ivan's smile falls, a frown now in its place. "Cally is not responding to the medicinal herbs as I had hoped. That wound appears to have been repeatedly infected." He rubs the gray scruff along his jaw. "The infection has spread and entered her bloodstream."

"What does that mean?"

Ivan's inhale is shaky, and I prepare myself for whatever he's about to say. "The resources we have here are not enough to save her."

I freeze, a tingling spreading from my chest to my arms as panic begins to take hold. "So, we need to get her to a healer."

"There is another, less risky option. An extract imbued with Fae magic, but it is only available in specialized apothecaries in hybrid towns."

The tingling abates. Thank the Mother. "Great. I'll go."

Ivan shakes his head. "Luca and I have already discussed it. He's prepared to leave soon."

If they think I'm not about to help fix the mess that I've created, they're wrong. And if they think I'm about to sit here by myself and not help save my best friend's life, they're insane. "I wasn't joking. I'm going."

Luca's face twists into a scowl. "Your Highness—"

"I'll use the dark magic sigil and I'll be fine."

Asmo stiffens. "There is a cost to using dark magic," he says gravely. "You can't just use it whenever you want. It chips away at you."

Luca storms from the kitchen. "Might I remind you, Your Highness, that the last time you ventured somewhere, a group of witches found us?"

I understand the risk I'm taking, but if I can't provide this one small thing for the only person who has been beside me for years, who was captured, thrown in a dungeon, and is now literally on the edge of death, because of me, then what good am I? All I've managed to do is endanger everyone around me.

At least this way, I'm only endangering myself.

"I need to do this," I admit.

Asmo watches me, dark eyes unblinking, jaw working. "Okay," he says. "We change our appearance and go get the extract. Princess, which House was friendliest to the High Crown?"

I can feel Luca's gaze burning a hole in my profile.

"Canis," I answer.

"You're sure?"

I nod. Canis will be the safest. August is a good male.

You thought Marik was, too, I chide myself. *Look how that turned out.*

"Okay then. Let's go." He stands abruptly and holds his hand out to me.

"You can't be serious," Luca says as he pushes himself from his chair. "We have to plan this. We have no idea where we're going."

"*You* don't need to have a plan. Mae and I are going. You're staying here," Asmo says, his hand still outstretched, eyes still on mine.

"Absolutely not," Luca says, nostrils flaring and voice turning shrill. "Your Highness, need I remind you that not even twenty-four hours ago, we were considering the fact that he might have betrayed us?" he asks, gesturing to Asmo.

"Your choice," Asmo whispers to me. His eyes are doing that thing again where they turn soft, like he's afraid I'll say no. Like it would hurt him if I did.

My body reacts before my brain does, and my hand reaches for his.

"Let's go," I say as I stand. Luca mutters something under his breath that sounds a lot like *stupid.*

Asmo leads me to the kitchen and hands me a knife. "Do you remember the spell? Do you know who you're going to transform into?"

I nod, the female deer hybrid etched into my memory. From guilt or necessity, I don't want to think about which. The blade is light in my palm. I lift my shirt and carve the mark into my stomach, whispering the words. *As are you, as am I.*

My blood turns black as it evaporates into the air.

Beside me, Asmo repeats the spell. But he's not the girl from before. He looks similar to his usual self, but his features are different. Gone is the defined jawline, the strong cheekbones, the fern-green slivers in pools of night. He just looks like an average male with black hair and dark eyes.

"Did you make yourself shorter, too?" I ask.

"I made myself average height."

"Are you not already average height?"

He clasps a hand to his chest. "You wound me."

Back in the living room, Ivan hands Asmo a slip of paper. "The name of the extract. You should be able to find it at any apothecary that specializes in Fae healing magic."

Luca glares at us as we walk toward the front door. "Mae, think about this. You could be walking into a trap."

"I'll have her back before sundown, Dad," Asmo says sarcastically before taking my hand and pulling me out the door.

When we're outside, Asmo stops and faces me. "We don't have to do this, Mae. We can walk right back inside and tell Ivan it was all one big joke."

I shake my head. "No. I'm tired of sitting around and doing nothing. Let's go."

He grins. "That's my girl."

"We should've thought about this more," I groan. The wind whips around us, snow falling slowly but steadily as we descend into the capital of House Canis. Bouldercrest is situated in the valley of the Wolven Peaks, known for its packs of wolves that roam the slopes. Unfortunately, Bouldercrest is also the coldest town I've ever been to.

"I didn't know it got this cold," I complain as we stomp through a blanket of snow that's at least a foot deep. Stubborn goosebumps pepper my skin, still lingering even after I rub my arms through my thin coat.

"My fault. I forgot you've never been here," Asmo says. "Would you like me to carry you, Your Highness?"

I shoot him a look. "How would that help?"

"You'd be against my chest. Nice and toasty," he says with a dazzling grin. Even in his *average* disguise, he still manages to have the same disarming smile.

I roll my eyes. "How close are we?"

He grabs my arm and stops walking. He looks around slowly,

pointed ears perked. Panic and magic flares in my veins. I know better than to ask what's wrong. But even with my sharp senses, I don't hear anything out of the ordinary. Only the silence of the forest cloaked in snow.

"Probably just a wolf," I say, but even I'm not so sure.

"Just be careful with what you say," Asmo mutters, lacing his fingers into mine and resuming down the path.

I refrain from asking why. My brain doesn't work anymore, anyway, with his hand in mine. Something so normal, like holding hands, isn't for us. His grip tightens, like he's thinking about the way our fingers are intertwined, too.

Silence falls between us for the rest of the walk, both of us on high alert. A pack of midnight-black wolves passes, watching us carefully before continuing up the mountain. The only sound is the crunch of our boots as they stomp through the thin layer of ice covering the snow.

The town comes into view, stone buildings built into the steep mountainside and descending into the valley. The roofs are capped with snow, smoke billowing from the chimneys. The scent of burning wood drifts toward me, reminding me of freezing nights beside the fire. And Willa—no, Cora.

A sharp wind cuts between the trees, and I lean closer to Asmo. We are miserably under-dressed and woefully out of place. We step into the first clothing store we find, my fingers and toes tingling as they start to defrost.

"'lo there!" a slim wolf hybrid calls from the counter at the back of the store. "Help you with anything?" The icy blue of his eyes reminds me of August.

Asmo clears his throat. "My wife and I are from out of town. Can you believe that we forgot our coats?" He chuckles as if the thought is just absurd. "Poor thing was shivering all the way from the portal!" He grabs my shoulders and rubs them.

I play along and throw a sheepish smile at the store clerk, but *wife* clangs around my head, making me buzz.

The wolf hybrid eyes us. For a moment, I think he's going to whip my shirt up and expose my mark. "Forgive me for saying this, but that wasn't very smart of you. You're lucky it's a warm day here. If you had portaled in during one of our snowstorms, you would have needed to portal right back. The weather conditions can be brutal up here. Where did you say you're from?"

A warm day? I was practically frozen solid the moment we stepped from the portal. I make a mental note to never come back during the peak of winter.

"My wife is from the Deer Court," Asmo says with a smile, as if that explains it.

"Ah," the male says.

I can't help but feel like I'm missing something. Thankfully, Asmo breaks the silence before it can drag on too long. "Can you point us in the direction of the coats?"

"Right back there," he says, gesturing toward the righthand side of the store. "Let me know if I can help."

Asmo throws his arm around me and tugs me toward the wall of coats. I grab a black one that goes to my ankles. Asmo chooses a plain black wool coat and a charcoal scarf from a stand near the register. We place our items on the counter and wait for the clerk to give us our total.

"Deer Court, huh?" he asks as he surveys our selections.

"Uh-huh," I confirm, unwilling to give any more information than that.

"What brings you two here?"

"We thought we'd do some traveling for our honeymoon," Asmo says, a warm smile on his face.

"Bad time to travel," the shop owner mutters.

"Why's that?" I ask, attempting to sound nonchalant. I think I pull it off, but Asmo squeezes my hand. *Be careful.*

The wolf hybrid raises an eyebrow at me. "Things must be just fine in the Deer Court then, huh?" I don't respond, not sure of what to say to that. The wolf hybrid leans closer and lowers his voice. "Just be careful, alright? Black-leather witches roam the streets now. But the night is when it gets bad. I would stay inside if I were you. The Cursed have begun to roam the streets when the sun goes down."

I freeze. The cambions haunt my nightmares. But since I got a glimpse of the Cursed, images of hollow-eyed bears and wolves now chase me in my dreams. Knowing they're now stationed throughout the kingdom and are controlled by black-leather witches—vicious, powerful witches who have climbed through the ranks and slaughtered countless —even their own kind—to secure their spot at the top...My stomach hollows.

"I've heard of black-leather witches...but the Cursed?" I play dumb. I will never forget the dread I felt when I saw them walking down the street in Briar's Glen.

He scowls. "Undead woodland creatures," he explains. "An abomination to the Mother and an affront to the sanctity of us all."

"Shit," Asmo mutters.

Shit, indeed.

The shop owner nods solemnly. "King Conall and Prince August themselves have been seen walking the streets more, keeping an eye on things. Scary times."

A silence falls as Asmo pulls the coin purse from his pocket and begins counting out the total.

"Erm—is there any chance you know of any healing shops near here?" I ask the shopkeeper, then turn to Asmo. "What kind did your mother need?"

He sets the total on the counter and slides it across. "She needs something from the Fae healers?"

The shopkeeper tilts his head. "Hm...There's an apothecary just down the way. Take a right when you exit and you'll see it on the right-hand side a few doors down. If they don't have what you're looking for, they should know how to help."

"Thank you. And thanks for the warning," Asmo says.

The shopkeeper dips his head in acknowledgement. "Wish I didn't have to give it."

We throw our coats on before we exit the shop. The door slams shut behind us, sending a final gust of warm air toward us as if in farewell. Asmo reaches for my hand and laces his fingers between mine. My cheeks warm, despite the freezing temperature.

"Wit—"

"Not here," Asmo says firmly.

True to the shopkeeper's word, the apothecary is exactly three shops down, with a door the color of pine that reminds me of home. The scent of earth and spices wraps around me as we enter—cinnamon and chamomile and other scents I can't place. Wooden shelves line every inch of the walls, filled with glass bottles and jars sitting in neat rows.

A gray wolf sits beside the counter, yellow eyes tracking our movements. My heart leaps into my throat when I see it.

"Hello," I say tentatively to the wolf, but it remains still as a statue.

Asmo pulls the slip of paper from his pocket and begins to survey the walls of jars. A door on the back wall opens, and a figure steps through, hunched over something as they walk backward through the door.

"Need some help with that?" Asmo asks.

The figure whirls, crystal-blue eyes wide, and glass bottles go tumbling from the top of the wooden box in her hands. "Oh n—"

On instinct, I send out a burst of magic that cradles the bottles midair.

She releases a sigh of relief and says, "Thank you so much. That would have been a pain to clean up." She walks to the wooden counter and sets the remaining items on its surface. "You can set them here, if you don't mind."

I float the remaining items to rest on the counter. "Close call," I say lamely.

The female huffs a laugh and straightens. "Sorry about that. What can I do for you? Looking for anything in particular?"

"Yes, actually," Asmo says. "We're looking for something with..." He glances at the paper in his hands. "*Agligella*, or any healing extract with Fae magic. Do you happen to have something like that?"

"What for?" She begins placing the glass bottles on shelves behind the counter, but she doesn't look away from us. She must know this place like the back of her hands.

"My mother fell and has a nasty wound that won't seem to go away," Asmo says. The lie snags against my net.

The shopkeeper frowns. "An extract like that is going to cost you. Those kinds of things are harder and harder to come by since the Fae fell."

"Do you have it?" Asmo asks.

She shakes her head and I want to squeeze my eyes shut, if only to pretend I didn't see her answer. "But I know where you can find some. There's another apothecary that specializes in rare tinctures and salves. They'll have what you're looking for."

"Where is it?" I ask.

"It's not exactly in town," she says. "Are you familiar with the portal on the cliff?" Asmo and I nod simultaneously. It's the only portal location I'm familiar with in this region. "There are two paths—one into town and one that goes up the mountain. If you follow that path all the way up, you'll stumble upon a tiny shack and you'll find what you need there."

Every word rings true, but it doesn't sound exactly...safe. "A shack near the top of the mountain?" Asmo asks dubiously.

The shopkeeper gives us a shaky grimace. "I know. Look, it's my father's shop. He isn't exactly fond of socializing, so he prefers to be out of the path of most hybrids. But he'll be able to help."

Truth again. Asmo looks at me. I nod. "Okay, thank you for your help," he says.

We turn to leave, but the shopkeeper stops us. "One more thing— He's only open to the public in the first hour before sundown."

I grit my teeth, then force myself to exhale. This male will have what we need for Cally.

"Thank you," Asmo tosses over his shoulder.

The wolf's yellow eyes don't leave us until the door closes.

"Fuck," I mutter once we're back on the streets of Bouldercrest.

Asmo shoves his hands into his coat pockets and leans against the gray exterior of the apothecary. "Well, princess, we have some time to kill."

I frown. "Should we just come back?"

Asmo grins, his eyes crinkling and his dimple appearing. "I have a better idea."

My stomach does somersaults at the way he's looking at me. "What?"

"What about a little date?" he asks, his smile flickering at the question, as if he's afraid of my answer.

My cheeks feel too warm, and I refrain from loosening the scarf around my neck. "A—a date?" We have so many other things to think about and a date is a complete and utter waste of time.

His smile falters again, and my heart lurches at the vulnerability that shines in his eyes.

"Okay," I say. "Let's go on a date."

CHAPTER 12
MAE

WE FIND A LOCAL TAVERN—THE Fox Den—sandwiched between a tailor's shop and an indoor market. The door chimes as we step inside and, like a gentleman, Asmo pulls a barstool out for me. The fabric is worn, as if thousands of people have sat here before me. The faded seats, the clinking of glasses, and the sharp smell of alcohol remind me of the tavern Cally and I used to visit every weekend. A wave of homesickness washes over me.

"This is my favorite way to learn about a town. Just listening to the conversations around us," Asmo's deep voice whispers in my ear, his breath hot on my neck. A shiver of pleasure rolls its way down my spine.

"And that's what you like to do on your dates?"

He pulls out the seat beside me. "I thought you'd learned by now that it doesn't matter what we do together. Training, arguing, people watching—it makes no difference."

"What do you mean?"

He signals the bartender, then looks back to me, his gaze searing. "You know exactly what I mean."

He's right. Before the wedding, it didn't matter what Asmo said or did—the pull to him was stronger every minute I spent with him. The fury he incited in me did nothing to lessen that.

"Get you?" the bartender asks, pulling Asmo's attention away from me.

"Two beers."

The bartender pours two tall glasses of the light ale and slides them over, not bothering to spare us another glance. Asmo leans back in his chair, his legs spreading until his knee is resting against mine. I don't move my leg.

He pulls my chair closer to his and throws his arm around the back of it, fingertips brushing against my shoulder, every graze feeling like a burst of fire.

He dips his head, lowering his mouth to my ear. "What I feel for you. It's always there." His voice is rough, low. My stomach does that thing again where it twists. "Even if all we ever did was fight, it would still be there. So, it makes no difference."

Every word is true, a caress against my net. From the moment I met him, all we've managed to do is clash against one other. Yet, that tug toward him remains, strengthens even. Even if it feels like a constant cycle of two beings colliding again and again, then trying to salvage whatever they can from the wreckage.

But right now, it doesn't feel like a collision. It feels natural, and warm, and maybe a little bit like home.

His thumb strokes rhythmic patterns on my shoulder, and we people-watch for another beer. A couple sits together in the corner, hunched over a game of chess. A group of hybrids sit around a table exchanging raucous tales of debauchery. A mother and her teenage son share a basket of bread and cheese.

I wonder if Asmo sees the couple in the corner. I wonder if he wishes that might be us some day.

It's been *months* since I've felt like a normal person, since I've even thought about sitting in a tavern. Since I've gone anywhere without a team of people looking after me. Since I've felt safe.

Asmo turns to me, a twinkle in his dark eyes. "Ever played billiards?"

A grin spreads across my face.

He downs his beer and places it on the bar. He offers me his hand, and I accept. I can't help but think about how this is the most our hands have ever touched. Asmo's hands, even in this body, are nice. They're big, his fingers strong, his palms rough and calloused.

He leads me to an empty billiards table, one hand on the small of my waist. As he meticulously racks the billiard balls, a sharp crack and raucous laughter come from our left. Two Canis males have just finished a game, and one of them toasts me with his beer when he catches me looking. Sometimes I forget how friendly Canis are, unlike the male beside me who's currently wearing a rare grin as he circles the table, as if he's already won.

Game on, Asmo.

We play two games, each of us winning one. He heads back to the bar for another round as I set up the next game, buzzing from the alcohol and the anticipation of kicking his ass.

"You know, you're not bad at billiards, but you'd do a lot better if you put some power behind your shots," Asmo says, returning with a frosted glass pitcher of the light ale.

I roll my eyes. "How badly were you beaten last game?"

His crooked smile is answer enough. "Mind if I show you?"

"By all means," I say, gesturing to the table.

He grabs one of the polished sticks and hands it to me. He steps behind me, lining his body with mine before gently guiding me to the edge of the billiards table until the fronts of my thighs are pressed against it. He slides his hand down my arm, stopping just above my hand.

"Bend over," Asmo whispers in my ear, his breath sending shivers down my spine again.

My body instinctively reacts, my backside pressing into his crotch.

Oh. I'm not the only one who's turned on. Heat rises to my cheeks.

His left hand guides the billiards stick up while his right hand guides my own into position.

"Now, bring this arm back and use some of your power to drive it forward," he whispers against my neck, bringing my right arm back and firing it forward.

The black cue ball shoots forward, sending the target balls in every direction.

I turn in his arms, a smile on my face. "That was my best one yet!"

"If you win this one, you have to give me the credit," he says, his voice husky and low.

"And if I don't?" I tease, desperately trying to cling to any sense of control I have when I'm pressed this close to him. Even in different bodies, our chemistry is undeniable. As if our very souls pull toward one another.

"You have to make everything hard, don't you?" he growls.

"It certainly *feels* like I do," I say a little breathlessly as I press my hips further into his.

His eyes dart to my mouth. My head feels light at the memory of his lips on mine. Of his lips on my—

"Get a room!" someone yells in our direction.

Asmo's eyes darken. "Sorry, man." He forces a smile, but it doesn't meet his eyes. He pulls away from me, revealing the two wolf hybrids watching us from the billiards table beside us. The taller one has sandy-blond hair and eyes the color of a storm cloud, while the shorter one has straight black hair and eyes the color of the sky.

"I'm so sorry," I say, not faking the blush on my cheeks. "We just got married," I lie, hoping that's enough for them to get off our backs.

"No way!" the taller male says. "Congrats!" He walks over to us and offers a hand to Asmo. "I'm Flint. This is Firo." Asmo takes Flint's hand and shakes it briefly. I offer them both a smile. "You two don't look like you're from around here."

Asmo chuckles. "Is it that obvious?"

"We're from the Deer Court. Well, I am. This is my first time traveling outside of my court," I say, feigning shyness and hoping it comes across as genuine. Technically, it's not a lie.

"Welcome to the Court of Wolves!" Flint lets loose a howl and pulls me in for a hug. Asmo goes rigid, but the wolf hybrid lets me go.

I can't help but laugh. "Thanks. Anything we should make sure to check out while we're here?"

Flint's smile disappears. "Actually, about that...It's not exactly a great time to be traveling around the town..." He looks at Firo hesitantly and rubs the back of his neck.

"Why's that?" I ask, even though I know the answer. *Witches.*

"Well, between you and me..." He leans forward, lowering his voice to a conspiratorial whisper. "The witches are becoming a problem. Not just around here, but across the kingdom. And we're seeing more of the Cursed..." he trails off, as if expecting me to gasp or ask him for more information.

I play my part with a sharp inhale. "The Cursed?"

He buys it. He nods apologetically, like he's sorry he's the one that has to break the news of the horrors that now plague the kingdom. "Creepy undead monsters the witches control. They only come out at night, but they're terrifying."

Just like with the shopkeeper, I don't fake my shudder. "How do you know that?" Even though we saw witches in the human town, I don't recall any mention of this being a kingdom-wide problem in any of the newspapers Ivan's brought home.

His grin threatens to split his face. "You have to promise not to tell anyone. I only tell my secrets to pretty girls. But you're taken, so I'm going out on a limb here, okay?"

Asmo stiffens beside me at the blatant flirtation. The balls on Flint...

I play into it and lean in closer to him, holding out my right pinky. "Pinky promise," I say with a flirtatious smile.

He wraps his pinky around mine and lowers his voice even further. "Prince August is my cousin, and he told me that the witches are becoming a problem. He told me all that." He beams.

I freeze at the truth in his words, then remember the role I'm playing. "You're kidding!" I say with a dramatic gasp.

Flint's expression is smug. He's either a fucking idiot or a hell of a liar. But I'm not feeling any deception. Fucking idiot, then.

"I've always wanted to meet him," I say, and a plan begins to take hold. A shoddy, spur-of-the-moment plan that only a fucking idiot would agree to. "You know what? I have a single friend. She's gorgeous. She might be a good match for August. Wait, now that I think about it...She might be a good match for you, too."

Flint's expression turns from smug to cautious. "Oh, I dunno."

Fuck.

"I think she mentioned recently going out with Prince Koa, didn't she? I'm not sure if she's still single," Asmo says from beside me, and I want to wrap him in my arms and kiss his beautiful brain for catching onto my last-minute plan.

"Oh, you're right. Too bad, huh?" I say in faux disappointment.

"Well, wait. She must be gorgeous, huh? And you think she'd be a good fit for me?" Flint asks hopefully.

He really is a fucking idiot.

I place my finger on my chin and look at the ceiling for a moment as I pretend to consider this. "I think it might be a good match, but I also think she would be good with Prince August from what I've heard about him."

"He does have a thing for deer hybrids," Firo mutters to Flint. I could kiss Firo right now, too.

Flint twists his mouth as he considers the offer. "But is she with Koa?"

I shake my head. "Not that I know of. Nothing official yet, at least. Maybe you and Prince August could meet her, see if anything clicks," I offer.

"If she's good enough for Koa..." Flint says, raising his eyebrows at Firo, who just shrugs. A man of few words.

"Hey, think about it," I say with a warm smile. "We'll be here for a little longer. I'm happy to bring her back with us one day soon. Just let me know."

I grab Asmo's hand and lead him back to the bar. We both order waters this time.

"You're lucky that happened. I was about to annihilate you in another game," I say with a wink.

"Bullshit," he says, nudging me with his elbow. "Hey, you did good back there."

"Don't act so surprised. But also, if we can pull this off...I'll never question my luck again. And if he really *is* August's cousin, August needs to know what he's up to. Who knows how many *pretty girls* he's telling this information to?"

My sloppy plan works. Only ten minutes pass before Flint walks back up to us.

We meet with August in three days.

CHAPTER 13
MAE

THE SUN HAS ALREADY BEGUN its descent behind the mountain peak, the dusk growing stronger with every passing minute. Bouldercrest looks a far cry from the bustling town it had been earlier. All that remains are vendors as they close their carts and head home. Doors are dead bolted shut and windows shuttered closed. The wind now cuts through the streets quicker, as if it, too, is in a hurry to pass through the town before the night falls.

"This should be fun," I murmur. The few remaining hybrids still out walk with their heads down.

"The second we get this extract, we're beelining for the portal," I say to Asmo, but he just smirks.

"We'll be fine."

Silence falls between us as we begin the trek back up the mountain. My legs begin to burn after approximately two minutes. I used to be able to sprint up hills without a second thought, but now, my muscles scream at me in protest and my breathing turns labored within moments.

"Let me know if you need a break," Asmo says, his breathing annoyingly normal. "Or a ride."

If my cheeks weren't already pink from exertion, they would have turned pink at the thought of riding him.

We pass the split in the path back to the portal location and continue up, the layer of snow growing thicker the more we climb. The temperature continues to drop as the sun descends, and the thin layer of sweat from climbing is only making me colder. To top it all off, my head aches, a slow but steady throbbing building near my temples.

The shack is exactly that—a shack. Smoke rises in lazy puffs from the stone chimney. A singular window is illuminated by a warm glow from the inside. The butter-yellow door's paint is chipped and weathered, but an apothecary jar is painted in white in the center.

Asmo enters first. I follow, and the overwhelming scent of spices hits me like a wall. The room is stuffy, but it beats standing outside in the cold. A small hearth blazes in the far corner of the room, surrounded by shelves of glass jars. A figure is bent over a wooden counter, gray tail swishing as he works.

The apothecarist from earlier said her father preferred to stay out of the way. Seeing the tail brings a new understanding to why. Although the Woodland Kingdom is comprised of hybrids with animalistic features, some of those features are deemed unappealing, though that's probably too kind a word. Hybrids with furry ears, tails, and hands that resemble paws often face prejudice, and use glamours to hide them. But some choose not to hide, and society makes them pay for that choice.

I clear my throat. "Excuse me."

He turns, his eyes the same crystal blue as the apothecarist from earlier. They flash to mine, then to the ground. "What can I help you with?"

"Your daughter sent us here," I say warmly. "My husband's mother is ill. We were hoping you might have *agligella,* or if not, any healing extract imbued with the magic of the Fae."

He mumbles something, then turns his back to us as he walks to the wall of jars. He plucks a small jar from a shelf near the top and sets it on the counter. "Sixty coins."

I blink. Sixty coins for that tiny jar? I look to Asmo, but his face is unbothered. He pulls the coin purse from his pocket and steps toward the wolf hybrid.

"Just put it there," he says, pointing to the counter closest to us.

Asmo narrows his gaze. "You don't want to count it?"

"It looks enough," the hybrid answers, refusing to look at us.

Asmo slides the outrageous amount onto the counter and reaches for the jar. The hybrid doesn't even take the payment, just leaves it and shuffles back to his spot on the far wall. He turns his back to us once more, bent over whatever task he was working on when we first arrived.

Asmo eyes the jar, an herb-green paste inside. "This is the right thing?" The apothecarist nods his head. Asmo looks at me pointedly, then asks, "This is the Fae-imbued extract?"

"Yes." Truth.

I nod and Asmo shrugs, then turns back toward the door. "Thank you," I say over my shoulder, the hybrid's tail swishing one last time as I shut the door behind me.

"Interesting male," Asmo says as we traverse back down the path.

"A little odd, but can you blame him? His tail has probably made his life difficult. I'd live up here, too, if I were him."

In the few moments we were inside, the sun dipped below the mountain, taking its light—and any remaining warmth—with it. I nearly trip over a fallen log, but Asmo's hand is there to steady me.

When I look back up, my breath lodges in my throat. A figure emerges from behind a tree, head tilted and golden eyes so bright, they're nearly luminescent. A witch, in all black. A Cursed wolf stands on each side of her. The undead wolves stare at us, rotten teeth bared. Ice crawls through my veins.

"Didn't the Golden Family warn everyone not to be out past sunset?" she croons.

"Anything out past sundown is ours to play with," a high-pitched voice calls behind us.

I whirl. Another black-leather witch stands before me. The wind gusts past us, but the witch's snow-white hair remains eerily still.

My head throbs again. Asmo shouts, and a snarl comes from behind me. A sharp slice of pain erupts along my calf. I stagger and drop to my knees. The witch yanks me back up. Her hand wraps around my throat, sharp iron nails digging into my skin. Not long ago, Marik's osseris had me pinned just like this.

Feet away, Asmo hurls black flames at the golden-eyed witch. He dodges a lunge from one of the Cursed wolves, then strikes it down with a slash of a sword made of flames.

"You shouldn't have been out at night," the witch whispers into my ear. "Now your little—"

I bring my head forward and rear back, a satisfying crunch sounding as my head collides with her nose. Her hold on me loosens. I duck out of her reach, summoning fire as I turn toward her. But she's too fast.

She grabs me again and pulls me toward her. I don't fight it this time. I collide with her, my white flames searing into her chest. She screams and jumps away from me, flinging her dagger toward me. It slices through my forearm. I hiss, but surge forward and hurl fire at her. It collides with her leathers, but does nothing. She smirks and surges toward me again, a writhing ball of dark magic in the palm of her hand.

I will not die today.

I summon wind and send it racing toward her, then channel fire. A wall of wildfire speeds toward her. Her face turns ghost white as it approaches, but she doesn't run. She doesn't have time. My wildfire consumes her, leaving a pile of ash in its wake. I drop my hands and let the flames die.

Behind me, Asmo still battles the golden-eyed witch. The Cursed lay on the ground, unmoving. Asmo slashes at the witch with his sword of flames, but she's too fast. She dodges every strike.

I reach for my magic that stems from the earth, focusing on the feel of the dirt beneath me, the twisting roots of the tree that run below the surface. My magic brushes against one, and I grab hold of it, forcing the roots upward, reaching for the witch as she avoids Asmo's blows. I push, urging the roots faster.

The witch stumbles as the roots find purchase, ensnaring her in their grasp. She glances down and screams in anger. It's all Asmo needs to land his sword in her neck. Her scream dies as her blood stains the snow black.

Asmo turns, eyes wild. "Are you okay?" He rushes to me, bloodied hands reaching out as he assesses me. Blood pours down my leg and drips from my forearm, but I'm okay. I'm alive.

"I'm fine," I say, as my gaze roves over every inch of him.

He grabs me, and the Canis forest disappears. A different forest materializes, the familiar cabin hidden behind the barrier.

As promised, Asmo and I technically arrive back at the cabin before sunset. A sliver of sun is still in the sky, but it's nearly gone here, too. The moment we step through the translucent barrier, the front door whips open. Ivan stands in the doorway, a relieved expression on his face that quickly turns to horror the longer he stares at us.

"Told you I'd have her back," Asmo says cheerfully, as if he didn't send Luca and Ivan into cardiac arrest only hours ago. As if we don't have blood all over us.

"What in the hells happened?" Ivan asks as he hurries toward us.

Fiery pain flares up my injured leg when I step forward. Then I'm weightless as Asmo scoops me into his arms and carries me inside. "Get a rag," he barks to Ivan.

"I'm fine," I protest, but everything hurts—my leg, forearm, and head throbbing in unison.

Ivan hurries behind us, veering into the kitchen before returning with a clean rag. Asmo wraps it around my ankle without warning and I hiss. He lifts my shirt and slashes the dark sigil, then mars his own. The throbbing in my head vanishes.

"Better?" Asmo asks, peering up at me. I nod. Already, the wound on my forearm begins to knit itself together.

Ivan eyes us wearily from across the living room. "What happened?"

"Witches," I grumble, expecting Luca to chime in with a lecture about why we shouldn't have left in the first place, but there's no sign of him. "Where are Holly and Luca?"

"Gathering wood for the fire," Ivan responds. "We were running low. Wh—"

"How is Cally?" I ask.

Ivan's jaw clenches. "She's stable, but she needs that extract. Did you find it?"

Asmo pulls the glass jar from his pocket and tosses it to Ivan. He catches it mid-air. "Are you going to tell me what the hell happened, or do I have to keep asking?"

Asmo quickly recounts our time in Bouldercrest and everything we learned. Ivan paces the living room the entire time, staring at the floor. He stops at the mention of Flint.

"Wait a second. August's cousin?"

I nod. "That's who he claimed to be."

"And he doesn't know your true identities?" Ivan asks, now staring at Asmo like his gaze might better serve as a knife poised to cut through him if he answers wrong.

Asmo glares back. "Despite what you might think, I only have Mae's safety in mind. Of course we didn't tell him who we were."

"So, he just *volunteered* that information?" Ivan asks incredulously. He walks to the kitchen and grabs a glass from the open shelves, setting it on the dark wood countertop.

"He's either an incredible liar or an idiot," I say. "We're planning to meet back up with him in three days."

Ivan turns back toward us, brows now pinched together. "What? How? How's that even going to work? What did you tell him?" He fires each question at me.

"I told him I had a gorgeous friend who would love to meet him and August."

His hand falls short of the glass whiskey decanter. He slowly turns back to face me. "And who is your gorgeous friend?"

"Holly."

He sets the empty glass on the counter with a little more force than necessary. "Absolutely not."

I put my hands up. "Ivan, hear me out. August *knows* Holly. I can't walk in there, but if he sees Holly, we can get him alone and tell him who we are."

"And what if he's with the witches? Then what?"

I wince as Asmo wipes the rag along the wound once more, muttering a half-hearted apology from the floor. "He's not! The shop-keeper said King Conall and August have been patrolling the streets to ensure everyone's safety. I *know* August. He would never condone this!" I exclaim. I nudge Asmo, who remains annoyingly silent on the matter. "A little help here?"

He huffs a sigh. "She's right, Ivan. August is annoyingly honorable."

"It's too dangerous," Ivan says.

"Good thing it's not up to you," Holly mumbles as she walks in the front door. "We could hear you outside. I'll do it."

Luca whirls his head toward her. "You will do no such thing," he growls.

"Luca," Ivan says in warning. "Take a breath. Holly—"

She holds up a hand to cut him off. "We don't have time to sit here and do nothing. We have a serious problem." Her tone is unyielding, so different from the female I first met. She looks at me. "Luca and I saw an osseris in the forest."

The air is snatched from my lungs at the word, at the unwelcome reminder of its talons scraping along my antlers, at its foul breath along my neck, at the bones protruding from its chest and pressing into my back.

Luca sits on the couch and begins to unlace his boots. "Most likely hunting for information to report back to the witch controlling it."

Or to the High King.

"It's a good thing you weren't here," Ivan admits.

Asmo turns and heads toward the bedrooms. "We need to leave. Now," he calls as he leaves us in his wake, his hands still covered in dried blood.

"Where the hell are we supposed to go?" I ask, looking from Ivan to Luca.

"There's another house I know of," Luca says as he laces his boots back up. "Gather your things. We leave in five minutes."

I hobble to my bedroom and shove my belongings into my bag. It doesn't even take an entire minute to pack everything. Asmo emerges from his bedroom, Cally limp in his arms, his own bag of clothes hanging from the crook of his elbow.

Ivan forms a portal big enough for three of us to step through at a time—Asmo, Cally, and I go first.

Our new home sits at the peak of a small mountain in the woods and looks almost identical to the old one, with warm wood siding and gray stacked stone columns on the front porch. A warm, red front door beckons us inside.

Luca gets to work on forming the protective barrier as the rest of us survey the cabin. I run into a chair as I enter the cramped living area. I back up, only to jostle a small end table. The space is crammed with furniture—overstuffed chairs and cabinets and a plaid couch running beneath a small window that barely lets any light in.

"It's going to be a tight fit," Ivan mutters before crossing the room in four strides.

Holly returns from inspecting the bedrooms and drops her bag on the couch, disrupting the thick layer of dust that has amassed with the cabin's disuse. "I'll take the living room this time, Ivan. You and Luca can take the room with two beds." She glances at Cally in Asmo's arms and says, "There's a primary bedroom and another small bedroom down the hall."

Asmo disappears down the hallway, Ivan close behind him. I sag against the armchair. I'm ready to fall into bed and sleep for a year.

"Ivan will take care of her," Holly says reassuringly. "She'll be back to it in no time."

My throat tightens when I think about my best friend. About what she's been through—what she's still going through.

"Guess it's you and me, princess," Asmo says as he returns to the living room. He grabs my bag from the chair and disappears down the hallway once more.

I follow him, limping with every other step. "What do you mean?"

He enters the primary bedroom, the bed taking up nearly the entire space. He sets our bags on a dresser crammed underneath a window. "Cally needs the separate bedroom. Ivan has to apply the extract every hour, and you need to sleep," he says, pulling the blankets from the bed and shaking the dust from them. "Ready for our sleepover?"

I muster the energy to roll my eyes. "That's not happening. You're going to sleep on the floor."

"Oh, am I? Scared to sleep with the big bad prince?" he asks with a smirk.

I chuckle and lean against the wall, watching him shake out the pillows. "You don't scare me, Asmo." I resist the urge to squirm under the intensity of his gaze, now fixated entirely on me, not the pillows.

"Really?"

"No. You never have," I answer. It's the truth. Of all the emotions

I've experienced with Asmo, fear has never been one. Unless, of course, you count being scared that he'll betray me, like Marik and Cora did.

He turns away from me with a quiet exhale. He tosses a pillow and blanket to the floor, making a sad version of a makeshift bed. He grabs a change of clothes from his bag and shuffles past me. Before he leaves the bedroom, he stops at the door. "You absolutely terrify me."

He shuts the door behind him. I peel my clothes off and collapse into bed, his words echoing inside my head as I drift to sleep.

CHAPTER 14
MAE

THREE DAYS LATER, Asmo and I return to Bouldercrest with Holly, all of us dressed appropriately this time. Snow falls heavily, wrapping the forest in its cold embrace.

"Bit chilly," Asmo mutters as he stuffs his hands into his pocket.

"No shit," Holly quips back. Mother, I love this version of her.

I survey the winter woods. "At least there are no witches here this time," I say. The blanket of white is all-encompassing, not a blur of black leather or Cursed creature to be seen. Holly re-adjusts the daggers hidden in a belt that loops around her hips.

Asmo and I wear the same disguises as before, the sigil etched into the space below our ribs. Holly, much to Luca's disapproval, is herself. She wears a scarf to hide her face, but that's the extent of her disguise. Her honey blonde hair is longer now, and she struggles to keep it tame against the wind.

We make the journey into town quietly. I can't stop picturing the Cursed, cambions, and osseri hiding behind every tree, and my nerves are shot by the time we make it into town. We cut through the crowded streets as a silent unit, me sandwiched between Asmo and Holly. Outdoor vendors stand nearly empty and blanketed in snow, while cafés are packed with hybrids desperate to escape the freezing weather.

The Fox Den comes into view as we round the corner, its interior looking barren through foggy windows. The entrance is blocked by two guards wearing suits of light blue and gray armor.

"This tavern is closed," the one on the right says firmly.

"May I ask why?" Asmo responds, using the most respectful tone I've ever heard come out of his mouth.

"Matters of the High Family."

I fight to contain my smile. Flint really did it. He got August here.

"Oh! Perfect. I believe those matters involve us." Asmo flashes the guards a charming smile. "We're here to meet Prince August and his cousin, Flint. Please inform them that we've arrived."

The guards don't move. I wonder how much it's killing Asmo to act so cordial. If the guards knew who hid behind the disguise, a simple command and sharpening of his gaze would have them rushing to open the doors.

Holly stirs beside me. "Is it possible that this meeting isn't for us and we got the location wrong?"

"No, this is it," Asmo says confidently, then cups his hands over his mouth. "Flint! We're here!"

My mouth falls open. "What are you doing?" I shout-whisper at him, which is pointless because the guards are standing four feet in front of us.

"If they're not going to tell him, then I'll tell him. We didn't come all this way for nothing. We had a plan. It's not my fault that Flint didn't tell us the secret password to get in."

The tavern door opens. Flint stands there, a smile on his face. "Hello!"

"See? I told you," Asmo says to the guards before pushing past them and pulling Flint into a friendly embrace.

Prince of Darkness, my ass.

"You made it!" Flint exclaims before turning his attention to me. "Hello again! I don't think I ever caught your name, now that I think about it."

I say the first name that comes to mind. "Amelia."

"And this must be..." he says, turning his gaze to Holly. His smile flickers when he sees her, his gaze lingering on her scars. He catches himself and pastes the smile back on.

My blood boils and I tamp down a string of curses. I shouldn't have asked her to do this.

"Holly," she says warmly, extending her hand. She either didn't notice his smile falter or, like me, she shoved it into a box to think about later. He takes her hand in his and places a brief kiss on the scarred skin.

"Holly, welcome! Let's get you out of the cold." He ushers her inside, and we follow, the tavern a ghostly version of the one we visited the other day. The only sounds are our feet shuffling on the floorboards below and a fire crackling. No billiards being shot, no glasses clinking together, no raucous hybrids shouting as they call for more beer.

The room is empty save for one figure seated on a green leather sofa next to the blazing fire, long legs crossed at the knee. His golden blond hair is neatly styled, pointed ears peeking through the glossy strands.

My breathing quickens. He's here.

"Cousin!" Flint exclaims. "Our guests have arrived!" I wish I could bottle his enthusiasm and drink it every morning instead of coffee.

August rises from the sofa and I'm taken back to the first time I met him. He is gorgeous. Tall and golden skin and blond hair and those piercing eyes the color of a glacier. They captivated me then and they captivate me now. But unlike before, they gloss over me and move right to Holly.

He freezes.

"Welcome," he says quietly, his eyes locked on Holly.

Flint doesn't notice. He heads to the bar to pour us all a round of drinks.

"And what did you say your names were?" August asks, gaze flitting between Asmo and me.

"We didn't," Asmo answers.

August stands still, staring at Asmo. It feels like a challenge—like he's about to demand Asmo give him his name.

"I'm Amelia," I say, walking to him and extending my hand. He hesitantly pulls his gaze from Asmo and shifts it to me. My hand hangs in the air between us before I remember. I form a curtsy.

"Lovely to meet you, Amelia," August says, but his usual charm is missing. He seems tired, deflated. Just like us. It gives me some hope, that maybe things in the High Houses aren't as status-quo as I thought. Maybe August has been fighting back against Marik behind closed doors.

He walks up to Holly and clasps his hands behind his back. "And you must be…"

"Holly," she says. She stares up at him, meeting the challenge he's laid out for her.

August's gaze snaps to me, then back to Asmo, before settling on Holly once more.

"Flint," he calls, his eyes still on Holly. "Out."

"What? Why?" Flint asks from behind us, disappointment in his tone.

"Go." His demand is harsh. Final.

Behind us, something is set on the bar before footsteps head to the exit, a draft of wind entering as Flint opens and closes the door behind him. Leaving us alone with August. Will he be with us or against us?

My power sits just below the surface, ready to strike.

"Sit," August commands.

Thankfully, Asmo doesn't quip back with a smart-ass response. We all take a seat on the green sofa while August settles into the matching armchair on the opposite side.

"What's going on here?" August asks, glancing between the three of us.

"Prince August," Holly says, her tone respectful. "It's so good to see you again."

"Who are these two?" he asks her, gaze flitting between Asmo and me.

"We'll get to that," Holly says. Again, I'm reminded of the timid Holly from before. This Holly has been through literal fire. Instead of it destroying her, it morphed her and hardened her into a weapon. She's been through too much and has too much to lose. Her home—the kingdom—hangs in the balance.

"No, Holly," he responds. "I don't think you understand how this is going to work. Let me remind you of some facts."

It appears August has changed, too. Gone is his carefree demeanor, replaced by a version of him who has also been hardened. *King Conall and Prince August have been seen walking the streets, keeping an eye on things.* Just how much has August seen? How much has his court suffered because of Marik? Because of me?

He settles back in the chair, arms draped along the armrests. He lifts his chin as he assesses us. "Witches and dark magic have spread throughout the kingdom. The last time I saw you, you were dead. The last time I saw Mae, she was dead. Now, miraculously, you and Mae are alive, seemingly resurrected. Do you see how this might be looking to me right now?"

Holly's jaw drops. "You think that Mae and I were brought back from the dead? By dark magic?"

He cocks his head. "Are you denying it?"

"Of course I'm denying that," she hisses. "It was close. Too close. But I never died. And neither did Mae."

"So, you're in touch with her, then?" he asks.

Holly nods curtly.

"And what does the Crown want with us?" His tone is careful, controlled.

Holly looks at me, unsure of how to play this. We decided that we wouldn't reveal ourselves to August until we were absolutely certain that he wasn't in support of Marik. But I never anticipated that he'd think we were with the High Court.

He grips the armrests and leans forward. "What's going on here? We've done everything you've asked." His tone is no longer controlled. Fury laces every word.

"August," I say softly. He turns to me in confusion, at the informality, the lack of title. "We're not with Marik."

"Who are you?" he asks, then looks back to Holly. "I don't understand."

Holly's mouth opens and shuts, and she looks at me again, mouth twisted into a grimace.

Here goes nothing. "August," I say softly. "It's me. It's Mae."

His gaze sharpens as he truly looks at me, head to toe. "You're not wearing a glamour."

I stand and undo my coat. I pull my shirt up and reveal the sigil on my ribs. "This mark allows me to change my appearance."

He shakes his head. "That's not possible."

"It's dark magic," Asmo explains, now standing beside me. In solidarity or protection if this goes wrong, I'm not sure.

August flinches. "What do you want?" he repeats, tone somehow even harsher than it was before. "Did Astrid report something that wasn't to her liking?"

"What? What are you talking about?" I ask.

"I have listened to and abided by every request. So, if there's nothing else, I'd like to return to my family," he says coldly. He stands and points to the door. "My guards will see you out."

"No, August, listen. We're not with Marik. Please, hear me out," I plead.

August extends his hand, and ice begins to coat the floor, slowly creeping toward us. I open my mouth to explain more, but before I can, Asmo summons a dagger from Elle's belt. In one swift motion, he snatches it from the air and slashes the sigil through my shirt.

I yelp, more in surprise than pain.

"Sorry," he mumbles, then takes the knife to his ribs. His features slowly shift back to his real ones—his frame lengthening, his hair turning a shade darker, and his eyes shifting back to their pools of darkness, the fern-green forming around his iris, the silver cutting right through its middle.

"What is going on?" August asks—no, commands. "What is this?"

"August, just listen to me," I say. "The Mae that's on the throne isn't *me.*"

He pauses. "What do you mean?"

"We're confident Elle is pretending to be me. We think Marik is using this same dark magic to change her appearance to make it look like me. But it's not. We've been in hiding since the wedding."

August looks at Asmo. "And what about you? That's your brother on the throne. You're telling me you have nothing to do with that?"

"That's exactly what I'm telling you," Asmo responds coolly. Normally, an insulting nickname would have been tacked onto the end of that.

Such restraint.

August looks back at me, his arms now crossed, the muscles strained. "And I'm just supposed to take your word for it?"

"Think about it. What's your last memory of me on the night of the wedding?" I ask him. He just stares back at me. "*Think*," I urge.

"Cora had just fired a bolt of lightning at you and you died."

I take a cautious step closer. "And? What happened after that?"

He stares up at the ceiling for a moment, but then says, "I don't...I think Luca and Ivan dragged your body away."

Asmo nods emphatically. "Yes. Holly and I defended them as they did."

"Have you been to the Deer Court since then?" I ask August. He nods. "And did you see Asmo, Holly, Ivan, or Luca while you were there?" I press.

He shakes his head slowly. Hope spreads through me. Maybe, just maybe, we convinced him.

"That's because they've been with me. We've been in hiding around the court while we healed," I say. "Ask me anything. Something only I know."

He hesitates, then says, "Tell me of our first date."

"You mean your only date," Asmo says wryly.

August ignores the comment, still staring at me with his arms crossed.

"You took me to the lagoon in the woods. I got scared. I thought you were leading me to my death or something because of how dark the forest got," I recall with a snort. "You had a picnic—kind of—set up. There was a canoe. We got in the canoe, but you left the picnic basket on the shore. You—"

He strides toward me and grabs my left hand. Asmo tenses beside me.

"You're not wearing the ring," he says. He yanks the scarf from my neck. "Or the necklace."

I don't even know what happened to my wedding ring. I shiver as I think of the weight of the sigil. I can't imagine how it must be to constantly wear a necklace made of dark magic.

"No, I don't. Because I'm not the one sitting on that throne," I say softly.

August sinks into the chair, putting his head in his hands. He runs his fingers through his hair, then looks up at me. "Okay, fine. I believe you." He looks at Asmo, then me. "You trust him?"

I nod firmly. "I do."

My net snags on my own lie, as if reminding me of the truth. I may be beginning to trust him, but I don't fully. Not yet, at least. I'm not sure it's a luxury that I have.

August's jaw clenches once, but he nods firmly. Acceptance. My knees threaten to give. "Okay. Now what?" he asks.

"We need your help," I say. "Is there another place we can talk?"

August funnels us away from The Fox Den, its wooden interior now replaced by shades of gray stone.

"Welcome to my humble abode. I'll have to show you the bedroom another time, Mae," August says with a wink as he drops his hands and backs away from us. The flirty comment is so quintessentially August that it fills me with a weightlessness that's been missing since before the wedding.

I gawk at his "humble abode." The living room is the size of my entire house in Pinebend. Rough stone covers the floor and travels up the walls, all the way to the domed ceiling. Oversized windows line one wall, offering a view of the slope down the mountain to the frozen river. From here, it looks like the thinnest of lines wending through the valley.

"Are we inside of the mountain?" I ask.

"Bit bigger than the mountains in the Deer Court," August says, plopping onto a massive fabric sectional in the center of the room.

Asmo surveys the room, hands clasped behind his back. "A little darker than I thought the Golden Prince would have," he mutters.

August shrugs. "Nothing I can do about the stone. Since, you know, we're inside of a mountain. I do try to soften it a bit though," he says, patting the white couch.

"Do you mind?" Asmo asks, glancing at the large fireplace, also gray. Fresh, unused logs sit in a tidy pile in the hearth. He doesn't wait for August to respond and instead fires a ball of black flames at the logs. They light, sending a delicious crackling and warmth through the room.

Asmo heads toward the sectional, but before he can step on the rug, his foot freezes mid-air. August's hand is outstretched as he stares at Asmo's foot.

"Please," August says, "no shoes on the carpet."

I stifle a giggle as Asmo bends down and plucks each shoe off, setting them neatly beside each other in front of the cream plush rug. Holly and I follow suit, placing snow-dusted boots next to Asmo's.

Holly takes a seat beside August on the edge of the sofa, hands on her knees. She looks more nervous than I've seen her in a while. Asmo and I sit on the opposite edge of the sofa, appropriately distanced. I swallow the desire to scoot closer to him.

We quickly fill August in on the last month—mine and Holly's recovery, learning to use the sigils, sneaking into the tithe, rescuing Cally, and killing the witches. August listens with rapt attention, nodding and grimacing throughout.

"Are they looking for you?" August asks. "Surely they know you're alive."

"I don't know," I admit. "We've been careful in laying low. So careful that our own knowledge of what's been going on has been limited. We didn't know witches were placed amongst the courts until we visited Bouldercrest a few days ago."

He sucks his teeth. "They're trying to *assimilate* them," he says with a roll of his eyes. "Just an excuse to justify placing them in our courts while they terrorize our people and slaughter our animals. Their goal, in my opinion, is to make us feel defeated. The fact that they tried to harm you means they're escalating."

I rub the nearly healed mark on my forearm from the witch's dagger. "We were lucky."

"How did you kill them?" August asks. "Their leathers make it difficult to harm them."

"They must be imbued with dark magic," Asmo says.

Ah, so that's why my flames did nothing to their leathers. "The only thing that worked was when I set her on fire."

August raises his eyebrows. "Impressive."

I barely contain my grimace. Holly stares straight ahead with an empty gaze, and I want to kick myself.

"Fire and beheading should work," Asmo says, completely oblivious.

"Noted. Okay, so...What's the plan?" August asks, leaning back on the couch and spreading his legs, also completely oblivious.

"We're not sure," I admit. "We know something needs to be done about Marik and Cora. But we've been pretty helpless since it's just been the five of us. We don't have access to any kind of army to remove them. We don't know what to do. We need your help."

August leans forward, resting elbows on knees. "I know it might not seem like it, but we do have an advantage. They must be nervous that you're out there somewhere and they have no clue where. So, we have two options. We can either tell the kingdom their secret—that Elle is pretending to be you—or we can use Elle on the inside."

"No, absolutely not," Holly says, shaking her head. "We can't leave her in there. We have no idea what he's doing to her."

"All due respect, Holly, but I think that's Elle's choice," Asmo replies. "It could work. We can find another way to get back in there and give her the option. Outing Marik and Cora would force their hand and give up the one advantage we have. Besides, who knows what they'll do to Elle in retaliation? I like the idea of letting them think we're weak while we're secretly working against them. It gives us time to prepare without them attacking. And it keeps Elle safe."

My body feels like it's shrinking into itself with guilt. I didn't even think about what they might do to Elle if we attack. And if I know her, she'll sacrifice herself to help get us the information we need. "If—and that's a big *if*—we're able to talk to Elle again, and she agrees to help us from the inside, you have to promise me that we'll get her out the moment it gets too dangerous," I say.

Asmo nods. "Deal."

"And how are we going to do that?" August asks, kicking his feet up onto the solid white marble coffee table centered on the rug.

"I don't know yet. We got in once. There's got to be another way in. But I need more information on what's going on. We've been secluded in cabins for the last month. We came to you for help," I remind him, staring at him expectantly.

"Well, I wasn't aware I'd be meeting with you all today. I would've prepared my notes if I had known," he says, then winks at me. Once, it would have made me blush. Now, it makes me feel warm in a different way. A familiar way. "Officially, the kingdom isn't aware that Cora is working with Marik. Right now, everyone thinks that you and Marik have retreated into your castle and shut everyone out while you play honeymoon. Citizens are pissed about the tithe, but they were told by the High Crown that it's necessary for the good of the kingdom."

"What a crock of shit," Asmo mutters.

"Something about taxes and increasing wages for farmers. Unofficially," he continues, "Dark magic is spreading throughout the kingdom and people are terrified. It sounds like the Deer Court is the last court to get hit with it, but we've been dealing with it since the wedding. As I said, the High Crown has stationed covens of witches in each court. Their *pets* have been responsible for citizens and livestock getting attacked at night. When I brought this to Marik, he said he'd deal with it, but it's only gotten worse."

He stands and walks to a dry bar built into the stone wall. "Better yet," he says with his back to us, "the witches are allowed to come into our manors at any time. And they're the only guests allowed at the High Castle right now. They report everything back to Marik."

"Is that what you meant when you asked me about—what was the name?" I ask.

He nods as he grabs a bottle of amber liquid. "Whiskey anyone?"

Holly and I shake our heads. Asmo waves his hand, floating the bottle over to him in response.

"Piss-poor manners," August mutters as he grabs two glasses from the built-in shelf.

I clear my throat pointedly. "The name?"

August sinks back into the chair and hands Asmo one of the glasses. "Astrid. She's been a problem. She's the witch in command around here."

"How many witches are there here?" Asmo asks as he pours the amber liquid. He floats the whiskey back to August.

August plucks the bottle from the air, uncorks it, and takes a swig. He grimaces as he swallows. "I think twenty-something, but more come every day. Two less now, thanks to you."

Asmo sneers at him, slamming his glass back on the table untouched. "You drink straight from the bottle, then offer the contents to your guests?"

August grins at him. "No, I offer my guests the first pour, then drink the rest from the bottle."

"Can you two focus?" I snap. "This is happening in every court?" I ask August.

He looks at me, taking another swig from the bottle. "As far as I'm aware, but I'm not sure about the Serpent Court," August says, glancing back to Asmo, who shrugs.

"Do you think Koa and Barrett would be willing to help us, too?" I ask hopefully.

August nods. "Yeah, they're sick of this shit."

Beside me, Asmo picks his whiskey back up and surveys the contents, as if looking for any sign of August's backwash.

"Can you keep this from your parents?" I ask August. "Do you think Koa and Barrett would be able to keep it from theirs? We need as few people knowing about this as possible."

August nods. "Yeah, don't worry about it."

"Thanks. And definitely keep it from your cousin," I say.

August rolls his eyes at the mention of Flint. "That little...I'm going to wring his neck when you leave." He glances at Asmo, still surveying the contents of his glass. "What—"

Three knocks rap on the door. I nearly jump out of my skin. *The witches are allowed to come into our manors at any time.* Asmo surges to his feet and reaches for me, but August holds two hands up. "Relax, for the Mother's sake." The footsteps retreat and the pounding in my chest lessens. August stands. "It's mid-day."

"And?" I ask.

"Daily briefings are delivered. Reports and such things to review before I meet with the Pack."

"The Pack?"

"Their version of the Herd," Asmo explains.

Sure enough, August opens the door to a neat collection of papers. He snags the bundle and shuts the door behind him, switching the lock in place. He scans through the documents, then gets to the newspaper at the bottom of the report. His eyes widen as he reads. "Looks like Elle is playing High Queen tomorrow."

He tosses the paper onto the coffee table, and all the blood drains from my face as I read the headline.

HIGH QUEEN MAE VIKANDER INVITES LOCAL TEACHER, ELIZA RAINEY, TO HIGH CASTLE TO DISCUSS EDUCATION REFORM

My name alone sends shivers along my skin. I wasn't prepared to see Marik's last name as my own. But the shivers turn into the clawing fingers of horror as it hits me.

Someone in the High Castle is summoning Asmo.

Someone knows.

CHAPTER 15
ELLE

Eliza and I sit in the rose garden at a white wrought-iron table. An eggshell-blue teapot and two matching cups of steaming tea sit in between us. A towering tray of untouched pastries sits on the edge of the table, pushed aside so as not to block my view of the female in front of me.

Eliza wears a black, fur-lined coat and plain black trousers. The informality of the outfit shocked me at first, a stark contrast to the gown that I was told—forced—to wear, its thin sleeves offering no protection from the cold.

"Thank you for joining me," I say warmly.

She nods curtly. "Thank you for the invite, Your Highness," she says politely, then glances around the garden. "Your garden is beautiful."

She's right. Somehow, the roses are unaffected by the cold. Shades of light pink, crimson red, and ivory roses surround us, their sharp thorns hidden among the foliage.

"It was the late High Princess's favorite spot. Like my sister, it's one of my favorites," I say, trying desperately to keep my tone warm, even though I want to choke on every word.

Eliza's gaze lingers for a beat too long before she picks up her cup and blows on the steaming liquid.

I clear my throat, sparing a look at the guards in every corner of the garden. When I told Marik I wanted to invite the teacher back, he initially dismissed the idea with an apathetic denial. Later, he came back to my wing and said that Cora said it would be a good idea, a good look for the High Crown. I swallowed the retort that rose, something about him being spineless.

I should've known he wouldn't allow me to meet with her alone. We had more privacy when she was locked in the dungeons. Eliza doesn't miss my glance to the guards. If she picks up on the reminder that we're being watched, she doesn't acknowledge it.

Steam wafts from my teacup, and I hold it in my hand, relishing in the warmth it provides. "I invited you here to discuss our education policies," I say, again, trying with all my might to come across as inviting and friendly. Even though I want to grab the butter knife and jam it into my throat.

"I'm not sure how much help I'll be," Eliza says, a regretful smile on her delicate features. "I'm not exactly well-versed in the kingdom's education policies."

It's a lie. Eliza continues to get more interesting.

"Oh, that's okay," I reassure her. "I'm not expecting you to be. I want to learn how we can help you as a teacher. How we can change our policies to make your life easier. Teachers do so much for the kingdom, and I want to ensure we're taking care of you."

She gives me a tight smile. "That is a wonderful first policy change for a new High Queen."

"Yes, well, as you may or may not know, my aunt homeschooled me. It's important to me that I learn more about your experience in the school system because it's so unfamiliar to me."

I swallow the hatred I feel at the mention of my fake aunt, who's actually Mae's fake aunt, who's actually Cora, the First Witch.

"Yes, I knew that," she says, her blue eyes piercing mine. Truth.

I resist the urge to shake my head to wave off the sudden intensity of her gaze. She stares at me expectantly. But I'm not sure what she's looking for.

Her gaze cuts to the guards, then back to me. "I am aware of Mae's —of your—history."

Truth.

I narrow my eyes for a moment, then remember myself, and paste a smile to my face. It feels like there's something I'm missing. I go out on a limb. "You seem so familiar to me. Have we met before? I mean, before the tithe?"

She smiles—a real smile this time. "Yes, Your Highness. We have. We've spoken before. Many times." Truth. She grabs a lock of her brown hair. "My hair's normally darker than this. It's grown quite a bit, so maybe you don't recognize me."

Underneath the table, I ball my hands into fists. I don't know what idiotic plan I had in asking her to join me. I have no idea who Mae knows or doesn't know.

"When did we meet?" I ask.

She considers this as she takes another sip of her tea, her eyes flitting back to the guards in each corner. She appears to be as aware of the guards as I am. Eliza is hiding something. I just don't know what.

She sets her cup down on the saucer and says, "It was a long time ago. But more recently, I also had the pleasure of meeting your companion. What was her name, with the red hair?"

My pulse quickens. Although her words are casual, she watches me like she's trying to drill a hole into my brain with her mind.

Her mannerisms...her tone...

"She brought you to meet my brother. Months ago."

I turn the words over in my head. She—Elle—*I*—brought Mae to meet her brother...I purse my lips as my mind fumbles, scrambles to put the pieces together. "What's your brother's name?"

She brings the cup to her lips, a smirk on her face as she takes a tiny sip. Her eyes don't leave mine as she gives me a nearly imperceptible shake of her head. Wrong question.

"How old is your brother?" I ask quietly, sparing a glance at the guards. They stand stock-still, black statues in a garden of roses.

Eliza watches me carefully. Her next words ring of truth.

"He's my twin."

My heart slams in my chest. I sit up straight, realization spreading through my body like an electric current. I pick up my cup of tea and bring it slowly to my lips as I think through my response. My hands shake. If I'm right, Eliza is wearing a sigil, too.

If I'm right, Eliza isn't Eliza at all.

If I'm right, Asmo is sitting in front of me. And I have no idea what his agenda is.

I set the teacup down delicately, willing it not to slam into the matching saucer.

"Twins have always fascinated me," I say, forcing a smile onto my face. "How close are you with him?"

Eliza—Asmo?—smiles slowly, bright eyes twinkling. "Not very. In fact, a recent family dispute has us estranged at the moment." Truth.

Sweet, sweet relief floods through me. "I'm sorry to hear that," I lie.

She waves me off. "No, don't be. Just a bit of a difference of opinions on a family matter," she says nonchalantly before twisting in her seat to survey the garden again. "Would I be able to pluck some flowers and bring them home?"

"Um, sure. Of course," I say.

She smiles. "Thank you, Your Highness." She glances around the garden once more and stands. As she does, she bumps into the table, sending both cups of tea toppling to the ground. The cups shatter into pieces as they hit the cobblestone.

She gasps. "Oh! I'm so sorry." She bends down, dropping to the floor on her knees, reaching for the shards of the broken cups.

This is my chance. The guards have glanced over here but make no attempt to come help.

Mother forbid I prick a finger.

I bend down and join Eliza on the ground, knees digging into the small pebbles underneath the table. Dozens of questions roar through my mind like a river threatening to break its dam.

Is Holly okay? Where's Luca? Ivan?

What are you doing to save the kingdom?

Can you save me from your monster of a brother?

But I swallow them. It's too risky.

When she reaches for a blue shard, she sneaks a folded scrap of paper underneath. I reach for it, sliding the paper up the sleeve of my blouse as I pluck the broken piece of ceramic from the ground.

It takes all my willpower not to look at the guards.

"I'm so sorry about that. I'm such a klutz," Eliza says with a huff as she stands back up and sits in her chair.

I laugh at the lie as it comes from her mouth. "Oh, don't worry about it. I've never been a big fan of tea, anyways. Shall we get down to business?" I ask her, motioning for the guards to come forward.

Eliza freezes at the summons.

I hand the guards the broken teacups. "Discard this," I say before ordering them away with a wave of my hand.

Eliza's posture visibly relaxes as they retreat. "Yes," she says with a smile.

O ne hour later, I walk Eliza to the front doors, guards trailing behind us. We spent the rest of our time discussing education policy, something she was surprisingly informed on. Well, I guess it's not surprising given that she's actually a High Prince.

The note tucked into my sleeve felt like an itch I couldn't scratch.

"Thank you, again, for inviting me, Your Highness," she says, dipping into a bow before the grand double doors.

"The pleasure was all mine. I'd love for you to come back soon so we can continue our discussion," I say sincerely. "Maybe next time I can give you a tour of the grounds."

Please don't leave me here.

Please save me.

"I'd love that," she says with a smile.

I open the double doors for her. With a glance back at the guards, I step outside. They don't stop me, so I escort Eliza to the top of the grand stairs that slope down the small mountain.

I pull her in for a hug. Tears threaten to spill, but I swallow them down. Later.

"She's alive," she whispers into my hair, so quietly that it could have been the whisper of the wind. She pulls away, and I have to remember to act normal. To act like those two words didn't just change my life. Like they didn't just spring a well of hope into my chest.

She's alive.

I wave goodbye to Eliza—Asmo—and resist the urge to sprint up the stairs and into my wing, lock myself in the bathroom, and unfurl the note still burning a hole in my sleeve.

"Your Highness," a guard says drily behind me.

I turn and walk back inside. They watch as I walk up the stairs and enter my wing, every step torturously slow.

When I enter my wing, the guards stationed inside don't even glance at me. I enter my private bathroom and lock the door behind me. I take a deep, shaky breath and sink to the marble floor. Slowly, quietly, I pull the folded note from my sleeve. I throw a small sound barrier up and unfold the note, the paper crinkling as I do.

I let loose a sob as I see the handwriting.

I would know it anywhere. I've seen it on official documents and on countless Herd meeting notes, his neat penmanship something I always admired.

Ivan.

We're okay. Everyone is okay. Stay strong.

That's all there is. I summon a small flame to the palm of my hand and burn the note.

Mae is alive.

And they know I'm here.

CHAPTER 16
MAE

THE PORTAL SPITS us in front of a quaint cottage nestled in the middle of a forest, filled with gargantuan trees with trunks as thick as the bears that climb them. Birds chirp, and brilliant beams of light cascade through the canopy. To the right, a massive wall of rock juts upward, small collections of trees and bushes adorning its granite surface as it stretches toward the sky. A chipmunk dashes past us and races toward the cabin, slipping into a hole where the forest floor meets the cabin wall.

"This is it?" I ask, eyeing the small cottage skeptically. The front door is the largest feature, its wooden façade almost reaching the roof.

The corner of Asmo's mouth twitches. "It's more of a grower than a shower."

My jaw drops as I burst into a laugh. He turns and heads toward the cottage, but I reach for him and grab the back of his wool coat. "Wait!" I say with a huff. "I know August said it's okay to come as ourselves, but should we put our marks on? Just to be safe?"

Asmo frowns. "I—"

The wooden door opens before he can answer the question. Asmo shifts to step in front of me, shielding me behind him. Over his shoulder, a mop of brown, curly hair comes into view.

Barrett.

He looks the same, but his normally tidy hair is loose, wavy locks curling just below his ears. I shove Asmo to the side and close the distance between us, slamming into Barrett and crushing him in a tight hug. The last time I saw him was at my wedding, his bear form vicious and cutting through cambions and dark creatures as he fought to defend me and my kingdom.

"It's really you," he whispers into my hair. He smells of clay and dust and I cling to him. He gives me one final squeeze before releasing me. "When August told me..." He trails off with a shake of his head.

I step back to Asmo's side.

"I can't believe it. I really can't believe it," Barrett says, pulling the front door open. "Come in. Let's get out of the cold." He ushers us inside and I freeze when I see what exactly is hidden inside this quaint cottage.

"Told you," Asmo mutters in my ear.

We stand at the top of a large stair landing. Beneath us, a wide stone staircase winds in lazy circles into the depths of a massive cave. The stairs lead to different levels, each entry alcove bright with lit candelabras embedded in stone walls.

Barrett turns to face us, a grin on his handsome face. "Cool, isn't it?"

I snort in response. *Cool* is an understatement. This place is grand, stunning, its size and depth staggering. He gestures for us to follow him. Although the stairs are wide enough for the three of us to walk side-by-side, one glance down at the emptiness beneath us has me walking behind Barrett and Asmo.

"Welcome to the Court of Bears," Barrett says, pride in every word.

We stop at the third level down, candelabras blazing brilliantly. Even from the top of the stair landing, this level was illuminated. A chandelier of branches hangs from a tall, sloped ceiling, highlighting two stone thrones and the figures perched in them.

King Torben and Queen Artis.

Torben wears a simple black robe with a light brown tunic and matching trousers. His short, brown curly hair is neatly styled underneath a crown of branches. His large hands rest on the armrests of his stone throne, thick fingers gripping the edges. Beside him, Queen Artis wears a loose blue gown the color of the sky on a cloudless day. Her straight, thick brown hair flows freely, resting behind her shoulders. Her eyes are warm, the color of milk chocolate, a stark contrast to her husband's hard and unyielding gaze.

One princess, both tall and broad in stature, stands on each side of them. Their gazes are soft, but their postures are ramrod straight. Barrett leaves our side and stands centered between them, a sudden look of apprehension on his face as his gaze flits between his father and me.

I form a deep bow. Beside me, Asmo huffs a sigh of impatience.

"Rise," a deep voice rumbles from the throne.

Unease prickles in my gut. I stand straight, tall. I am still the High Queen. Barrett gives me a brief nod. That's all I need.

"Hello," I say, projecting my voice. "You must be King Torben." His face remains impassive. I dip my head toward Queen Artis. "And you, Queen Artis." Her eyes twinkle, but her features remain neutral otherwise. "It's lovely to officially meet you both."

Less is more, Holly's voice echoes in my head. *Quiet is confident.*

So, I wait.

The King and Queen of the Bear Court watch me carefully. I don't take my eyes from them, not even to glance at Barrett. They could both shift and tear me to shreds in an instant.

"Welcome to our court." Torben's tone is official and lacks any warmth. "We received a visit from Prince August. He informed us of the meeting you had with him. Of the tale you weave." Every sentence is a statement of fact, devoid of any emotion. He's careful to hold his cards close to the vest, but his words tell me all I need to know—he doesn't believe me.

I shift on my feet. "It is no tale. He speaks the truth." He doesn't say anything, so I continue, "We've come to seek your help in destroying the usurpers of the throne—High King Marik and his...consort," I say, the word tasting like ash on my tongue. "The First Witch."

Torben tilts his chin upward. "You mean to tell me that the First Witch is on the throne? And everyone thinks it's you?"

I shake my head. "No, not exactly. My advisor and friend, Elle, is on the throne."

He quirks an eyebrow. "Your friend?"

Damnit, Mae. I regain my composure, my confidence, and project my voice again. "Yes, we believe the First Witch and Marik are compelling her to use dark magic to transform her appearance. To pretend to be me. Although there is an imposter on the High Throne, that imposter is a prisoner."

Torben steeples his fingers together. "And? How do you expect us to help? You got yourself ousted from the throne, and expect us to divert our limited resources to helping you get it back?"

I suck air through my teeth, trying to bottle the rage I feel, but it slips through. "If you don't, then Marik and Cora will ruin the kingdom. You're a fool if you think they'll stop with my throne."

Torben directs his gaze to Asmo. "And you, boy, your brother is responsible for this? And you had no hand in it?"

Asmo bristles at the title, or lack thereof.

"Might I remind you, I'm the same status as your son," he says, and I swear I can feel darkness radiating from his every word. "I'll tolerate your disrespect toward me, but I will not tolerate, nor will I forget, the disrespect you've shown the High Queen today. We come to you seeking your assistance out of respect, but Mae could easily order you and your entire court to go to war for her. She could send your court to their deaths to fight for her. But she stands here, in front of you, *bowing* to you, while you sit on your thrones and treat her like she's beneath you."

Torben shifts in his seat. He opens his mouth, but Artis speaks first. "Forgive my husband," she says, placing her hand on his forearm. "When August came to us, we were skeptical. And we remain so. High King Marik has visited us several times, trying to place witches in our court, and we were under the impression that you stood beside him and supported this. We've been noncompliant, at least in his words," she says with a shrug. "We are just trying to protect our home. Forgive us for our caution, Your Highness."

She rises from her throne. Despite her large frame, every step toward me is fluid. Her pale blue gown flows behind her on the rough stone floor. She stops in front of me and sinks to one knee in a deep bow.

"Please rise," I say, still hating the way the words feel on my tongue.

When she does, a smile graces her face. She returns to her throne, long brown hair bobbing at her waist. Torben stands next. I thought Barrett was tall, but his father is colossal. As he walks toward me, I can't help but feel like I'm shrinking with every step.

He drops to a knee before me, the top of his head coming to my chest. I let him remain on his knees for a few moments longer than Artis. "You may rise," I say, not hating it as much this time.

He stands, offering me another tilt of his head before returning to his throne with a deep sigh.

"My wife is right," he says gruffly. "I apologize, Your Highness. We are, of course, happy to see you are unharmed. We are also undoubtedly glad to hear it is not you behind the witches' resurgence. But it seems we have a long road ahead of us," he says, exhaustion now weighing down every word. "I know time is of the essence, but I'd like to meet with my family before we speak further. Shall we reconvene in the morning and discuss how to defeat the usurpers?"

I swallow hard at the dismissal. I'm eager to get back, to see how Cally's doing, to finally get some kind of direction, some answer on how the hell we're going to move forward and defeat Marik.

Barrett comes forward. "I'll take you to our guest quarters."

We offer the King and Queen a final, albeit brief, bow before following Barrett from the throne room and onto the landing. The moment we step from the throne room, I feel like my lungs can fully expand.

Barrett is silent as he leads us down three more levels, the light from above fading with every step downward. We reach the third landing down and turn toward another caved hallway.

"There's a private kitchenette and a private bathroom in the guest suite. You should have no need to leave, unless, of course, you'd like to." He places his palm on the center of a door at the end of the hallway and mutters something under his breath. "Give it a try. The spell should recognize both of your magic now."

I place my hand on the mahogany door, feeling a click as I do. Asmo does the same, the door clicking back to locked. I turn to Barrett. "I'm sorry. I think there's some confusion. Asmo and I need separate rooms."

Barrett blinks. "Oh. Sorry, I—"

Asmo cuts him off with a charming smile. "No need. One room is great."

Barrett's eyebrows draw together. "Okay, well just let me know if something changes," he says awkwardly before opening the door.

As I pass Asmo, I nudge him in the ribs with my elbow. I swear I hear him chuckle as I enter the guest suite.

The walls are crafted of rough, uneven stone the color of sand, as if the room was carved directly into a mountain. In the corner, a basin of water is cut into the stone floor, steam rising from the clear water. There's a small kitchenette and a private bathroom on the other side of the suite, and an oversized bed draped in white linens is centered on the back wall.

Asmo excuses himself and makes his way to the private bathroom.

"You did great back there. My father..." Barrett rubs the back of his neck as he searches for the right words. "He's great, but he's very protective. The last few months have been tough on us."

I guess I was naïve to expect King Torben to welcome me without question. "Thank you for convincing him to see us."

"You're the High Queen," he says, like my throne wasn't just stolen from me. Like my title has any meaning right now. "When August came to us and told us the truth, I believed him. I tried to tell my father that there was no way you would allow the witches to roam free, not after what happened that night. But my father...Well," he says with a grimace, "He didn't get the chance to know you before the wedding. He didn't believe August."

"But he saw me fighting Cora. He was there. He knows what Marik did," I protest.

Barrett sighs. "You have to understand. It's been a month of silence. And with reports of you on the throne...We just assumed you were in on it now. When August came, I was so ashamed."

I give him a sad smile. "It's okay, Barrett. Thank you for vouching for me. I would be skeptical if I were your father," I say truthfully.

He smiles, but it falls quickly. "How long are you staying?"

"Just for the night," Asmo says, sauntering back to us. "We'll leave after we speak with your father tomorrow."

Barrett gives us a curt nod. "There's a lot to discuss, but I'm confident they'll help. I'll send someone to wake you early, if that's okay."

I nod in approval. "I don't sleep much these days anyways," I admit.

His answering smile is sad and full of pity. I hate it.

"See you in the morning, Mae," he says, then gives Asmo a curt nod. "Asmo."

Asmo returns it. Cordial, professional. At least he's not slinging insults or pet names like he tends to do with Koa and August. Barrett closes the door softly behind him, leaving Asmo and me alone for the first time in months.

The last time we were truly alone, with no one in the room next door or down the hall…Well, the last time was when I was telling him I was marrying his brother. The silence between us feels stifling and suffocating, yet charged with something that feels almost tangible. Something that I want to grab and cling to.

There are a million things to say. To ask.

Did you want one room because you can't stand to be apart from me, like I can't stand to be apart from you?

Why did you choose me? Why did you reject me?

What are we doing?

Asmo clears his throat, and my chest feels too tight. I mutter some excuse about needing to shower and escape into the private bathroom, desperate to create some distance between us.

The shower is nestled inside a small, stone alcove with a built-in stone bench. With barely a thought, I twist my hand in the air and turn the shower on.

Regret sits on my shoulders as I remember Elle teaching me how to do that. I feel so heavy, so weighed down by everything that's happened. Everything that we still have to do.

Water rushes from the showerhead, falling onto the stone floor in a soothing, rhythmic pattern. I peel my trousers and blouse from my too-slender frame and toss them into the corner.

My hip bones jut out farther than they did before, and my stomach is flatter than it's ever been. My body is a collection of black marks—the one on my chest from Cora's lightning, the dark magic sigils, and scars from dark creatures' teeth. Apparently, dark magic takes a while to heal, but the marks fade with every day.

The one on my chest from Cora's lightning is still sore. It doesn't hurt like it once did, but a brief pain still lingers. The scar on my ankle from the cambion has faded, but a black outline of its teeth still mars my pale skin, now joined by the black outline of the Cursed wolf's teeth just above. I wince as I think about the cambion embedding its sharp teeth into the delicate curvature of Elle's neck.

Like everything these days, I shove the thought away.

Just like I shove aside the effects of the dark magic whenever we use it. Every time we carve the marks into our skin, my head pounds and my magic comes slower. I swear it gets worse every time.

I can't imagine being forced to do this every day.

The shower water is freezing, and I don't bother warming it. The cold water pelts my skin and makes me feel alive, reminds me that I'm still breathing.

I throw my clothes back on and step out of the bathroom. Asmo is already fast asleep, curled up on the floor in a pile of white pillows and blankets. I stop and stare at him, waiting for him to move. But he doesn't. His chest rises and falls in deep breaths. His long lashes rest against his cheeks, fluttering slightly. He looks so calm.

My feet are quiet as I pad to the bed, already messy and unmade because of what Asmo stole from the top layers. I sink into the soft mattress and close my eyes.

CHAPTER 17

ELLE

FOUR DAYS HAVE PASSED since Asmo last visited me. Four days since I learned Mae is still alive. Since then, I've spent every day waiting for Marik to reveal he knows who I met with. Luckily, he's been too busy with Cora to pay me too much attention. I've never been so happy to be locked in my wing.

The days have been filled with pacing my room and trying to distract myself as I read through every novel in Mae's private collection. The slim forest-green book slides from the bookshelf, the embossed stag head on the front cover shining as it catches the sunlight. The stag is smooth to the touch, but the rest of the cover feels rough and weathered.

The spine cracks as I open it. I flip through several blank pages, each one stiff and brittle. On the fourth page, *The First Deer Queen* is written in neat cursive.

I skim through the tale, finding some comfort in the familiar words. My mother used to tell me this story to help me fall asleep, her calloused hands gently rubbing my back as she wove the tale of Wrena's true daughter. The story would always seep into my dreams, images of me wearing a crown sticking with me for the next day.

But this isn't the tale I was told. No, the tale I was told was Mae's prophecy.

The story in my hands tells of Wrena's creation of the High Houses.

This tale is about Mae's grandmother. Mae's mother, a High Fae princess, was the daughter in the story. Has Mae read this? She must have, since this was in her private library. This is not a book that was housed in the royal collection. How did she get this?

I flip through the rest of the book. At the end, there's a hurried script written on a singular page. The words are nearly illegible, but I can make out some—*flowers, moss, blood, essence, two, light,* and *She.*

Someone pounds on the door and I nearly jump out of my skin. I shelve the book and roll my shoulders as I mentally prepare myself for a visitor.

Marik stands in the foyer, lanky frame leaning against the wall. His head snaps up when I clear my throat.

"What do you want?" I ask.

He raises an eyebrow. "Is that how you wish to speak to me?"

I force a very-clearly fake smile to my face. "What can I do for you, Your Highness?" My voice is full of faux sweetness, as if I just bit into a rotten candy apple.

And suddenly, my back is against the wall, every muscle and joint locked. Marik stalks toward me, features darkening with every step. He stops inches from me. His eyes, the perfect embodiment of a solar eclipse, pierce into mine.

"Is that how you wish to speak to me, Elle?" he repeats, spitting my name like venom.

I refuse to look away from him. Rage has my blood pounding like a drum. "Yes."

The corner of his mouth lifts in a smirk. "And yet, it changes nothing." With a crook of his finger, my chin tilts upward, exposing the column of my neck to him. I still don't look away. His chuckle is low and derisive, his breath hot on my throat.

He could end my life in an instant. He's already killed Etta, Silas, Adelaide, and who knows who else.

He takes a step back and smooths the wrinkles on his shirt. He runs a hand through his hair, returning it to its orderly state. "We have somewhere to be, little fawn. Can you behave? Or do I need to control your every move?"

I swallow the vitriol I want to hurl at him and say as calmly as I can, "Fine."

The other corner of his mouth lifts. "Good girl." He turns on his heel and walks to the door. "We need to be in the throne room immediately. Go change." By change, he means change into Mae. He snaps his fingers and my body slumps as his control vanishes.

I trudge to the bathroom, to the blade, and the smothering blanket of dark magic settles over me.

The throne room is empty when we enter, save for one ancient, raven-haired witch. She sits in one of the berry thrones, slender arms draped on the armrests, legs crossed. Desire fills Cora's bone-white eyes as she tracks Marik's every move.

The snort comes from nowhere, and I clap a hand over my mouth. Cora's head cocks as her gaze lands on me. In any other instance, the expression on her face would chill me to the bone. But I've found that I no longer care what happens to me. What I *do* care about, however, is pissing these people off. I drop my hand back to my side and smile.

"What's so funny?" Her tone is curious.

"Oh, nothing," I say dismissively, not even deigning to look at her.

I expect what comes next. My foot freezes mid-stride. Icy fingers crawl up my throat before forcing my chin to tilt toward Cora.

She stares at me from the stolen throne, a single dark eyebrow raised. "What is so funny?"

I lock my jaw. Again, I'm expecting it when her shadow fingers pry it open. Although I have no choice but to look at her, I do so with pride as I say my next words. "You look at him like a love-sick teenager. It's embarrassing."

Anger flashes in her eyes, but only briefly. It doesn't matter. It's enough. It's a win.

What happened to behaving? Marik's voice whispers in my mind. I don't respond.

Cora addresses Marik. "Are you prepared to speak with them?"

Marik nods and stops in front of Cora on the throne. He bends down and she reaches for him, wrapping those pale, slender arms around his neck before pressing her lips to his. I look away as a sour tang fills my mouth. Disgusting.

Marik clears his throat, now perched on the previously empty throne. He motions to the space behind him. "You will stand right here and you will not speak unless spoken to *by me*. Is that clear?"

I walk to the dais and take my spot. Cora's earlier expression didn't scare me, but this upcoming visitor has me nervous.

The throne room doors open and Marik's control slips over me. For once, I'm thankful for it. Without it, I might have sunk to my knees in defeat.

"Welcome, House Panthera," Cora says warmly.

MARIK

For once, Elle doesn't fight the hold I have on her. Every time I've controlled her, she is a constant force bashing against my grip, like waves in a hurricane crashing into the rocks lining the shore. The first time she fought it, I was shocked. The second time, I was prepared. By the third time, I was impressed. By the tenth time, I was jealous that she had the strength and the hope to not succumb.

But now, she sags against it.

And my skin prickles in disappointment.

House Panthera comes to a stop in front of us. They all bow, like good little, spineless soldiers. Katze stands and stares at Cora with something like worship. I'd love to hear Elle snort at him right about now.

"Welcome back, House Panthera. Lovely to see you again, Cassia," I say, forcing myself to look at her with hunger. Forcing myself to play my part.

She stares back at me, her rage barely concealed behind her emerald eyes. "Lovely to see you, Your Highness," Cassia says, but her tone tells me she'd rather be shoveling horse shit.

"Koa," I say, dipping my head toward him.

Unlike his sister, his stare is hollow. "Your Highness," he responds drily.

I wish rolling my eyes was kingly. "Give your reports," I command.

Katze grimaces. "Our subjects are not as keen to invite the witches in as we initially thought."

I lean back, placing my elbow on the armrest and resting my chin in my hand. "Make them," I say. Again, he grimaces. He might be the weakest, most spineless of them all.

"It's not as easy as that, Your Highness," Katze says, casting a nervous glance toward Cora.

"What do you expect me to say, Katze?" I ask him, voice hardening. "The problem lies in your court, not mine. You're responsible for your subjects, not me."

"We've been thinking..." he says, turning toward his wife. Issa's full lips curl into a cruel smile, and Katze straightens. "We'd like to begin executing the dissenters," he says, chest puffed in pride.

Koa doesn't flinch at the words, but Cassia balls her hands into tiny fists before hiding them behind her back.

Elle screams in my head. I tighten my control on her so she doesn't sprint at the Panthera King and claw his eyes from their sockets.

"Are you sure that won't push them in the opposite direction?" I query.

Before Katze can respond, Issa says, "We are confident that it will provide the right motivation, Your Highness." Her voice is lined with cold, cruel pride. Mother always liked her.

"Fine," I say, prepared for Elle to thrash against my hold. But it doesn't come. I resist the urge to look back at her. Her fight is a constant that I've grown used to over the months. Her silence, although rare, is concerning. Not for the first time, I wonder if bringing her to this was a good idea. I tried to warn Cora that it would be too much, but she insisted that House Panthera see "Mae" involved.

"Kill everyone who disagrees," Cora says.

I shift in my seat at the order, but give a curt nod of agreement. There's no room for sympathy on a stolen throne.

Elle was silent for the rest of the day, even when I released her from my control. After House Panthera left, she followed me back to her wing without protest. The last time she was like this, she was trying to take her own life.

The next morning, I knock on her door. I wait, hoping she'll open it on her own.

She doesn't.

I shove it open anyway. She's curled on the couch, a novel clutched in her hands. Her crimson hair is a mess, wavy strands tangled in her ivory antlers. She wears a pair of navy-blue cotton pajamas, the blue accentuating the bags under her eyes.

"You look like shit," I mutter. She doesn't respond, nor does she look up at me. "Elle." Still no response. I could make her, but the thought is tiring. I stand there, waiting for her to say something.

She doesn't. I settle into the armchair across from the couch. Thanks to my parents, I can wait. Mother and Father used to force Asmo and me to sit in silence for hours, any sound or movement punished with a quick slash of the snake-skin whip. The whip's end was meant to resemble the tail of a rattlesnake, studded with an iron tip. Sometimes, after dozens of lashings, I would have preferred the deathly kiss of a rattlesnake.

I don't have to wait long, but it's not Elle that breaks the silence. The front door opens. Vicente's dark head of shiny, black hair pokes through the archway.

"What is it?" I ask.

"Your Highness," his whiny voice starts. "It's important, sir."

I sigh. I don't care about whatever the hell Vicente has to say, if I'm being honest. He's a snively second-in-command chosen by Father. If only Cora's black magic hadn't saved him and Mother from the brink of death. Then I wouldn't have to deal with Vicente.

With a sigh, I stand. Elle still hasn't moved.

"I didn't realize you were a statue," I toss over my shoulder as I turn toward Vicente.

He refuses to be in this space longer than he must, so he stands outside awkwardly, picking dirt from beneath his fingernails.

"What is it?" I ask as I shut the doors behind me.

Vicente drops his hands to his sides and straightens. Detritus still hangs from one of his nails. "Sir, they've done it again."

Again, I sigh. "Fine, lead me to it," I order, then stop. "Wait here." I turn and enter the wing again. Surprisingly, Elle is capable of moving, as she's currently staring at me from the couch, novel discarded on the coffee table.

"What does he mean?" she asks. Her vocal chords sound like they were made of gravel.

"Come on," I order. But it's not really an order, if I'm being honest. This time, it's more like a request. She could easily deny it, but she doesn't. She stands, and I swear I see a flicker of that normal fire in her eyes, if only for a moment.

She doesn't change out of her pajamas or put on shoes. I don't object. Her silence has been a form of torture that I never expected, nor can I explain why. Not rationally, at least. Her fiery attitude had been a reminder of a boy long gone. One who fought against his parents and what he was destined to become. But her current silence reminds me of a boy hardened into a man who grew too tired of fighting.

Vicente doesn't acknowledge her as we step from the wing, but I don't miss the flash of disgust that flickers over his features.

"Lead us."

Like a good boy, Vicente heeds my command and sets off down the stairs. Outside, he takes a right down the path that winds around the mountain. I hate this mountain. Well, maybe I just hate mountains in general. I much prefer the flat plane of home. The City of Sand. Regardless, we descend, until Vicente comes to a slow stop. He doesn't need to explain what happened. This is the fourth time this week. This time, the blood displays the message on the mossy forest floor. Last time, it was on the marble stairs of the castle.

Every time, it spells the same thing.

THERE ARE TWO

Cora and I have puzzled over the message a dozen times, each of us drawing blanks for what it could mean. Every few days, the same message appears somewhere on the castle grounds. Every time, it's written in fresh blood. And nobody has any idea who's writing it.

Elle stands beside me as she stares at the message.

"What is this?" Her voice is monotone.

"We're not sure."

She surveys the scene in front of her. The sun peeks through the canopy of trees, shining down on the smooth slope of her nose, then to freckles the same color of her eyes.

I inhale sharply and wrench my gaze back to the scene in front of us.

"We just noticed it, Your Highness," Vicente says, hands clasped behind his back as he watches me.

I glare at him. "It's been dry for at least an hour, and you just noticed it?"

He shifts uneasily on his feet and refuses to meet my glare. "Yes, Your Highness."

I withhold the sigh that I so desperately want to let loose. "I thought I told you to increase the patrols," I say. My voice is low, and I don't need to be a psychic to tell that my change in tone has Vicente feeling nervous now.

Another thing Mother and Father taught us—presentation is everything.

"We did, sir, but they missed the culprit again."

I summon midnight flames and fire a ball at Vicent's greasy head of hair. He ducks and I pull back before they collide with the ancient tree behind him. The last thing I need is a forest fire on my hands.

"It is your job, Vicente, to ensure they are doing theirs," I hiss as I take slow, measured steps toward him.

He shrinks back toward the tree, helpless prey caught by the predator.

"Y-y-yes, Your Highness," he stammers.

"Get to the bottom of this," I spit before turning on my heels and leaving him to clean this mess up. I don't need to turn to know Elle follows behind me. I can sense her proximity. Ever since I put that damned necklace on her, she hasn't left my mind.

Although she's my prisoner, I can't help but feel like she's the one I can't escape.

CHAPTER 18
MAE

Asmo's back is rigid as he follows Barrett to the throne room. He's barely spoken two words to me this morning. All he's done is shove a bagel in his mouth and grunt in approval or dissent when I reviewed our talking points for our meeting with Torben and Artis.

"How bad has it been, Barrett?" I whisper as he leads us down the hall.

He doesn't turn, but I can hear him all the same. "Marik keeps trying to force us to house witches in our court. Every time we say no, we receive fewer resources from the High Court to support our own. Not to mention, cambions and the Cursed haunt the forest. Every morning, there are more animals for us to bury."

I wince. That's worse than August's report.

Torben and Artis are already seated on their thrones when we arrive, Torben in another set of brown pants and shirt, Artis in a loose shift dress the color of a fern. She gives Asmo and me a gracious smile as we enter. "Welcome back. Sleep well?"

No, I tossed and turned as I thought about undead animals ripping me and everyone I loved apart. I dreamed of Marik's grin as he choked an innocent male with writhing wildfire. I dreamed Asmo held the flames next. "Yes. Thank you for your hospitality."

Torben clears his throat. "Right, well. I think it's best if we dive right into it, don't you?"

I don't miss the fact that Torben still looks at me with distrust, nor does the fact escape me that Asmo and I have not been offered a place to sit.

My palms turn clammy, but I nod. "Perfect."

Torben leans forward. "You said yesterday that your friend is a prisoner on the throne. That's how Marik and Cora are getting away with this, forcing an unwilling female to use dark magic to pretend to be you. Is that correct?"

"Yes. Her name is Elle. She was an advisor to the High Throne. To me and to my father. She was responsible for helping me escape the First Witch and Marik on the night of my wedding. Without her, I'd either be dead or chained in the dungeons. Although she is a prisoner, we've found a way to make contact with her, and we can use her imprisonment to our advantage. She can get us information on guard placements, shift changes, potentially even information on Marik's plans."

Sweat pools under my arms. We have no idea if Elle can do this. We have no idea if she'll even agree to try. Telling Torben our hopeful plan, without telling him it's not a concrete plan, is all a huge gamble. But Asmo and I agreed this may be our best shot at securing Ursidae's support. And therefore, our best shot at getting Elle out and my throne back.

Torben raises an eyebrow. "And what happens when Marik realizes what she's doing? She'll be dead with a snap of his finger."

"She's careful. She won't—"

Torben laughs, but Artis's smile is now gone. I bristle as I'm reminded of another male sitting on a throne of branches, laughing at me like I'm the kingdom's biggest fool. Barrett straightens, jaw clenched as he looks at the stone floor.

"This is your plan? This is how you expect to get the kingdom back?" he asks, placing a hand on his belly as he leans back on his throne and snickers.

My lip curls. Months ago, I would have folded at the challenge, at the insulting laugh. Now, it just pisses me off. I will ice and steel into my tone. "I'm coming to you for help. I cannot do this alone. Marik and

Cora have the Royal Guard, the Serpent House, and the witches to protect them. I have nothing. I need your court."

Torben's laugh dies. "This war might as well be over. Our court alone cannot help you, girl."

Asmo bristles beside me, tension radiating from him.

I'm the fucking High Queen, not a *girl*. Inhale, exhale. When I'm back on my throne, I can be picky about the insulting pet names that grown males use to belittle powerful females.

"We also have the support of House Canis," I counter. "I feel confident that House Panthera will assist. We have to get Marik and Cora off the throne."

"No." Torben's answer is a sledgehammer to my heart.

"All due respect, Torben," I say, intentionally refraining from referring to him by his title. Although he is *a* king, I am *the* Queen, and he answers to me. "I do not accept your answer. If you refuse my aid, you're dooming the rest of the kingdom to the same fate that your court will eventually succumb to. Make no mistake, Cora and Marik will succeed in starving your court or overrunning it. Either way, you will have to face them. Do it alone, or do it with me and whatever allies I procure. The choice is yours."

Torben's features grow taut, and the throne room goes silent, save for the *tap, tap, tap* of his meaty finger on his throne of branches. The one crafted after the High Throne. My throne.

"Father," Barrett says cautiously. "She is our High Queen. She is coming to us for assistance, and she is right. If we do nothing, our people—innocent people—will die."

Torben turns his head toward Barrett. His voice is low and grave. "Son, it is my responsibility to protect our court. I can protect them here, but if we send our young males to fight in a woefully understaffed army against witches, we are just signing their death certificates. The witches were responsible for the fall of the Fae Kingdom. They are strong and they are merciless, and they will stop at nothing. My answer is no. We cannot help. This war is lost already."

My magic roils underneath the surface, as if begging to unleash on Torben. I swore an oath to protect. It's in my blood to do so, and this buffoon of a male is denying me aid.

Artis clears her throat. "We will send aid if you can secure the support of Houses Canis and Panthera. However, we will not mandate our citizens to fight. We will provide them with the facts of what they will be facing and give them the choice."

Torben's face turns red, his hands balling into tight, angry fists. "Artis—"

She holds a graceful hand up to her husband, her gaze still fixed on mine. "You are young, Your Highness. You have a hard road ahead of you, regardless of which path you choose to take. I hope you understand we are just doing what is necessary to protect our own." She stands. Torben reluctantly joins her. "Our son will walk you out," she says. Although her eyes are warm, her tone is firm.

My hands threaten to shake, and I clasp them behind my back tightly. I want to collapse, to beg, to offer anything for their help, for the promise of hope again. But I straighten my spine and say, "You said you would help us."

Artis's smile falters. "My husband and I had to discuss our options. We went through every scenario last night. Unfortunately, we are limited in the support we can offer you. We must protect our citizens first. If you return with Houses Canis and Panthera's support, we will offer you what little we can. Until then, we must keep our resources within our court." She turns to Barrett and gestures toward us. "Please, son."

Barrett steps forward, his brows drawn together as he stares at his mother. She refuses to acknowledge it. He walks toward us and gestures back to the landing. "This way," he mumbles, refusing to meet my gaze.

"Did either of you leave anything back in your rooms?" Barrett asks as we approach the stairs. I shake my head, but he looks at me with wide, expectant eyes. "Are you sure?"

"I did," Asmo lies. "Do you mind taking me back there before we leave?"

The walk back to the private guest quarters is silent, save for the sounds of our footsteps on the hard, worn dirt of the cave floor. My thoughts are a frenzied mix of shock and anger. I thought he would help us. How dare he not?

The moment we're back inside the private room, Barrett turns to face Asmo and me.

"What the fuck was that, Barrett?" Asmo hisses, taking a menacing step toward him. I reach for Asmo's arm to pull him back, but it does nothing.

Barrett drops his head into his hands. "I don't know," he groans. "When I spoke with my father last night, the plan was to help you. They must have changed their minds after I went to bed." He lifts his head. "Mae, I am so sorry. I really thought...I wasn't expecting that to go that way."

I sigh. Asmo takes a step back to stand beside me. "It's okay, Bar—" I begin to say, but Asmo jerks his head toward me, eyes narrowed to slits.

"I wholeheartedly disagree, princess. Barrett made it seem like this was a done deal. And now, it's contingent on two other courts agreeing to help?"

Once, his expression would have made me shrink. Now, all I can focus on is the silver that cuts through his fern-green iris. His gaze softens, jaw unclenching as he stares at me.

"We already have August's help. I feel confident that we can get Koa's," I say, more calmly than I feel.

"We thought we had his help." Asmo throws a wild hand toward Barrett, who now stands by the door watching us. "Plus, we haven't talked to August's parents. Just August. It could be the same damn thing."

"August's court will help you. He gave me his word," Barrett says.

Asmo turns back to him. "And what good is his word? You as good as gave me yours, and it was useless," he snaps.

Barrett's mouth tightens into a frown. "I'm sorry, Mae." He turns and opens the door, quelling any response Asmo or I had to give. The three of us climb the steep flight of stairs without speaking, light blooming around us the higher we climb. Barrett exits the underground palace first. Asmo doesn't give him any form of salutation. He just walks away, his hands tucked into his pockets.

"I'm in as much shock as you are," Barrett mutters.

I offer him a half-assed smile. It's all I can muster right now. This was a blow. We were counting on House Ursidae to help, and we're leaving without it.

"Be safe, okay?" I say before turning and walking back to Asmo.

Leaves crunch beneath me as I walk toward him. He stands still, his back turned to me. His tall frame is bathed in sunlight, broad shoulders cutting through a ray as it tries to reach the forest floor.

"I could use a drink right about now," I say.

He turns to me, a lopsided smile on his face. It jars me. A smile is the last thing I expected after the crushing conversation we just had with Torben and Artis.

"Let's go then."

I narrow my eyes. Surely I didn't hear him correctly. "We have to go back ho—to the house. Ivan will be worried. And what about Cally? I need to check on her."

He dismisses the idea with a wave of his hand. "Come on," he says, tugging me against him. "They won't be expecting us for hours. Let's be normal for a second and just go grab a drink before we have to think about what comes next."

The memory of sitting at the tavern with Asmo, of forgetting everything for an hour as we played billiards...of being normal hybrids. "Okay," I whisper.

The air blurs around us as we funnel out of the Ursine forest and land back in Bouldercrest. Luckily, nobody—human, hybrid, or witch —is at the portal location when the funnel releases us from its grasp. Asmo and I, stupidly, didn't think to use our sigils to change our appearances before we left.

I fumble for the knife at my side and begin to press the blade into my skin, but Asmo's hand clamps around my wrist. He takes the knife from my hand and kneels before me, reminding me of a time from before. Him on his knees, pushing the hem of my dress up, his thumb grazing my scars.

"I hate that you have to do this," he whispers, holding the blade to my stomach.

"Me, too," I whisper breathlessly, feeling the tingle of goosebumps erupting at his touch. But if it keeps me from being hidden away,

secluded in a dusty cabin, if it helps me *live*, it's a sacrifice I'll make—
again and again.

He carves the mark into the plane of my stomach, over the still-
healing scar of the last one. "As are you, as am I," I whisper.

Asmo changes into his usual disguise and reaches for my hand. We
walk down the path in silence, then join the bustling foot traffic. We
come to a stop outside of a dilapidated building. Pink paint peels from
the façade, and a shattered window reveals an empty bar. A sign hangs
precariously from a rusted nail above the door. *The Famous Peaks Inn.*

The inside is no better than the outside. The stench of beer and stale
food grows stronger with every step closer to an empty bar that's seen
better days. Asmo pulls out a barstool, the cotton on the seat stained
and pilling. I refrain from crinkling my nose in disgust before I take a
careful seat, praying to the Mother that it doesn't fall apart.

To my immense surprise, Asmo looks right at home. He places his
elbows right onto the sticky counter and motions toward the bartender,
a male who seems to be as old as the inn. His clothes are disheveled and
stained, gray hair shaggy and out of place. Gray, furry ears peak out from
his hair. I almost miss them with how perfectly they blend in.

"What can I get ya?" he asks Asmo.

"Pitcher of light ale. Two glasses."

The bartender slides the glasses toward us, then sets a full pitcher in
front of us. Asmo chills a glass with his magic and fills it with the ale. He
offers it to me, and I nearly down the whole glass.

It's crisp and light and sends a delicious buzz straight to my head.
It's undoubtedly the best beer I've ever had.

Asmo watches me with crinkled eyes as he downs his own glass. He
pours himself another and tops mine off.

"Good, right?" he asks, leaning back onto the creaky stool.

I take another sip. "I didn't know beer could taste this good."

"I'd never lead you astray, princess." He reaches for my mouth,
wiping away the foam from the quick pour with his thumb. I avert my
gaze as I remember the last time his thumb was on my mouth—when I
asked him to marry me and he said no.

I down the rest of my drink and pour myself another. "How did you
know about this place?"

He shrugs. "I didn't. Lucky guess based on its appearance. Places like this are the best for a cold beer. That's just one of the rules of the world."

He might have a point. Cally and I used to visit the most popular taverns and pubs on nights out. Although the music and atmosphere were incredible, the drinks were always too expensive and frankly, gross.

"How did you discover that rule?" I ask.

He looks straight ahead, the light from the window hitting the sharp line of his jaw. "Whenever Marik and I wanted a normal night out or to go for a drink without having to be *us,* we'd search for a pub on the outskirts of the court."

Marik. His brother. My husband. The one who betrayed us both.

We both fall quiet. Asmo takes another huge swallow of his beer.

"This sucks," I mutter.

Asmo snorts. "What in particular?" He wipes a bead of condensation from his glass.

Great question. Everything. Hiding in abandoned dusty homes. Waking up and feeling the weight of the kingdom on my chest, so heavy I feel like I can't breathe. The feeling that nobody believes in me to save this kingdom. The fact that I don't even believe in myself.

What am I supposed to do against all of this? I've only just begun to grasp my magic, but I still don't even know how to funnel or portal or —"Can you teach me how to shift?"

Asmo cocks his head. "You don't know how?"

I kick him under the table. "Save it. Don't you think I would have already if I could? I don't even know if I can," I admit.

He takes another swig of his drink, then sets it on the table gently. "I didn't mean it like that. I would bet my life that you can."

"What makes you so sure?" *Why do you believe in me so much when I don't believe in myself?*

"Have you forgotten that you're the first of Wrena's line?"

"What good is that when I've spent the last almost twenty-six years of my life barely skimming the surface of my magic?"

He shrugs. "Fair point. When we get back, I'll teach you to shift. While we're at it, is there anything else you'd like me to teach you?" he asks with a mischievous grin.

I bump my shoulder into his. It barely moves him, but his beer sloshes in his glass. His answering chuckle rumbles through his chest, sending warm embers into my own.

CHAPTER 19
MAE

THE LIGHT BEGINS to dim as the sun slips behind the Wolven Peaks. The bar, already dingy and dark, now grows even more so. I'm not sure how much longer the bartender is going to be able to continue his current task of cleaning dirty dishes unless he lights a candle soon.

Asmo and I have almost finished another pitcher, both of us feeling unquestionably tipsy and bordering on drunk, when the barkeeper clears his throat. "You folks planning to stay the night? You'd be the only guests, so I'll give you the room for cheap."

Asmo sets his glass down. "We'll just finish this pitcher and then we'll be out of your hair."

The male's hand freezes mid-scrub on a chipped plate. He eyes Asmo carefully. "You're going to miss the curfew."

His words sober me. Now it's Asmo's turn to freeze. "What curfew?" His voice is low and threatening.

The barkeeper is unaffected by it, rinsing the soap from the dish in his hand. "Not from around here, then?"

"What are you talking about?" Asmo leans forward, placing a hand on the bar top.

"Mandatory curfew in effect at sundown to keep Canis citizens safe," he says flatly, now focusing on a stubborn stain that looks like it's a permanent fixture of the plate by now.

"From what?" I ask, but I have a feeling I already know the answer. The last time we were here, being inside before dark wasn't a mandate, just a strong suggestion. Granted, we didn't listen to it, and we nearly paid the price. The wound on my calf throbs at the reminder.

"Damn witches and their pets," he says with disgust.

I glance out the window at the empty streets, now cloaked in darkness.

"Shit," Asmo grumbles. "You didn't think to mention this before sundown?"

The barkeeper shrugs. "Figured you were either staying the night or you were locals who knew better." He glances around the empty bar. "This isn't exactly a tourist destination."

Asmo stands and tugs me from the barstool. "Come on."

The barkeeper chuckles. "You can take your chances, but I wouldn't if I were you. Entire town is spelled against any kind of portaling. Guards roam the streets, hauling people to their homes or the dungeons if they have none. All in the name of protection against the witches," he says, setting the plate down with a little more force than necessary.

Asmo stops and turns slowly. He does a good job at looking calm, but the hunch of his shoulders and the clench of his jaw tell me otherwise. He tosses another handful of coins on the bar and holds his hand out in a silent demand.

The barkeeper tosses a key onto the bar and gestures toward a staircase on the opposite end of the room. "Second floor. Room eight. Gave you the nicest of the lot to make up for my mistake. Free breakfast at first light. You'll be able to leave then."

Asmo storms up the stairs and I hurry after him. Behind us, the barkeeper mutters an unenthusiastic, "Enjoy your stay."

Ivan's going to kill us.

Room eight isn't as awful as I anticipated. An empty bowl and a fresh canister of water sit on a small wooden dresser shoved against the wall by the door. A double-paned window looks out onto the snow-capped mountain range, its peaks shrouded in the shadow of night. Other than the window, the other hallmark feature is the bed that dominates the room. A white duvet hugs the large bed, looking comfortable and surprisingly clean.

One bed. And there's absolutely no way either of us can sleep on the floor, unless we want to sleep in the hallway or at the bar downstairs.

Asmo stares at the bed and ruffles his hair with his hand.

"Well, this isn't how I was expecting the night to go," he mutters.

He shrugs off his jacket and tosses it onto the wooden dresser, then sits on the bed and unlaces his leather boots. I turn away, my chest too tight at the thought of spending an entire night alone with him in this room with no real escape.

I pull my knife from my boot and mar the sigil on my stomach. Without looking, I toss the knife on the bed for Asmo to do the same. I pour some of the water from the canister into the empty bowl and splash my face, hoping to wash some of the grit from the day away.

When I turn, the real Asmo is on the bed, back against the bedframe, long legs stretched out and crossed at the ankle. "I hope Ivan isn't too worried," I mutter as I toss my boots toward the wall.

Asmo snorts. "He's not your dad. He'll be fine."

I turn to face him, a lick of anger rolling up my spine. "You're right. I must have somehow forgotten my dad is dead." *Murdered at the hands of your brother, actually.*

His eyes narrow, and he opens his mouth, then shuts it. Probably a smart move.

I take a deep breath and sink onto the bed. Underneath the duvet are freshly laundered sheets. I lay down, my back turned to Asmo, and stare at the scuffed wall.

The sheets rustle as the bed shifts. "Mae," he says, "I didn't...I'm sorry for how today turned out. With Torben."

I don't want to think about how today turned out. I don't want to think about the predicament that we're in and how the well of hope I felt this morning was drained by the afternoon. I don't want to think about anything.

"What are you even still doing here?" I ask, unwilling to face him as I voice the question that has plagued me for weeks. Since I first woke up to find him leaning over me, eyes full of pain. "Why aren't you with your family? Why aren't you with your court?" Tears well, and I resist the urge to swipe them away. But it's not sadness. It's anger, frustration, hurt that he chose his court over me when I chose him.

My relationship with Asmo isn't the only thing that has me feeling emotional. It's a messy conglomeration of the entire month, of losing him, Elle, my father, my aunt, a sister I never knew, of nearly losing Cally. I have no idea how to make this okay, how to save myself, let alone an entire kingdom from the betrayal of the people I once trusted.

Okay, and maybe the alcohol isn't helping either.

I expect Asmo to respond with equal amounts of anger. I expect him to play the game back, the one that we've been so good at playing since we first met. The one where we circle each other, firing insults and hurling cruelties.

What I don't expect is his hand on the dip of my waist, the feeling of him sliding me back toward him, only inches apart. Heat radiates from him. It's not just the chill in the air that's making my body yearn to be pressed against his warmth. It's a need that I've tried to suppress for months now.

We lay there, my questions hanging in the air, his hand cupping my waist. My heart twisting in my chest.

When he finally responds, his voice is a whisper. "I left everything behind for you. I should've made the decision sooner, but you have to understand my entire life has been my court. I grew up thinking I'd be placed in a loveless marriage to someone my parents chose. I never expected...you. Every interaction with you left me wanting more. And that was terrifying for me. That's not how my life was supposed to go. But what terrified me even more was being without you."

I freeze. This is not the game we play. No, this breaks all our unspoken rules. The rules that say we walk around our feelings, that we avoid mentioning the lingering looks, the too-long touches, the way our eyes connect and can never seem to pull away. We're supposed to tiptoe around anything that resembles a conversation about what we've done to each other and what the world has done to us—how it's pushed us together by sheer force and how we continue to push back.

He takes a deep breath, his thumb now stroking the slope of my waist. "The day you asked me to marry you, I panicked. I wasn't ready to make a decision. I still hadn't given up the idea of leaving my court, of throwing my future away in favor of a different one. When you told me you picked Marik, I was devastated, but I was also...happy. At least I'd get to keep seeing you. How fucked up is that?" He snorts.

I don't say a word. The lump in my throat feels too thick and my vision blurs with the hot burn of unshed tears.

"But then, my idiotic brother, in the most fucked up way, gave me another chance to be with you. When I stepped toward my family on that day, it was like my heart faltered in my chest. It was like moving through quicksand. Everything felt miserably wrong. Being next to you feels right. It's always felt right. Even if you were the villain in this story, I'd still choose to be next to you."

Tears silently stream down my face in warm, salty rivulets.

"When Cora..." He inhales shakily, and his hand grips my waist tighter. "I thought you were dead. It felt like my soul flickered when that bolt hit you. And in my own selfish way, when Torben said he wouldn't help us today, all I felt was relief. I saw a path that meant we didn't have to fight. That meant I could just take you and hide you away, keep you protected from everyone and everything." He pauses, a huff of warm laughter stirring loose strands of hair against my neck and sending shivers down my spine. "And then you stood up to him. Like you stand up to me, every day. Like you stood up to Marik and Cora. And I realized you're not meant to hide. You're meant to fight, to lead, to protect. I want to be beside you for all of it, if you'll have me."

I can't say anything. I physically don't think I'm capable of forming a sentence right now without my voice cracking. My silence is a dam holding back floodwaters. All this time, I've been terrified to lean into my feelings. I don't know how I can trust anything I feel, especially when what I feel for Asmo is like my wildfire—burning and uncontrollable. The idea of giving myself to him feels reckless, selfish, and idiotic. But it also feels right.

Every word he speaks is the truth. Every single word. And every choice he's made has been for me. He's done nothing to indicate he was ever a part of Marik's plan.

"If you don't want me, I get it. I've been an insufferable asshole to you at every turn. When I said I wasn't good for you, I meant it. There are plenty of other perfectly charming males out there who will treat you the way you deserve, but I think you feel this, too, Mae. I think there's more to us than a normal relationship. I think..." He trails off as I turn to face him.

I don't bother wiping the tears from my face.

His face is inches from mine. His perfect, angelic, beautiful face. I've thought of it so many times, I've yearned for him, I've dreamed of him, I've pictured him as I've kissed the other High Princes. He's right. There's something between us that's not normal. It feels...otherworldly, like what's between us was crafted from magic itself.

His hand leaves my waist to brush the tears from my cheeks. "I made you cry again."

"What's new?" I ask, lifting one corner of my mouth.

His gaze darts to my mouth, then back to my eyes. "I'm sorry. I'm so sorry," he whispers as he brushes away another tear.

I've spent so much time trying to keep myself away, and it feels like I'm hitting my breaking point. It feels like I've been underwater for too long, like my lungs are about to burst if I don't open my mouth and *breathe.*

So, I do. I breathe.

I close the distance between us, crashing my lips against his. This time, there are no butterflies that take flight in my stomach. This feels like dragons soaring through my blood, breathing hot flames into every vein, setting every part of me on fire.

His hand grips the back of my head, fingers wrapping in my hair. I scoot closer to him and press every inch of my body against every inch of his. His mouth over mine stifles the groan when I feel him against me. When I feel how ready he is for me.

And I'm done. I'm done holding myself back, forcing my feelings into a box and shoving them away. I'm done minimizing what I feel for Asmo, done ignoring the way my heart somehow calms and pulses at the same time when he walks into a room, the way my body sings when he's near.

I reach for the fastening of his pants, but he grips my wrist, pinning it over my head as he rolls on top of me. His mouth shifts from mine and moves to my ear, his tongue licking and biting down the slope of my neck. My back arches at the feeling. He slides one hand underneath me, bringing me flush against his chest, like he can't stand to be apart from me.

He lifts my shirt, and the cool kiss of the winter air bites at my skin. But Asmo's warm hands set every inch of me on fire. His hand cups my breast, thumb flicking over my hardened nipple.

"Mae," he whispers, and it sounds like a prayer.

I reach for his pants, desperate to feel him inside of me. Desperate to know what he feels like, what it's like to be one with him. He doesn't stop me this time. He lifts his hips and helps me pull his pants down. I lift my hips in a silent request for him to remove mine, our tongues still colliding. He throws my pants into the corner of the room.

He breaks away from me and gets on his knees to stare at my center, giving me a full, unobstructed view of him.

He is perfection. His abs ripple down to hips that form a V pointing directly to his...

My mouth dries, while another part of me floods.

His smile at my glistening sex threatens to make me climax. It's not the animalistic desire in his eyes as he stares at me, it's the vulnerability of sharing this with him. Of baring everything to him. I lift my hips, yearning to feel him against me. My center brushes against him, and he goes still at the contact.

I can't take it anymore. I pull him onto the bed and climb on top of him, spreading my legs over his impressive length. He stares up at me with a wicked grin, chest already heaving.

"Mae," he growls.

When we cross this bridge, is there any going back? Is there any possible way I could never hear my name on his lips again?

I lean down, pressing my chest against his. His hands find my hips and guide them, lining my entrance just over his erection. Slowly, so, so slowly, I lower myself onto his perfect length. Pleasure rolls through me as he fills me. My instincts take over, hips rocking as all my thoughts explode at once.

All I can feel is him, every thought and sensation hyper-focused on that and that alone. Asmo beneath me, inside of me. This male who's pushed me away and pulled me back, who's sacrificed everything for me, who's held me in my darkest moments.

He groans, eyes closed as I rock against him. He fills every inch of me, our bodies moving in perfect rhythm as one. It feels like we're two pieces of a puzzle, like the Mother designed us to fit perfectly together.

His hands grip my backside, and my orgasm rips through me like a wave of wildfire. Exactly what I thought it would feel like to give myself to him—burning and uncontrollable. But my wildfire is a part of me, and so is Asmo, in a way. He will always be a part of me, and a part of what made me the person I am today.

So, I give myself up to him, to the uncontrollable, to the burning, and I let it take me.

I smother my moans into his shoulder, biting down as the flames crest. He wraps his arms around my waist, and stifles his own moans into the hollow of my neck. His entire body goes rigid as he explodes into me.

Our breathing fades from a panting frenzy to a calmer rhythm. Sweat slicks between us, but neither of us moves. He holds me with a possessive claim, fingertips digging into my curves. I cling to him, thinking of all the mistakes I've ever made, and wondering if this is the biggest one yet.

We lay like that, two hearts beating against each other as one, until sleep takes us both.

CHAPTER 20
MARIK

I ALMOST—ALMOST—JUMP when I open the door to Cora's bedroom. Two cambions stand stationary, one on each side of the open double-doors that lead to the grand balcony. Somehow, their empty eyes follow me as I enter the room.

Cora stands on the balcony, hands resting on the wrought-iron fence overlooking the rose garden. The black aura around her is dim today, but her white silk robe still pops against it. Her inky hair stirs with the breeze, then shifts as she turns toward me. Her eyes are the color of bone and moon and white roses.

"Hello, darling," she croons. I force myself to reach for her.

She pulls me closer and locks her arms around my waist. She is so small against me. It's easy to forget about the ancient power that lurks within her. I forget more and more with every passing day. When we first met, I was terrified. Mother and Father stared at her in a way I had never seen before, their worshipping eyes clinging to her. Only something powerful could warrant that look from them. Asmo had begun to earn that look, but not me. Not until I agreed to work with Cora. To kill the High Family.

Her hands find the hem of my shirt, sharp nails dragging upward as she works her hands up my back.

"You called for me?" I ask.

Her nails dig into my spine. Tiny pinpricks of pain give way to blood, and I fight the urge to shove her away from me. I knew my response to her greeting would irritate her, but my patience is thin these days.

"Try again," she says in the kind of calm that can only be viewed as a threat.

"Hello, beautiful," I say, forcing my gaze to meet hers. Every instinct in every cell of my body screams at me to run, to flee, as I peer into her eyes. Her normally white irises are surrounded by a band of black flames. I can't look away, fixated on the way the flames flicker and writhe.

The corners of her eyes crinkle with her smile. "Better." She leads me into the bedroom, white sheets rumpled and pillows askew.

Cora's sexual appetite is nearly insatiable, but an unmade bed always indicates she's not interested. She likes order and cleanliness when we defile each other. She perches on the bed, then cuts her gaze to the floor in front of her. I kneel, hoping that I didn't misread the room. I almost send a prayer to the Mother, then think better of it. She'd probably receive it and force the opposite to happen.

It's what I deserve, after all.

Thankfully, Cora doesn't spread her legs. She crosses them and leans back on the bed, surveying me with a disinterested gaze.

"Have there been any reports on the girl?" she asks.

"Who?" I know exactly who she's talking about, but my back still stings and I'm in a foul mood.

Her gaze narrows. "You know who."

My hands clench behind my back. Mae. "No, there have been no sightings of her since the last update," I say, even though the last update was the same—Nobody has seen her since Asmo dragged her from the throne room and vanished.

"Hopefully she's lying dead in some ditch after that injury. It was enough to kill her," she says with a smile, even though she fumed for days afterward about the fact that it, in fact, didn't kill her. The one fucking objective of attacking during the wedding. "Anyways. I called you here for a different reason. We need to establish them as a High House."

I blink. This time, I truly don't have a clue who or what she's talking about. "Who?"

Her hands clench as she grips the sheets, and I fight back a flare of panic. The last time I pissed her off, she thrust a fire poker into a blazing hearth and then pressed it to my ribs. Every time it was about to heal itself, she'd do it again. And again. And again. I still have the scar, now smooth and white. I breathe through the panic, force it down. I can handle pain. Father made sure of it.

"The witches," she says through gritted teeth.

This again. I shake my head. "Canis and Ursidae will never vote in approval."

The black aura around her swells. "Make them."

I rein in the sigh I was about to let loose. "It's not that simple," I say for what feels like the hundredth time. Cora is cold, calculating, manipulative, and cruel. But she does not understand the Woodland Kingdom like she does the underworld. Mae's botched assassination is a perfect example. I told Cora we should do it after the wedding, when Mae was alone. But she wanted the show. She wanted the other High Houses to see. To learn who was really in control. And what it would cost them if they didn't fall in line.

It didn't matter how many times I told her it wouldn't work.

"I grow tired of this, Marik," she says, tapping her foot on the ground beside my knee. "We've been circling around this for months. You promised you'd be able to get them to agree, yet here we are. It's time to consider the other options."

"What you're suggesting will destroy the kingdom and is the very opposite of the goal," I argue. "We're supposed to have a kingdom to rule. Not destroy it."

"Not if we contain it."

I raise an eyebrow at her. "And how do you suggest we do that?" Despite my attempt to not sound like an asshole, it doesn't work. My knees ache from kneeling before her, and my mood only worsens the longer I stay here. I brace myself for the sting of her hand on my cheek, but it doesn't come.

She leans back onto her palms, raven hair cascading over her shoulders like a glossy wave. "We've planted the witches in their courts. We need to start using them. Start forcing them to comply. They vote in agreement or we begin implementing the back-up plan." It always comes back to this, to threatening the kings' and queens' children. "I'll give them one more opportunity. Arrange the council meeting. If they don't agree, we give them the ultimatum."

My mind reels. Even with the ultimatum, Canis and Ursidae won't submit. "Cora, they won't respond well to that. Up until now, we've been a peaceful kingdom. We have to try to sell them on the witches, make them believe that the witches are *good*. Scare tactics won't work."

Her face contorts into a sneer. "Then we'll wipe them from the face of the kingdom. I won't tolerate their disrespect, and neither will you. You're High King. Your word is law now." She stands abruptly in one eerie motion that forces me to scuttle backward. "Arrange the meeting."

The door to Mae's—now Elle's—wing clicks open. I swear it takes longer this time, as if the ancient magic embedded inside revolts against my presence. Or maybe it's the ring on my finger that reeks of dark magic. The ring that connects me to Elle's necklace, that allows me to speak inside her mind, that now beckons me closer and pulls me toward the bedroom.

The knife comes from nowhere, flying through the air with the speed of lightning.

I slow its trajectory with a burst of wind and pluck it from the air. I descend into the bond that connects me to Elle. The first time I reached for her, I nearly jumped out of my skin. Of all the times I've used this magic to control another, I've never been able to see into the other person's mind.

And Elle's was a blistering inferno of rage. But underneath it all was fear. And yet, she didn't show an ounce of it.

That was something I was never able to master. And Father made sure I knew I fell short.

Now, when I look down the bond, Elle's rage is once again burning hot and bright. The last time I saw her, she was torturously silent, reminding me of myself from long ago. But now, she reminds me of a different, newer version of myself. The version that relies on rage to get out of bed.

It would be so much easier if Elle gave into the despair. If she just did what was asked of her. If she let the dark magic consume her. That would be the path of least resistance.

And yet, for some reason that goes against everything I'm working toward, I stoke the fire that fuels her.

Come out, come out, little fawn, I whisper down the bond.

Her answering shriek is full of hate. I want to bottle the sound and keep it in my pocket.

The second knife bites against my throat, the blade cool against my skin. My chuckle jostles it, and a warm drop of blood runs down my neck—the second time a female has made me bleed today. Normally, I'm the one doing the bloodletting. I wonder how much she'd like it if the roles were reversed. How much more—or less—she'd hate me if I used my tongue to lick up the blood.

"Drop it," Elle orders.

Sister damn me, but I do. The knife in my hand clatters to the floor. A gust of wind sends it scattering across the room.

I grasp her wrist and press the blade further into my neck. "Do it," I whisper. *Please.*

"Give me one good reason not to," she growls in my ear, and I can't help the small part of me that thrills at her tone.

I try to think of a good reason, any reason at all. But I can't. I'm a terrible male. I have betrayed my kingdom. My own brother didn't care or trust me enough to join me. I have slaughtered innocent people to get what I wanted. I have used my tongue to lie and manipulate my way to the throne beside a witch with a heart of onyx.

It would be easier to just let Elle spill my blood, to slump against her body, limp and lifeless. I know the slash wouldn't kill me, but it's nice to pretend it would. My breath shudders as I pull it to my lungs.

"It won't change a thing. Cora will never stop. With or without me."

Elle is silent, but the knife shakes against my neck. Another drop spills.

I could easily make her drop it. But my soul protests at the thought of forcing her back into a silent husk of herself.

"I came to ask you to join me for dinner this week." I don't know what compels me to say it. It's not true. Actually, I don't know why I came here.

"What's the point in asking? You'll just force me to join you anyways," she hisses.

I turn, the knife grazing my throat, and face her. Her amber eyes promise death. Her lips chapped and bright-red and parted. I tear my gaze from them.

I shrug. "Perhaps. Now, will you pretty please remove this from my neck so I can leave? I do have High King duties to attend to." Another lie. But the way she's staring at me is constricting my chest and I need to get out of this room and away from her.

She clenches her jaw for one, two seconds, then drops her hand to her side. She stares up at me with a fire that I can only imagine is straight from Hell. I would know. It's the exact way I look at myself in the mirror.

She steps back and motions toward the door. "After you, Your Highness." Detest drips from every word.

Another time, I would have punished her for it. But now, I ignore it. My foot is barely out the door when I hear the plunk of the knife landing in the wooden door frame inches from my pointed ear. I ignore that, too.

But what I can't ignore, no matter how hard I try, is the way my heart lurched when I stared down at her. How I was only inches away from making a move that would have ended my life in an entirely different way.

CHAPTER 21
MAE

At some point, Asmo and I become disconnected in the middle of the night, but I still cling to him like a piece of driftwood in the middle of the ocean. His arms are wrapped around me, one thumb lazily stroking the small of my back.

I pull my cheek from the dried puddle of drool on his chest and glance up. He watches me with a smirk on his face. Early morning light filters into the room and onto the bed, rays of sunshine landing on his messy locks of hair.

"How do you still manage to look that good with drool on your face?" he asks, voice rough and low.

I laugh into his chest, then lift my head and wipe it away. "Asmo."

"Princess." His voice is soft, and it threatens to undo me again.

His words from last night echo in my mind, his vulnerability something fresh and new. Something that I'm not sure how to deal with. I'm not used to this version of him. I'm used to him being predictably prickly and pissed off, not...sweet. Our usual script is gone, erased by his speech, waiting to be rewritten.

But we don't have the time to delve into this. We have a kingdom to win back, Elle to rescue, an entire people to protect from his brother. From my husband.

"We have to go," I say lamely.

One corner of his mouth quirks up. "I've just been waiting on you."

"You could have woken me up," I retort.

"Who am I to wake a High Queen?"

I roll my eyes and push myself up, but Asmo pulls me back down and wraps his arms around me.

"Wh—" The question dies on my lips as he shifts underneath me, then rolls us both over, pinning me beneath him. My body arches into him without a thought, but then he's gone and I swallow the protest as he stands before me, all of him on display.

All thoughts go out the window as I devour every inch of him. And I mean...every. Inch.

"If you keep looking at me like that, princess..."

I shake my head, forcing my gaze from his sculpted body. We dress quickly, my mind reeling as I mull over the news that we have to share with the remnants of my court—that Ursidae's support comes with conditions that I'm not sure I can meet.

We carve the sigils into our stomachs and toss the key onto the bar on the way out. The town is nearly empty as we walk back to the portal location in silence, neither of us daring to attract any attention to ourselves.

Ivan wrenches the front door open the moment we step through the barrier. His eyes are wild with panic as they rove over me, then Asmo.

"What happened?" Ivan orders, the question directed at Asmo.

But I answer it. "We're so sorry, Ivan. We're fine. We left the Bear Court and went to grab a drink. By the time we went to leave, we couldn't because of some curfew in place, so we had to stay overnight in an inn."

Ivan's expression goes from panicked to irritated, a scowl darkening his features. "You couldn't just break the curfew? Mother, what if something had happened?"

"It wasn't exactly that simple." I explain the protections put in place —the wards that prevented travel, the guards roaming the streets.

He huffs a breath. "Well, probably smart of you not to test it. Last thing we need is you getting hauled into a prison cell. Been there, done that, as the kids say. Anyways." He gestures us inside. "Come on, then."

We step inside, and I'm fully prepared for everyone to be waiting for us, but the living room is empty. "Where's everyone else?"

"Holly and Luca are out looking for you. Cally is asleep," Ivan answers. He takes a seat on the sofa and stares up at us expectantly. "Well? What happened with Ursidae?"

I sigh as I settle into the armchair across from him. "Shouldn't we wait for the others?" I ask, pointedly, looking around the empty room.

"They won't be back for hours. Just tell me."

"Torben refused," Asmo says gruffly as he plops onto the couch beside Ivan.

"Well, not technically," I object, giving Asmo a side-eye. "He promised to help us if we can get Panthera and Canis to promise their support."

Ivan leans forward and steeples his hands together. "Tell me everything."

I recount the entire visit, Asmo grunting in disapproval when we get to Artis's ultimatum.

"What do we do, Ivan?" I ask. It comes out desperate. Defeated. We thought Torben would be what we needed to get back to the throne. But with his conditions, it feels like we were in a carriage—albeit, a very shoddily assembled carriage—and one of the front wheels just went flying off.

"You're sure Canis will help?" Ivan asks.

I nod eagerly, despite the creeping doubt I have. My answer is based solely on August's promise. Ivan runs his hand along his jaw, thumb rubbing the short stubble that's begun to grow. "I don't see another option," I say. "We'll have to visit Panthera next and hope they'll agree to help."

Panthera, who's more aligned with House Serpent than any other court. The thought does not sit well with me. But we don't have another option. We need their help if we want Ursidae's. If we have any chance of winning this war.

Ivan and Asmo begin to discuss the logistics of our trip to Panthera, and I find myself drifting off. The surge of emotions from our visit has left me drained. My hope flared when Torben said they'd help, then was doused by the morning. Then, Asmo's speech and everything that followed...

My heart feels wrung out.

I try to slip away, but I feel Asmo's eyes on me as I leave. Just like the first day we met, when I felt him watching me as I left the terrace.

Cally's bedroom door is cracked open, and a soft light from within pulls me closer. I nearly drop to the floor when I peer inside.

She's awake, propped up on the bed against a stack of pillows. The sickly pallor is gone, replaced by healthy, rosy cheeks. Her hair is no longer matted, damp curls now resting on her shoulders. Her cheekbones are still too sharp, her frame entirely too small.

But she is alive. And awake.

I push the door open. She grins when she sees me, and my knees nearly buckle with relief. I was so scared I'd never see her smile again.

"Hey," I whisper, terrified that speaking any louder will somehow shatter her.

Her smile turns soft and her eyes turn glassy. "Hey." The first word I've heard her speak in over a month. I swallow the thick lump that's formed in my throat. Tears well, and I force myself to breathe, to hold myself together.

"Ivan said you were still asleep. I didn't realize...I didn't mean to..." I thought he meant she was still *asleep*, still on the edge of the death, not just taking a nap. That salve... I inhale a shaky breath. What would have happened if we didn't have Ivan? What if he had never heard of that salve? What if Asmo and I couldn't find it?

Cally scoots closer to the wall, freeing a space on the bed. She pats it in silent command.

"How are you feeling?" I ask as I perch on the edge of the bed.

"Better." She pulls her shirt up, revealing a pink—but healing—wound the size of my thumb. Gone are the red veins spreading from it like sprawling fingers. Gone is the smell of death.

"How did it happen?" I ask.

She lowers her shirt and pulls the blanket up to her chest. "I don't know. It was chaos. Everybody was trying to get out, and I was trying to get to you, and there were these freaky monsters in the crowd, grabbing people and ripping into them. I think I caught a knife, maybe? Then they dragged us all to the dungeons, and it just kept getting worse." She stares at her hands, now wringing in her lap. "What happened that night? I remember you walking down the aisle, Marik laughing...and then it all went to shit." Her voice is a whisper, as if she's scared to learn the truth.

I tell her everything—what Marik did, Cora pretending to be Willa, nearly dying from her lightning. Then I tell her about the witches and the Cursed, Elle pretending to be me. She stares at me in mute horror the whole time.

"This is..." she trails off, raking a hand through her damp curls.

"Fucked?" I offer.

"Yeah. That's a good word for it." She reaches behind her and winces as she tries to readjust the pillows.

"Here. Let me do it." I grab another pillow from the end of the bed and place it behind her. "Better?"

She settles back against the stack and nods. "Thanks."

I sit back at the foot of the bed and gesture toward her stomach. "Does it still hurt?"

She frowns. "Yeah, but it's better than it was. Thank you for getting that salve, by the way. Ivan told me what happened when you went. You shouldn't have gone. It was way too risky."

I wave my hand in dismissal. She shouldn't be thanking me. She should be cursing me out, screaming at me for allowing her to be thrown into a dungeon, for almost getting her killed. "It was my fault you were down there anyway," I grumble.

She scoffs. "It was your fault you were tricked by a thousand-year-old witch and her boy toy? Please, Mae." She nudges me with her foot. "Hey, I mean it. Thank you. You saved me."

But I didn't, did I? I'm the reason she was sent to the dungeons, and Asmo was the one who got her out. I know a part of me will always blame myself for her being there in the first place. My shoulders slump as regret returns.

"Where were you? Last night?" she asks. A subject change, for which I am immeasurably grateful for, even if the question isn't exactly what I want to talk about.

Getting the hope beat out of me with a bat named Torben. Then Asmo and I...

My cheeks warm, and I stare down at my hands. "We left Ursidae and got stuck in Canis for the night because of some town-wide curfew." If Cally notices my blush, she doesn't say anything.

I fill her in on the visit to the other two courts, leaving out the part about my night with Asmo. It doesn't feel right to share. Not yet at least. Not until I know what Asmo and I are doing.

"Well. Shit," Cally says after I tell her about Torben She stares past me, gaze fixed on the empty wall. "What the hell do we do now?"

I want to tell her I hate that question, that I hate being in charge, that I never wanted this, that I'm fully incapable of figuring this fucking mess out.

"I don't know," I admit. It's the only answer I have.

She nods, and it somehow feels like the perfect response. There is nothing else to say, but a grim, silent acceptance of the facts.

H olly and Luca return just as the snow begins to fall. "No sign of them," Luca huffs, slamming the door behind him with enough force to rattle the kitchen walls.

I'm in the kitchen eating with Asmo and Cally. She flinches at the sound, tea spilling over the rim of her mug. Asmo sets his bowl down and pokes his head into the living room. "Looking for me?" he asks, devilish smile on his face.

"Where is she?" Luca responds, voice low and threatening.

What is it with these males?

"I'm here and I'm unharmed," I call from the kitchen. "We got caught up, but we're fine."

Holly comes around the corner, a smile forming as she sees me. Luca gives me a quick once-over, then nods curtly and turns back toward the living room. We all settle into our usual seats in the living room while Cally remains in the kitchen.

Asmo lights a fire in the small hearth. The crackling of the kindle does something to my soul, calming it in a way that I didn't know I needed.

Ivan catches Holly and Luca up on our failure of a visit to House Ursidae. "We'll be visiting Panthera in a few days to speak with Prince Koa," he says.

Luca grimaces. "We have a problem."

Dread twists in my gut. "What?" I ask.

"I'm not so sure that Panthera will be willing to help us," he says as he shifts in his chair. "They've begun publicly executing witch dissenters."

My blood runs cold, and the fire stutters in the hearth. "Witch dissenters?" I ask. "As in, people who disagree with the witches?"

Luca's answering nod is grim. A shudder works its way through me, the slow crawl of horror. I close my eyes, as if that will do anything to stop it.

"No," I say. "They wouldn't do that. They *can't* do that. Koa would never agree to it."

Ivan's face is as white as the snow falling outside. Holly stands against the wall, silently bobbing her head. Asmo's thigh is rigid against mine. Cally stares at us all in mute horror, frozen in the kitchen, still clutching her mug.

"Koa may not be doing this, but his parents are nearly as ruthless as mine," Asmo mutters. "Fuck. There's no way they'll agree to help us if they're already in bed with Marik."

I shake my head. "Forget that for now. When did this start? Why is nobody stopping this?" My voice is a weird mix of desperation and disgust.

"We visited Beckinsdale this morning, hoping to glean some information about your whereabouts," Luca says with a pointed glare. "Instead, we found a female cougar hybrid hanging in the town square. She was the second execution in two days, according to a local shopkeeper. The next one will be tomorrow at sunrise."

Bile surges upward, and I can't take it anymore. I can't hear about bodies hanging, about innocent hybrids being slaughtered, about prisoners left emaciated and children being thrown into dungeons. The door bangs shut behind me. I storm into the forest, thick snowflakes falling like ashes all around me. The soft thud of footsteps follows close behind. I don't have to turn to know it's Asmo. I have always known when he's near.

I face him. White snowflakes rest on his raven hair, his rosy cheeks. His hands are shoved into his pockets and his shoulders are hunched.

And I can't stand it. I can't fucking stand it.

I close my eyes, ball my hands into fists, and scream. Birds take flight, their answering calls shrill as they cut through the night. Do they scream, too, for what we have become?

I scream until my face is red and I'm hunched over and gasping for air and all I can think about is the roaring in my head.

Asmo pulls me into his arms. The ball of panic inside my chest begins to calm. The roaring quiets.

"What the fuck am I supposed to do?" I whisper into his chest.

"Why do you think you're alone in figuring this out?" His voice is low.

I pull back, but he's staring at the line of trees, his gaze distant, glassy.

"Because it's my job. It's what I was born to do. You can walk away, any time. You can leave whenever you want and all of this will still be on me."

His jaw clenches. "Do you really think so low of me? Besides, I don't think I could walk away if I tried."

I shove against him, but he grips me tighter. "You did though. Remember? You walked away from me." I don't know why I say it, but I'm pissed and hurt and terrified that he'll do it again. Some part of me feels a little guilty for bringing it up, but only a very small part.

"Stop," he says, now looking down at me. "Don't turn this into an argument about us." He turns away from me, and the cold wraps around me once more. I fight the urge to reach for him again. "So Marik and Cora are ramping up their plans. Stop wallowing and do something about it."

I cross my arms over my chest and glare at him, gnashing my teeth together as I bite back a litany of responses. He's right, but I don't know what *to* do. "I feel helpless," I admit. "I can't do anything to save anyone. Even if I wanted to go help the Panthera hybrids, I have no idea how to make a portal. I have no idea if I can even funnel. What the fuck am I supposed to do?”

“You say you feel helpless, so start by taking some control back.”

I grit my teeth. “*How?*”

“Shift.”

“I don’t know how to, Asmo.”

He draws in a deep breath, then releases it, as if *I’m* the one testing *his* patience. “Everyone’s method of shifting is different. You have to find what yours is on your own.”

“Well, what’s yours?”

He shrugs, his hands stuffed in his pockets. “I just do it. It’s become ingrained in me. But when I was first learning, I’d picture myself as a snake, slithering in the sun.”

“There’s the other thing. You’re a snake.”

He gives me a blank look. “So?”

“You have fangs. That’s dangerous.” I gesture to my antlers. “What the hell kind of threat does a deer pose?”

He pulls a hand from his pocket. “Speed, stealth, heightened senses, weapons built on top of your head.” He extends a finger for each advantage.

“I guess,” I grumble.

“There you go again. Enough.”

I ignore him. “How do I funnel?”

“If you can shift, then funneling should come naturally to you. Envision yourself in another location, then imagine the wind rushing around you and the scene fading as you step into your destination. You have to believe it will work. Otherwise, it won’t.”

“Where am I supposed to go?” I ask, uncrossing my arms and looking around the desolate forest.

“Somewhere you can see.”

I quirk an eyebrow. “Then how am I ever supposed to funnel to new places?”

“That comes with practice. Just focus on this for now.” His voice is calm, despite my blatant and misdirected attitude. He places a warm hand on my shoulder and turns me, pointing toward a large, snow-covered rock. "Imagine funneling there. You can see it. Picture the wind swirling around you as you step toward it."

I stare so hard at the rock that it feels like I might burn a hole through it. I inhale, then exhale and concentrate on doing what Asmo said. I focus my mind, imagining every other time I've funneled, the wind spinning around me like a vortex. I move forward, but I'm only one step closer to the rock.

"Try again," Asmo whispers.

This time, I settle into my magic, focusing on my connection to the earth. Instead of thinking of wind, I reach for it, pulling it toward me and coaxing it around me. I don't have to imagine the wind whipping around me—I can feel it. I stare at the rock, envisioning the wind whisking me away in its gentle embrace. Suddenly, the rock is within reach. A grin steals across my face and I turn to Asmo. He stares at me through the trees with a smirk.

"Now come back!" he yells.

I close my eyes and think about the wind transporting me into Asmo's arms. It whips around me, then dies. Warmth radiates from Asmo as he stands before me. I grin up at him.

"You caught onto that so quickly." He beams. "Do it again."

Normally, I would protest at the idea of being ordered around. But I funnel again, this time directly onto the rock, staring at Asmo with triumph. "Come ba—"

I funnel directly in front of him, the wind stirring strands of his hair.

He was right. I already feel like I have more control. I could go anywhere. My breath hitches as I think about where I can go now, and what I can do.

"What?" Asmo looks at me, one eyebrow raised.

"Nothing." My net tugs with the lie.

CHAPTER 22
MARIK

THE URGE TO hurl the crown from my head is overwhelming. Mother and Father sit on my left, beside King Katze and Queen Issa. Both Mother and Father survey the others with cool disinterest, a gleam in their eyes. They are proud to be here, Cora sitting on one end of the grand table in the castle's great hall, me on the other. On my right, Kings Torben and Conall sit next to their queens—Artis and Sasha, respectively. All four of them sit with postures stiff as boards and gazes cold as ice.

"We've already agreed to house your witches," Queen Sasha says tiredly. "We've had to implement a mandatory curfew because their creatures attack our citizens at night. Those who break the curfew are collected by guards and placed in our dungeons until first light. Our citizens are beginning to turn against us. And you expect us to allow *more* witches in *and* vote on them as a High House? Even though they're responsible for the deaths of woodland animals and injuries against our citizens? Have you lost your minds?"

The High Council meeting has only been in session for five minutes, and already the air is thick with tension. Cora hasn't said a single word, but that hasn't stopped Houses Ursidae and Canis from shooting death glares at her. I told her that Mae's crown and the black aura wouldn't help, but she insisted.

"I don't think you're understanding what I'm saying," I say coolly. "Should you vote no today on the matter of the witches becoming a High House, there will be consequences."

"Where is Mae?" Conall asks. Do I detect a challenge in his frosty blue eyes?

I grit my teeth. I knew this would be a problem. Given Elle's most recent attempt on my life, I didn't think it particularly wise to bring her to this meeting. Granted, I could have forced the issue. But, call me selfish, I don't particularly like it when she gets all silent on me. It reminds me too much of someone I used to know—a version of myself that I broke free of long ago.

"She is indisposed," I answer. "Cora is her trusted advisor and is attending in her place."

Conall snorts. "You really expect us to believe that? What have you done to her? There's no way she's behind this. Behind her." He waves his hand at Cora dismissively.

Wrong choice.

Cora doesn't move, but her end of the table begins to rot, black mold and mildew spreading across its expanse. It stops at Sasha, then forms into a tiny hill of mold before growing an arm and reaching for her.

The chair shrieks against the floor as Sasha shoves away from the table and stands. "You intend to threaten us? Is that why you invited us here under the guise of a High Council meeting?" she spits at Cora.

Cora's voice is low, almost a growl. "No. I intend to threaten your children. You will vote the witches in as a High House. Or your children will succumb to the blade. Do you understand?"

I grip the edges of my armrests at the threat. Conall stands, joining his wife. They link hands, ice forming at their feet.

"No, no," Cora's voice has turned pleasant, as if she just told them their children will be on the receiving end of an inheritance, not the wrong end of a sword. "There will be none of that. My witches and my creatures are on standby, black magic ready. Each of your offspring are in their sight. And if you so much as threaten me one more time, you will lose them one by one."

"Liar," Sasha growls.

Cora unfurls her wrist, and a hand mirror flies toward her. She strokes the edges, then flips it toward Sasha and Conall. An image of Princess Lola is reflected in the glass. She walks through stone hallways, her pink dress trailing behind her, long blonde hair unbound and cascading down her back in soft waves.

Sasha's face pales. "H-how?"

Cora sets the mirror on the table. "Magic," she says with a grin. *Magic, and the witches that we forced the Houses to allow into their homes.* "Now. Sit."

They do. The King and Queen of House Canis sit on the edges of their chairs, but every inch of them is poised to attack.

Cora smiles, and I know she thinks she won. I know she thinks that her threats are working, that everyone is going to listen to her with their children's lives on the line. But I know better. It will only piss them off. And an angry, scared predator is a dangerous enemy to have.

"Where is Mae?" Sasha asks through gritted teeth.

Cora settles back in her chair, fingers draped over the edge of her armrest. "Since we're being honest with each other now," she says, luminescent smile matching the gleam of her eyes, "Mae is dead. I'm High Queen now. Your subjects are not to learn this information, or my threat will ring true."

My mother and father smile at her words, but the rest of the High Families flinch. It takes all my self-control to school my features. I warned Cora not to divulge this information, and yet, here she is. A headache begins to bloom. What the fuck is the point of giving my advice if she's not going to listen to it?

Cora stands and leans over the table, both hands face-down on the rotten wood. "Now. Here's what's going to happen. You're going to vote yes today, and you're going to tell your citizens that the witches are *good* for the kingdom. If you're unable to convince them, then your children will die, and so will your citizens. House Panthera has already executed two of their own, with a new execution scheduled every day for as long as there are dissenters." She smiles at Katze and Issa, who stare back at her with empty gazes.

It was their idea. The least they can do is pretend like they're proud of it.

Artis and Torben are silent, but Conall stares at Panthera in horror. "Is this true?" he asks. Katze nods, staring straight down at the table. "You—"

Cora waves her hand, and the arm of mold grows closer to Sasha, cutting off any retort Conall had.

"They're just doing what needs to be done. And their children will live for it, isn't that right?" Cora asks House Panthera pleasantly.

"Yes, Your Majesty," Issa says with a soft smile.

Cora returns the smile. "That's right. Because I would *so* hate for Princess Cassia to die before she's had the chance to truly live. That would be such a shame, wouldn't it?"

Issa's smile fades. "Yes, Your Majesty," she repeats in a drawl. Katze stares ahead, unwilling to look at Cora or his wife.

The last time I saw House Panthera, Issa was all for the executions, Katze nearly panting for them. I wonder what changed. Maybe it's no longer fun to play games with the devil when what you love hangs in the balance.

Cora turns her gaze to Mother and Father next. "Just look at the Serpent Princes. Asmo chose Mae, and he died for it." The words are full of conviction, but there's no evidence to suggest he's dead. If I know my brother, he found a way out. He always did when we were young. "But no matter, because Marik chose the right side," Cora continues, beaming at my parents. As if they did the world a favor by raising me.

They return the smile, but it looks like a puppet is pulling the corners of their mouths up, one yank at a time. Asmo will always be their proudest accomplishment. And now he's gone, leaving them with second-best—me.

Cora brings her hands together in a loud clap, and Sasha jumps in her seat. "Now, does anyone object to the forming of the witches as a High House?" She looks around the table.

Every single king and queen of the High Houses stares at the table in silence.

"Wonderful!" Cora exclaims cheerfully. "It's official, then. The witches will be recognized as a High House. I'll throw a ball to celebrate. And remember the warnings you were given today, won't you?"

Murmurs of confirmation ring around the table.

Cowards.

But then again, I don't have anything I care about enough to lose. Not even myself.

To my immense surprise, Elle doesn't attack me when I step inside her wing. To my even greater surprise, she's already dressed and ready for our dinner. I thought I was going to have to bring her meal to her wing.

She sits on the couch, her red hair hanging limp at her shoulders. At least it looks like it was brushed. The black necklace is clunky around her slender neck. She wears a shapeless navy-blue shift that cuts off halfway down her thighs. It looks like...

"Is that a pillowcase?"

She lifts her chin. "I refuse to wear any more of Mae's clothes. It was this or nothing."

I shrug. I don't particularly care what she wears, if I'm being honest. She stands, and I can't help but gaze at her defined legs as they work to push her to standing.

I offer her my hand, but she declines, pushing past me and throwing the front door open. She doesn't stop to put on shoes or anything else, just walks out barefoot in the pillowcase. I follow her, trying not to watch her in wonder. She places one foot on the steps, then turns to look back at me.

"Where are we going?"

I shove down whatever the hell this feeling is and walk around her, resisting the urge to brush my hand against her as I pass. The feeling almost vanishes with her out of my sight, but the desire to turn back and look at her is too strong for my liking.

We walk in silence, guards eyeing Elle as we pass, their gazes catching on her legs. I hover a hand over the small of her back on instinct until we're in the formal dining room.

The table is set for two, a floral arrangement of black roses and white peonies sitting in the center. The floral scent is cloying, and I resist the urge to order a servant to remove them. Ebony plates sit on opposite ends of the table, centered atop ivory placemats with gold branches embroidered along the edges.

Elle sits, and I take the opposite seat, watching her carefully as she eyes the cutlery in front of her. She doesn't pick up the knife and hurl it in my direction. Someone's full of surprises tonight.

I clear my throat. "Thank you for joining me tonight," I say. And I mean it.

She scoffs. "Like I had a choice."

I summon the waitstaff with a wave of my hand. A male deer hybrid in an all-black uniform steps forward, pouring chilled water into two glasses.

"You did have a choice, you know," I say. "I wasn't going to force you to come."

She doesn't respond. Instead, she peers up at the male hybrid. "Thank you," she says to him. It sounds like a plea, not a sentiment of gratitude.

He doesn't look at her, doesn't answer at all. "They've all been instructed not to respond," I explain, and her face falls as the hybrid disappears.

I take a sip of water as I try to think about what to say. I'm not sure what I was expecting tonight. Although we've had dinner before, this feels different for some reason. I still don't know why I invited her to dinner, or how I fooled myself into thinking it would go well. The silence blossoms between us, and I try not to look at her, but it's like my eyes act before my brain can.

I fidget with the cloth napkin in my lap. "Everyone on the castle grounds is aware of who you really are. I don't think there's any need for you to be locked in your wing anymore. You're free to leave it if you would like, but a guard will need to escort you."

I smile, expecting her to be happy at this news. But she doesn't return it. The doors to the kitchen open and the male waiter enters again, two steaming bowls in his hands. He sets them down in front of us, then exits silently. I pick up my spoon and stir the liquid inside. Soup, some kind of creamy chowder. I set the spoon back down, uninterested in the first course.

Elle doesn't touch hers either.

"I think it's a chowder," I offer. She doesn't acknowledge it. I clear my throat and pull at the tie around my neck that suddenly feels too tight. "Elle, there's something you should know." Again, no acknowledgement. I continue, "The witches are to become an official High House. The High Council voted on it this morning. There will be an announcement and a ball to commemorate their new status."

Her jaw tenses. I peek down the bond the necklace gifts me. The simmering heat of her hatred is all I can feel.

Logically, I know that my actions have been despicable. I know that I have manipulated not one, but two innocent females to steal their crowns. I know that what I've done has resulted in the deaths of many. However, feeling empathy, compassion, or sympathy has never been easy for me.

Asmo was always better at that. He used to lecture me about morals and integrity and blah, blah, blah. It was easier to shut that part off and do whatever was necessary to get the results I wanted. That's all that matters. Results. Winning.

But now, as I peer into Elle's mind, I can feel the way all of this has impacted her. And it makes me want to...apologize. Me on my knees in front of her, begging for her—I blink the image away.

"Why?" Elle's voice croaks from the other end of the table. She stares up at me, hands still in her lap, soup growing cold.

"It's complicated," I answer as I stir the soup in my bowl.

"No," she says, eyes like honey boring into eyes like ash. "Why am I allowed to walk freely now? Why all of a sudden?"

"Cora told the High Houses that Mae is dead." I take another spoonful of soup. But it's hard to swallow as Elle's horror floods my mind. I set the spoon down with as much grace as I can muster and look back up at her. Her face is devoid of any color, her freckles seeming to pop even more against her ghost-white cheeks.

"But she's not…Is she?"

I shrug. "I have no earthly idea." The cold flood of horror is now replaced by that raging heat again. I tilt my head. "Why are you angry?"

She stills. "What do you mean?"

I ignore the question. "What if I told you Mae *was* dead?" The slow crawl of confusion spreads down the bond. "That I found her body washed up along the river that cuts through this very mountain?" I smile as the cold returns, horror joining once more, a familiar friend. "What if I told you that Cora hanged her body on the flag posts in the turrets?"

Her face blanches, and yes—there it is, the full force of her horror, the darkness of oblivion.

I used to loathe the feeling, but I now relish it. I am horror's master.

And what if I told you I was lying? I whisper into her mind, delighting at the flash of anger, at the pink that returns to her cheeks. A flicker of uncertainty dampens my delight, but only for a moment. Pissing her off is the only way to keep her from slipping back into her shell.

She shoves away from the table and rises. "You're a monster," she spits at me.

I lean back in my chair as she storms away from me. She's right.

I am a monster, for I was forged in the oblivion where horror resides.

CHAPTER 23
MAE

SOMEONE HAS LOCKED me inside my room. The handle only twists by a fraction, then stops. I consider beating on the door for someone to let me out but think better of it. That would defeat the entire purpose of trying to sneak out.

The window also refuses to budge.

I don't have time for this.

I throw up a sound barrier, then summon wind as cold as ice and pour it into the lock. I use the hilt of my dagger to smash the ice into bits. And just like that, the door swings open.

I manage to slip from the cabin undetected. Not even Holly stirs on the couch as I tip-toe through the living room and click the door shut behind me. I spent all night arguing with everyone about rescuing the next execution victim. Luca and Ivan were firmly against the idea, while everyone else remained silent.

"You'll get yourself killed," Luca said tersely.

But what the hell is the point of living if I sit back while innocent people die? I stopped arguing and went to bed without another word, then spent the entire night planning how to sneak off in the morning.

I make it to the edge of the forest and turn back to the safehouse.

Nobody follows. I turn, preparing to somehow funnel myself to a court I've never visited, when a voice cuts through the silent forest.

"Where do you think you're going?"

I whirl. Asmo leans against a pine tree, one foot propped against the thick trunk behind him, his all-black outfit blending in with the dark. Dawn is still far off.

"Fuck!" I gasp. My hand flies to my chest, heart hammering against its cage.

"Well?" He raises an eyebrow.

"Nowhere," I say.

He scoffs at the answer. "At least come up with something creative."

"Fine. I'm going on a hike."

He shoves away from the trunk and stalks toward me. "Mae."

I cross my arms and plant my foot in the thin layer of snow. "Asmo."

He reaches for me, placing a warm hand on my forearm. "If you're going on a rescue mission, at least let me tag along."

"Me, too," a voice calls from behind me. Asmo's hand tightens briefly around my arm, then relaxes when he looks over my shoulder.

I turn. Holly's honey blonde hair catches moon beams as she walks between the trees. Like Asmo, she's dressed in all black.

A grin spreads across my face.

"Where are we going? The truth this time," she says, arching a thin eyebrow.

"Panthera. To rescue the citizens that are going to be executed," I say firmly. There is no room for negotiation on this. I will not watch more people die for this war if I can do something about it. All I've done is sit and watch people get hurt. Asmo's words echoed through my head all night. *Do something about it.* I'm done feeling powerless. I have power and I can—and will—use it to help.

"Alright then," Holly says. She forms a portal and we all step through at once, landing in a deserted building. A hole in the dilapidated roof reveals a sliver of the moon.

"Where are we?" I ask, nose scrunching at the smell of dirt and rotting wood.

"An old barn on the outskirts of Beckinsdale," Holly says, shutting the portal behind her. "I used to come here to hook up with a Panthera hybrid a couple years ago."

Asmo grabs a knife from his boot and pulls his shirt up, cutting his sigil into his perfectly chiseled stomach. He transforms in front of me, then hands the knife to Holly. "Do you remember your person?"

"We used them yesterday," she says in confirmation as she carves the mark. She hands the knife to me, and I cut mine into my stomach. "What's the plan?" she asks, staring at me expectantly.

"I don't know," I admit with a laugh, because it's absurd to have a rescue plan without a plan at all. Holly's face falls and I hurriedly add, "I was thinking we'd try to find the prisoner before they can even be brought to the town square." I resist the urge to wring my hands together. "But if I'm being honest, I have no clue where to even start looking for them."

"Mother's sake princess," Asmo mutters, running a hand through his hair. "Well, they must be keeping them in the dungeons."

"Great," I say cheerily, ignoring the first part of his response. "Let's go, then."

Asmo stares at me, eyebrows raised. "You can't just waltz into the dungeons."

"I'm not going to. You are."

He scoffs. "What makes you think I can do that?"

I motion toward him. "You're...you. You've been here before. You know where they are, don't you?"

"Well, yes..." he says cautiously, lips pressing together in a frown. "But that doesn't mean we can just walk in there. Don't forget that Panthera is now a friend to the High Court. They're going to be guarding the dungeons. And if we get caught..."

I wave him away. "I know, I know. I just need to get eyes on the prisoner and see how tight their security is."

Asmo lets loose a sigh that borders on insulting. "Mother help us."

Something soars through the night air, inches from my face. I jump back with a squeal, heart racing and magic flaring as I look around the room.

Holly's laughter fills the dilapidated barn. "It's just an owl," she says between laughs. She points up in the corner and sure enough, a tawny owl is perched on a wooden beam, yellow eyes watching us.

Just as I feel my heart rate returning to normal, the owl soars from its perch and shifts mid-air. Into a human male. The last time I saw someone shift, they ended up naked, but this male wears a pair of trousers covered in dirt and patched holes. His linen shift was once white, but is now a worn gray with fraying cuffs.

Asmo throws up a protective barrier around me as Holly fists a dagger in one hand and moves to stand in front of me. The male shifter holds his hands up.

"I come in peace." His voice is calm and steady. He speaks the truth. "I'm here to help."

"Who the fuck are you?" Asmo asks, voice low and thrumming with power.

"My name is Basil." Truth.

"And what do you want, Basil?" Asmo asks, all but spitting his name at him.

He takes a step forward, posture relaxed and hands loose at his sides. "First of all, you guys were being loud as all sin in here. We could hear you. Ever heard of a sound barrier?" Basil asks nonchalantly, as if completely apathetic to the fact that Asmo could obliterate him with a flick of his hand.

But then again, I'm forgetting that Asmo doesn't look like Asmo.

"So, it's true, then," Basil says. "You're alive." He stares at me now with those wide, yellow eyes.

I shake my head. "What?"

He snorts. "Come on. You're the High Queen." He cuts his gaze to Asmo. "And you're Prince Asmo." He looks back at me. "We knew you'd come. We've been waiting."

Again, his words ring true. They jar me, and my skin tingles— either from nerves or magic ready to defend me and my friends, I don't know. Maybe both. I don't move an inch.

"Oh, come on," he repeats. "I see the way you both guard her. It's your instinct to protect her. Plus, I can see your auras." He gestures toward Asmo and says, "Yours is black, like the High King," then to me and says, "Yours is white, like King Silas's. Well, mostly white, just like yours, is mostly black." He gestures back to Asmo. He glances at Holly and says, "No clue who you are, though, if I'm being frank."

Auras? What is he talking about? The only person with an aura is Cora, and hers is black. Asmo doesn't have an aura, and I certainly don't.

"It's my gift. Auras aren't visible to everyone, but I can see them," he offers in explanation. "I don't know why or how, but I can."

Truth.

Asmo reaches for me. "Let's go."

"Wait," Basil says.

"What do you want?" Holly asks.

"I already told you. I'm here to help. We've been waiting for you to come."

Holly doesn't ask what the hell he means by *we*, but instead asks, "Help with what?"

"Rescuing Rain."

"Who is Rain? And who is *we*?" I ask.

He huffs impatiently. "We don't have time for this. First light grows closer the longer we stand here."

I don't need to look outside to know he's right. The darkness within the barn is slowly but steadily waning. But I'm not willing to risk everything without hearing more from him. I narrow my eyes at him in silent demand.

He catches the movement and says, "Rain is the next hybrid to be executed by the Crown."

"Who is *we*?" I repeat the question, more forcefully this time.

His foot taps against the dirt floor and he frowns, cutting another glance to the barn exit. "Rain is a lynx hybrid who has connections with the Lower Houses. There are several of us—yours truly included—who have been fighting the Cursed the witches have been setting loose in our forests," he says, his words hurried. "We've been trying our damndest to fight back against them in the only way we can. But we need you to save Rain, Your Highness. We can't do this without you."

This is only bringing more questions to mind, but Basil is right about the impending first light.

He continues, "This isn't how we anticipated asking for your help, but we already have a plan to rescue her. We just can't do it alone. We need someone more powerful."

I look at Asmo, but he's watching Basil with a dubious expression on his face. So far, Basil has only told me the truth. I steel myself, then say, "Fine." Holly whips her head toward me, but I hold a hand up. "He's telling the truth."

Asmo's eyes are wild as he stares at me. "Are you crazy? Marik was telling the truth and look where that got us."

Ouch. "Fuck you."

His face softens. "Mae, I didn't mean...I just meant it as a reminder that there are ways around the truth."

Basil makes the sound of a clock ticking. Every second we stand here is another that we could be helping. Someone's life hangs in the balance. This is the closest I've felt to helping, to actually doing something for my kingdom.

Asmo stares at me for another silent moment, then dips his head. "Okay, if you trust him...Let's go." He turns to Basil and stalks toward him. "If you even think about hurting her, I'll rip out those talons and use them to gouge—"

"Asmo!" I hiss.

Basil bows his head. "Yes, Your Highness." He takes his right hand and places it over his heart. "I swear to the Mother that I'm here to help. My sole purpose right now is to rescue Rain, then to work with the High Queen to rescue the kingdom in any way I can."

Truths, all of them. Whatever they mean.

"Let's go," I say. "Lead the way, Basil."

He shoots one last worried glance at Asmo, then walks out the barn and into the darkness. Tall grass surrounds us as we follow Basil down a well-trodden trail. He stops in front of a thick tree, a gaping hole at the bottom of its trunk. He crouches and gestures for us to follow him. I stop, not dumb enough to follow a random owl shifter into a hollowed-out tree trunk.

He looks back at us, yellow eyes quickly darting between all of us. "Are you okay if I bring out my first-in-command?"

"What?" I ask. "Are you not the leader of your group?" I assumed as much, since he was the one who came out to speak with us.

He straightens a bit and says, "No, Your Highness. I do not lead the resistance."

Truth. My blood chills at his choice of words. Resistance? What the fuck is he even talking about?

"Um, sure," I say, and he disappears into the tree trunk.

"I don't like this, princess," Asmo whispers. He shifts on his feet as he looks around us, hands open and ready to fight, defend, or funnel us away.

Holly steps closer to me. "Me either. This feels weird."

My ears pick up on shuffling, two pairs of footsteps coming toward us from inside the tree. We move back, hands splayed and ready.

Basil returns, a stunning female beside him. Her chestnut hair is pulled back into a braid, but her amber eyes match mine. Her build is tall and rail thin, but she bears the hallmark features of a deer hybrid.

Holly stumbles back.

"Etta," Asmo whispers in disbelief.

PART TWO

CHAPTER 24

MAE

My dead sister stands before me.

She is a different version of me—one with darker features, but the same honey eyes. Her cheeks are rosy pink, but without freckles. Her chocolate-brown hair hangs over her shoulders, the same lackluster waves as my white hair. She bears no antlers. And no crown.

"I—" I start, then close my mouth as I fumble for what to say. My thoughts swirl, each one vanishing the moment I reach for it. Everything I ever thought I'd say to her is gone.

"Blimey, Ett, I didn't think bringing you would cause this much of a reaction. We don't exactly have time for this," Basil says.

"She's a dead High Princess," Asmo says in disbelief. "What did you think would happen?"

I still. She's a dead High Princess...with the right to the High Throne. What if she wants it back? What if all of this is for nothing? What if I'm scraping and clawing for a throne that isn't even mine? Am I about to risk my life for something that doesn't even belong to me?

"We have to go," Basil urges.

He's right. Someone—Rain—will die if we don't get moving.

I swore an oath—that wasn't mine to swear, apparently—to protect the people of the Woodland Kingdom. And that is what I am here to do.

I wrench my gaze from Etta. "What's the plan?" I ask Basil.

"We've had several of our shifters scouting the dungeons. They've reported there are only a few guards watching Rain."

"Why do you need us, then?" Asmo asks.

Basil grimaces. "The guards are witches."

Asmo nods. "Yeah, that's a pretty important piece of information." Sarcasm drips from his tone.

Basil claps his hands together with a nervous smile. "Right, well. The plan is for our familiars to cause a distraction in the dungeons. When the guards—"

"The witches," Asmo corrects.

Basil's smile falls, and he shoots a glare at Asmo. I can't help but think if Asmo weren't in his disguise, he would be rethinking that glare. "When the witches are distracted, we make our move. Which is where you two come in," he says, beaming expectantly at Asmo and me.

"How so?" I ask.

"We were hoping you could take care of the witches. We also...well, the cell door is stone and we don't really have a solution for breaking into it. We were hoping you might be powerful enough to do it." He gestures to Asmo and me, his hands hanging in the air.

"So, you expected her to do everything?" Asmo asks.

I can't help but snort. "I'm sorry to have failed your expectations, Basil, but I have no idea what I'm doing. I can try, but I don't know how to break a *stone door*." I look at Asmo. "What about you? Can't you do that sword thingy that you did to kill that cambion in the woods?"

Asmo turns to me slowly. "It's called a shadow sword. But yes, that should work. I can always shoot a ball of fire at the walls."

"No, you will not," Etta says. Her voice is melodic. "We want to minimize the damage and the casualties. Our objective is to rescue Rain, not destroy the place. If your shadow sword will be effective, that is what will be done."

Asmo cocks his head at her, then purses his lip. He opens his mouth, then appears to think better of it, and closes it. I look at the ground to hide my smile.

"When the cell is breached, you will grab her and run. Do you understand?" Etta's eyes are cool as she directs her question toward Asmo.

He clasps his hands behind his back and nods once.

"Wait," I say. "How are we even going to get into the dungeons? Surely there will be more than three gu—witches—that we'll need to get past."

Basil's yellow eyes light up. "Our cave has a direct tunnel to the dungeons. It's how we're able to get our familiars and shifters in so easily." He begins to turn back to the tree trunk, then looks at Holly. "Do you want to stay here? You still look a little pale."

Holly shakes her head. "I'm fine."

"Holly's always that pale," Asmo mutters.

Etta jumps when she hears Holly's name.

"Right then," Basil says before turning on his heels. "Follow me."

He crouches down and enters the tree trunk, disappearing from view, just like stepping through a portal. When I follow, I realize the hollowed-out tree trunk is an entrance shrouded in shadows. It opens to a cave with sloped ceilings, reminding me of the hallways in the Bear Court. Wide tunnels cut through walls of packed dirt and clay, branching in all directions and winding through the underground.

"What is this place?" I ask as we pass an archway leading down a dimly lit tunnel.

"You're inside the underground city of Squall's End, the central location for the Lower Houses. They don't have an official court or town to call their home, so they created one," Etta says from ahead.

The Lower Houses? I look back at Holly. She stares forward, eyes locked on the back of Etta's head. Not helpful.

"It's been in development for the last several decades. And it's remained undetected by the High Houses," Etta says with a pointed glance in my direction. I mimic locking my lips and throwing away the key.

An entire court living underground. The High Court has no clue this place exists. Until now. They just risked ruining everything to save their friend.

Basil leads us further, the ground slowly sloping downward.

"How much longer?" Asmo calls to Basil.

"Just around this bend here," he calls back.

"When we get there," Etta says, "you must be silent. We cannot give up our advantage. Asmo, can you cloak everyone in darkness? That will keep the guards from noticing our entry and exit point."

Her familiarity with Asmo pricks at me, but I chide myself. They knew each other before I knew him. Besides, I have no claim on him. I may feel like I do, but we have yet to establish what's between us. We continue to dance around it, desperate to avoid the actual conversation. Well, maybe it's just me that's desperate to avoid defining whatever this is. Doing so would mean adding another person to my list of people that I care about. The list of people that, if anything happened to them, it would undoubtedly break me. And admitting to myself what I feel for Asmo...well, it would be just another name on a list that's already too long.

Asmo nods. "Just let me know when."

We turn the corner, and the hallway abruptly stops. I look around for any sign of a door, but there isn't one. It's just a dead end.

"Wh—"

Etta glares at me, a finger raised to her thin lips. Asmo shifts slightly in front of me and flares his hands at his side. Basil presses his palm to the cave wall and whispers something under his breath.

My jaw drops. I can't help it. A portal forms on the wall. A fucking portal on the wall. Well, at least, it resembles one...It swirls with the same darkness. But unlike other portals, I can see through the wall— right into a dark alcove filled with brooms, buckets, and mops stained with something that resembles dried blood. Great.

"Now, Asmo," Etta whispers.

Darkness descends over us like a blanket. Asmo's free hand rests on the small of my back and I resist the urge to lean into him, to feel him pressed against me again. Basil goes through the portal and gestures for us to follow.

"Asmo," Etta whispers. He doesn't move. "You need to go first to keep us cloaked as we exit," she urges him.

His hand reluctantly leaves my back, and the darkness follows him as he steps through the portal. I follow behind him, and we walk forward, carefully sidestepping galvanized buckets and stained mops. As we exit the alcove, the only sounds that can be heard are the solitary drips of water coming from the ceiling.

"This way," Basil whispers as he begins to travel through the dank, freezing tunnel, avoiding puddles of slushy, gray ice.

I've only been in this space for minutes and I'm fighting shivering. But this is a different kind of shiver, one that has nothing to do with the temperature. It works its way up my spine as I think about Cally forced to remain in these conditions for weeks. Of the way she laid limply in Asmo's arms.

We pass abandoned cells as we trek upward, their doors hanging open, revealing dark rooms covered in moss and slick algae. I jump as a noise comes from within one of the cells. I clutch my chest, then drop my hand as a rat scuttles from the shadows. My lip curls in disgust, and it disappears down the tunnel, back to the way we came.

The hallway grows lighter as we travel further, but we remain cloaked in the shadows. Skittering feet approach from down the hall, and I brace myself to see another rat, but it's just a chipmunk. It launches itself in the air and lands in the palm of Basil's outstretched hand.

He watches the chipmunk with rapt attention as it taps its feet. Finally, Basil nods and releases the chipmunk. It races forward, toward the light just around the bend. He whispers to us, "There are only two witches guarding Rain's cell. I'll send in the distraction, then we'll strike. Got it?"

No, I don't *got it*. *Only* two witches? There were *only* two witches in Bouldercrest and Asmo and I struggled to escape. And what the hell is the distraction?

Asmo gives a curt nod. I don't ask any of my questions. I just give Basil a shaky smile. What other choice do I have?

"Keep us in the shadows for as long as possible. Let's keep this as quiet as we can," BAsil says.

We wait in silence for what feels like an eternity. Finally, Basil steps forward. We follow, and my heart pounds in my ears. I press my palms to my side to steady the slight shaking as adrenaline spreads.

"—I was telling her that I don't like—" a voice says.

"I know," another voice hisses. "I'm not an idiot."

The two distinctly female voices grow louder as we approach until they sound like they're only feet away. Basil points to a closed stone door with a small square cut into the stone near the top.

This must be the door to Rain's cell.

"Wait, what the—ow!" the first voice hisses.

"Now!" Basil whispers.

"Just kill it!" the second voice yells.

Asmo steps forward and raises his hand toward the door. With one swift motion, he carves a line through the stone door.

"I'm trying," the first voice snaps.

The door cracks.

"Wind," Basil commands.

I summon and pull the cracked stone portions away with a gust of wind, leaving half of the door open. A body lies on the floor curled in a ball, dark hair matted against her head. Her slight frame is swallowed by a dingy gray blanket and I thank the Mother that she at least has that to keep herself warm.

She lifts her head, one hand held against the sudden burst of light.

"Lessen the shadows," Basil orders. Asmo abides, and Basil motions to Rain, urging her to run to us.

Her face pales, and she shakes her head furiously. She casts a terrified glance back to the witches, who are doing Mother knows what, and then back to us with a final shake of her head.

"Damnit," Basil hisses. "More shadows."

Asmo, once again, abides, and then Basil darts forward. He dashes into the cell and scoops Rain up. He turns back to us and steps out of the cell, but one of the witches notices.

"Hey!" she shrieks.

I freeze, watching in horror as she raises her hand.

And then she's bent over, clutching her stomach as blood gushes from a wound. Basil wastes no time, tearing past her and sprinting back down the hallway, back in the direction of the alcove.

"What the fuck just happened?" I ask.

"Sword thingy," Asmo says with a wink. He grabs my arm and pulls me down the hallway.

I look back, waiting for voices and shouts commanding us to stop.

But nothing comes.

Basil opens the portal again, Rain still cradled in his arms. On the other side, Holly is rooted to the same spot, gnawing on her fingernails. The moment we're back in Squall's End, Etta slams the portal shut. I swear I hear a scream of rage as it closes.

My long legs struggle to catch up with Etta and Basil as they race down the hallway. It's been so long since I've run, days spent jogging through Pinebend long gone.

Etta and Rain lead us to a room the size of the throne room at the High Castle. The ceiling soars above us, strung with lanterns lit by white flames. Neat rows of cots are stationed uniformly throughout the space, only a few currently occupied. Along the walls, wooden tables are lined with sanitary solution and healers' tools. Although dirt covers the floor and the walls, the smell of antiseptic clings to the air. A healing center.

Basil sets Rain down on the closest cot, and a male healer rushes over.

"We just got her back from the Panthera dungeons," Etta says to him.

"Alright, then. Exposure, malnutrition, superficial wounds. I'll check her vitals first, but give me a little room," he says. He extends his palm, hovering it just over Rain's forehead.

"I'm fine," Rain croaks.

But she doesn't look it. Her black hair is affixed to the top of her head, still matted in clumps. Gray dirt is crusted along one side of her face, and purple lines her eyes.

The healer removes his palm and looks back at Etta. "Yep, dehydrated and malnourished. Nothing more."

"Thank you, Max. Get her taken care of, please," Etta says warmly.

"Of course," the healer—Max—says before walking toward the wall of supplies.

"I feel fine," Rain grumbles from the cot, but she makes no move to get up.

"You heard Max. You will let him take care of you, and then you will be released," Etta says firmly.

Rain mumbles something, then turns her back on all of us. Etta motions toward the door and we follow her out. Now that the adrenaline of the rescue mission has worn off, my muscles turn weak again as I face Etta. My sister. My *dead* half-sister. We stare at each other in silence for several moments, each of us assessing the other.

"I thought you had antlers," she says with a frown.

I lift my shirt, exposing the mark on my stomach. "Sigil."

She winces, like I just showed her an infected wound. "Dark magic?"

I don't answer. Instead, I grab a dagger from a holster and destroy the mark. Etta's gaze roves up and down again, but she doesn't say anything. I offer the dagger to Asmo, who switches back to his usual appearance instantly.

"Etta, you have a lot of explaining to do," Asmo says.

Her amber eyes narrow and her tone is harsh as she says, "I don't answer to you, Asmo. I never have, and I certainly don't now."

He quirks an eyebrow. "And who, pray tell, *do* you answer to?" He looks to Basil, who stands beside Etta. But he shakes his head when Asmo's gaze falls on him.

Etta's mouth twitches into a smirk. "Nobody. Not anymore."

Asmo huffs a sigh. "Well, now you've exposed yourself to the High Queen."

No, no, no. I hold my hands up quickly. "No, I'm not here in that role. I'm not going to tell anyone, Etta."

She gives me a half-smile. "Unfortunately, sister, you *are* here in that role. We need you in that role. If you have the heart I think you do, I was hoping you'd come rescue the prisoners set for execution. And I was right. We've been on the lookout for you for days now. If I didn't want you here, you wouldn't be here."

"What do you mean?" I ask.

"You lost your throne. I lost mine." She walks toward me, her gaze so intense that I fight the urge to step backward. "Let's destroy it together."

CHAPTER 25
MAE

"Have you lost your mind?" I ask, because that's the only plausible response to Etta's proposition.

Her head jerks back, like my question was a slap to the face. "No. I'm perfectly sane," she says in a completely rational tone.

"You want to...destroy the throne?" Holly asks from behind me, her first words to Etta since she miraculously returned from the grave.

Etta's nod is crisp, and her smile is soft, a stark juxtaposition to the idea of destroying an entire kingdom. My kingdom.

My eyebrows inch upward. "Um...Okay, let's say you do...Then what?"

Her smile widens, now revealing pearly-white teeth. It's genuine, her eyes now crinkled and twinkling. "We remake it."

Asmo crosses his arms and says, "Into...what exactly?" His tone is skeptical.

"Into a better kingdom that recognizes the Lower Houses and improves conditions for the humans," she says simply. "Oh, and one that re-establishes the Fae Kingdom."

I blink. "Sorry, the Fae? They're gone."

Their kingdom has been gone for twenty-five years, and the Fae people haven't been seen for nearly a decade. My mind races as I recall

Holly's lessons on them, but there wasn't much. The kingdom fell and they disappeared. That was the short version, but Holly only had a limited amount of time to teach me everything I needed to know.

"The Fae were never gone," a rich, velvety voice says behind me. I turn, but Asmo's back blocks my view. I crane my neck to look over his shoulder.

The female walking toward us is the embodiment of ethereal. She reeks of power, her build muscular and her stride graceful. Her skin is a rich dark brown, complemented by white, swirling tattoos covering both arms. Her hair and eyebrows are white as snow, but her eyes are blue as a lagoon. They meet mine over Asmo's shoulder. "We've just been in hiding." She stops and bows, deep and low, before rising once more. "A pleasure to meet you, Your Highness. I am Amaris."

I step around Asmo, about to repeat the sentiment, when he asks, "And who are you?"

"You are protective of her. Good. It is in your blood," Amaris says.

"Who are you?" Asmo repeats, but it's less of a question now and more of a growl.

"I am the delegate to the Fae Kingdom. And that," she says, gaze cutting back to me, "is my queen."

She draws a dagger from a hidden compartment of her leather vest. Asmo throws up a barrier, but Amaris bends down on one knee and draws the dagger across her palm, blood sprouting in its wake.

"With my blood, I vow to protect and serve you, granddaughter of Wrena and daughter of Orla." She wipes the dagger on the leather vest and sheaths it. "I mean you no harm."

My net bobs along the surface of the calm river. Nothing snags. "She's telling the truth," I tell Asmo, but he doesn't drop the shield.

"What is this, Etta?" Asmo asks, turning back to my sister.

"I already told you. *This*," she gestures to Amaris and Basil, "is the resistance."

"How are you even alive?" Asmo asks Etta. "And you," he turns back to Amaris, "Who are you and what the fuck is happening right now?"

Amaris rises. "You know as well as I do, Prince Asmo, that a blood oath is enough to prove my loyalty to your ma—"

Asmo snarls at her, and I flinch, nearly bumping into Holly.

"The Fae Kingdom has been gone for decades," he says, "So, forgive me if I'm cautious of you and a princess that's supposed to be six feet under right now."

My stomach tightens at his crass words, and Etta stiffens. I place a hand on his shoulder, and feel the muscle relax. "Az, let's just hear them out," I whisper. "Please."

Basil watches Asmo carefully, as if he thinks he's moments away from exploding. But Asmo's shoulders drop and he dips his head—albeit tersely—in silent acceptance. He shifts to the side, and I move to stand beside him as his equal, not something he needs to protect.

"I will explain everything," Etta says placatingly. "But first, I want to make it clear what our mission is. We want to remake the kingdom."

Wrena's granddaughter will rebirth the kingdom—for better or for worse.

"You said earlier you wanted to destroy it, not remake it," I point out.

Etta looks at Asmo. "Prince, tell me, would House Serpent recognize the Lower Houses as a formal House?"

He doesn't have to think about it. "No."

No surprise there.

Etta's smile brightens. "Exactly. And neither would Panthera. Therefore, the old Houses cannot remain."

Asmo guffaws, and Etta's smile falters infinitesimally. "Well," I say, "I have good news for you. Marik and Cora are about to destroy everything. I guess we can just wait for them to finish it off!" I shoot her a sarcastic smile.

She rolls her eyes. "That's not what I meant. Obviously, we have to stop Marik and the witches. If we don't, then they'll break it beyond repair. We need to break it ourselves."

"What you're saying makes no sense," I say, crossing my arms.

She sighs, and it has me bristling. *Is this what it's like to have a sister?*

"We have to stop them, then change the way things are done within the kingdom," she explains, still speaking in that maddeningly rational tone. "We re-establish the Fae, establish the Lower Houses as a formal High House, and improve conditions for humans. I'm not saying burn the castle down. It needs to be figuratively destroyed, I guess." She looks to the dirt ceiling in speculation, and nods firmly. "Yes, that's a better way to put it."

"Then what? You take back the throne and rule?" I look at her, one eyebrow raised, as I ask the question that's been tugging in the back of my mind since I saw her alive.

She snorts. "No. I don't want your throne. I was lucky your brother tried to kill me and got me away from it," she says with an accusatory glance at Asmo.

Asmo shoves his hands in his pockets, and based on the clench of his jaw, I get the feeling that he's resisting firing back a smart-ass comment. Amaris watches the exchange with a bemused expression, the white tattoos swirling on her arms like galaxies in the night sky.

"Then what's the point? What do you get out of this?" I ask.

Etta rolls her eyes. "The feeling of being a good person?"

"Etta, come on," Holly mutters.

Etta straightens, her face sobering. "Sorry. It's a good question. It's not right that our kingdom has shunned the Lower Houses. They deserve a place at the table. I would like to make that happen for them."

Obviously, I was not expecting Etta to be alive. The purpose of coming here today was to rescue a prisoner, not forge an alliance with an unsuspecting, formerly dead princess and a formerly fallen kingdom. Of course, I could walk away. Maybe that would be the smarter thing to do. I have no idea who Etta truly is or if she has an ulterior agenda, but with Torben's refusal to help, I'm running out of options here.

"Our goals are aligned—we both agree that Marik, Cora, and the witches need to go," I begin, lifting my chin and straightening my spine. "But if you want my support on the other end of this war in remaking the kingdom, you have to agree to fight with us against the witches. Canis and Ursidae have agreed to help, but that's not enough, especially since Panthera is now against us." I turn to Amaris. "I have no clue about the Fae forces, but we will take any help we can get."

"We stand behind the fallen princess," Amaris says. "Our forces are theirs to command."

I tilt my head. "You just swore a blood oath to protect and serve me. Not Etta." Her mouth parts, then shuts. A new gleam shines in her eyes as she assesses me. I don't give her an opportunity to respond. "But I don't want to come in between whatever deal you had previously with Etta."

It's not the truth. Not entirely, at least. We have zero allies, and forcing the Fae to fight for us might screw me out of any opportunity for an arrangement with Etta and the Lower Houses. I'm not exactly in a situation where I can turn away help, let alone create enemies. And I get the sense that Etta is not someone I want to make an enemy of.

Etta takes a step forward, hands clasped in front of her. "Let me be crystal-clear, High Queen," she says, and the title surprises me. Just moments ago, she looked at me like she felt sorry for me, like she thought me naïve. "I expect you to re-establish the Fae and the Lower Houses as official governments within the kingdom. I expect you to ensure they are treated equally under the law and in our society. In return, we will provide you aid in defeating the witches. In addition, you will help us rescue the prisoners that are to be executed."

I grind my teeth as I think through the implications of this. Agreeing to something like this without consulting the Herd is downright stupid. Sure, it sounds logical and empathetic—why wouldn't we want to help other groups succeed? But there is so much I don't know about the Fae and the Lower Houses. What if they're dangerous? Ivan's tale comes to mind, along with everything I've heard about the Fae, which is all, frankly, terrible. But my mother was Fae, and I am half-Fae.

I rub my temples as I think through the other considerations she just added. Agreeing to help rescue prisoners puts us at risk, but it's the only option we have for securing the allies we need to fight the witches. Losing Ursidae was a blow that we couldn't afford, and this is a solution. But if I don't agree, then we risk losing allies and the forces necessary to save the entire kingdom.

Asmo steps forward. "Mae..."

I hold my hand up. "Deal."

Etta extends her hand, and I grasp it. It is shockingly rough and calloused, and I wonder who she has had to become since facing death's door. "Come back tomorrow. Same time."

Asmo, Holly, and I exit the cave and I throw my hand up to block the sun rays that now shine down in full force. Asmo grabs Holly and me and funnels us back to the cabin.

The front door flies open as we step through the translucent barrier. Luca emerges, shoulders tensed, hands fisted, chest puffed. He descends the front porch stairs in a rush, stalking toward Holly.

"What is wrong with you?" he seethes at her.

She throws her hands up. "We're okay, Luc," she says calmly. "Everyone's okay. Take a breath."

She walks past him, but he grabs her forearm, jerking her to a halt. She tries to pull from his grasp, but he won't let go. "You're hurting me," she says calmly, but I can hear the strain in her voice.

Although I've begun to see snippets of anger from him, of disrespect and harsh tones, I've never seen him act this way. "What do you think you're doing?" I yell, hurrying toward them.

He turns to me and drops her arm, which is a smart move, but then he jabs his finger in my face. "And you? How could you be so *stupid*?" he hisses at me.

I stop mid-stride. "Excuse me?"

Behind me, Asmo chuckles quietly.

Luca steps closer to me, a flush of red tinging his cheeks. "How dare you? You do whatever you want, waltzing around here like you own the damned place, like you can do no wrong, like you don't have a care in the world, like we don't have innocent people's lives at stake."

Every word feels like a slap.

The cabin door bangs open. Ivan runs toward us, reaching for Luca, but he shrugs him off. "Elle's life is on the line," Luca hisses at me.

So, I guess I know who locked me in my room.

I get in his space, my face now inches from his. "You think I don't know that?" I whisper. "Do you honestly think I don't think about her every day and wish I could take it all back? Do you think I've forgotten my role in the bodies that hang in the gallows? *I'm* responsible for all of this, and I'm trying to fix it."

I pause, gritting my teeth as I stare at him, daring him to speak back to me. The breeze stirs, and with it, the pungent smell of liquor from the male before me. My lip curls in disgust.

"I am your queen. I may not be on the throne, but I will return to it one day. You do not touch another member of my court again, you do not touch another female again, you do not point your finger at me, and you do not insult my intelligence or my virtues again. If you have a problem with me, you can speak to me respectfully. Do you understand me?" I whisper.

His face is still red, his features pulled tight. The silence between us stretches as he considers his response. And I hope he considers every option, because I will not forget this moment.

"Do. You. Understand. Me?" I repeat, my voice low.

"Yes." His voice sounds pained, like it took every ounce of his willpower and strength to say the word. He forms a bow and when he straightens, there's a cold smile on his face. "Your Highness," he adds, but the title borders on a sneer.

"Fantastic," I mutter before shoving past him.

Inside, Holly's clothes are strewn about the couch, and I toss them into the corner.

Cally emerges from the hallway. "What's going on? Where were you? Is everything okay?"

"Everything's fine," I say, shoving the couch against the far wall, and setting the two armchairs in a semi-circle. "Hand me that chair," I say, pointing to one of the dining chairs in the kitchen. Cally obliges, dragging it and placing it next to the others.

Holly and Ivan walk back inside, both of them watching me carefully. I offer them a tight smile, but they stand there in silence like scolded children. Luca enters next, his posture still rigid. He won't meet my gaze. Asmo follows behind him.

"Sit," I command the group. "You, too, Cally," I add softly. "Please."

Everyone finds their seat amidst the circle, and I perch on the wooden dining chair.

"I understand that our sudden disappearance may have caused some...upset," I say, even though that's not the right word. Anger and a childish response is probably the better way to describe it, but alas. "I apologize for not informing you of my plan. Moving forward, if I think something is in the best interest of the court or someone's life, I will inform you instead of hiding it."

Luca leans forward in his seat, his shoulders hunched as he stares at the chipped hardwoods.

"I did not plan on Asmo or Holly joining me. My intention was to go alone." Luca's head snaps up, mouth parting with what I'm certain is a string of insults. I hold my hand up. "I'm still speaking."

His jaw works, but he drops his burning glare back to the floor.

"I understand it was reckless," I say. "For that, I am sorry."

Ivan clears his throat, "Your Highness, if I may…We're all frustrated by the situation we've found ourselves in. It is our duty to protect you, and we're happy to do so, but it does make it harder if you—"

"Leave without saying a word, I know," I say.

Ivan gives me a half-smile, and I think that means I'm forgiven. Or at least, he's not angry with me in the way Luca is. I can take Luca's criticism, but Ivan's makes my chest tighten. His support has been unwavering, and the regret on my shoulders feels a little heavier every time he sighs.

"Well, where did you go?" Cally asks from beside me, the last person I expected to have any input in this conversation. But the question returns me to some sense of normalcy. Of course Cally wouldn't be mad at me for going. She'd just want to know what happened and where I went. I want to leap from my chair and squeeze her for asking it.

But my stomach twists again as I think of the information that's left to share. "Panthera." Ivan's fingers grip the armrests, but he doesn't say anything. "We were able to rescue the hybrid that was set for execution. We also…" I trail off, struggling with how to share the other part of our rescue. "Have you ever heard of Squall's End?"

Ivan stares at me blankly. "No, I don't think I have. It doesn't sound familiar. Why?"

"What do you know of the Lower Houses?" I ask.

His eyebrows knit together. "They encompass the remainder of the woodland creatures—squirrels, chipmunks, birds, rabbits, and other Lower hybrids. None of them have ever been considered a formal House, but they were governed by the High Court as Lower Houses. They petitioned to be removed from the High Court's rules…well, generations ago, and have been governing themselves ever since," he says. "Why? What's going on?"

"The Lower Houses are involved in something called the resistance," I say, the word feeling difficult to form on my tongue. A new kind of guilt twists in my gut as I think about the need for a resistance to form under my throne. That there are injustices and inequities throughout the kingdom that I didn't know existed—or that the Crown turned a blind eye to—me, included.

"A resistance?" Ivan asks.

I nod slowly as I think through how best to share the next part of the news. *The princess you all thought was dead is actually alive. Surprise!*

Across the circle, Asmo catches my gaze and offers me an encouraging nod. I fill my lungs and blurt, "Etta is alive, and she's leading it."

Cally gasps, Luca's posture goes rigid, and Ivan stares at me silently before turning to Holly. "Etta is...alive?" His voice is a whisper, but it cracks nonetheless.

Holly's features soften as she dips her head in confirmation. Ivan's face pales, and he runs his hands through his gray hair.

"And the Fae are back," I add lamely. It's another huge revelation, but not as big as learning Etta is alive.

I can feel Cally's stare boring into my profile. I twist my hands in my lap as I consider the next bit of news I have to drop. The deal I made.

The fire crackles in the stone hearth, embers popping and wood settling. The silence that descends upon us is heavy, fraught with unasked questions.

What does this mean for us? What do we do next? How is Etta still alive?

"What do you mean, a resistance?" Luca's voice is gruff.

I recount the last several hours, Holly filling in when necessary. Asmo remains a silent observer throughout, gaze mostly locked on Luca.

Ivan leans back in his chair, a deep sigh coming from some part of him that I'm sure is bone tired. "Okay," he says. "Okay." He steeples his hands together as he processes the news. "Etta is alive, the Fae are back, and the Lower Houses have formed a resistance. So, now what?"

I bite the inside of my cheek. Here goes nothing.

"Etta and I made a deal," I say cautiously. Ivan's gaze instantly narrows. "She has agreed to help us fight the witches with Canis and Ursidae. We will have the power of the Lower Houses and the Fae to attack Marik and Cora."

Ivan raises a single eyebrow. "And what do we have to do in return?"

"If we are successful in defeating Marik, I promised to remake the throne with her," I say.

Holly clears her throat, looking at me expectantly. She tilts her head.

"And we have to help them rescue the prisoners that are set to be executed," I add hurriedly. "I'm not asking for your permission, though. This is what's going to happen. I would like your help with planning this. If you do not agree, you can leave," I say, but I feel like I might pass out. My head feels too light and my palms are sweaty.

To my surprise, Luca doesn't get up and walk out the door.

"Good," I say. I place my hands on the armrests of the chair and stand, my gaze traveling over each of them. "We return tomorrow morning before first light."

I'm getting ready for bed when the knock on the door comes. Probably Asmo checking to see if I'm decent before he comes in to grab something. Although we've been sharing the room, he always comes to bed after me and wakes long before me. He's made no attempt to recreate what happened between us the other night at the inn. Sometimes, I'll turn over and find him facing me, his hand inches away, as if he fell asleep reaching for me. Sometimes, I stare at him until I fall back asleep, warring with myself to rest my hand on top of his.

The other night was everything I needed to hear from him. It was perfect and raw and messy and felt like it was the first step to fixing the crack in my heart. But I'm terrified. I'm so terrified.

"Come in," I call, then shove my dirty clothes into a pile on the floor by the dresser.

The door clicks open. "Can I speak to you for a moment?"

It's Ivan. Mother, he looks exhausted. If we make it back to the throne, I'll find some way to make all of this up to him. He deserves it.

"Sure. What's going on?"

He looks around the room. "Mind if we speak outside?"

"Yeah. Give me a second. Meet you out there." I grab my coat and shove my boots on, then follow him out the front door. "Is everything okay?"

He glances at the floor, then back to me. "I—yes. I just wanted to speak about Luca earlier. He's having a very hard time."

I cross my arms. "We all are." My mind is roaring with anger. Is Ivan about to try to justify Luca's outburst? "Ivan, he locked me in my room."

"Mother. I didn't...I had no clue." He sighs, a white puff of air in the freezing night. "You're right. It's just..." He trails off, looking past me into the forest as he searches for the words.

Ivan has a heart of gold, and I try to remember that. He's known Luca for years, has worked beside him, has spoken with him almost every day. Although he's technically known of me since I was a little girl, he is closer to Luca. The roaring in my head quiets.

"We all join the guard for different reasons. Mine was for your father. Luca's was for his daughter. She died when she was fifteen. She was rebellious and head-strong and I think you remind him of her in a lot of ways. When she passed, he went off the deep end. Began drinking heavily and became volatile. He...I don't think he ever found a good way to deal with it."

An ember of sympathy begins to take place, but only an ember. While I feel sorry for him and can give him some grace, I also find myself not caring. We've all experienced unimaginable tragedies in the last few months. I watched my friend die. I watched Holly burn. I watched Elle bleed out. I have been betrayed by the people I loved. A snappy response here and there is fine, but yelling at people and name-calling is not tolerable.

"While I am sorry to hear that, I don't find that an acceptable excuse for his behavior."

His face falls, a flicker of sadness now etched on his features. "You're right. I just—I thought maybe that might help explain what happened today."

"It does," I say, refraining from adding *But it doesn't matter.* "If there's anything I can do, please let me know."

Ivan twists his hands together. "Thanks." He turns back toward the door and pauses. His gaze is heavy and I fight the urge to look away. "For what it's worth, I think you're doing a great job. I know you're doing everything you can to get Elle back. Just...Talk to us, okay? No more solo missions. If we lose you, it's over. For everyone."

I stay on the porch until I can't feel my fingers, the weight of his words, of the kingdom, hanging over me.

CHAPTER 26
MAE

Thump.

Thump.

Thump.

Asmo hurls three daggers at the tree trunk in quick succession, each one landing a hair's width apart in a neat row.

"What can I do for you, princess?" he drawls as he walks to the tree, his back to me.

"How did you know it was me?" I ask, leaning against a nearby trunk.

"Snakes have an excellent sense of smell." He plucks the daggers out, drops of liquid leaking from each hole like tears.

He turns to face me. His hair is unkempt, as if he's been running his fingers through it repeatedly. After the tense scene from earlier, I don't blame him.

I came out here with a purpose—to talk about the plan for tomorrow, but I find myself asking, "What do I smell like?"

He faces the tree, sets his feet shoulder-width apart and raises the dagger. He pauses and turns to me. Through his white shirt, the black ink of his snake tattoo is visible. One corner of his mouth quirks, his dimple making an appearance. "You smell like pine and wildflowers."

My own mouth quirks up in a soft smile. He throws his favorite all-black dagger at the trunk. It lands with a thump.

He walks to the trunk and yanks it out, a strand of sap hanging from the obsidian metal. Asmo lifts the dagger to his full lips and licks the sap from the knife, tongue expertly flicking along the blade. Those dragons take flight again, low in my stomach.

"What kind of flowers?" I ask, surprised I'm able to even get the question out.

He smirks. "Remember those bleeding-hearts we got from the market?"

I tilt my head. "Why do you think of *that* flower?"

He twirls the dagger in his hand, then shoves it into the holster strapped around his hips and walks toward me, stopping a few feet away. The sun has begun to set, highlighting one side of his face and leaving the other in the shadows. The silver band circles his iris, a perfect comparison of the light and the dark that resides within him.

"You remind me of them." He smiles that half-smile again, and it threatens to undo me.

"But why?" I whisper.

He looks down as he fidgets with the dagger in the holster. "The first day I met you, you basically tore a piece of my heart and took it with you," he says with a huff of laughter. "You left it bloody and torn, and I fought to get it back. But there was nothing I could do. You took it, whether you knew it or not, and you've had it ever since." He says the words simply, as if they are facts. But his smile is shaky and he stares at the ground. "So, you remind me of bleeding-heart flowers."

My heart constricts in my chest at the vulnerability in his words, at the truth he's chosen to share with me. He cups my cheek. I close my eyes and nuzzle into it. "Does your heart still bleed?" I whisper.

He chuckles, but it comes out breathy. "My heart will always bleed for you, as yours will always bleed for mine."

My eyelids flutter open and I meet his gaze. "When will it stop?"

"I don't think it will ever stop, princess. And that's okay. I'll bleed for an eternity if it means I'm bleeding for you."

"Asmo," I whisper, pulling him against me. That damn dimple is back on his face, and I brush my thumb over it.

"Mae," he answers, the smile on his face deepening.

"Do you want to kiss me?" I ask cheekily.

"Yes," he whispers. "Forever."

My heart flips at the truth that rings in that one little word: forever. This broken High Prince, who fought the chemistry between us, who pulled away from me at every turn.

He leans forward, his lips parting. My blood heats, but I freeze.

What if he does it again? What if I choose him, and he leaves again?

Despite the way my heart seems to be beating out of my chest to be closer to him, I force walls around it. I take a step back. "No, I don't...I can't." I clench my teeth, but that fire in my veins is barely lessening. But it doesn't matter how much my body yearns for him, or how much I want to be with him. My heart—my crown—is too fragile to give away. I have to be certain. I will not make the same mistake again. "I'm sorry," I mutter.

"Mae," he says, his fingertips brushing along my forearm. "Why do you keep pushing this away?"

A different High Prince once warned me that sex is an easy way to manipulate and gain power. Holly once warned me that that exact form of manipulation is House Serpent's specialty. I've already fallen for it once. How stupid do I need to be to do it again?

Even with my ability to detect lies, I feel like I'm floating in the ocean, pulled by two different currents—my heart and my mind. My heart pulls me toward Asmo every chance it can, while my mind comes racing in the opposite direction, warning me away from him. I'm caught in the middle, and I'm so close to drowning.

I turn on my heels and walk back toward the cabin.

The last thing I hear before I enter the cabin is the *thump, thump, thump,* of the daggers sinking into the tree.

W e find Basil in the barn. He wastes no time on introductions. He ushers us into Squall's End to begin preparing for the next rescue, hurriedly sharing the details as we walk.

Etta and Amaris are waiting for us. Etta's chestnut hair is pulled into a knot on the top of her head, wisps framing her delicate face. Amaris's thick, white braid is tossed over one shoulder. Her leather vest is outfitted with no less than a dozen daggers. She offers me a bow and Asmo a smirk.

Someone behind me gasps.

Etta's lips curl into a smile, her eyes softening as they land on whoever is behind me. I step aside, not wanting to be caught in some sort of awkward embrace that isn't meant for me. I bump into Asmo in my haste to get out of the way, his solid chest unmoving behind me.

I try to elbow him out of my way, but he catches my arm, holding it steady. "I may have compared you to a bleeding heart yesterday, but can you please stop with the violence?" His whisper sends chills dancing along my skin. He removes his hand, but his fingers drag along my skin as if it was the last thing he wanted to do.

Etta and Ivan pull apart, and he stares at her with unshed tears. "You're alive," he whispers.

Etta gives him an animated nod, her grin stretched wide and her cheeks rosy.

Holly watches them with the biggest smile I've ever seen on her face, the expression pulling at the burn scars that grace the edge of her jawline. My own heart squeezes in my chest.

"I can't believe it," Luca mutters. He turns to Asmo and me, both of us standing near the door, watching the scene before us. "Are you sure this isn't one of those marks?"

"I'm sure," I say confidently. I've gotten no sense of deception from Etta, and my net has been up constantly, its presence now something I don't even have to think about.

Basil clears his throat from behind Etta. "Mind if we postpone this reunion?"

Etta nearly jumps at the reminder, and I chide myself for forgetting the real reason we're here—to save someone from execution. "He's right," Etta says. "Time is of the essence." She turns her gaze to Asmo and me. "Are you two ready to hold up your end of the bargain?"

I want to correct her. I'm the one who made the deal. Asmo can leave whenever he wants. He is not beholden to me or my court, I remind myself. "We will assist in the rescue, but we must discuss details of our arrangement once the prisoner is safe," I say firmly.

She nods. "Done. Did Basil fill you in on the details?"

"He said that it's essentially the same rescue mission as the last time."

"That's right."

Luca swings his head toward me. "You failed to inform us that we'd be rescuing anyone today, Your Highness."

I raise an eyebrow. The title is without the near-sneer this time, and I can't help but wonder if he's had an attitude adjustment, or if it's due to our present company. And, if I remember correctly, I implied that was our purpose today. Not to mention, Basil was just reviewing the details. What did he think that was for? A ball? Whatever.

"That's part of our deal."

Etta slides past me, heading down the hallway in the direction of the front entrance. "Fill them in as we go. We're running out of time," she calls behind her.

We follow Etta, and Basil recounts the details of our rescue mission to Ivan and Luca. Ivan falls in step behind me. "Mae," he whispers. "How do you know this isn't a trap?"

"Nobody here is lying."

"Yes, but...There are ways around that. Just think of Marik," he says, but he winces.

He's right. Oh, how Marik got around that line of defense. "Asmo was kind enough to give me that reminder already, Ivan," I say curtly. I regret it as soon as it's out. Ivan has been one of the few people I've been able to rely on. To trust without a shadow of a doubt. But like Asmo, he can leave at any time.

He rubs the back of his neck. "Just don't only rely on that."

I force a smile to my face. If only he knew how much I've been thinking of Marik's betrayal and the ease in which he did it. In fact, not a day goes by where I don't think of it. It clings to me like a stain. "You're right. Thank you."

"Excuse me, Your Highnesses," Basil mutters as he squeezes between Asmo and me. He joins Etta at the dirt wall.

The portal opens slowly, starting as a pinprick, then spreading outward until it reaches the tunnel's sloped ceiling. "Trickier than yesterday," Basil mutters. "They must have put some additional precautions in place."

"Be on your watch, princess," Asmo mutters to me. "And stay behind me." He glances down at me, then adds, "Please."

I mumble an agreement. Amaris looks at Asmo, a bemused expression on her face.

"Ready when you are," Etta says.

Asmo's shadows fall over us, and I swear they linger on my skin as they brush past me and form around us. The dungeons are even colder today. I rub my hands along my arms, my breath forming small clouds in front of me. We creep down the hallway, carefully avoiding slushy puddles of melted gray ice.

My heart drops to my stomach as something splashes in a puddle behind me, entirely too close.

Dozens of rats sprint toward us. I raise my hands, ready to blast them all the hell away from me, but Basil shoves Asmo and me against a freezing cold wall of stone. He looks at us, a finger pressed against his lips.

The rats race past us, an angry mob of four-legged, long-tailed creatures. Basil pointedly looks down the hallway, then back to Asmo and me.

Today's distraction, then.

I give him a shaky thumbs up. We wait another minute before resuming our slow walk down the hallway.

That's when the screaming starts. Around the corner, two figures are squirming. They're covered in rats.

"Get them off of me!" one shrieks, firing balls of magic in the air. I duck as one flies toward me.

Amaris moves toward the witches and extends two hands, splendid bursts of shimmering magic striking and freezing them in place. "Hurry," she says. "It won't last long."

"Why didn't we just—" Asmo starts, but Basil points to a single door. Asmo strikes, shadow sword cutting a jagged line down the middle. I don't wait for Basil's command. I pull the wreckage away. This time, the figure rushes out as soon as the door is cracked open. Judging by his bright-green eyes, this prisoner is a Panthera hybrid.

Basil emerges from the shadows and gestures forward, urging the male toward us. He sprints toward us, almost slipping on a patch of ice. His dingy gray blanket falls from his shoulders, revealing an almost-naked male. Dirty, but otherwise healthy.

Basil pulls him into the shadows with us. The male starts as he sees us, but we take off down the hall, and my heart hammers in my chest.

The screaming starts again, but nobody follows us. Basil all but shoves the male through the open portal, and it closes behind us with a pop.

"Where am I?" the male asks. He rubs his biceps, at the goosebumps that still linger.

I shrug my coat off and hold it out to him. It's entirely too small on him, but it's better than nothing.

"You're in a safe place," Etta says, her tone calm and reassuring.

He eyes her dubiously, then looks around the dirt hallway, carefully assessing each of us. "Where am I?" he repeats.

"Squall's End," Asmo answers. Etta shoots him a glare as sharp as a knife.

The male's brow furrows. "What is that?"

Etta answers before Asmo gets the chance. "We'll explain everything. First, I'd like to have you checked out by a healer, if that's okay. Once that's done, I'm happy to answer your questions."

He blinks rapidly, as if trying to make sense of everything. "Sure. Yeah. Okay."

Etta smiles softly, gesturing down the hallway. "This way." We wait several moments before we follow. The male was already skittish and clearly confused. Having a pack of hybrids trailing you in an unknown location would be enough to send anyone over the edge and straight into panic.

Asmo's hand brushes against mine as we walk, each touch a spark. I glance at him, but he stares ahead. His hair is neatly styled today, black locks combed and tame, but that one errant lock of hair is loose and bouncing with every step.

Etta makes sure the rescued prisoner is with a healer, then leads us to a private room. The walls are rough, made of hewn rock and dirt. A black fabric couch sits in the middle of the room. Several armchairs are scattered on the opposite side, their armrests faded by use over time. Two large, repurposed barrels sit in between the couch and chairs. Along the back wall, light wood cabinets form a small kitchenette. Dark wooden shelves line the walls, an assortment of dishes, mugs, and cook-ware neatly organized on their surfaces.

"This is one of our common areas," Etta says, walking to one of the armchairs and sinking into it. Everyone squeezes into a seat, save for Holly, who heads to the nearest wall and leans against it. Her favorite spot.

"Etta," Ivan starts, staring at her with a pained expression. "You're alive."

She smiles. "Yes, I am." She looks to me and says, "We didn't get the chance to discuss the details around my disappearance from the court, but it was not by choice." She takes a shaky breath, then turns to Asmo with a cold expression. "Your brother tried to kill me, Prince. And he nearly succeeded."

Asmo's expression remains unchanged, her words appearing to bounce off him like pebbles thrown at a statue. He stares back at her, long legs crossed and hand dangling from one of the armrests.

"But...We buried you," Luca says. "I—I saw your body. You were dead."

Etta places her hands in her lap, dropping her gaze to her hands as she wrings them together. "Yes, you did." She sits in silence for a few moments, her posture rigid as she gathers her words. I can't imagine the courage it's taking her to relive this.

"I found her." Basil breaks the silence. "In the forest. She was barely alive. Anybody would have missed it. But I can see peoples' auras. Every living being has one. When you die, so does your aura." Etta still doesn't look up. "I was on a scouting mission," Basil continues. "Something we do often. We walk through the different courts and look for any signs of Lower House members. Several of us were patrolling the High Court's grounds, and I saw an aura...barely there, on the edge of flickering out. Thank the Mother that we don't bury the dead like the Fae. Otherwise, the dirt would have suffocated her. I was so lucky that we had a healer with us who was able to stabilize her. We took her back to Squall's End and nursed her back to health."

The blood drains from my face. I was right there the whole time. I laid flowers on her body, cried for her, and she was alive the whole time. We abandoned her in the forest. We left her to rot. I feel sick.

Ivan's hands are clenched into fists in his lap.

Then, they're pummeling Basil's face.

CHAPTER 27
MAE

IVAN REARS BACK and strikes Basil in the face again. Basil throws his hands out, and a burst of magic sends Ivan flying. He lands on the barrel with a thud. He scrambles and launches himself at Basil again. Luca jumps out of the way, just narrowly avoiding Ivan's fist. Basil throws a hand up and deflects the blow.

Asmo sits back in his chair, a grin spread across his face. "Do something!" I hiss. But he just sits there, eyes twinkling as he watches Ivan and Basil.

Males are useless. I throw a shield around Ivan as Basil prepares to go on the offense.

"Sit," I command. "Now." Basil watches Ivan, jaw clenched and hands balled into fists. "*Now*," I repeat.

"Yes, Your Majesty," Basil whispers. He sits on the edge of the couch, unfurling his hands and cupping his knees. He angles his body toward Ivan, who sits on the opposite side of the couch, Luca sitting awkwardly between them.

Etta raises her head and looks at Ivan. "They saved my life."

"They stole you from the throne," Ivan fires back.

Etta shakes her head. "No, Ivan. I don't think you understand. I was going to die out there. They took me in. They saved me."

What would I have done, in her shoes? I was lucky enough that Asmo was there to save me, not someone I didn't know. I don't blame Etta for staying.

"They could have brought you back to the castle. *We* could have saved you."

Etta takes a deep breath, fidgeting with the material on her pants. "They would have risked everything. It would have exposed their entire operation."

"I don't give a damn," Ivan says incredulously.

Etta's eyes shutter closed, as if she's torn between Ivan's anger and Basil's decision. Torn between a before and after. "They didn't know what to do. They made a choice. But it was mine to stay."

My mind races. Etta has been alive this whole time. She knew I was on the throne but didn't make a move to restore her position. My life could have remained unchanged if she had taken the throne back. I could have avoided so much pain—physical and emotional. We wouldn't be here right now.

But that's not entirely true. Cora would have found another way.

"I took months to heal," Etta continues, "But when I did, I was given the choice to leave. I declined. The people here are good, selfless, and working toward something more important than me returning to the throne. They're fighting for their rights, the rights they should have had all along. So, I decided to stay and help them." She turns to me and says, "I apologize for the hell you've found yourself in, and that my decision to stay forced you into that."

I nod in silent forgiveness. Although I've been grumbling about my position and its burden, I wouldn't step away even if I could. I'm surprised to find that even if I could go back and force Etta back to the throne, I wouldn't. Because then I wouldn't have my friends, nor would I be this version of myself—the one that has found another piece of my heart in magic.

"You truly abandoned your birthright for this?" Ivan asks. He sounds sad.

Etta's answering smile is tight. "Yes. It's important." She looks around, to the walls of dirt, the bare-bones furniture. "This place, these people, are good. Since staying here, I've learned more about the state of this kingdom. Humans need our assistance and the Fae need help re-establishing themselves. Maybe I abandoned my birthright so I can make it better."

Her hands have stopped twitching and her posture is straighter. She's confident about this. No—proud.

Ivan stares at her, then looks at me. "And you agreed to this?" I nod. His face is blank as he asks, "You agreed to destroy your own throne? Both of you truly want this?"

Etta smiles, reminding me of the way she was yesterday when she explained everything to us. "We would like to rebuild it," she says, "Make it better. Make it something to be proud of. The Lower Houses and the humans are a part of this kingdom, but they have never had the same rights as members of the High Houses. And the Fae deserve to return home." Ivan's face pales at the reminder of the Fae, and I wonder again what I've agreed to. "We want to rid the throne of the black rot that is Marik and the witches, then start over with a new kingdom, one that takes care of *all* its subjects."

"And which one of you will rule?" Ivan asks, eyes darting between Etta and me.

Etta dips her chin toward me.

"I'll continue to rule," I say, as confidently as I can. If I'm being honest, I feel like an imposter on the High Throne again now that I know Etta is alive.

"She is the eldest sister, after all. The throne is rightly hers," Etta says.

I blink. She's right. Despite my mother not being Queen Adelaide, it doesn't matter. All that matters is my father's lineage. And I am the elder sister.

"Remind me of the conditions of the deal," Ivan says to Etta. "Please," he adds.

"Mae has agreed to help us rescue the prisoners set for execution. In exchange, we will assist you in fighting Marik and Cora."

"That seems like an unbalanced trade," Luca says. "What does that even mean, that you'll assist us in fighting?"

Amaris leans forward. "Between the Lower Houses and the Fae, we have hundreds of citizens that are willing and able to fight. They are yours if you decide to take up arms."

Luca raises an eyebrow. "In exchange for rescuing a few citizens?"

Etta nods, that smile still on her face. "And in exchange for your help in establishing the Lower Houses as a formal House."

"And restoring the Fae Kingdom," Amaris adds.

Ivan shifts in his seat.

"Once Mae is back on the throne, of course," Etta says.

Luca leans back against the sofa, still sandwiched between Ivan and Basil, who scoots further to the side. "Okay then," Luca says. "What's the plan?"

It feels like a weight has been lifted. I was prepared for a bigger argument. Not that it would have mattered, because there's no way we're backing out of the arrangement anyway.

"Well, that's why we're here today. We need to come up with one," Etta says. "I think you all should move into Squall's End. I don't know where you're staying, but this has got to be safer than wherever you are currently. Plus, it will be convenient for arranging our rescue missions, will allow you to train with our army, and familiarize yourself with our citizens."

I tilt my head as I consider her proposal. It's not a bad idea, but I'm curious to know what the others think before I agree to it. Moving here was not a part of the deal, and I don't want to force them to do anything else if they're not on board. I've already agreed to enough without their input.

"We can achieve all of those things regardless of our living arrangements," I respond. "Either way, I think one of the next steps is to get in contact with August and Barrett to inform them of our alliance."

Etta's jaw twitches. "I would like to wait on that."

I freeze. "Why is that?"

She hesitates, glancing down at her lap. "You have to understand, Squall's End has been hidden for decades. I don't want to show our hand too quickly. What if this arrangement doesn't work?"

"So, you want to stay hidden...while also becoming a formal House?" Asmo asks dubiously. His fingers drum on the worn leather armrest. "Those two are mutually exclusive. Which is it, Etta?"

She doesn't answer. She watches him, lips pursed, then snaps her gaze to me. "You're sure about him?"

"Yes." My answer is quick and decisive, my net bobbing along the river undisturbed.

She huffs a breath. "Well, if I'm being honest with you, Mae. His presence gives me pause. His brother just tried to kill me, then stole the throne. Who's to say Asmo isn't Marik's backup plan to finish you off?"

"I would never hurt Mae." Asmo's tone is deadly, ice cold. It rings with truth.

Etta turns her gaze to him, as if seeing him through a new light. "Did you have anything to do with Marik's plan to steal the throne?"

He doesn't take his eyes from her. "No."

"Did you know of it?"

"No."

She stares at him for a beat longer, then turns back to me. "Fine." I tilt my head at her easy acceptance of his answers. Can she detect lies, too? "I agree with you. Speaking with Barrett and August should be next. But I would appreciate some time to do so. Do you agree to hold off for another week?"

I freeze. A week? Another week of Elle being in Marik's hands? "No, I'm not okay with waiting a week. Elle is being held as Marik's prisoner."

She rolls her shoulders back, as if sitting here and working with us is proving to be a monumental test to her endurance. "The extra time will give us time to plan for the conversation with August and Barrett. It's arguably the most important conversation we'll have, and it needs to be thoroughly thought out." Her features soften, and she adds, "Getting Elle out is a priority. She was my friend, too."

I inhale a shaky breath. "Etta, we have reason to believe that Marik is controlling her using dark magic."

Her eyelids shutter, and she sucks in a sharp inhale of air. The softness is gone. "Well, while I am sorry to hear that, all of the citizens in Squall's End are counting on me for their safety and their futures. Like I said, Elle is a priority, but we do not risk the mission or the safety of others to rescue her."

I don't care. Marik is a monster, and Elle is at his hands. Elle sacrificed herself not once, but twice, to save my life. And I've left her to rot in that castle with him. I swallow every word, each one thick and sharp. Instead, I nod. Etta has offered me more hope of getting Elle back than anybody else. The rest of the kingdom has abandoned her. Without Etta and the Lower Houses, we'd be back at square one.

"I would welcome the opportunity to stay here and learn more about Squall's End and its citizens," I say. "However, I would like to speak with my advisors. With my friends."

One corner of her mouth quirks up. "Of course. We'll be outside," she says.

Basil shuts the door behind them as he, Etta, and Amaris exit the room.

"Well?" I ask, looking around. Holly still stands against the wall, arms crossed. Ivan and Luca sit more comfortably on the couch, both leaning back with relaxed postures. Asmo's legs are still crossed, one arm now slung across the back of the chair. "What do you think?"

"I think the argument to live here is sound," Asmo says. "What do *you* think?"

I lean forward. "I agree." I look to the couch, to Ivan and Luca.

Ivan is slowly nodding. "Me, too," he says.

Luca grunts in what I assume is approval.

"Thank the Mother," Holly says. "I need to get out of that house and into a real bed."

"To be fair, I don't know if they have real beds," I point out.

She chuckles, but her smile fades as she says, "I trust Etta. If she's been safe here and she trusts them, I feel comfortable with it."

Alright then.

"Let's do it."

A smo tosses the empty leather bag on the bed. I grab it and start shoving my meager belongings inside, the collection small enough to carry everything in both hands.

He opens the drawer that holds all his clothes. Only one drawer, and it's not even full.

I can't help but huff a meager half-laugh.

"What's so funny, princess?" he asks, gathering his collection of black shirts and turning toward the bed.

"The fact that we told Etta we had to come back and get our belongings. We have almost nothing."

He re-folds his shirts, making sure each one is as neat as it can be before setting them in a tidy pile. "Ah yes. How I miss my fashionable clothing items in the court that sold its soul to be on the throne," he says. "If this bag is my only closet, then I am proud of the choices I have made."

I look back down at the bag and shove my well-worn socks inside. I stop when I find the pair of socks I stole from Asmo's drawer.

"Hey," I say abruptly, "when you were in the dungeons, I looked through your clothes."

He quirks an eyebrow. "Snooping? Or just missing me?"

I ignore him and hold up the black pair of socks. "Why do you have a wine cork inside of this pair?"

His eyes narrow in on the pair in my hands. "I was wondering where those went."

I toss them to him. He snatches them mid-air and unfolds them, reaching his hand inside and extracting the wine cork. He holds it in the air between us.

"Our first date," he says. I blink. He smiles. "The very first one, when you stormed away from me. I complimented you and you accused me of finding you a plaything, then you left me at the table. Remember?"

I cross my arms. What a way to spin the truth. "You didn't compliment me. You said you found me...intriguing."

"Is that not a compliment?"

My answering sigh is impatient. "You treated me like I was trivial, like I was something you wanted to explore, not someone you wanted to marry."

His smile disappears. "That was never my intention, Mae."

My name on his lips sends a shiver up my spine. I'm always *princess.*

What started as a rude nickname has turned into something endearing. But him saying my actual name always conveys a sense of gravity or vulnerability.

"To be clear, I did—I do—want to explore you. I want to explore every inch of you. Of your body, of your mind. You are intriguing to me, in every meaning of the word. Every female I've ever been with... They've always been so quick to please me, to agree with me, to be liked by me. You are the only one who's ever challenged me, who's been brave enough to push back, to not take my shit."

Although his words give me butterflies, I roll my eyes at them. "This just sounds like the same thing, Asmo. You find me interesting, so that's why you're attracted to me."

His jaw clenches. "No. That's not what I'm saying." He rakes his fingers through his hair. "But even if it is, why is that a bad thing?" Although his tone is calm, I can tell he's fighting from saying more.

"Because then I'm just something you've never had. At what point do you get bored and throw me away?"

"Mae." He takes a step toward me, and the shiver turns into something warmer. This room is so small, that single step nearly backs me against the wall. He takes another, and this time, I'm forced against it. "I threw my future away. For you. I threw my family away. For you. I threw everything away to *have you*. What makes you think I would throw you away after I fought so hard for you?"

I snort. "So, the reason you want me is because you have nothing to go back to?"

His hand flies up, the movement quick as a snake striking, and cups the back of my neck. His fingers intertwine in my hair and tug, forcing my gaze upward. Pain lines his eyes. "What are you doing right now?" he whispers. "Why do you keep pushing this away?"

Because the person who raised me only did so to throw me to the figurative wolves and steal my throne. The person who I hoped to marry only did so after murdering my father and then nearly killing my sister, all for the purposes of tricking me into marrying him. Then he tried to kill me.

I have no idea if I can trust myself again, if I can ever trust another person again. I have no clue how to love when it comes with so much risk—not just my heart, but the safety of my kingdom.

I close my eyes. Being vulnerable with others has never been my strong suit.

"Talk to me."

I take a deep breath and force the words to come out. "I have a bit of a difficult time believing anyone," I admit. "After...After Marik and Cora. Do you blame me?"

He reaches for my hand and brings it to his chest, to the space above his beating heart. "Do you not feel what's between us? Are you so blinded by what my brother did?"

His heart beats against my palm, and I can't think with him so close to me. "I—"

He grips my hand and squeezes. "Did he damage your heart so terribly?" His voice breaks. He presses his forehead against mine, and my breathing hitches. "Did he kill what's mine?" His words feel like a plea, and my heart cracks.

I'm suffocating under the weight of what he's done to me. I can't breathe when I look at you, but I can't breathe when I think about being with you.

"Asmo, it's—"

But the moment is interrupted by three knocks on the door and Ivan yelling, "Ready?"

Asmo's jaw clenches and his hold on my hand loosens. I slip away from him, his words clinging to me like a stain.

Did he kill what's mine?

Every muscle in my body strains to turn back to Asmo, to scream and cry and hand him my heart and beg him to fix it. To put back the piece he stole from it.

But I can't.

I have a kingdom to lead.

My heart can wait.

CHAPTER 28
MARIK

ELLE DOESN'T WEAR a pillowcase to dinner tonight. Well, not exactly. Instead, she's wrapped a cream sheet around her slender figure, cinched at the waist by a curtain rope. Her shoulders are exposed, and they're somehow both smooth and sharp. She shoves past me when I open the door, her stringy red hair bobbing against her shoulder blades as she descends the staircase.

I reach to pull out her chair, but she stops me with a glare. It feels like every nerve in my body lights up at the defiance in her stare, like something ancient within me stirs. *She's here. She came to play tonight.*

I stride to my chair, the ornate legs dragging along the ancient wooden floors. She sits opposite me, posture straight and gaze stony. I don't need to descend into the bond to know what she's feeling. The pointed glare of her amber eyes tells me all I need to know, the flame of the candles flickering in them like a living symbol of the hatred burning inside of her.

The first course is brought out, the waitstaff floating plates of salad behind them.

"Thank you." Elle's gratitude is warm, the upward tilt of her mouth offering me a glimpse of something I haven't seen from her since before

I was High King, but it disappears as the waitstaff turns from her without a word.

"Why do you do that?" I ask.

She snatches her fork from the table and stabs it into the bed of lettuce. "Do what?"

I tilt my head toward the exit. "Try to speak to the staff."

"Why wouldn't I?" she asks around a meager helping of the salad.

"They're the help," I explain. "Nobody. Nothing."

She scoffs. "Says the High Prince who has never had to grovel at another person's feet."

I could correct her on the title. I'm High King now, after all, but I remain silent. She has no clue how wrong she is. I've been groveling all my life. The feet may have changed over the years, but it never stops. Once, it was Father's snake-skinned boots, now it's Cora's black leather heels.

"What?" Elle asks. "Do I not speak the truth?" I shrug away the question and take another bite. "Is this how you won Mae over? Silence and brooding over all the things you had? Oh, poor High Prince. Born with everything but a soul."

I can't help the laugh that comes.

She quirks an eyebrow. "Funny?"

I shove my plate away, barely touched. "You're right."

She grunts something, then finishes her salad without another word. I signal to the waitstaff that hovers by the door, and he rushes toward me. Embarrassing. Why would anyone deign to speak to them?

"Wine."

He returns moments later, reaching to pop the cork. I stop him and motion for the bottle. But before I wave him away, I force myself to say, "Thank you." The words taste like dirt, but a peek down the bond reveals a new emotion from Elle—shock, tinged with curiosity.

The male skitters off. I rise, popping the cork, and walk to Elle's side of the table. She watches me with fascination, the green flecks of her eyes, mixed with honey, now sparkling. It makes my skin feel too tight.

I pour the red wine into her glass, marveling at the way it fills as it sloshes. Father used to always call red wine *blood wine*. He used to joke that it was the blood of our enemies, then clink his glass with Mother's. Then, when I got older, with Cora's.

"Why does that make you so happy?" I ask as I return to my seat, my back turned to Elle.

"What?"

"Why did it make you happy when I thanked the waiter?" I clarify as I sit.

She gulps down her wine. "Because it's a nice thing to do."

"But why is it?"

She sets the glass on the table, stroking the base with her thumb. Again, my skin feels too tight. I adjust my jacket, but it doesn't help. "You've never had to be anything less than, because you've always been on top. You have no idea what it's like to be treated like dirt on someone's shoe."

But I know exactly what it feels like to be treated like that. I know the feeling of being kicked when I'm down—of being stomped on when my face is caked with blood. I know the bite of the whip, the kiss of the blade over thick scars, the sinking of a fist into black-and-blue skin, again, and again, and again.

I know exactly what cruelty is like.

I snort as I reach for my glass. "Being nice does no favors for anyone and gets you nowhere. I just don't get the sentiment."

"And do you like that about yourself?" she asks me.

No. I don't like a single thing about myself. "It's gotten me where I am," I answer.

She raises an eyebrow. "You're a murderer on a stolen throne," she says drily.

Now it's my turn to quirk an eyebrow. "Careful, Elle. You're beginning to speak of murder with a nonchalance that resembles...well, me."

"I will never be anything close to the person you are," she hisses.

Funny. She's exactly who I used to be—willing to fight everyone that punished me, willing to spit on anyone who wronged me. But eventually, you stop fighting for yourself. And instead, you become the one that swings the blade.

Oh, but you could, little fawn, I croon down the bond. *Don't forget that monsters are created.*

"Nothing could turn me into the pitiful creature you've turned yourself into," she sneers.

"Do you think I was born this way? A monster?"

She glares at me, her nostrils flaring and cheeks flushing pink.

I was made into what I am, carefully crafted and sculpted by others who wielded hammers and swords. Although I've shoved every experience that's helped make me who I am into a box, sometimes I pull them out. To remember I wasn't always this way. I send a memory down the bond, fighting a shudder as I'm forced to remember it, too.

Small hands grasping for purchase on a concrete wall, fingernails clawing at the door, tiny fists banging on its unyielding surface. Chubby cheeks crusted with dirt and tear tracks, a throat grown raw from screaming. Impenetrable darkness surrounds me and steals my vision. My other senses were always stronger than my brother's. A blessing and a curse.

In this moment, a curse.

The vibrations along the floor as the undead creature lumbers toward me tells me I'm locked in a room with something massive. A bear, likely. Or what used to be a bear. The huff of its breath along the back of my neck sends me skittering to the other side of the locked room, and it lets loose a bellow that curdles my insides.

What would Asmo do? What does Father want?

I curl into a ball, knowing this is the incorrect answer. But I can't think, I can't breathe, I can't I can't I can't.

My heart beats in my chest like a wild thing, pumping blood through my veins as Father's instructions play on a loop in my head.

Give into the fear. Become its master, Marik.

I inhale, exhale, inhale, exhale. I breathe through gritted teeth and force myself to my feet, stumbling to the center of the room and dropping to the floor as my knees give out. If this monster doesn't kill me, my heart might.

I scream before I can change my mind and force myself to lie on the ground. I squeeze my eyes shut as I wait for the bear to come. Tears slip down my cheeks as its footsteps grow closer, as the stench of its rotting teeth grows stronger, as I remember what it feels like for those teeth to sink into me. Over and over again.

Even in the dark, I can see the bear's outline. Its jaw opens and sinks into my chest.

I pull myself from the memory before Elle can see what comes next. Maybe it's a mistake to shield her from it. Maybe I should let her see exactly how a monster is made.

I don't have to look closely to feel what she's feeling. The emotions are so strong they're practically screaming at me down the bond. The icy crawl of horror. The soft glimmer of pity.

"How old were you?" she whispers.

"Does it matter?"

"Yes, Marik. Of course it matters."

"Six." I lean back in my chair, summoning the bottle of wine. I don't bother pouring it into my glass. I swig from the bottle.

Elle shakes her head. The candlelight shines on her glassy eyes.

"You feel sad for me," I say. "Why?"

She studies me. My heartbeat quickens in my chest and my palms tingle. For fuck's sake, Marik.

"Nobody deserves that."

I roll my eyes and take another swig from the bottle. "It made me stronger." I resist the urge to laugh at the irony of this conversation, so similar to one that I had with my dear wife.

"Was it one of the Cursed?" she asks. I nod in confirmation. "Who..."

"Who do you think?" My voice feels too rough, too thick with emotion. The unfamiliarity of it makes me uncomfortable. Her eyes turn soft again and I speak before she can voice the answer. "Anyone can turn into a monster. Even you," I warn. Because I used to be just like her —full of rage—until one day I gave up and became something other. Something worse.

Her smile is full of pity, and I regret the decision to share this memory with her. This isn't what I wanted. I didn't expect her to feel this way toward me. I didn't want pity. It was a warning. And maybe, a small part of me wanted to show her that I wasn't always this way.

"But how? I had never even heard of them until the witches..." Her eyes widen as she puts it together. "How long have you been working with them, Marik? How long has this been going on?"

I shake my head. Too long. There was no stopping this. If I hadn't agreed to it, Cora would have found a way to use Asmo. My brother is too good, too strong, too pure. But that wouldn't have stopped her. She would've done exactly to him what I'm doing to Elle. Bile threatens to rise, but I tamp it down.

"You don't...I'm sorry that happened to you," Elle whispers across the table. "You know, you could use your strengths to do good. You didn't have to..." She trails off, searching for the right words.

"Become the devil?" I ask with a snort. Because that's what I am. To her, at least.

Her brow furrows. "No. That's not what I was going to say. It's a different kind of strength, isn't it? To continue to live, even when the world seems unbearable?"

It's my turn to look at her pointedly. "You tell me, Elle. And then tell me that if I subjected you to the same horrors, would you still be who you are today? Would you turn into a shred of the person you were supposed to be? Or would you be forced to become something entirely different to survive?"

She doesn't have an answer. I float the bottle of wine to her. She snags it from the air and downs the rest, draining it in three gulps. She sits there, staring at the table until she finally whispers, "None of that changes anything you've done."

I lean back in my chair. We sit in silence until the waitstaff returns with the next course. I rise from the table and take the two plates from them. I set mine on the table, then walk to Elle. Her head snaps up as I send a breeze toward her, carrying the scent closer. Her face pales again, then flushes red.

I walk behind her and lean over her, catching a whiff of rosemary-scented shampoo. I set the ivory plate delicately in front of her, the gamey scent of venison wafting toward me. "No, it doesn't change a thing. Dinner is served. Enjoy," I whisper into her ear.

The moment I step away, she hurls the plate at my back. I figured that was coming. I let it slam into me, the plate shattering into pieces as it strikes me.

I stride from the room and don't look back.

Don't forget who I am, little fawn.

CHAPTER 29
MAE

MY PUNCH barely grazes Asmo's cheek, but it's the closest I've come to striking him in the last hour of training. To my irritation, he gracefully dodges the blow. To my satisfaction, he takes the bait and doesn't see my follow-up strike coming. With my knee.

He stumbles back, one hand clutching his groin.

"Fuck," he swears. "Watch it."

I roll my eyes. "Males are so weak. If your dick is so valuable, maybe don't leave it exposed."

His eyes darken. "I could've sworn you loved it when I—"

I strike again. I summon wind and aim it at the ground, my magic brushing against the dirt-packed floor as the wind travels over it. I summon earth—the dirt mixing with the wind—and aim straight for Asmo.

He throws up a barrier to block the blow. My wind dies and the dirt falls to the floor as it hits his shield. I huff a sigh. "What am I supposed to do against that? How do I break a shield?"

He drops his hands, and the shimmer of the barrier disappears. "It depends." He walks closer to me, running his hand through his hair to restore some sort of order to it. "The more a barrier is attacked, the weaker it becomes. You could continue to strike it, or you could fight smart."

I raise an eyebrow. "Meaning?"

"Think about it." He flares his hand once more, and the barrier reappears. "It's not possible to hold up a barrier to protect yourself and continue to attack your opponent," he says, firing a burst of black flames that die when they reach his shield. "It's also not possible to hold a barrier forever. You could wait your opponent out and essentially be in a stalemate."

He pulls me through his barrier. He steps outside and summons his flames, creating a controlled fire on the ground. "Or you could use your environment to see what else you could do to entice them to drop the barrier," he says, coaxing the flames higher. I resist the urge to adjust my clothing as sweat begins to bead along my back. "Then, you could quickly attack when they drop it, or they'll attack you, in which case, you should be prepared to provide a strong counter-attack."

"So, in that instance, what could I have done?"

"Hard to answer, since we're not in battle," he says. I cross my arms and glare at him. He continues, "There are a number of things that would have made me drop my barrier. Don't forget, although the barrier protects against strikes, it does not make the user immune to their environment. You need to get creative. You have to make the environment around them unbearable."

"Like what you did with your fire?"

He nods eagerly. "Yes, exactly. You could surround them with fire or burn things around them to create smoke and make it hard for them to breathe."

My brain swirls with possibilities, with images of me surrounding Marik in a wall of wildfire. I grin. "Again."

He hurls a wall of black flames at me and all I can do is throw a barrier up to avoid being scorched. He's right. There's no way I can attack him while I have my shield up. But there's also no way I can drop it without being burned alive.

So, I do what any sane female would do. I start screaming.

He yanks his magic back to him. His eyes are wide, concern and panic etched across every line in his face. Good. "Wh—"

I hurl my own fire back at him, and it speeds toward him. He throws up his shield and I pour more magic into my fire, the white flames licking at every surface, searching the unyielding shield for some entrance.

They find none. I pull back, letting the fire recede but still surrounding Asmo in a writhing circle. He watches me over the flames, the reflection dancing in his dark eyes. His black locks are now curled at the ends from brushing against his sweat-slicked forehead, and my heart skips a beat.

His words from yesterday have been on repeat in my mind since we left the cabin. *Why do you keep pushing this away? Did he kill what's mine?*

What if this male is who I was destined for? What if he's the one who can heal me? What if I dare to give it a chance? What if I just stopped fighting it and gave in? Would the regret ease? Would the pain of my decisions lessen? Maybe it would help me make sense of it all. Maybe I had to choose Marik to have Asmo.

Maybe my heart had to bleed, a sacrifice for a love worth having.

"Asmo," I whisper, striding toward him, coaxing my flames to part as I step through them. Heat pulses from them, but they don't burn me. He drops the shield and I reach for him. For the male who brought me back from the brink of death. For the male who threw away a life for me. For the male who has held a piece of my heart in his hand since I first met him, just as I've held his.

"Mae," he whispers.

I wrap my arms around his neck and press my body to his. My heart riots in my chest. "Nobody could ever kill what's yours."

It's the truth. Despite all that we've been through, what I feel for him has only strengthened. It feels immortal. In life, and in death, somehow, I know it will be there.

My hands find their way to the bottom of his shirt. I peel it over his head and toss it to the ground. I toss mine next. Asmo's eyes drift from my face, down to the peaks and valleys of my chest, the small buds that harden at his stare.

"What's mine?" he asks, his thumb stroking my cheek.

I nod, my eyes never leaving his. "All of it."

That's all it takes. His teeth, his tongue, his mouth collide with mine. His movements are frenzied, every stroke of his tongue forceful and hungry, sending delicious fire down every vein of my body. One hand cups the back of my head, fingers tangled in my hair. The other holds me against him.

Every inch of him is hard and taut.

His mouth breaks away from mine to place fevered kisses along my jaw, my neck, my collarbone.

"Mine," he growls in my ear.

My blood hums.

I am his. I was from day one. The other princes didn't have a chance. It was always him.

I fumble with the fastening at his pants, desperate to see all of him. Desperate to have him inside of me again.

He bites down on my neck, then soothes the ache with his tongue. I gasp, trying desperately to focus on unbuttoning his pants, but it feels impossible with his mouth and teeth and his hands sliding lower. His erection strains against the band. His chest heaves and sweat from the fire glistens along his chiseled pecs.

Finally, the button bursts free and I reach to pull them down, but his hand clamps around my wrist. "Wh—" I start, but he swirls me around, bringing my backside flush against him. My mouth dries.

"I need to be inside of you," he growls against my neck, voicing the urge that's been throbbing inside of me, too.

He pulls my pants down and rubs my center with his fingers, moaning as he finds the pool of wetness waiting for him. His hardness, now entirely free, nudges against my opening. I gasp, desperate to have him inside me, to be one with him again.

Last time, it felt like I had finally found something I had been searching for—something that I had no idea I needed until it slid into place. It felt like I could breathe, like I could finally see clearly. Despite the way I've pushed him away, I've thought about that moment count-less times. And right now, he's acting like he has, too.

He gently guides himself inside of me. I tilt my head back and gasp at the utter pleasure that shoots through me at his entrance. One hand holds me firmly against him, while the other hand wraps around my throat.

His hips begin to rock back and forth in slow motions, sending my blood into a heated frenzy. Sweat drips down my back, but I don't care. I need more. He groans in my ear, and I grind my hips against him in rhythm, already feeling the crescendo build.

"You feel so perfect." His voice is breathy and low.

I can't form words. The only thing I can think about is him moving inside of me. His pace quickens. He huffs in my ear, his moans growing louder and matching my own.

The wave crests, and every muscle in my body tightens around him, every sense focused on him pounding into me as I ride the wave of my orgasm. I arch my back and let out a gasp as it peaks and peaks and peaks. I dig my nails into his forearm, his hand still around my throat.

"Fuck," he barks as he explodes inside of me.

I can't breathe I'm on fire I'm in heaven I'm in love I'm floating I'm burning burning burning

"Shit," he hisses. He pulls out of me, his seed dripping from me and spilling onto the floor. I ache to have him back inside of me.

I twist. The flames—my flames—are now licking at the ceiling. Asmo summons sand and begins to smother them. I shake my head, post-coital bliss now over as the realization that I could burn this place to the ground replaces it. I wrench my magic back to me and the flames die.

Asmo turns to me, his length still hard and glistening. My mouth dries and my mind turns hazy at the sight of him. "We should talk about this," he says as he tosses me my clothes.

I nod. Yes, we should. We have so much to talk about—what this means, what happens next, what the hell we're doing. First, I need to figure out what hell *I'm* doing. Every instinct in my body is screaming at me to just be with him, but that one part of my brain is holding me back.

We get dressed and head back toward the residential wing. My mind races, my heart and my brain playing tug-of-war again.

"Your Highness!" someone calls behind me. I turn. Rain is racing down the hallway, her black, wavy hair flowing behind her as she runs.

She looks like a different version of herself now, such a contrast to the shell of herself we pulled from the dungeon. Her eyes are wide, frantic.

"What's wrong?" I ask.

She comes to a stop before us, and her breathing is labored from the exertion. "The witches are attacking the citizens in the square."

Horror drags its nails down my spine. How is Koa allowing this to happen?

"Where is everyone else?" I ask.

"Etta is preparing a group to portal there and fight. Having you both there would be helpful," she says, then adds, "Please."

"Take us there," Asmo demands.

She leads us to the main training room, where a dozen hybrids and two towering Fae males are strapping all manners of weapons to their person: daggers, swords, and small axes. One female straps a bow and arrow to her back.

Etta is locked in conversation with a Fae male who looks like he might eat me for breakfast. She turns as the door thuds shut behind us. "Oh, great, Rain found you. Suit up," she says, tossing me a dagger. I slow its path with my wind and snatch it from the air.

"What do you know?" Asmo asks Etta as he stalks toward the wall of weapons.

"One of our scouts returned from a patrol early. Apparently, a group of citizens thought it would be a good idea to chain themselves to the gallows in protest of the executions. The witches caught wind of it and decided to execute them there. Citizens and shopkeepers decided to fight back this time. It's a bloodbath," she answers, helping a yellow-eyed female secure a massive sword to her back.

Asmo grabs his belt of daggers and secures them around his waist. "How many witches?"

"Ten. Black-leather," the yellow-eyed female answers. "Their pets are also on the loose."

Great.

"Has anyone killed a witch before?" I ask as I glance skeptically around the room.

"That's why we need you two," Etta says. "You have to burn them. Fire is the only thing I know that works. Some of our hybrids can summon fire, but not with the range or intensity that I've seen you two demonstrate."

My heart drops into my stomach as I process what she says. Asmo and I are going into a real battle. Because we are the only ones capable of defeating the witches. Ten of them.

Asmo must catch the expression on my face, because he grabs my hand and squeezes it once before letting it go. He stands tall and clears his throat, crossing his hands behind his back as he lifts his chin and puffs his chest out.

A leader.

I mimic him, trying to summon the kind of confidence he emanates. He's had a lifetime of building it. I've had months.

"Listen up," Asmo booms. "There are black-leather witches and the Cursed. Mae and I will keep our eyes and ears open, ready to assist you in any way we can. The best way to handle this will be if you all distract the witches long enough for us to sneak up behind them and torch them alive. But I'm open to any other ideas."

He glances around the ragtag group of fighters, waiting for someone to offer a better idea. Nobody does.

"Anything to add, High Queen?" He glances at me and my heart swells.

I stifle my smile and force myself to look at every single male and female in front of me. I etch their faces into my memory. I could be signing their death warrants. "I'm not sure what kinds of creatures will be there, but I have fought—and killed—many cambions. Cut their head off, burn their bodies, or chop them into pieces. The Cursed are scary, but they can be killed. Kill the witches and it kills the creatures they control. We can do this. We have to do this. We are the only hope for these people. Be brave and be strong."

They nod in unison.

"Can any of you funnel?" Asmo asks the group. Several raise their hands. "Good. Take two or three hybrids with you and funnel into separate locations, then we'll attack from a different side. I'll leave you to figure out your funnel destinations. We leave in five minutes."

Etta stands in the corner of the room watching us. She wears a simple white linen shirt and leather pants, but no weapons.

"Aren't you coming with?" I ask as the group disbands to strap even more weaponry to their bodies.

"I can't, but Amaris will be joining in a moment."

"Why can't you?" I press. If I'm going, why can't she?

She shakes her head once, a look of shame written across her face. "I don't have powers anymore. They're gone."

I cringe, both at the thought of losing my magic and for pressing her. "I'm sorry," I whisper. My magic is something that feels like another, living extension of me, of my soul. To have it ripped away would be like losing a part of me.

Etta crosses her arms and looks back up at me, her gaze now hardened. "Don't be. Just make them pay."

I nod, but what I really want to say is, *I have no clue what I'm doing.*

Amaris strides in, a look of determination on her face. If anyone knows what they're doing when it comes to fighting, it's her. She's in her usual uniform—black leather pants, black leather vest, dagger hilts from every pocket. Her posture is strong, and her stride is steady, measured. She acknowledges me with a brief bow, then heads to the two Fae males in the corner.

Asmo carves a mark into his stomach, but it's different from the usual one. It's two slashes, a third one cutting between them. "What is that?" I ask.

"Keeps me clothed after I shift. Don't want to be running around naked fighting witches, do I?" He smiles, but he seems nervous.

This is just another reminder of how much he knows about dark magic. How much he's hiding from me. He carves a second sigil next to it, the oval and the X, then hands me the knife.

"Let's go," Asmo barks after I carve my sigil.

We walk toward the group of Lower House members willing to fight and defend the citizens of a kingdom that tossed them to the side.

Let's make them pay. Let's make them *all* pay.

CHAPTER 30
MAE

Asmo funnels us into a dank alleyway. The sound of screams and the metallic scent of blood hang in the air. I turn, adrenaline and the burn of my magic beginning to take hold, but Asmo grabs my forearm.

"Wait," he says, turning me to face him. "How are you feeling?"

Despite the adrenaline, my pulse races and my palms are already slick with sweat. "Nervous," I admit.

"Come on," he scoffs. "You've taken on an army of cambions before and you fought off the First Witch."

But his words only remind me of my failures. "The army of cambions nearly killed Elle, and Cora nearly killed me," I grumble.

"We handled those witches at Bouldercrest without a problem," he says. *Yeah, when that Cursed wolf sunk its teeth into my leg?* Asmo pulls me into his arms. "You're powerful and you're smart. We can do this," he says, brushing my lower lip with his thumb.

We can do this, not just me. I don't have to do this by myself. I have my...whatever Asmo is to me to help me. Boyfriend feels too trivial. We've been through too much together. Partner, maybe. Because that's what he feels like—he's been with me through everything and stood beside me through it all. I press my lips to his, wishing I could melt into him.

"You're their queen, Mae," he whispers against my lips. "Show them."

He's right. I am the rightful High Queen. I am of Wrena's line. I have a well of power in me that continues to grow, and I grow stronger every day.

Show them.

My boot heels strike the cobbled streets as we fly toward the square. Rage courses through me, and my magic churns as the screams grow louder and the scent of blood grows stronger.

But it stutters when I come to a stop at the end of the alleyway.

Three bodies hang from the gallows, their feet floating as they gently sway from nooses. Below them, three more lay face down in still pools of blood, arms reaching out, as if they were slain while trying to save those above from their fate.

They swing in a rhythm known only to them. I'd like to think it's to the tune of a beloved song, or maybe the ghost of an "I love you" to their partner as they thought of their goodbyes.

Innocent people executed—*my* people executed. People with families, with dreams, with jobs, and favorite foods and colors and laughs and dog-eared books. For what? Having an opinion that doesn't match Marik's?

A hand grazes my shoulder. "I'll cut them down," Asmo says. "Use your wind to slow their fall."

He stands beneath the first body—a female with tight black curls that tumble to her waist. With a slash of his shadow sword, she falls. The magic that once felt so difficult to summon bursts through me and slows her landing. Asmo catches her with ease and lays her down gently.

When all three are down, I walk to those lying in pools of their own blood. The blood has turned tacky and sticks to the male as I flip him. He looks like he's sleeping, his long eyelashes resting against lifeless cheeks. I turn the other two over and commit their features to memory. I will not forget.

I step to the gallows and summon fire, resting my hand on its wooden platform. The blaze takes hold, and my flames lick and bite and consume the structure within moments. Heat radiates from the writhing mass of smoke, and I move away.

From the alleyway, the gallows appeared huge, like some monster that might scoop me in its meaty fist and hang me with the crook of its finger. But up close, it feels more like a stray dog that can be scared away. Like it was just a terrifying shadow that's actually nothing at all. Something that can be beaten. Destroyed.

Just like Marik and Cora.

"Princess," Asmo says, a warning and a reminder.

"I know." If we don't get moving, more people will die.

My throat burns as I scan their features once more—a crooked nose, high cheekbones, a birthmark in the shape of a leaf—before turning to the square.

It's chaos. Cambions and the Cursed race through the streets while creatures resembling massive bats fly through the sky. Elemental, Fae, and streaks of dark magic zing through the air, finding purchase against their victims or striking the buildings around us. Glass shatters, wood splinters, and blood spills.

Citizens stand their ground against witches and cambions, clutching anything that can be used as a weapon—broken chair legs, wooden stakes, frying pans.

Across the square, Lower House members dressed in fighting leathers spill through another alleyway, weapons and hands raised. Amaris leads them. She wastes no time, slashing the back of a cambion's neck with her sword.

I narrowly avoid the ball of black magic that flies toward me. It hits the ground with a hiss, charring it upon its contact. A raven-haired witch stares at me from the roof of a bakery, her telltale black aura writhing around her.

I grin at her in invitation.

She leaps from the roof, landing on her feet with an otherworldly grace, and immediately begins her attack. I barely get my shield up, but every blow slowly eats away at it. She doesn't let up, a grin splitting her face as each one lands. Asmo is right—I can't attack her from inside my shield.

She fires another shot. I drop the shield and duck, summoning wind and fire, sending it blazing toward her. She leaps out of its path with a giggle, then fires at me again. I dodge it. I funnel more magic into the path of wildfire, but it's too slow to catch her.

She turns back to me, hand raised to attack again. But she doesn't get the chance.

Asmo slams his hands over her ears and sets her ablaze. Her shriek dies as her body slumps against him.

One witch down.

Across the square, two Lower House hybrids fight another witch. Although they're hurling fire at her, she dodges each blow with effortless speed, while somehow still hurling strikes at them. Her back is turned to us. Good news for us, bad news for her.

"Want the honors this time?" Asmo asks me, a smirk on his face.

I don't bother responding. I sprint toward the witch and leap, my palms already on fire. I wrap my hands around her and force my flames down her throat. Her body collapses, and I tumble with her.

Two witches down. Eight to go.

The hybrids offer me a quick thanks, then speed off in search of another target. A few feet away, three Panthera citizens face off against a witch, her all-black leathers shielding her from everything they fire at her. I watch in horror as she hurls a writhing ball of black magic at the group and finds her mark, catching a female hybrid in the gut. Her body thuds as it hits the ground.

Asmo leaps into the air and shifts into his serpent form. He races to the witch and rips her head from her body. I blink. Between the shadow sword and whatever that was, just how powerful is Asmo? Someone screams for help, and it snaps me out of my thoughts. I rush to the fallen female, who now lays still. I close her eyes and commit her face to memory.

"Watch out!" someone shrieks. Two cambions race toward me. These fucking things.

I summon water and douse them, then summon an icy wind to freeze them. I stab both of them where their eyes should be, and they explode into icy shards.

A witch jumps from a nearby roof and lands directly on Asmo's serpentine back. He thrashes, but it's no use. Her sharp nails are embedded into his scales. If she summons her magic...

Fuck, fuck, fuck.

The square blurs past me and I jump onto Asmo's back, then pounce on the witch's. She wrenches herself from Asmo's scales and reaches back for me, razor-sharp nails grazing my cheek. I hiss as pain erupts and the warmth of blood spreads. Asmo writhes beneath me, and the witch and I go flying.

My head smacks onto the street with a burst of pain. I blink furiously, hot blood pouring down my face. The witch reaches for me, and I brace for the feeling of her nails raking across my skin again. But it doesn't come. A sword slashes through her neck, and her head goes flying. A blond Fae male stands behind her, holding an enormous sword, now covered in the witch's blood. His golden hair reminds me of August, but his eyes are pits of black. He offers me a bloodstained hand and helps me to my feet.

Four witches down.

"You okay?" he asks.

I nod. "Thanks."

"Don't mention it," he says before taking off and disappearing into the crowd.

Nearby, a Lower House hybrid is in a losing battle against another witch, barely able to fend off the her blows as she advances upon him. Asmo slithers toward them, unlocking his massive jaw and sinking his teeth into the witch's side. She shrieks and tries to turn, to escape, but she can't.

Her shriek turns into a full-blown scream when she sees me running toward them. Music to my ears. My flames already burn on my palms. I shove them down her throat, suffocating her and burning her from the inside out. She stops squirming, and I pull back my fire before it reaches Asmo. It wouldn't be very helpful if I set him on fire before we had a chance to figure out what's between us. He shifts back into his human form. The witch tumbles to the ground as his fangs disappear.

His hands fly to cup my face. "Shit," he curses as he surveys the cut on my cheek.

"I'm fine," I say, shaking his hands off me, but the movement makes my cheek throb. "Only five more," I say.

"You've been keeping count, princess?" he asks with a smirk, but he watches me carefully.

A massive black bat shrieks through the air, swooping down with large, membranous wings. Asmo and I duck, narrowly avoiding his reaching claws. If I were in my actual body, he would have struck my antlers.

"What the fuck are those things?" I hiss as I watch it circle the sky.

"Drabar," Asmo says grimly.

It swoops from the sky and hovers over two witches standing on a nearby roof, who both fire at citizens on the ground.

"Cowards," I mutter as I scan the scene. "They won't even come down and fight."

"Then let's go to them," Asmo says with a wicked grin.

My eyes catch on a group of cambions surrounding three Lower House members. They stand with their backs against each other as they try to fight the cambions off, but there are too many. They're going to be overwhelmed in a matter of seconds.

"Meet you there," I say, leaving him and rushing toward the crowd of devil children, daggers drawn.

I slash the necks of two cambions simultaneously, then stab two more. Some of the hollow-eyed freaks turn to me, giving the Lower House hybrids the perfect opportunity to strike with their backs turned. More cambions fall to the ground. I summon fire and torch them, risking no chances of them popping back up.

One of them leaps up and sinks its sharp teeth around a female hybrid's exposed arm. She screams and tries to pull it from her arm, but the cambion is latched onto her.

A flash of red hair flits in my mind, but it's not Elle being bitten this time. I shake the memory away and rush to the hybrid. The cambion dies with a burst of ice and the kiss of my dagger.

It crumbles away from her. "Thanks," she says, exhaustion lining her voice. She turns away from me and strikes another cambion, sword embedding in its neck.

I scan the scene. Asmo is locked in battle with the two witches on the roof, but I don't see the remaining witches.

Bodies litter the ground, witches, cambions, drabar, Cursed, and

Panthera citizens. Too many lay lifeless in the town square. I spot two fallen bodies in the familiar black leathers of the Lower House hybrids, both of them laying facedown, crimson blood pooling around them.

"Help!" someone—a child—screams. "Please!"

I don't even think about it. The scream comes from an alley. I rush toward it, jumping over piles of trash and puddles of still water and blood. I follow the sounds of sobbing down the narrow back alley. Every movement jars the wound on my cheek. I'm going to need a healer.

"Mama," the voice whimpers just ahead. My heart squeezes. Was their mother one of the many laying dead in the square?

The crying grows louder, then fades slightly as I run past a bakery. I backtrack, stopping in front of its ivory front door, the fancy scrawl of the bakery name painted in bright pink in the center. The cries are coming from inside. I peer through the bay window. There are scattered chairs and half-eaten croissants, but no crying child.

I step inside, pulling my daggers out just in case. I pass small bistro tables covered in white linens, plates of food left in the chaos. In the back hallway, boxes are filled with imported fruits and unopened bags of flour. A soft glow comes from another room at the end of the hall.

"Shh, it's okay, Mama," the voice whispers as it chokes back tears.

The child sits on the ground in the empty, windowless room. A little girl. A lit candle sits on the floor beside her, illuminating filthy clothing, covered in crimson and black blood. Her hair is dark and stringy, hanging limply down her back. She looks down at her hands as they quiver in her lap.

"Hey," I whisper, but her head remains angled downward, toward her shaking hands in her lap. "Hey," I repeat. "Are you okay?"

I take a step forward. "Do you nee—" The girl's head snaps up. The hair on the back of my neck stands. I drop my daggers and scream for my magic, but I'm too late.

Cold hands clamp around my arms, and my magic stutters at the touch.

The girl stares up at me with dark eyes and a cruel smile, then rises to her feet. Her dark aura writhes around her as she shifts.

Into a witch.

"Got you," she whispers.

CHAPTER 31
MAE

MY HEAD BEATS LIKE A DRUM, its pounding incessant and fierce. I keep my eyes closed as I try to gather my bearings. I'm lying on my side. My cheek rubs against something gritty, and pain blooms at the movement. I crack my eyes open, but all I see is gray stone, the scattering of dirt and pebbles.

And a small puddle of dried blood.

I reach to push myself up, but my wrists are bound by something cold and unyielding. My hands are shoved against what feels like a stone wall. Maybe I can blast a hole through the wall behind me. I summon fire, but nothing comes. I dig deeper, but I know it's gone. Something's muting my magic.

I take a deep breath, forcing myself not to panic. Thankfully, my feet are unbound. A very, very small victory. I tilt my head to look down. Dirt underneath my cheek punishes the movement and I grit my teeth as another wave of pain radiates through my face.

Good news—my extremities seem to be intact. Another victory.

But my hope dissipates when I see more dried blood on my stomach, then the white-blonde hair that falls over my shoulder. The sigil was destroyed.

I've been captured. And they know who I really am.

Motherfuck.

Every atom in my body, every nerve that runs beneath my skin, flares. Normally, this would be the part where I summon some element that would help get me out of this Motherforsaken place. But it's all muted, and my chest is rising and falling too fast and now it's constricting and I feel like I can't draw a breath and—

Stop it. You are not going to die here. This is not the end.

In. Out. In. Out.

I blink back tears and force myself into a sitting position. I gasp as pain shoots through my stomach, the skin pulling as I move. Fresh blood begins to seep through my already blood-soaked shirt.

Whatever is muting my magic must be preventing my blood from healing my wound. Or wounds—the gash on my cheek pulses, the cold air biting it now that my face is off the ground.

I grit my teeth and get my feet underneath me, then push into a standing position. My wound throbs and I force deep breaths as my stomach churns—in through my nose, out through my mouth.

The room is covered in stone. A small window, blocked by iron bars, looks out over the mountains disturbingly high in the air. Large, pointed rocks jut up from the blanket of snow in a threatening collection of jagged teeth.

Another, smaller window is affixed to the door. I shuffle to it, every movement jostling the wound in my stomach. Hot blood trickles along the flat plane of my belly. I lean against the window, finding several guards stationed in the hall outside, their backs turned to me.

Okay, so I'm not in just any room. I'm in a cell. High up in what I'm assuming is the Banfolk Mountains.

I leave the windowed door and slide down the stone wall. My vision blurs. I close my eyes and let salty tears fall. They mix with the gash on my cheek, each sting reminding me that I'm alive. That I'm here. That there is still so much to fight for.

Cally. Holly. Ivan. Etta.

My kingdom.

Asmo.

I repeat the names, my wounds throbbing and my cheek burning, until the light from the window disappears and the cell grows dark.

Cally. Holly. Ivan. Etta.

My kingdom.

I cry myself to sleep, Asmo's name on my lips.

A *pregnant woman leaned over a dusty wooden dining table, hands gripping the sides with such force that her knuckles flashed white.*

"This is all I could find," another woman said, entering the room with two dingy towels in her hands. "Careful, or you'll break the table."

"Shut up, Willa," the pregnant woman hissed through gritted teeth.

The other woman—Willa—chuckled, brushing black, wavy hair behind pointed Fae ears. "Do you want to try laying down?"

The pregnant woman took a deep breath, knuckles still white as bone. "No, the bed is filthy."

"We should have mailed ahead. 'Dearest Unknowing Citizen of the Deer Court, please ensure you have fresh towels prepared for Her Royal Fae Princess,'" Willa said in a haughty tone, coaxing a ghost of a smile from the other woman. "Orla, you really should lie down. The contractions are coming too close together. What if you pop and the baby goes flying?"

"Babies," Orla corrected her. "The oracle said two girls."

"Whatever she said. You're going to kill them if they fly out of you and land straight on the floor."

BANG!

Orla spun toward the sound. "What was that? Is it her?" she managed to ask before she bit down on a groan, a contraction working its way through her.

Willa peered out the window. "No, but we have to get these babies out," she whispered.

Orla, eyes shut tight as the pain of the contraction ebbed, nodded tightly.

Willa led her into the abandoned home's only bedroom. She snatched the dusty quilt from the bed and flipped it over, laying it on the ground. She helped Orla settle onto the blanket and then sat between her and the wall, supporting Orla's back.

"I can't believe we didn't make it to Silas before my water broke," Orla muttered.

Willa rubbed her sister's arms. "I know. At least Levana gave us enough warning to get you out."

"Could have given us a little more time," Orla snorted with a glance toward her belly. "You have to keep them from her, okay?" Sweat was beginning to line her forehead, her white hair clinging to her clammy skin. "Promise me," she begged.

"I will," Willa whispered. "I promise."

"I mean it. You heard what the oracle predicted," Orla said. "You can't let Cora—" She gasped in pain, belly rolling with the contraction.

Willa reached for her sister's hand and grasped it. "I know. It's my fault we're in this mess. I'll protect them with my life. I mean it."

A streak of black darted past the window. Willa glanced at the window nervously. "Can you push?"

Orla whirled her hand and one of the pillows flew from the bed. She caught it mid-air, took a deep breath, gritted her teeth, and pushed. She shoved her face into the pillow, muting the sounds of her groans. Her face turned pink with strain, and, after a moment, she collapsed against her sister.

"Good, good," Willa soothed. "I can sense it. They're almost here. Hang in there."

Orla sat back up and gritted her teeth once more. Spittle flew from her mouth, veins popping along her neck as she pushed.

And just like that, out came one rosy, pink baby girl, tiny hands balled into fists, ready to fight the world. A mass of fire-red hair covered her tiny head, two pedicles dotting the top. She opened her mouth and let loose a scream.

Willa extricated herself from behind Orla and rushed to the baby, scooping her up in her arms. She grabbed the blade from her satchel and cut the umbilical cord. The baby whined in her arms, her face red and angry.

"Orla!" Willa exclaimed. "Look at her!" She held the baby to her sister, who sagged against the wall.

Orla took her daughter in her arms, a warmth spreading through her like a summer's day. "Ellysia," she whispered.

A soft smile stole across Willa's face. "That's perfect, Orla. For the light. Just like the oracle said."

Orla's face fell, and she handed her daughter back to her sister. "Take her."

"What? Don't you want to hold her?" Willa asked, face wrinkled in something like pity, or sadness. Or both.

Another contraction began to roll through her. Orla shook her head. "No," she moaned. "Get her out of here. Take her somewhere safe."

Willa paused. "Wh—no. You still have one more. That wasn't the plan."

"Go, Willa," Orla commanded. "Cora is close. If you can't save both, at least save one."

Willa's face contorted in protest. "I can't leave you here like this."

Orla snarled, her teeth flashing. "You made me a promise. You put us in this position when you summoned Cora. Go. Now."

Willa's face fell, but she grabbed a discarded blanket and wrapped the baby in it, swaddling her tiny body tightly. She tucked her to her chest and fled the abandoned house.

After waves of contractions, nearly cracking a tooth from gnashing her teeth together, and straining every muscle in her body to push, the second baby finally came. Orla leaned over and scooped her up, desperate to have her in her arms. This one, also born with two pedicles, had hair as white as snow, just like her mother.

"Maerellis," she whispered. "Another source of light to shine upon the kingdom."

Orla cradled her in her arms, eyes twinkling as she surveyed every inch of her daughter—her tiny nose, her delicate pointed ears, her scrunched fingers and toes. A tear spilled from her eye, landing on her daughter's forehead with a tiny plunk.

The front door opened with a creak. Orla set the baby between her and the wall, shifting her body to defend her daughter's life with her own. She snatched the knife from the floor and readied herself. The bedroom door opened, but it was only Willa.

She held her hands up. Empty.

Ellysia was gone.

"She's safe," Willa whispered. "I found a family for her."

Orla had dozens of questions, but she swallowed them. None of them mattered.

The baby with hair white as snow cooed softly behind Orla, and Willa's eyes lit up at the sound.

Orla reached behind her and picked her daughter back up. "Her name is Maerellis. You have to take her and go. Now," she plead, eyes filling with tears.

A bang came from the front room. The sound of the front door being broken down, splintered into pieces.

The color drained from Orla's face and she severed the umbilical cord in one motion. She held her daughter out to Willa with trembling arms, and Willa tucked the baby against her chest. Orla tried to get up but stumbled and fell back to the floor. She pointed to the window in the bedroom in silent plea and Willa sprinted toward it.

But it was too late.

Living shadows had already begun slipping through the crack under the door, twisting and forming into Cora's monsters. They stared at the child in Willa's arms with hunger and delight. Willa clutched her to her chest, eyes wild as she stared them down.

Orla bared her teeth in challenge. But cold sweat dampened her brow and her body sagged, every part of her spent. She rose to her feet, legs shaky but strong enough. She fired at the monsters made from shadow, but it went wide as she lost her footing. She collapsed to the ground again. She was too weak.

The bedroom door creaked open. She knew it was a death sentence.

Cora filled the door frame, a cruel grin on her face. She held her hand out to Willa. "Give me the child."

Orla managed to rise again, blood trailing down her legs. She shielded her sister and her daughter with her body. An animalistic sound came from her throat. A growl. A battle cry. A final stand. "Never."

"Leave, Cora," Willa said from behind her. "There is no place for you in this kingdom."

Cora smirked. "How pitiful that you think only of your kingdom."

Orla stared back at her, hands splayed, blood pooling at her feet.

"Last chance. Give me the child," Cora demanded. The black shadows multiplied, turning into a pack of wolves as they circled the Fae princesses.

"Silas will never let you get away with this," Orla spat.

Cora chuckled. "He'll die, too." Her wrist twitched and the wolves attacked, shadowed teeth sinking into Orla's calves. She went down with a shriek and fired a burst of magic at Cora. But it missed her entirely, colliding with the ceiling instead. Chunks of wood fell, but Cora easily sidestepped it. Cora attacked, shooting black lightning right into Orla's chest. She fell, hitting the ground with a sickening thump. She didn't rise again.

"Too easy," Cora mumbled. She stretched her hand toward Willa and the baby, fingers splayed. They both went flying toward her. Cora snatched the baby from Willa's arms, then whispered something in Willa's ears. Willa slumped against her, but her chest still rose.

She dropped Willa to the ground and walked from the bedroom, where a small group of witches in black stood staring at her, cold smiles affixed to their faces.

Cora held the baby up. "It's time," she said with a gleeful grin. "Grab the princess and let's go."

She looked down at the baby. "Hello, Maerellis. I think I'll call you Mae."

B elow me, a bed of moss. Above me, a blazing sun. Beside me, a babbling creek.

Songbirds tweet, gentle melodies spurring me from the images of my aunt unconscious on the ground, my mother sprawled dead next to her, and my sister gone.

I push myself into a sitting position. My hands are unbound. I call upon my magic, but it still doesn't come. Something moves in my peripheral.

It's a younger version of me.

I look to be about six years old. Sunflower-yellow butterflies rest on my antlers. Light pink flowers adorn the two braids that spill over my shoulders. The sun filters through the canopy of trees, shining upon my pale skin in a soft glow.

Younger me walks closer, footsteps barely making a sound as they step gracefully over fallen branches. She stops a few feet away, gaze fixed on me. Eyes that are not mine.

My eyes are a warm amber, but this girl's eyes are ocean-blue and... moving. Just like the waves reflected in the Mother's eyes from the first time I dreamed of Her.

The girl stares at me, then begins to speak in a voice that is also not mine.

"Once upon a time," she begins in a high-pitched, sing-song voice, "the land was wild with the forest. Luscious greenery covered rolling hills and creatures roamed free. Flowers hung from the trees and bees danced in the air. Creeks cut through forests and wildflowers bloomed along their banks."

She smiles as she looks around the forest, at the moss and the bees now buzzing through the air. Bees that weren't here before. A rabbit hops toward me, pink nose scrunching.

The girl waves her hands. The rabbit skitters off and the bees fall to the ground, black bodies hitting the moss like pebbles. Her voice turns grave and deep. "Now, the rabbits hide. The birds are silent. And the moss is soaked with blood."

Blood seeps from the moss, between my fingers, and into my clothing. I try to squirm, desperate to get up, but I can no longer move.

"The creeks continue throughout the forest, but they are no longer the source of life they once were. They are too contaminated by the blood of the beings that they used to quench. Flowers wilt at the magic that swirls in the air, its very essence evil and damning. Even the sun has abandoned this world, as if it is too scared to shine its piercing rays into air now rife with the poison of dark magic."

Her ocean eyes don't leave mine as the sunlight fades, the once-cheery forest now dark and foreboding. The scent of blood coats the air, thick and metallic, and a cackle sounds through the night.

"Witches run rampant through the forest," she continues, her voice surrounding me now, "leaving a trail of blood in their wake. The Mother sends clouds of her tears, hoping to heal Her dying child. But there is so much damage, even for Her. She knew this was coming. She did everything She could to stop it. But it was not enough. She came so close to stopping it in the beginning. But in the end, even She couldn't rid the world of the dark magic that plagued her creations. So instead, She did everything else in Her power to stop them—to stop Her sister."

The forest is still dark, but the girl's hair, white as snow, glows in the dark. Her braids are now untangled, and her hair begins to stir. But there is no wind.

"When Her sister descended from the heavens to destroy the world that the Mother had created, She created the Fae. But the Fae were too weak, too set in their ways, too concerned with themselves to stop the evil that was spreading. So, the Mother drew elements from each of Her five favorite creations—the deer, for their beauty and innocence."

A stag dashes through the forest, hooves landing in puddles of blood, before disappearing through the tall line of trees.

"The bears," the girl continues, "for their fierce loyalty and bravery."

A hot huff of breath on my neck sends a shiver down my spine. A grizzly bear lumbers past me, its paws the size of my head.

"The wolves, for their speed and grace." A black wolf stalks from the trees, watching me with eyes as white as the moon. It joins the bear, then darts back into the woods. The bear bellows and chases after it, the ground shaking with the impact.

"The wildcats, for their stealth and strength." A black panther slinks between two trees, gaze locked on something over my shoulder.

"And the snakes, for their curiosity and tenacity." Behind me, a hiss grows closer, and the hair on the back of my neck raises. A snake as thick as my thigh slithers closer. I try to move away, but I'm still frozen in place.

"She spun their magic with the Fae and created the first woodland-Fae hybrids. She gifted them the strength of elemental magic."

With a snap of her fingers, the snake and the panther disappear. As if they were never there.

"Even then, it wasn't enough. She plucked three pieces of Herself: one from Her heart, one from Her mind, and one from Her soul. With each piece, she created three more hybrids. But three was still not enough, so She created a final hybrid, one that had elements of all three pieces of Herself. Because the day cannot exist without the night, the Mother crafted the females after the light, and the males after the dark."

She flares her hands and gazes toward the sky. Four people float near the treetops, hands grasped as they spin slowly. The moonlight casts an eerie glow on the group, yet none of their features are identifiable. Their hair floats around them, unbound and drifting through the air as if suspended in water.

"Two sisters and two brothers were created, each pair destined to cross paths with the other. Two pairs of mates to serve as the perfect balance to each other and save Her creation. Together, they would be strong enough to defeat the evil that was consuming the world She so lovingly created."

The girl walks toward me, stepping into the light of the moon. The four above jerk their heads back into silent screams, and a river of blood now flows past me. I want to vomit, I want to crawl away, but the girl's gaze holds me still. Her eyes reflect a thunderstorm, dark gray clouds writhing in her irises, her pupils white and slashing through the storm clouds like bolts of lightning.

"But even that failed. And now, the Mother is too weak to defeat Her sister. And soon, the oceans will fill with Her blood."

CHAPTER 32
ELLE

WHEN I WAS LITTLE, my mom used to whisper stories of brave males and females with the kind of strength that can only be gifted by the Mother. Powerful hybrids and High Fae, only made possible by the blessings provided to them by some deity.

My parents were devout believers in the Mother, never missing a single service or religious holiday. In Redwick, religious meetings were held daily, once at first light and again at second light. Without fail, my parents would drag me to every single one.

"Listen up, Elle," my mom would always whisper in my ear. She had an uncanny ability to tell when I wasn't paying attention. My dad, on the other hand, would squeeze me tight, as if he knew I hated every second we were there.

Every night, my mom would revisit the lessons taught by the priest, whispering them to me in the dark as her warm, calloused hands rubbed my back until my eyes closed and my mind drifted far away from the stories of the Mother. She used to credit her blessings to the Mother— our plentiful food, the safety of our home, our health and wellness. As if my dad didn't spend every waking moment working for those privileges, as if the Mother had something to do with his hard work and provisions.

My mom always used to credit Her with me. And so, naturally, I spat on the Mother. I was nobody's possession and certainly nothing to be gifted. As I got older, I turned away from my parents and the religion that I was raised to believe in.

But now, I cry on bloodied knees to Her, praying, begging, screaming for Her to help me. For Her to do something. I spend hours apologizing and repenting for my sins. I spend nights clenching sheets and crying for Her to listen. She is the only thing I have left to cling to.

And She has abandoned me.

CHAPTER 33
MARIK

THE TASTE of Cora coats my tongue, nearly as vile as the taste of my shame as I lay beside her. She's sprawled on the bed, her midnight hair wild on the crisp white linen sheets. The scent of sex permeates the air, and I long to shut off my senses.

We lay in silence as her breathing calms. I fight to control my own as my mind wars with itself, just like it does every time.

This is what you agreed to.

This is what must be done.

This was the price you knew you'd pay.

A knock raps on the door to the bedroom. I ignore it, but it comes again. "Your Highness," someone says on the other side. "It's urgent."

I swing my legs over the side of the bed and throw a robe on before padding to the door. I crack it, careful to shield Cora's nude form from our visitor.

"Your Highness, sir," the messenger says as he bows his head. "My apologies, but the Panthera Court has arrived with urgent news. They request an audience immediately."

Anger flares at the surprise visit. I stoke it. It's so much easier than the abyss that beckons me every time I lay with Cora.

"What do they want?" I ask.

"I'm not sure, Your Highness. All they said was that it's urgent. They're waiting in the throne room. Would you like me to tell them you're..." He glances over my shoulder. "Indisposed?"

I summon the writhing shadows that I rarely use and create the illusion of my own black aura. I hate using them, if I'm being honest. They remind me too much of the miseries that lurk in the depths of my mind. The male takes an involuntary step backward, and a corner of my mouth ticks upward in satisfaction.

"I'll be down in a moment," I say in dismissal, then shut the door behind me. Cora is up, already pulling a black gown over her slender frame. She looks over her shoulder and beckons me to help with the buttons that line the back.

I button each one, her knobby spine slowly disappearing with each movement. I don't bother to ask if she heard what the messenger said. She hears everything. She is everywhere.

There is no escaping her.

I throw on my black trousers and the white linen shirt that's now rumpled. A combination of fire and water is all I need to fix them, and I hover my hand over the wrinkles to smooth them out.

Cora watches me with a satisfied smirk. She steps closer, runs her long fingers through my black locks.

"So handsome," she mutters before turning and walking out the door.

I shut my feelings away, forcing them into the room in my head where I send them to die.

Cora is already halfway down the hallway by the time I exit, but my long legs have me by her side in moments.

"Should we bring Elle with us?" I ask.

"Why?" she asks disdainfully.

"Why wouldn't the High Queen be at this meeting?"

The truth is, it's been about a week since I last saw her at our disaster of a dinner. Cora has kept me busy with her pets and useless tasks that have prevented me from visiting her. Even so, I've been keenly aware of Elle's movements because of the necklace. She's been a good girl—no murder attempts on the guards, no screaming at the walls, no attempts to drown herself.

But her silence has been too loud, and every day that passes without seeing her makes my skin crawl in an unfamiliar way. An unpleasant way.

I can't stand it. I need to see her.

"But they already know that's not Mae," Cora says.

"Do appearances no longer matter?"

She gives me a long look, but mutters, "Fine."

We walk in silence to Elle's wing. Two guards are stationed outside, one on each side of the double doors, bowing as we approach. I knock on the door, and as usual, Elle doesn't answer.

"Why do you bother knocking?" Cora sneers.

Because I want her to choose to open it.

I ignore the question and open the doors. The answering stench is foul, like unwashed body odor and stale food.

Cora gasps. "What is that smell?"

"Elle?" I call, but only silence greets me.

I turn toward the guards. "When's the last time anyone checked on her?"

The one closest to me grimaces. "It's been several days, Your Highness."

An image of the guard's head on a stick flits through my mind. "*Days?* You're supposed to be checking on her multiple times a day, you fucking morons," I snarl at them.

"She's a prisoner," the guard says with a shrug.

My pathetic attempt at self-control vanishes. I turn to him, black flames already in my palm. His face pales, the whites of his eyes glistening. To his credit, he doesn't back away. I close the gap between us and hold my flames to his face. Sweat begins to bead on his upper lip.

"Do you consider yourself above my rule?" I whisper.

"N-no, Your Highness," he stammers, gaze fixed on my flames as they purr in my palm.

I've always found solace in them. Whenever Father left me in the dungeons, they would comfort me like a friend. A friend that could never leave me. They've always been quick to listen to me, my earliest power that developed.

"You know," I whisper as we both watch my flames inch higher, now darting wildly beneath his chin. "I used to think I was Mother-damned, and that my black flames were more Sister-given, that they belonged in Hell. The next time you disobey a direct order from me, you'll meet one of them and you can ask them which one blessed me."

"Y-yes, Your Highness." His eyes are basically as wide as dinner plates by now, and I want to shove my flames into them.

But I don't. I turn and stalk back through the doors.

Cora follows behind me. "Your father would be proud," she croons.

I used to yearn for those words. How ironic that they make me sick now. I once thought of my father as strong, but it turns out, he's as weak as the rest of them. He is a boot-licking excuse of a man who craves the scraps of power that he is allowed. And I am his son, through and through. I am no better.

I am worse.

I take a deep breath and clench one hand into a fist, smothering the fire that threatens to return. Sometimes, my anger feels like a living extension of me, like it might take over any day and ruin everything I've worked for.

I follow the bond to the bedroom and fling the door open. The stench is even stronger in here. I rip the curtains open and yank open the window. Elle doesn't flinch as a cold gust of wind floods the room. She lies on the bed, eyes wide but vacant.

"What do you want?" she asks, but it's weak. There's no fire behind it.

"We have visitors," I say as I assess her. Her red hair is limp and tangled. She's so fucking thin. Her cheeks are sunken and her shoulders look angular inside her sleeping gown. It's only been a week.

"Get up, girl," Cora orders from the edge of the bed.

Elle just stares at me, those lifeless amber eyes shredding into me. Until they're not. Her head snatches back as she's yanked up by an invisible string.

"I said get up," Cora says. "We don't have time for this."

"Cora," I say placatingly, despite the way my muscles have gone rigid and how my entire body flushes with that fucking anger I'm barely keeping tame. "She can't join us like this. She's a mess. She needs to bathe."

She cocks her head to one side and purses her lips. "And? They're waiting."

I force myself to breathe. "I would appreciate not having to force her to do every little thing so I can concentrate on the conversation with Koa," I lie.

Cora stares at me with a blank expression. I'm ready for her challenge, but it doesn't come. "Fine," she says, then turns on her heels. "Ten minutes."

The door slams, and Elle's body collapses against the bed as Cora relinquishes her control.

She looks so small. So different from the fiery female I first met all those years ago. I don't know what in the world compels me, but I scoop her from the bed. She's all bones and sharp angles. I carry her to the bathroom and set her in the oversized tub, flip the spigot, and warm the water with my magic.

She leans her head against the edge, the column of her neck exposed.

"I feel sorry for you," she croaks.

I snort. "No, you don't."

She doesn't respond. The water weighs down her sleeping gown, clinging to her skin. I grab the lavender soap and lather it on her hands, across brittle fingernails and blue-green veins. I rinse the soap away with warm water, watching as it washes away the suds and reveals the freckles that line her forearms.

I set down the bar of soap and exchange it for the bar of shampoo. It smells of lilies, just like Mae's hair. When I look back up at Elle, I find her in the same position, neck still exposed as she stares at the ceiling. Her throat bobs. A single tear tracks down her cheek, then down her neck.

I can't resist the urge to brush it away with my thumb.

Her hand snaps forward, and she grabs my wrist with a speed I didn't know she possessed. At least, not in this shell of herself.

"Don't." Her command is full of power, and it stops me. I remove my hand slowly and instead offer her the bar of shampoo. She takes it from me and slides down into the water, dousing her hair. She emerges, beads of water clinging to her long eyelashes as she blinks the water away.

"I'll let you finish on your own," I mutter, knees aching as I rise and exit the bathroom.

I sit on the wooden throne that I fought so hard for. That I keep having to claw for.

King Katze and his family stand in front of me. Elle sits beside me, a glamour hiding the bags under her eyes. Cora stands on my left, looking at House Panthera with disdain.

Something is different about Koa today. Cassia looks at me with her usual hatred, but Koa now seems to have joined her. The last time I saw him, he appeared apathetic, but certainly not full of rage.

"Your Highness," Katze begins, eyes locked on me. "Thank you for meeting with us. We are aware it is a surprise, but we come with urgent news that we think you will be happy to hear."

I motion forward with one hand, wishing he'd spit it out already.

Koa watches me with a cold, calculating stare. He stands rigid, the only flicker of movement in the way his jaw works. Mother, I always fucking hated him.

"Well?" I ask.

A smirk pulls at one corner of Katze's mouth. "We caught Mae."

I reach for Elle and slam her walls shut to block any reaction from her. I almost flinch at the white-hot fury that emanates down the bond. It makes me wish I could open my walls to her and show her that it lives inside of me, too.

"Her and your brother have been responsible for the rescues of the prisoners we wrote to you about, and the deaths of the witches guarding them," Katze says.

Ah, that. Part of the reason Cora has been keeping me so busy. Katze did, in fact, write us a letter detailing the deaths of several witches and the loss of several prisoners. Cora raged for a full day, then tasked me with training the witches to ensure they know how our magic works.

"She's alive? And you caught her?" Cora asks, pure glee in her voice. If I turned, I know I'd see her leaning forward, a smile splitting her face.

Katze nods, his smirk growing wider. "Well done, King Katze," she praises.

He averts his gaze and tries to quash his grin. He looks so bashful. It makes me want to pummel his face in.

"Where is she?" I ask, shifting in my seat. "And what of my brother?"

Katze turns back to me, the smirk now fully gone. "She is secured in our dungeons. Your brother escaped us."

I raise an eyebrow. "The dungeons that they managed to break into?"

He shakes his head. "No, Your Highness," he says, attempting to hide his scowl at the title. "She is in our personal dungeons, reserved for the most dangerous offenders, constantly guarded by our most powerful. She will not be escaping."

"Good." I bite my cheek as I consider the development—Mae is caught, but I can't use that to my advantage when she's in another court. "You will bring her here."

"And what do you plan to do with her?" Koa asks from beside his father.

Katze whirls toward his son, a vein beginning to pulse just below his ear. A perfect place for my fangs to sink into. The venom would spread within the span of a singular breath. He'd be dead on the floor within three.

"How is that any of your concern?" Cora responds.

"It's not," Katze quickly responds before his son can. "We'll bring her."

But Koa's not done. He stares at me and says, "Well, if I may make a suggestion, Your Highness..."

I smirk. He's playing the game now. "Of course, Prince Koa. What is it?"

He dips his head in gratitude. *Really laying it on thick, huh, Koa?* "Thank you, Your Highness." He gestures toward Elle and says, "I'm assuming you'd like to keep the kingdom under the guise that this is Mae, so I would not recommend a prisoner transfer. We have ancient wards in our dungeons that prevent portaling, which would mean we'd need to take her to a separate location before transporting her. To do so would require more guards to ensure it can be done successfully. The fewer people that know of her existence, the better."

Cora's next words have me fighting to contain Elle.

"Fine. Kill her there."

After Cora assigned House Panthera with Mae's death, she left the throne room with Katze to discuss the details. She didn't ask me to join, and frankly, I didn't want to.

The moment the guards shut the door behind them, I released Elle from my control and ordered her to leave. I didn't care where she went. I just needed to be alone in silence. To sit with my thoughts and think through what comes next.

I stand and stretch the ache from my back. I fucking hate this throne. Every day, I wonder a little more why I wanted this so badly to begin with.

All I wanted was power, but Cora holds onto all of it with an iron fist.

The silence that I yearned for quickly becomes overwhelming. My thoughts threaten to pull me into the darkest corners of my mind as I question everything I've done, and it's too hard to pull myself back from that place once I go there. I exit the throne room. I don't know or care where I'm going, I just need to get away.

The frigid air bites against my skin as I exit the castle. Bare trees and gray clouds are my only companions as I walk the cobblestone path. Even the birds are silent, or absent. I wouldn't blame them if they chose to flee this place, too.

My steps lead me to the pool terrace. A singular figure sits on the edge, feet soaking in the water.

Elle.

A guard stands watch over her. She wears nearly nothing, her skin pebbled as the wind gusts past. I can't help but wonder if she's trying to kill herself slowly, or if she's just punishing herself for every choice she's ever made that has landed her here. It's what I would do. It's what I do.

Leaves crunch under my black loafers as I approach, but she doesn't turn. Her head remains down, fixed on the swirling water at her feet.

I stand there, watching her, wondering why the fuck I'm here.

Her blood-red hair running halfway down her back. What would it feel like to run my fingers through it?

She pulls her feet from the frigid pool and rises. She turns to me. Her eyes are empty, devoid of any emotion at all, except, maybe, for hopelessness. My heart does a weird thing as I find myself wishing for her anger. For the way her eyes narrow to slits, how her cheeks flush with the lightest burst of pink, how her lips part, ready to hurl insults sharp as the edge of a blade.

My heart squeezes again, and I turn to the guard. "Get her a towel," I say, "And find her some shoes."

He disappears, and I'm about to turn back and ask Elle why she's out here, but jagged nails dig into my cheeks, clawing at my eyes.

"Fuck!" I curse, trying to fling her off me. But it does nothing. Her legs are wrapped around my waist.

"Your Highness!" the guard exclaims, rushing toward me.

I wave him off. "Stand down," I growl as I try to unlock Elle's legs. How do they look so frail, yet still have this much power?

"You motherfucker!" she screams as she wraps her hands around my neck. I grab her wrists and yank them apart. She flies from my back and lands in a heap on the ground. She jumps back up and I grab her wrist again, twisting it behind her and pulling her back flush against my chest. I wrap one arm around her neck, her chin resting on the crook of my elbow. She struggles, but she can't break free. Asmo can barely escape this hold.

I ease the pressure around her neck. We stand there in silence, her back pressed against my chest, her breath hot against my arm.

"Am I next, *Your Highness*?" she spits. "First Mae, then you'll kill me?"

That was always the plan, wasn't it? Anybody who got in the way—Silas, Adelaide, Etta. Mae was next, but she escaped and took my brother with her. Elle is disposable, her life just a tiny part of this story.

I could end it right here. The truth is out. Replace her with some other poor, unsuspecting hybrid, or human. It doesn't matter.

But then Elle would be gone.

And I'd be all alone.

Horror slithers through me as something ancient and primal stirs, somewhere deep inside of me. Something that rarely happens to hybrids.

But that's not the plan. I'm not supposed to feel this way. I'm not supposed to depend on anyone. *Nothing* is supposed to get in the way.

And yet, the thought of killing her...I would sooner rather rip out my own beating heart and offer it to her to toss into the flames.

No.

No, no, no.

The pulse in the side of her neck, pressed against my bicep, slows with every inhale. Dread fills me at its rhythm. At the exact same way my heart beats with it. I hold my breath, feeling my heartbeat slow, then feeling hers slow in response.

Two hearts beating as one.

No. This can't be. There's no way.

I take my free hand and prick my finger on my extended fang. Blood wells, and I smear it onto the necklace. It unlocks with a hiss and drops to the floor.

I reach for the bond between us, and every muscle in my body turns to stone.

The bond is still there.

It's still fucking there.

My mind races, but it's all white noise. None of it makes sense.

With shaky hands, I release Elle and step away from her. I take off, nearly sprinting down the path. The guard calls for me, but I ignore him. And leave my mate behind.

This time, the screaming in my head is mine.

CHAPTER 34
MAE

FOR THE LAST THREE DAYS, dinner has been served right as the sun begins to dip below the tallest peak. Today is no exception. The stone door opens right on time and a tray of food is shoved through the opening. It slides toward me on the gritty floor, dirt underneath scraping the bottom as it comes to a stop before me.

The brown soup looks abnormally lumpy, and I eye the meal with distaste. At least it smells better than whatever they gave me last night. Giving a prisoner soup while their hands are bound behind their back is another level of depravity.

The wound on my stomach protests as I scoot toward the tray, but I don't have the luxury of missing meals. I have no clue what's about to happen to me. As much as I'd rather kick the meal back to them and scream a hearty *fuck you*, I lay on my stomach and bite the edge of the bowl. I shove my disgust away and tilt it back. It spills over the sides, into my mouth, down my neck, and onto the floor. It tastes like ass, just like the last few nights' dinners.

I lay there for a moment, the wound in my stomach pulsing and sending waves of pain through my midsection. I wrangle my way back into a sitting position and slump against the stone wall once more. My heartbeat echoes in my ears. My breathing is shallow and the air feels too thick. All from that one bout of movement.

My wound continues to get worse. Laying on the ground and inviting dirt and Mother knows what else isn't helping it heal. Every time I have to eat, the wound is ripped back open. But I don't know what else to do. I have to eat. I need every bit of strength I can get.

I rest my head against the stone wall, resisting the urge to bash my skull against it.

The dreams of my mother and the girl with oceans in her eyes have barely left my mind since I woke. I've spent every waking hour dissecting them and committing them to memory. Every night, I pray for more. But nothing else has come.

The first dream is clear. If it's true, then Elle is my sister—my twin. I wanted to snort when I woke up from the dream. Of course she's my sister. She's the only other female I've ever met with antlers. We have the same eyes. We both share the truth-telling ability. How could I have missed it? From the moment we met, she felt familiar to me.

But the second dream...The girl told the tale of a world that has begun to come true. *The rabbits hide. The birds are silent. And the moss is soaked with blood.* The ground isn't soaked with blood yet, but the animals—and the hybrids—are in hiding as the witches spread. *Witches run rampant through the forest, leaving a trail of blood in their wake.* Yes, that one is clear—Asmo and I experienced it ourselves. *She couldn't rid the world of the dark magic that plagued her creatures.* Could this be the Cursed?

If this is all true, then the world is about to die. And the only ones who can save it are two pairs of mates that the Mother Herself created. *Because the day cannot exist without the night, the Mother crafted the females after the light, and the males after the dark.* Elle, the epitome of fire—of light. Me, with hair as white as the flames I wield. Asmo and Marik, brothers who control the darkness and flames of night.

If the second dream is true, the Mother has given Elle and me mates who are brothers...which means Elle's mate has to be Marik. Or Marik is mine, and Asmo is hers.

No.

Although I know very little about mates, I know they are physically incapable of causing harm to one other. If Marik was my mate, he would never have been able to do what he did. My first kiss with Asmo was electric, different than any other male I've ever been with. Every kiss, every touch, has been a shock to my system. Marik's touch, on the other hand, felt like any other.

If the only way to defeat Cora is for both pairs of mates to work in tandem...How in the Motherfucking hell is that supposed to work if Marik is the villain and Elle is his captive? Not to mention, how am I supposed to do anything trapped in this cell? I have no clue what's about to happen. Am I about to be walked to my death? Am I the next one to be hanged? Or will Cora waltz in and finish what she started?

I swallow tears of frustration. What I wouldn't give to have my old life back, to be stuck in Bound with Cally. I shake my head. No, that's not true. That life was a lie. Hell, before this, my entire life was a lie. If I had to discover that so that I could truly live, then I would do it all over again.

The sun continues to dip below the mountains. I watch as it goes, leaving me and my thoughts in darkness for the third night.

W hoever opens the door is silent, their footsteps light as they approach me. Two different scents waft toward me—one familiar and one unfamiliar. I lean away, but there's nowhere else to go. My hands are tied behind my back, which is literally against the wall.

There is nothing I can do.

You have weapons built on top of your head, Asmo once said.

I leap to my feet and bow my head, antlers ready to spear whoever's come for me. The movement has my stomach and face throbbing, but I won't go down without a fight. I'm not helpless Mae anymore. I'm the High Queen. I'm a direct descendant of Wrena. I will not be taken. Not again.

"Mae!" a familiar voice whisper-shouts. I stand on the balls of my feet, teeth bared. "It's me!" the voice says. A ball of light materializes in the air, bathing the cell in a soft glow.

I lift my head.

Koa.

But when I see who stands beside him, I shuffle backward and bare my teeth again.

He stands beside a fucking witch. Her eyes are golden, the color of the sun. Her raven hair is pin-straight. She watches me with curiosity, like she's a cat and I'm the mouse.

"When did you turn?" I seethe at him.

Koa holds his hands up. "It's not what it looks like. We're here to get you out."

With a sinking feeling, I realize I can't use my magic to tell if it's the truth. I narrow my gaze. "And do what? Take me to my death?"

"We don't have time for this, Prince," the witch murmurs to Koa, eyes never leaving mine.

Koa casts a glance backward, then turns back to me. "Mae, listen to me," he says pleadingly. "We have to go. The guards are incapacitated, but they could wake up any second. Trust me. Please."

Koa was never a liar. He was the first one to warn me about who to trust when I first became High Queen. He's never given me a reason to be wary of him. Except, of course, for the fact that his House sided with Cora. And that he's currently standing next to a witch.

"Koa..." the witch mutters as she glances back toward the open door. "Just knock her out and let's go."

He winces at the suggestion, and I back up, baring my antlers toward him once more.

"Mae, please. Levana and I are here to get you out. She's on our side. Just trust me."

I freeze at the name. Levana. Willa mentioned that name in my dream. I lift my head again. "You helped my mother," I say to her.

She raises an eyebrow. "Yes," she says.

Again, I want to pull my hair out because I can't use my net. *Mother, I'm trusting you...*

I turn back to Koa. "Fine. But if you're lying to me, I will kill you."

He swallows. "I promise. But please, we have to hurry."

I don't have any other options. I close my eyes for a moment, then snap them open. "Fine. Let's go."

Levana turns and stalks from the room, magic already swirling in her hands. Koa motions for me to follow her. Before I can think better of it, I do. I hurry through the threshold of the door and follow the witch down the dim hallway, Koa following closely behind me. The guards lay unconscious and slumped against the walls.

Levana darts down a hallway to the left. I follow, going as fast as I can with my hands still bound behind me.

"Just a little more," Koa whispers behind me.

We come to a dead end. Koa steps around me and presses his palm flat against the wall. It clicks underneath his touch and a hidden door opens, revealing a steep staircase. He sprints up the stairs and Levana shoves me forward. I bite back a curse as I catch myself and begin climbing the stairs. My thighs scream at the climb and every quick movement only opens my wounds further, but I force myself to keep going.

The stairs are dingy, narrow, and dangerously slick from melted snow and ice. I watch my step to keep from slipping and tumbling back to the bottom.

"Ow!" Koa yelps as my antlers collide with his back. He jumps forward, straight into another dead end.

I lift my head and grimace. "Sorry."

He gives me an exasperated look before placing his hand on the wall and opening another hidden door. He braces himself and steps onto a roof. Frigid air whips against me, stinging every inch of exposed skin and sending goosebumps erupting. It feels like I'm inhaling crisp scents of pine with a side of glass, the air so cold that every breath is a stab to my lungs. Bouldercrest was a tropical vacation compared to this.

Above us, gray clouds drift past, almost close enough to touch. The moon hangs nearby, its white glow shining upon the snowy peaks of mountains that surround us.

Levana joins us on the roof, sandwiching me between her and Koa. I swallow hard when I realize how high in the air we are. How alone I am with the two of them. With my hands bound behind my back. And no magic.

What the fuck have I done?

Koa reaches for me and I back away, right into the witch. He retracts his hand and holds it up in surrender again. "It's okay," he says soothingly. "I'm getting you out of here. Is there a safe place I can take you?"

"Get the cuffs off me and I can do it myself," I say.

He hesitates. "I'd prefer to do that once we're out of here. Just to be safe."

"Safe from *what*?" I growl. I don't particularly care to have my hands bound when he takes me to a new location.

He glances behind him to the closed door. "If anyone finds us out here and your hands are unbound—"

"Oh, it wouldn't look good for you?" I scoff.

He takes a step closer. "Please, let me funnel you out."

"We don't have time for this conversation, Prince. Mae, I will destroy the link the moment we're out of here. I swear it," Levana says.

I grit my teeth. I don't really have a choice. They're not budging and every second we waste here is another second that someone else could find us and drag me back to my cell. "Fine."

Koa's shoulders relax. "Where can we take you?"

I consider Bound, but I have no idea if it's safe. Maybe Cora and Marik have witches stationed there. Squall's End is the only place I know is undoubtedly safe, but I can't let Koa know about the underground court. I can't risk exposing them to him when I don't even fully trust him. "Take me to your other dungeons," I blurt. "Have Levana walk me in. Pretend like I'm a prisoner. You can keep the chains on, then release me once we're in the clear."

Koa gives me a dazed look. "What? That area is crawling with witches."

"I can take care of myself," I fire back, even though my hands are bound and I have no magic.

"If that's really what you want, we need to leave now, or we're going to miss the change in shift, and pulling this whole thing off will be much harder," Levana says.

Koa looks to the night sky and runs a hand through his hair, dark brown locks shining in the moonlight. "Are you sure?"

No, but I don't know what else to do. "Yes."

Koa sighs. "Your choice. Let's go."

I shake my head. "Wait." I turn back to Levana. "Give me your cloak. Throw it over my face and antlers. Nobody can know it's me."

She shrugs from the black cloak and tosses it over me, dampening my vision. I'm either a genius or the biggest fucking idiot in the kingdom.

"Get me the fuck out of here," I mutter behind the cloak.

A hand grips my bicep. The air thickens and the ground changes from the roof tiles to loose gravel as we materialize in a new location. I can only hope this is the entrance to the dungeons.

"Sister," a female voice says in rough greeting. "Who did you round up?"

"Dissenter," Levana says, her hand now gripping my arm tightly. "Out of my way," she hisses as she shoves me forward. My feet barely catch me, and I swallow the string of curses that rise.

"Lock them up, then come join us for supper."

Levana grunts in agreement before pushing me forward again. I can hear footsteps leading away from us, and the thud of my heart grows quieter.

"Where are you planning on going, anyway?" Levana whispers through the cloak.

"Just take me to the cells where you keep the execution victims," I say.

She guides me in silence for several moments, our feet crushing the gravel beneath us. The air grows colder as we descend into the bowels of the dungeons. After what feels like forever, she stops. She wrenches the cloak from my head, revealing the cells where Asmo and I rescued Rain.

I'm here. I'm so close. I hold in a shaky laugh.

Levana shrugs her coat back on and stares at me. "Okay, off you go then."

I shake my hands, wiggling the iron chains. "A little help here?"

She smirks. "Oh yeah, almost forgot."

I offer her a sardonic smile. She wiggles a finger in the direction of the chains, a slash of dark magic aiming for it like a knife. My hands fall to my sides as the chain linking them splits. My magic rushes to me, my knees buckling at the force of its return.

"Good luck," Levana whispers before turning and disappearing down the hall.

I turn toward the familiar exit, to the alcove. I run. It comes into view, and I skid to a stop. I can only hope that this wall is connected to Squall's End and wasn't just how they portaled in. If it's not, I've most likely signed my death warrant.

I place my hand on the wall where the portal appeared last time. I coax my magic into the stone wall, searching for the dirt on the other side. I imagine my fingers reaching through the stone, grappling for the brush of dirt.

There.

The dirt is softer. I splay my fingers and pull back until it feels like my hand is halfway embedded in the stone and halfway in the dirt. I twist, envisioning opening up an actual hole in the wall instead of opening a portal between the two locations. I imagine the stone and the dirt twisting and compacting, not seeking to destroy, but simply to manipulate.

A tiny pinprick of light bursts through the wall. I swallow the celebratory shout and focus on more, more, more. I lift my other hand and make another hole. My teeth gnash together as I focus on maintaining both at the same time. The stone is unwilling to give easily, but it eventually does. The circles grow wider and wider, eventually fusing together and revealing the hallway I've traveled so often in Squall's End.

I launch myself through the hole, and it slams shut behind me. My knees buckle and I hit the ground hard. My hands slide through the dirt and I fist it in heaps, reveling in the grains in my hand. I never knew this feeling would mean I'm safe.

I push myself to my feet and begin stumbling down the hall. My foot catches on a rock, but I keep moving.

My friends are here. Cally. Holly. Ivan. Etta. Asmo.

My court. My mate.

A squirrel hybrid I haven't met comes strolling down the hall. The papers in their hand go flying. They turn, disappearing down the hall and yelling, "It's the queen!"

I want to collapse, but I stay on my feet. A sob escapes me as it hits me. I'm safe.

Through my tears, a figure dressed in black rushes toward. He tilts my chin and forces my gaze upward, to the fern-green and the silver and the darkness of his eyes.

He brushes my tears away, and I allow myself to collapse.

My mate.

CHAPTER 35
MAE

ASMO REFUSES to let me go when the healer comes, which makes her job significantly harder, but I don't care. I can't stomach the thought of being away from him.

"The wound on your cheek has begun to heal already," she says with a smile, then glances at the dried blood on my shirt. "Prince, I need to look at her stomach," the Panthera female says, but he's silent and unmoving.

Asmo lets me remove his arm from my midsection. I peel my shirt up and hiss as it pulls at the crusted, dried blood.

The healer observes the wound, then hovers a steady hand above it. "I can feel your Fae blood beginning to heal it, but there is another force that is resisting against it."

"Black magic," I explain. She quirks an eyebrow. I pull my shirt up further to show her the scar from Cora's lightning bolt. Although the mark has lessened, it's still there. "So far, any wound with black magic has taken longer to heal. The one on my stomach was initially from a black magic mark to alter my appearance."

The healer nods as she considers my words. "Because of the magic-blocking cuffs and conditions you were kept in, its healing process was significantly delayed. I can heal the stab wound, but the dark sigil will have to heal on its own." She takes a closer look at my stomach. "I'll need to remove all the dirt and debris from the wound before I can heal it. Otherwise, I'll just be sealing all of that in, which could make for a nasty infection. It's going to hurt," she says with a nervous look toward Asmo.

"I'll be okay," I say reassuringly, more to Asmo than to the healer.

"I'll just go gather some materials, then."

Asmo stares straight ahead. His eyes are dark, the fern green only a sliver. I cup his cheek with one hand and force his gaze to mine. "I'm fine," I whisper.

His jaw clenches in my hand. He opens his mouth to say something, but slams it shut.

"Hey." I stroke his cheek with my thumb. His gaze returns to mine, but his eyes are glassy now. "I'm okay."

He nods hastily and looks away from me.

The healer returns with a shiny instrument in her hand with two pointed ends. Great. This is going to be even worse than when the healer had to disinfect the burn from the cambion.

"Ready?" she asks me, shooting another nervous glance toward Asmo.

I nod, and she begins. It doesn't take long, but it feels like an eternity, every brush of the wound sending shivers of pain through me. She sets the instrument down, then hovers her hand over my stomach. It begins to itch, and the skin knits itself back together.

"All done. You're officially free to go." She offers us one last smile, then takes her leave.

Asmo wastes no time. He carries me from the healing center. Just outside the door, a small group of people are whispering back and forth. I smile when I see them. Ivan, Etta, Basil, Holly, and Cally stand in a small group, faces tight with worry.

"Cally!" I exclaim, squirming in Asmo's arms to be put down. He just holds tighter. "Put me down, Asmo."

But Cally backs away as she looks at Asmo. "I think maybe you two should have some alone time. We'll catch up later. Dinner?" she says with a shaky smile, then turns away from us to rejoin the group.

"What was that about?" I ask Asmo. But he doesn't say a word.

Come to think of it, he hasn't said a word this entire time. He heads to the residential quarters with a frenzied pace, not even bothering to turn the knob when he gets to his door. No, instead, he just fucking barrels through it. It crashes open.

"Asmo!"

He slams it shut behind us and takes me to the bedroom. His private quarters look identical to mine: rough, uneven, dirt-packed walls, standard bed with red bedspread, worn sofa in the living space. His room is uncharacteristically messy. My heart breaks as I take in jagged pieces of broken ceramic and glass littering the floor.

He sets me on the bed gently, but he doesn't join me. He just stares at me, eyes dark.

"Come here," I whisper, reaching my hand to him. "Please."

Normally, I'd expect a snarky response. Something like *Since when do you say please, princess?* Instead, he lowers himself to the bed and envelops me in his arms, pulling me against his chest. His fingertips dig into my skin. We cling to each other in silence, and all I can think about is how this feels like home. I knew I felt something special for Asmo, but I didn't know it was this deep. I didn't know it penetrated my soul. Then again, I had no clue our souls were made for each other.

"Az." I glance up at him.

His stony gaze won't meet mine. I reach up, pressing a gentle kiss to his cheek, but he doesn't move. I cup his cheek, forcing him to look at me, then press my lips to his. It's like slipping a key into a lock. He unleashes, his lips moving against mine, tongue probing where our lips meet.

Asmo.

My mate.

I shift in his lap, facing him and wrapping my legs around his torso. His hands grip my back, and I straighten, deepening our kiss. My fingers splay through his hair, grabbing locks and tugging. Soft moans emanate from his throat.

My mate.

I need more.

I need him.

I raise myself upward and break away from the kiss. "Off," I say, reaching for his belt buckle.

He obliges, tossing the belt from the bed and crashing into something I don't care about. I lean back on the bed and shimmy out of my pants, desperate to get them off.

When I look back up at him, his gaze is fixed on my center, his own attraction evident. He looks like he wants to eat me alive. I rise quickly. All I want right now is to be one with him. I climb back on top of him, resting my center just above every hardened inch of him. I lower myself, but he stops me before I can settle onto him.

"Mae," he croaks. I cut my gaze upward. Unshed tears line his eyes as he stares at the cuffs still around my wrists. "I...I thought..." His voice cracks. "I'm so sorry. I was so..."

"I know. It's okay," I whisper. I lean in and press a soft kiss to his lips. "It's okay."

Because it is. It's okay. We're back together, and everything is okay. I don't care if the entire kingdom crumbles around us. As long as we're together, everything is okay.

I lower myself onto him. Pleasure shoots up my spine as every inch of him fills every inch of me. Perfectly made to fill every space and hollow.

"I thought you were gone," he whispers against my neck as he begins to rock himself inside of me.

Pressure builds with the rhythmic motion. His nails scrape my back, and I let out a moan at the sharp sting, the sweet pain.

"But I could feel you, right here." He takes my hand and places it against his muscled chest, the broken chain dangling against him as he slowly moves inside me. Against his heart. It beats wildly against my hand. I slow my hips to focus on his heartbeat, then I reach for my own chest, feeling the rhythm that thumps against my own ribcage.

They beat in the same rhythm.

I bring his hand to my chest and place his palm over my heart. "Do you feel that? Do you feel how they're the same?"

One corner of his mouth twitches upward, and my heart threatens to melt. I missed his smile. And that damned dimple.

"I know," he says.

I pause, even though my body protests the interruption. "What do you mean, you *know*?"

"I've known since the night of your coronation dinner."

"Known *what*, Asmo?" I ask.

His eyes soften. He brings a hand up, tucks a piece of hair behind my ear. He drags his thumb along my jawline. "I could feel that something was wrong with you. I don't know how. It was some instinctual, primal feeling in my gut. I just knew you were in danger. When Marik returned, when he told me what happened, I knew." He pauses, then whispers, "I knew you were my mate. There was no other explanation."

My heart threatens to implode. "Why didn't you say anything?"

His smile is sad. "Oh, come on, princess. You wouldn't have taken too well to that." His thumb slides down my neck, his hand now resting against the base. Intimate and possessive and carnal. "Plus, wasn't this way more fun?"

I open my mouth to protest, but he shuts me up with his lips, his tongue, his hips moving back and forth, and I lose any coherent thoughts I had.

We collide with a ferocity that could only be described as a wreck. Because that's what it feels like. Two people so drawn to each other that when they meet, it can only be a crash. It can only be some combination of tongues and teeth and lips and hands grabbing and nails clawing and lungs expanding and backs arching and hips meeting and thrusting thrusting thrusting and mouths wide open as waves roll and roll and roll through each of them.

I don't try to stifle my moans. My blood warms and my skin feels like it's made from pure fire. Beneath me, Asmo lets out a long moan and stills, his fingers digging into my hips as he releases himself deep inside of me.

I collapse against him, head resting on his shoulder, one hand splayed against his chest.

"If we're mates, why did you say no? When I asked you to marry me?" I whisper against his collarbone.

"Would you believe me if I said I'm stubborn?"

I snort. "Yes."

He lifts a hand and strokes my hair, playing with the tips, sending gentle aftershocks of pleasure shooting down my spine. "Good, because it's the truth." He sighs, and it feels bone deep. "I was still clinging to the future I planned for myself, but it all changed when Marik threatened your life. Something snapped in me. And when Cora..." He shudders. "When she fired that lightning bolt at you...when you dropped, I felt my own heart stutter. That confirmed everything. I've just been waiting on you, princess." He twirls a piece of my hair around his finger.

"Do you accept the bond now, then?" I stare up at him, heart quivering.

His chuckle reverberates through his chest, the vibrations tickling the palm of my hand. "What do you think?"

I close my eyes and focus on the feeling of his heart beating against mine. A warm ember of peace settles in the center of my chest, lighting and spreading through me. At the thought of being loved, of being safe, of knowing this male was made for me.

"How did you know?" he whispers. "When did it click for you?"

"The Mother visited me in a dream." I recount the dream to him, summarizing the words from the younger version of me-who-wasn't-really-me.

His eyes are wide by the time I finish.

"So, Marik's mate is Etta?" he asks, rubbing his forehead.

"Oh, yeah...that. The Mother also gifted me with a vision from my birth." I pause. Saying the words out loud makes it real. "Elle is my twin...meaning Elle is Marik's mate."

He snorts, his sudden laughter making my own mouth twitch into a smile. "Motherfuck, huh," he chuckles. "What a mess. Your husband is your sister's mate."

I give him a playful shove. "I really need to dissolve that marriage."

"Actually, I think I found a way around that." The smirk on his face is so damn kissable. "Ever since I suspected what's between us, I've been looking into the whole premise of mates. They're so rare with hybrids these days, so there isn't much current information on them. But from what I read, hybrids used to marry all the time, only to stumble upon their mate. They would perform a mating ceremony, then the marriage was dissolved. So, all we have to do is perform a mating ceremony." He grins at me.

"And how do we do that?" I ask skeptically.

His grin widens. "It's incredibly simple. Mating ceremonies can be as grand as weddings, but most are intimate and small-scale. It can just be us. Unlike wedding ceremonies, there isn't an exchange of vows or rings. It's a blood oath."

I roll my eyes. "Why does everything have to involve blood?"

He flips my wrist over, then traces a fingertip along the pale blue web of veins beneath my skin. "It holds our magic, our essence of life. And when I accept you as my mate, I accept you as mine. I accept you as the very thing that keeps me alive, just like the blood that courses through me. When we mix our blood, we really do become one. Metaphorically, at least. I am yours, and you are mine. We are one."

I smile at his words. "We are one." I press a kiss to his cheek. "Can we do it now?"

His eyes crinkle. "Are you sure?"

"Yes," I say. I've never been more certain of anything before.

He opens his mouth and two fangs pierce through his gums. I start at their sudden appearance. "I didn't know you could do that."

He shrugs. "Party trick. My venom is locked away, but I can prick your wrist if you want. Or I can get a knife, if you'd rather." He bends down, placing one fang to his wrist and dragging down slightly, blood bubbling in its wake.

I offer him my left wrist. He repeats the movement, a kissing sting biting my wrist.

He holds his hand up, fingers splayed. "Hold my hand." I lace my fingers in his, the blood mixing on our wrists. "Until the end of time, princess. Until we are taken by fate, let it be known that you are mine," he says.

His eyes shine with vulnerability, and my throat turns thick with emotion. He's always had a hold on me, always held a piece of my heart in his hands. It feels surreal to be here with him now, repeating these words to him.

As I do, Asmo's serpent tattoo begins to move. The black ink spreads up his chest. The tattoo elongates before branching off, forming a set of antlers. They begin at his collarbones, extending up his neck and wrapping around, the tips stopping just behind his ears. The snake now winds around the left side of the antlers before coming to a stop below his left ear, fangs bared.

"Asmo," I say in awe, reaching for the tattoo. "Your tattoo just grew antlers." But he's staring at my chest. I glance down, shocked to find black ink now between my breasts. I climb from Asmo's lap and rush to the mirror on the wall in the tiny bathroom.

I wince at what I see. My hipbones jut too far, my hair is matted and hangs limply over my shoulders. But in the center of my chest, over the scar from Cora's lightning bolt, are two intertwined snakes—one black and one white. Their heads are pointed upward, their tails trailing beneath my breasts. Both snakes' fangs are bared, as if they're biting the scar itself.

Asmo pads over to me. He pulls me into his warmth, his strength. He wraps his arms around me and meets my gaze in the mirror. He crooks his finger, tracing the snakes' path underneath my breasts, stopping at my heart.

"If you're ever taken from me again, I will burn the world down to get you back. And that is a promise to you, and a promise to anyone who thinks of it."

Chills skitter along my bare skin. He trails his hand up my neck, then forces my chin upward. He leans down, pressing his lips to mine in a deep kiss.

His threat hangs in the air, his lips tasting like the promise of death.

I savor it.

CHAPTER 36
MARIK

THE CAMBION SPRINTS TOWARD ME. I spin and crash my sword through its neck. Its head goes flying, landing with a thud halfway across the training center. Three more come. I run toward them and leap, lobbing their heads off in one motion.

Another group runs toward me, but I hold my hand up. They come to a stop.

"Go back to your creator," I mutter. They skitter away, all of them moving in unison and out the doors. Back to Cora. I clean their blood from the sword and sheath it.

I hate those fucking things. I always have. When Cora first showed them to me, my skin crawled. But they get the job done and they're easy to control. Since I no longer have a brother to train with, I've been using them to spar with. But all they know to do is run and try to bite. Elle is better at attacking me.

I exhale a frustrated sigh. My thoughts won't stop. I came to the training center to get my mind off everything and yet, here I am thinking about Elle again.

How is she my mate?

How did I get this all so fucking wrong?

What the hell have I done?

From the time I was little, my parents pushed the ideas of power and control. Power over everyone. Control over everything. They knew Asmo would take over our House when the time came, but they wanted me to have something of my own. I just didn't know it would be this.

Despite all they did to us, they did care for us in their own way. Asmo has always resented them for the way we were raised, but not me.

It made us stronger.

It left me always desiring more, something Asmo has never had to think about. He was always destined to rule. He's never had to consider how he's going to leave a legacy behind, how he'll be remembered in House Serpent history.

I have.

When my parents first agreed to work with Cora, I was excited. It was a chance for me to have a future of my own. And now, I finally have it all. Power. Control.

But none of it matters because there's something inside me that I have no control over, and I can feel it all slipping away.

"Fuck!" I hurl the sword at the window. It collides, but the window doesn't break.

I want to tear my hair out.

I stomp to the window and snatch the sword from the ground. The stairway to the weapons room is dark, but I descend anyway.

When we were younger, Asmo and I were forced to stay in the dungeons for weeks without any form of light. All to "sharpen our senses." We were five. But it worked.

Even so, dungeons and basements have unsettled me ever since. But I force myself to overcome the fear, the discomfort, as I always have. My eyes acclimate within seconds and I locate the weapons door, placing my palm flat on its surface. It unlocks and I toss the sword on the floor. Someone else will put it back. Probably.

The door clicks shut behind me as I exit and ascend the stairs. Vicente is waiting for me when I return. I could smell his greasy hair from the other room. He stares at the decapitated cambion bodies littering the floor.

"Vicente," I mutter in greeting.

He whirls, his gaze flicking to the cambion blood on my shirt, then to my face. "Your Highness," he snivels before forming a bow.

"What do you want?"

"Cora wants to see you."

Of course Cora wants to see me. She always wants to see me. "Where is she?"

"In her bedroom, sir," Vicente says with a grin.

I want to tell him he can go service her, then. No, what I really want is to fall to my knees and beg the Mother—or the Sister—to kill me.

"Thank you, Vicente," I say, less so in gratitude and more so in dismissal. I grab two of the cambion bodies and haul them toward the door. Vicente clears his throat. I stop and turn back to him. "Yes?"

"My apologies, sir, but she made it clear she wants to see you now."

I close my eyes and focus on not exploding into a ball of unchecked rage. I drop the bodies to the floor. "Handle this," I say, waving a hand toward the dozens of cambions now laying dead on the training center's floor.

Vincente's nose crinkles. "Yes, sir."

He gets to work, a clump of greasy hair falling forward as he reaches for one of the fallen cambions and grasps its shirt between two fingers. I smother my smirk with a hand and exit. Vicente could have warned me it was freezing out here. The City of Sand is never this fucking cold.

Something darts through the woods in my periphery. Cora's witches' pets coming out to play as the sun goes down, probably. A rabbit leaps across the path in front of me. Since I've been on the throne, the woodland creatures have mostly gone into hiding. Gone are the deer that used to graze through the forest, that used to watch as you trudged along the cobblestone path.

"Better go hide, little bunny," I mutter. "They're coming." Wraiths and cambions and drabar, to name a few.

I'll never forget the first time I saw one of the Cursed. I was six. Asmo and I had been playing outside. We were covered in red sand and dirt, and I was fully expecting to be yelled at by Mother for tracking it inside. We walked into the living room, and there was Cora. Sitting on the vintage black leather sofa, an undead wolf at her feet, its massive head resting on her lap. Asmo shifted me behind him, and I peered over his shoulder. Its milky eyes stared right through me. I wanted to sprint far, far away.

But I didn't. Father wouldn't have liked that. Between Father and the wolf, I knew the greater threat.

Days later, he made us fight it. Then, he made us fight every single one of Cora's monsters. Cursed bears with teeth the size of fingers and panthers with claws sharper than daggers. Wraiths and osseri, made of shadows and malevolence. Cambions, who I thought were just sick kids, but were just another nightmare come true.

It didn't take long for Asmo to beat every creature. Even at that age, he was better than me—quicker and stronger. But I was the one thinking three steps ahead and making the plans to get us out of whatever hell Father had put us in. I would usually go down first, but Asmo was there to pick me up or defend me while I got up. He always had my back.

Except for when it really mattered. When he abandoned me for Mae.

He didn't trust me enough to see the long game. Cora was always going to win. There was no stopping her. She would have found a way to the throne, with or without me. By agreeing to help her, I just ensured I wouldn't die. I secured power and security for my family, my court. And my brother walked away from me for it.

I run a hand through my hair as I push open the door to Cora's bedroom. I'm instantly assaulted by the sound of her voice, and I grit my teeth. I follow it, finding her on the balcony. She stands against the railing, holding a handheld mirror as she talks to someone on the other side. Most likely one of the head witches stationed in the other courts.

Mother used to use a dark mirror to communicate with Father when they were apart. Asmo and I have used them plenty of times, against Mother's direct instructions not to touch her items. Alas.

Cora eyes me over the mirror and smiles. I resist the urge to shove her over the railing. She wouldn't die, though. It would only succeed in pissing her off and earning her suspicion. Something I can't afford right now. Now that I have a fucking mate.

I have to get Elle out of here. I don't know what Cora has planned for Elle, but she's wasting away while she waits for Cora to make up her mind.

The game has changed. And I wasn't prepared.

Cora steps away from the railing, raven hair brushing against her silky white robe. The mirror hangs at her side. She walks to the wardrobe and opens it, placing the mirror delicately inside.

"How are things in the other courts?" I ask.

"Ursine still won't budge, but that's fine," she says in a sing-song voice. "It's no matter. We'll kill them soon enough." She turns, white eyes settling on me. "And now it's time to celebrate."

I lean against the wooden bedpost, arms crossed and one eyebrow raised. "Why's that?"

"Mae is to be executed, the other Houses are in line, and now the witches are about to be a High House in a matter of days. It's time to announce the ball."

"For?" I ask. It comes out bored and apathetic. Her smile falters, and I refrain from smirking.

"To celebrate the witches becoming a High House, of course! We've been hunted and persecuted for years. It's about time we're treated with some respect around here."

I sit on the bed. "Cora, what's the plan here?" For the most part, I usually go along with whatever she wants. I give feedback and make suggestions, but she's always the one with the final say. I'm not exactly the type to ask an ancient witch about her plans, let alone push her on them, but my patience is wearing thin these days.

Her gaze narrows. "What do you mean? I thought we were on the same page."

I consider taking a moment to reconsider this line of questioning, but I dismiss the idea. "You want the witches to be accepted as a High House, but you've been using them to maintain your law and order since you took the throne. The kingdom will never accept them if the witches are killing everyone they care about. They're even killing their pets and animals."

She scoffs. "I can't do anything about the animals. It's a dog-eat-dog world. If the woodland animals can't fend for themselves, that's not on me or the witches. As for the hybrids, they will accept the witches or they will die. There would be no need to execute anyone if they'd just shut up and accept them. And if they don't, then I'm fine ruling a kingdom of just witches."

"And what of Elle?" I ask before I can think better of it. "Do you plan to have her pretend to be Mae forever?"

She tilts her head. "Why do you ask, Marik? Are you too weak to control her for much longer?"

I breathe through my irritation. "No. But eventually, she's going to die being our captive. You know as well as I do that dark magic has a cost to the soul, and hers is already depleted. I'm not sure how much longer she'll be able to continue using it. There has to be another plan."

She waves away the concern. "I just need her for a little longer, then we can kill her."

In that moment, I've never been more thankful for Mother and Father's lessons. If I were anyone else, Asmo even, I wouldn't have been able to school my features well enough. Not from the First Witch, at least. I act like her words don't burn a hole inside of my heart, like my very being isn't writhing in protest at her words.

Just in case, I turn my back to her and face the bed, hiding my expression. "Good." I peel my shirt from my torso and toss it onto the floor, then stand before the bed.

Cora's footsteps grow closer and I brace myself for her touch. I force my mind to empty, to go to the happy place I always envision, the only thing that gets me through this as I let my body operate on autopilot.

The little cave that Asmo and I would play in on the grounds of the Serpent Court. Our safe space away from Mother and Father. Where we would read books to one another and travel away from the hellscape we were forced to endure, where we would pretend to be voyagers to different kingdoms and live different lives. When we got older, it became a place to drink in secret, to split a bottle of wine and commiserate over our problems, to just be ourselves.

But today, the landscape has changed. Instead of the usual cave, it's a bathroom. Elle lays inside a clawfoot tub, her red hair splayed over the porcelain edge. There's a smile on her face and freckles dancing on the apples of her cheeks. She holds out a bar of soap. "Come on, Marik."

I have no choice but to obey. Not that I would refuse even if I could.

It's like my feet have lost any will of their own. I take the soap and kneel before her, knees hitting the stony floor. I don't feel it. She holds her wrist out to me and I begin to lather the soap. Her head rests back on the tub's edge, and she exhales a deep sigh.

"This is my favorite part of the day," she murmurs.

"Mine, too." My voice comes out rough.

I can't resist the way my mouth tugs upward at her voice, at the fact that I'm able to give her this. I rub the soap in soft circles, careful to scrub every inch of her, loving the way it washes over her freckles.

"How was your day, my little snake?" she asks with a cheeky grin on her face. The water sloshes as she leans closer to me, her honey gaze flitting to my mouth. I close the distance between us and press my lips to hers.

The vision shatters as I erupt, spilling my seed all over Cora's stomach, her skin so pale that black veins can be seen weaving their way down her hips. Black veins that pulse as she climaxes. I shudder, glad I can pretend it's from my orgasm.

I collapse on the bed beside her. She rests her head on my chest, staring up at me with chilling bone-white eyes. I force myself to smile at her. It's not hard once I picture the way Elle's mouth quirked upward when she saw me.

CHAPTER 37
MAE

AFTER CONSUMMATING our bond a fourth time, Asmo and I emerge from his living quarters. His arm is slung around my shoulder and I lean into him as we walk down the dirt-lined hallway. He nods toward my door as we pass it.

"Do you want to move in with me now? Or should we move into yours?" he asks.

I hesitate. Sharing a room together sends a message that I'm eager to avoid. But now, I know Asmo's not just a boyfriend or someone I'm dating.

He's my mate.

"Mine," I say, "I saw the state of yours."

"I don't think I should be held responsible for the way I behaved when my mate was being held captive," he drawls.

I give him a shove. "Yes, you should be. You're still responsible for your behavior."

"You're right. Plus, if I'm to be High King, I can't be throwing dishes in anger."

"I think you're already High King."

His answering chuckle fuels my soul. Despite the circumstances, this is the happiest I've felt in months. I feel whole. Complete.

We walk to the mess hall together in time for the dinner service. As we enter, the sweet smell of maple syrup hits me. My stomach growls as a hunger pain moves through me. I haven't had real food in days, and breakfast for dinner was always my favorite.

I beeline to the buffet and snag a plate. My mouth salivates as I see the spread before me. Fresh biscuits, grandiose stacks of pancakes, sweet maple syrup, ripe strawberries, steaming scrambled eggs, and thick slices of bacon. I pile my plate full—one of everything—and carry it to the closest table.

Asmo approaches, his own plate overflowing with food. Mostly bacon and eggs. Fine, more pancakes and biscuits for me. He watches me shovel food into my mouth with a frown on his face.

"What?" I ask around a bite of syrup-soaked bacon.

"Did they not feed you?" he asks as he sits beside me. His question comes out quietly, as if he's scared of the answer.

I set my fork down. "They did, but it was disgusting."

Their aim was to keep me alive, nothing more. In the three days that I was there, I lost even more weight. Living in hidden cabins and jail cells hasn't been the best diet for the curvy figure I've always longed for.

His frown deepens, but he doesn't ask any more questions. He fingers the end of the chain that's still attached to my wrist. "We need to get these off."

I hold my wrist up and dangle the chain around. "You don't like the prisoner look?"

His gaze narrows. "I would like it a lot better if they were cuffs that I put on you. But these...these make me angry. Plus, I think it's making the others uncomfortable." His gaze pivots to the Lower House hybrids that now watch us with blatant curiosity.

I shrug. "I'm more concerned about eating right now." I shovel some combination of pancakes, syrups, and eggs into my mouth. I demolish every single bite, then stand and go back for more food.

Asmo eyes the overflowing plate as I walk back to the table. "I'm not so sure you should be eating that much, princess."

My answering glare shuts him up. But to my dismay, he's right. My stomach roils when I lift my next bite to my mouth. I place my fork back down with a huff and slide the plate over to him.

He plucks a piece of bacon from the plate and eats it in two bites. Males.

"Hurry up. I need to speak to the Herd," I say. "They need to know about the dreams."

He picks up the next piece of bacon with dramatized slowness. I snatch it from his hands and plop it back on the plate, then grab the plate and stand. "We can take it with us then if you're going to act like that."

We exit the mess hall, eyes following us as we go. Just outside, Rain leans against the wall. She pushes herself from the wall at the sight of us and forms a bow. "Your Highness!"

I smile. "Hi, Rain. How are you?" I used to hate that greeting. I've always found it disingenuous and overused. But I really do want to know how Rain is doing.

She returns my smile, her blue eyes brightening. "I'm doing well. Thanks to you. How are you?" she asks cautiously.

"Better now," I say, "Do you know where I can find Etta and the Herd?"

She nods. "They're waiting on you. Right this way." She turns and sets off down the hallway. Asmo falls in step beside me, taking bites of bacon as we walk. Rain turns down another hallway. How anyone memorizes the layout of this place is beyond me. She comes to a stop before a set of double doors, then opens them. "Princess Etta, she is ready."

"Thank you, Rain," Etta's voice comes from inside the room.

Rain stares at the plate in Asmo's hand. "Do you want me to…take that for you?" she asks awkwardly.

Asmo hesitates, but I shoot him a glare, and he gives her the plate.

Rain suppresses her smile and hurries back down the hall. Inside the room, Cally, Etta, Amaris, Ivan, Luca, Basil, and Holly all sit around a massive flat rock serving as a table. Etta sits at the head. Everyone stands as their eyes fall on me, then on the cuffs that still dangle from my wrists. They all form bows, and I shift the cuffs behind my back.

Cally is the first to approach me. She pulls me into a tight hug, and I squeeze her. "I'm okay," I mutter into her chestnut hair. Her arms tighten around me. Over her shoulder, my gaze snags on Ivan. The look on his face threatens to break my heart. He watches me carefully, like I might fall apart any second. I pull away from Cally, then turn to address them all.

"I'm fine. I promise. I learned a lot while I was gone, so I'd prefer to just dive into it." I take a seat in the closet chair. Asmo snags the seat beside me and scoots it closer to mine.

Across the table, Luca stares at me with a look I can't quite interpret. His gaze falls on Asmo's neck, eyes widening as they land on the tattoo.

"Tell us everything," Etta says. Or more like commands. Her posture is erect, her hands folded delicately on the stone table, her gaze sharp. She was born to be a leader.

I recount the story of how I was lured and captured, how I was kept in the dungeons at the top of the Panthera mountains, and how Koa helped me escape. I tell them of the dreams that I was gifted by the Mother and of the truths she revealed. Nobody speaks at first, the silence feeling like a thick, suffocating blanket.

"You didn't tell me Koa helped you escape," Asmo mutters beside me.

"You didn't exactly give me a chance," I shoot back.

Ivan is next to speak. "Elle is your twin?"

I nod slowly. It feels impossible, yet it also feels impossible that nobody noticed. We are somehow opposites, while also being identical.

"So, you two are mates, then," Etta says, nodding between Asmo and me. I don't miss the fact that she ignored having another half-sister. But I don't blame her. Learning there's another person in the world that you share blood and bone with, that you're a little bit less alone, is a lot to digest. Now isn't the time for her—or me—to dive into those emotions.

Amaris watches me, a knowing twinkle in her eye.

I nod. "Asmo and I completed a mating ceremony to officially accept the bond. That should make him High King, correct?"

Ivan blinks twice. "Yes, that would be correct."

Luca drops his head into the palm of his hand. "For the Mother's sake," he mutters under his breath.

Asmo leans forward in his seat, placing his elbows on the table and steepling his fingers as he stares at Luca. "What was that, Luca?"

Luca shifts in his seat. He doesn't meet Asmo's gaze. Instead, he looks directly at me as he says his next words. "Have you forgotten the mission here? Rescue Elle and get the throne back? It didn't work out with the first Serpent Prince, so you—" He slams his mouth shut and shakes his head.

I take a measured breath and tilt my chin up. "Finish your thought, Luca." His cheeks turn pink, and his jaw works silently. "Go on," I order calmly. "So I...What?"

He looks around the room, as if someone will jump to his rescue. Ivan stares at the table, despite Luca burning a hole at his profile. Everyone else watches him silently, unmoving.

He turns back to me, and—I'll give it to him—has the balls to look me in the eyes. "So you went with the other one?"

Although anger warms my veins, I smile. Because that is exactly what I expected from Luca. "Did I or did I not say that the next time you disagreed with me, you would speak to me about it respectfully?" I ask, again, calmly. He grips the armchairs of his seat. "Did we or did we not have a conversation about you questioning my virtues?"

Black shadows have begun to fill the room like wisps of smoke. Cally glances nervously at Asmo.

Luca sits up straighter. As if that would help him regain any ounce of reverence I once had for him. "All due respect, Your Highness—"

I hold my hand up. "No, not *all due respect.* You treat me like I'm beneath you. I warned you, Luca. There's no place for males that disrespect females in my court. Basil, please escort him from Squall's End immediately."

The color drains from his face. Etta whips her head toward me. Ivan doesn't move an inch.

"Mae, we can't just let him free," Etta objects. "He could tell someone of our location."

"Make him swear a dark oath," Asmo suggests. "There's no way he'll be able to lead anyone to Squall's End or tell them of our existence."

Etta's lip curls into a scowl. "I don't feel comfortable encouraging the use of dark magic. How does that make us any better than them?"

Asmo shrugs and leans back in his chair. "The only other way is to kill him, then. Or keep him locked in your dungeons."

Amaris extracts a blade from her leather vest and dangles it from her hand. "I'll do the honors." Her smile is wicked as she stares at Luca.

Etta's jaw twitches. "Fine. Do the dark oath," she orders.

Asmo grins. "So merciful, Princess Etta." He stands and pulls a knife from his belt. He offers it to Luca and says, "Draw blood and repeat after me."

Luca grips the knife in his hand, and Amaris sheathes hers with a frown. He turns to Ivan beside him. "Do something!"

Ivan looks up. His face is ashen. "There is nothing I can do, Luca. You were out of line and you have pushed her too far." Ivan looks as if he's aged decades in the span of minutes. "Would you prefer the dungeons? Death?"

"Ivan," Luca begs.

"What did you expect?" Ivan says, tone tinged with sorrow. "You tried to take things into your own hands more than once. But you're not the ruler of this kingdom, Luca. Mae is. It's her choice. Everything is her choice. We are supposed to be there to guide her, but you've taken it a step too far." He shakes his head. "I cannot support this. There is nothing to be done. I support her. She is my High Queen."

Luca's knuckles turn white as he grips the knife even harder. But he places it to his forearm, and blood wells. He lifts his head and meets Asmo's gaze in a glare of fury.

Asmo grins at him. "Perfect. Now, repeat after me: With this knife, I vow to forfeit my life, should I break the vow that I will make now." Luca repeats the words, and his blood begins to evaporate, turning into a black mist that hovers over the wound. Asmo continues, "I vow to keep Squall's End and its entire mission a secret from anyone. I vow never to bring anyone to the location of Squall's End or the barn nearby. I vow to never speak of Squall's End, the Fae, or the Lower House resistance to anyone."

Luca repeats the words, each word a hiss of hatred as he stares at Asmo. Black droplets of his blood continue to evaporate into thin air. The wound on his wrist closes, now a dark scar.

"Now, Luca, tell me of Squall's End," Asmo says cheekily.

Luca opens his mouth, but it slams shut.

Asmo leans back and throws one arm around my shoulders. "There." He grins at Etta.

"Fine." She jerks her head toward the door. "Basil, get him out."

"Where am I supposed to go?" Luca asks as Basil guides him from the room. He turns, glaring at me over Basil's shoulder. I don't look away.

"Not our problem," Asmo calls without turning to watch him leave.

Ivan watches him go with a frown. "Don't you think that could have been done a little more...tastefully?"

"He's lucky I didn't cut his tongue from his mouth and shove it up his—"

Amaris leans back in her chair and chuckles.

"Enough!" I hiss at Asmo. His smile falters. "Ivan, you know it had to be done."

Ivan nods in resignation. Holly places a hand on his arm. "I didn't recognize him by the end, Ivan. His attitude was...I've never seen him act like that. Not toward anyone. This time felt different than before."

Before, when his daughter died.

"I agree," Amaris says. She looks to me. "I'm not sure what happened prior, but it was good of you to give him another chance. A shame he squandered it."

Her words serve as a comfort, but also as a reminder of the position I hold. I straighten in my chair. "Let's move on. To answer everyone's questions, yes, Asmo is my mate. As such, he is now High King. Yes, Elle is my twin sister and Marik's mate. Yes, Koa helped me escape. A witch, Levana, also helped. I think Koa is working with her to help things in his court, maybe even acting as a double agent and betraying his family." I suck in a deep sigh and continue, "That means we can't count on Panthera to help us fight against Cora, but it is useful information. It's time that we go back to House Ursidae and inform them that we have the forces of the Lower Houses to help us fight against Cora."

Ivan is the first to speak. "This is a lot to digest. Prince, do you think this changes anything for your brother?"

I clear my throat. "King," I correct.

Ivan closes his eyes, and I regret making the correction. "Yes, I apologize, Your Highness."

Asmo waves the apology away and drums his fingers on the table as he considers the question. "Yes, actually. I do. When I felt the bond with Mae for the first time, my entire future shifted. While it's true I fought it, it didn't matter in the end. The bond made death preferable to doing anything that would hurt Mae. If Marik knows of the bond, he will do anything to save Elle. He might be our best bet to getting her out."

Ivan leans back in his chair, his forehead wrinkled as he stares down at his hands.

"So it changes things...We just don't know how yet," Etta says.

"There is a Fae princess in the enemy's hands as we speak," Amaris says gravely.

I nod in agreement. "And we have to rescue the enemy, too. Either willingly or unwillingly, Marik must join our forces to defeat Cora. There is no other way."

"However," Asmo adds, "I think it's likely that he comes willingly if it means saving his mate." He places his hand on my thigh underneath the table.

"We need to go see Torben," I say, "Today."

We spend the next hour preparing for the discussion with Torben, a sense of urgency permeating every sentence, every question.

Elle is a long-lost Fae and Woodland princess who is in the enemy's hands. Yet, the enemy might be our best way to save her.

We dismiss, each of us rising to grab last-minute weapons before heading to Ursidae.

"Mae," Etta says as I step through the double doors to leave. I turn, Asmo right behind me, holding the door open. "Can I talk to you for a second? Alone?"

I blink. I've never had a moment by myself with Etta. Every time she's near, she's with Amaris or Basil. She's made no attempts to speak with me, but neither have I.

"Sure. Of course."

Asmo gives me a look and I tilt my head towards the door. "I'll be fine."

He frowns. "I'll be just outside," he says before placing a kiss to my forehead. My heart flips in my chest.

Etta stands on the other side of the table. She snorts. "I never thought I'd see Asmo take to someone like he has with you."

It's so odd to think about him before me. To realize I knew of him before he knew me, technically. I knew his name, I knew the handsome cut of his jaw from the images in the newspapers. It's hard to imagine that people like Etta grew up with him.

I smile at the thought of a six-year-old Asmo fighting with Etta on the High Castle grounds. "What was he like when he was little?"

"They didn't come around much when they were young. When they did, they were terrified of everything. Marik more so."

My smile vanishes. I know they had a hard childhood. That their parents were cruel and abusive. I push it to the side. Another time. I'll deal with that another time. "What did you want to talk to me about?"

Etta sinks into her chair and sighs. She reaches for the braid slung over her shoulder and tugs on the end. "Yeah, right. I just...I wanted to say I'm sorry for avoiding you since you've been here. Probably shitty of me to pop back into your life and then never address the elephant in the room, huh?" She smiles, but it's flat. Dull.

She's right. But I don't blame her. I haven't exactly gone out of my way to find her and force the conversation. If I'm being honest, I'm scared. I don't know what to say to her. There's so much. And yet, every time I reach for something to say, I come up blank.

I wave her away. "No, don't worry. Please. I get it." I should say more. I should tell her I'm sorry, that I want to know her, that I feel uncomfortable and awkward, too. But I don't.

She nods slowly, the chair creaking as her head bobs. "Yeah. Well, anyways. We should get ready to leave."

"Etta," I say, "There will be plenty of time on the other side. We'll figure it out."

Her shoulders droop, and I feel mine do the same. We don't have to figure out the complicated mess of a relationship of two people brought together by immeasurable tragedies. Not yet anyway. We have a lifetime to know each other. I, for one, am looking forward to it.

CHAPTER 38
MAE

WE GET MY CUFFS OFF—THANKS to a hybrid who used to work as a blacksmith—and Asmo funnels all of us to the entrance of House Ursidae's court. This is not the same forest we visited before. The scene before us is a wasteland. Trees are scorched and barren, the ground is black and charred, animal corpses lay rotting in piles. The sickly-sweet stench of death hangs in the air. Asmo pulls me closer to him.

"Mother..." someone curses under their breath.

Chills skitter across my skin as I recall Her warning to me. These woods are too close to the prophesized end that She warned me of.

Everyone is silent as we walk to the now charred entrance to the cabin, as if someone fired flames—or black magic—at it repeatedly. But it held strong.

It swings open as we approach. Barrett stands in the doorway, his eyes hollow, his face gaunt, and his cheery affect long gone. He ushers us inside quickly, eyes wild as he watches the forest behind us.

"Bar—" I start, but he whirls toward me with a finger over his mouth. *How bad is it here?* He ushers Etta in without so much as a second glance. He gestures for us to follow him before flying down the stairs.

We do, our footsteps hurried as we try to keep up with him.

Nobody speaks. The court is darker than last time, the lights extinguished as we descend. The only light comes from the windows that line the very top of the building.

Barrett's tension seems to ease the further we descend. He comes to a stop before a set of double doors and places his palm flat on their surface. They unlock and he pushes both doors open.

The room inside is massive, roughly the same size as the throne room floors above. Love seats, sofas, and armchairs take up the center of the room. Chess sets sit on worn tables and stacks of books serve as end tables. Blankets are thrown over the backs of every sitting surface. Hallways branch off, leading to more doorways and hidden destinations.

Barrett turns back to me. "Sorry about the welcome. It's been...Well, I'm sure you saw how it's been since you were last here." He glances around and throws his hands up. "Welcome to our bunker, also called The Den. We've moved down here just in case."

"In case what?" I ask, but I saw the way the front door had been attacked.

He rubs his jawline, at the week's worth of stubble that lines it. "The witches have been trying to get in. Every night it gets worse. As soon as the sun goes down, the screaming begins. The magic that protects the door is ancient and it should hold, but...You never know with dark magic."

The terror they must feel every night, hearing evil literally knocking at their door, wondering if each blow will be the last.

"I'm so glad to see you, though," Barrett says, forcing a smile to his face. "We've been waiting for your return," he says, gaze now roaming over the small group of people that I guess I now call my court—Amaris, Holly, Ivan, Asmo, Basil, and Etta. "I assume everyone here is a trusted member of your..." He trails off when he gets to Etta. He raises a shaky finger in her direction, mouth falling open, then snapping shut. "H-how?"

"It's a long story, but it's her," I say.

"How do you know?" he asks as he stares at her.

"I was gifted the ability to discern truth from fiction," I answer. "It comes in handy."

His jaw drops again. "That is not something you've shared before, Mae." He attempts a smile, but it falls flat.

I return it anyway. "There's a lot to share. Where are Torben and Artis?"

He motions down a hallway. "They'll be eager to see you."

Hope blooms in my chest, but I squash it. I was hopeful they would provide more assistance last time, and they didn't.

He opens a curved walnut door. Over his shoulder, I get a glimpse of King Torben and Queen Artis seated around a table. They turn at the intrusion. Artis's hand covers her mouth, and she sets a fork down on the table. We must have interrupted dinner.

"Barrett—" Torben starts as he pushes back and stands from the table. His protest dies as our gazes connect. He forms a deep bow, as does Artis.

Huh. A very different reception than the last time we were here.

"Your Highness," he greets me.

"Hello, King Torben, Queen Artis," I say pleasantly as I nod toward each of them. "I'm sorry at the intrusion, especially during your meal. However, I come with some important updates that are a bit time-sensitive."

Torben nods quickly, his beard shaking at the impact. "Of course, of course. Barrett, more chairs, boy."

Wow, I get a chair this time? I bite my tongue, the question barely restrained. Even if Torben's attitude is different today, I will not forget the way he treated me last time. Like I was some naïve girl. Not the High Queen.

Barrett disappears down the hallway, returning moments later with several wooden dining chairs floating behind him. He arranges them into a circle, and I motion for everyone to sit.

"Where are your daughters? The princesses?" I ask Torben.

He waves the question away. "They're off reading their books somewhere."

"I'd actually like for them to join, if you don't mind."

He furrows his brow at the request. "Why?"

I motion to Barrett. "Your son is here. Why should your daughters not also be involved in this conversation?"

Barrett hides a smile, then stands and exits the room, presumably to find his sisters. It doesn't take long; he returns within moments, Princesses Arella and Eden in his wake. They bow when they see me, then offer a shy glance at Asmo beside me.

"Wonderful," I say. "Arella and Eden. Thank you for joining us." They dip their chins, cheeks turning pink. "King Torben, Queen Artis. Thank you for allowing me into your home once more."

Torben leans back in his chair, one hand gripping the arm rest, just like on his throne. He clears his throat, but Artis speaks first. "Thank you for coming, Your Highness. We have been awaiting your return." Her tone is gracious and welcoming.

I narrow my gaze. Again, I can't help but notice how this reception is vastly different than the last one. The chair creaks as I lean back and survey them. Torben's shoulders are slumped, and there's an air to him that wasn't there the last time. His gaze, previously unyielding, feels softer. "All due respect, but the last time I was here, you laughed in my face and all but kicked me out. What changed?"

A pink flush crawls up Torben's neck. "Yes, well. You were right." The admission is gruff, like it took all of his effort to say it.

I tilt my head. "About?"

He shifts in his chair, looking like he'd rather be anywhere but here. "Marik and Cora called all the kings and queens for a council meeting. Cora told us that you're dead, which we knew to be false. But then she threatened our children's lives if we didn't unanimously vote the witches in as a High House."

I glance at Asmo, who watches Torben like a hawk. I wonder what he thinks about his brother agreeing to kill the other princes and princesses. He did try to kill Etta, after all. What would it matter to Marik to kill the others?

"After the meeting, she instructed us that it was time to host a witch inside our court," Torben continues, "But we refused. That wasn't a part of the deal."

"So, they've been attacking your court ever since?" I ask.

Torben nods, gaze falling to the floor. Funny how quickly the bravado fades when a man realizes he's wrong.

Artis places a comforting hand on her husband's thick forearm. A topaz ring glints underneath the overhead light. "We fear that you were right," she says softly, "If we do nothing, our people will still die."

The urge to yell *I know I'm right!,* to lean back in my chair and laugh, to give them the same treatment they gave me, is overwhelming. I sigh and force the thought away. They still haven't outright said they'd help us. Yet.

"Alright," I say, "Then there's a lot to discuss. Before we do, I'd like to introduce you to my court."

Artis smiles and squeezes Torben's forearm, then drops her hand back into her lap.

"You've met Ivan and Holly before. They are my advisors." I gesture to each of them. "They sacrificed a lot to be here with me. I owe them my life." I gesture to Basil, who straightens and puffs his chest. "Basil is an owl shifter. He has also been instrumental in advising me."

Amaris remains leaned back in her chair, one leg crossed over the other. "This is Amaris." She grunts when I motion to her. Their eyes flare when they see her. I don't blame them. Seeing her for the first time shocked me, too. It's not just her, impressive and intimidating as she is. It's the swirling tattoos, the raw power emanating from her, the size of her. It's the fact that she's clearly Fae.

I gesture to Etta, and Torben and Artis do double-takes.

"Basil is responsible for saving Princess Etta's life," I say. "In return, Etta has been leading a group of Lower House members and the Fae who have been fighting against the witches. We have assisted them with facilitating the rescues of several prisoners set to be hanged." I leave out the bit about the resistance. I'm not sure where Torben and Artis fall on their approval of the Lower House becoming a formal House, and I'm not particularly interested in losing their help yet. "I do not bring you the support of House Panthera, but I do bring you Etta's forces. They are prepared to fight."

Artis nods once. She doesn't look at Torben or even pretend to consider my proposal. "We will help you."

Relief floods through me. Even though Artis and Torben have been thorns in my side, I resist the urge to fall out of my chair and worship at her feet for those four words. We have a fighting chance. Or at least, we have a greater chance than we did previously. A flicker of hope settles in my chest and I want to cup my hands around it, to protect it from extinguishing. Ever since Marik took the throne, I've felt like everything we've done has been a failure. Until now. Finally, we have some help. We're not doing this alone.

"Our citizens are eager to fight, to put a stop to the torture of our wildlife and our forest. The witches have done enough. We are ready to take up arms," Artis says.

We spend the remainder of our meeting discussing everything that's happened since we last saw them—Etta's revival, my capture and subsequent escape, the Mother's dreams, the prophecy, the victories we've had, and the lives we've saved. Barrett agrees to meet with August to share all the information from today. By the time we've finished speaking, postures have slumped and eyes have begun to grow heavy.

Artis stands and clasps her hands together, her sage green gown shifting. "Our guest quarters in The Den are not as spacious as the quarters above, but they will serve their purpose until the sun rises."

"Thank you, Artis, but that's alright," I respond as I rise. "I haven't slept in a bed with my mate in...quite some time." Asmo inches closer to me, and I swallow my smile. "If we can't defend ourselves against a few witches and their creatures long enough to funnel back to our home, I question our ability to defend ourselves against an army of them."

Torben eyes me with something like respect. I always underestimate the weight of brute strength in a male's mind.

"Thank you for believing in me," I say to the King and Queen of Bears. *Even though you didn't before and now you have no choice.* The words are on the tip of my tongue, but I force them back down. Instead, I smile. "Barrett, would you mind escorting us out?"

When we're back in the hallway, Barrett turns to me, thick brows drawn together. "You're not really planning on going out there, are you?"

"I am."

Asmo chuckles behind me. I look back to my ragtag group, to my friends, my mate, my family. "If anybody is uncomfortable going outside, you're welcome to stay here and portal back to Squall's End tomorrow."

Amaris extracts two newly sharpened daggers, the white tattoos on her arms swirling. "You know my answer."

Basil's smile widens. "Not a shot, Your Highness."

Etta tries—and fails—to hide her giggle, and Holly glances at her with adoration. Ivan looks at me with...something that I think might be pride. And Asmo, of course, stares at me like I'm the sun.

We exit the safety and warmth of The Den, and Barrett gestures for us all to be silent as we begin the long, arduous trek back up the stairs. No more light filters in through the top windows, so we climb in silence and darkness. Over the sounds of our breathing, faint animal screams and bellows filter in through the walls, growing louder with every step.

We crest the stairs, and Barrett pulls me into a silent hug. He gives me a look that I interpret as *Are you sure you want to do this?*

I place a hand on his shoulder and squeeze, meeting his warm brown eyes once more before turning and facing the door. Asmo joins me, lacing his fingers with mine.

The night air is frigid, the cold wrapping me in its grip like a fist. A scattering of stars peeks through trees that have been scorched, yet still reach for the sky.

The Mother created this forest eons ago, and it still stands. She created me and my mate to protect this forest. She gifted me with the ability to pull from Her creation, to funnel its life and vitality and pour it into my magic. To help, to defend, to protect those who cannot protect themselves. To serve as a beacon of hope, a symbol of strength and courage.

An animal growls in warning, followed by the cackle of a witch. I look to my right, to the night-drenched male standing beside me. Who once told me it's okay to be scared, that all that counts is what you do in the face of terror. He looks at me now, a soft smile on his handsome face.

"Make them wish they were back in Hell, princess," he says.

I match my mate's smile over the sounds of witches screaming, knowing it will be the last time they utter a sound. I look back over my shoulder. Amaris, Holly, Etta, Ivan, and Basil all meet my gaze, hands out and ready, looks of determination on their faces. "Not too late to get out of here," I say.

"We're with you, Your Highness," Ivan says, shoulders back and stance wide. Steady.

"Etta?"

She smirks. "I may have lost my magic, but Basil has been teaching me a thing or two since." She nudges him, and a gleam shines in his yellow eyes. Holly's mouth twists into a frown, but it's gone just as quickly as it appeared.

"We will protect you, my queen," Amaris says, dipping her head in reverence.

"Who said I need protecting?" I ask.

She offers me a flash of a smile, then pulls a third dagger from her vest. Once I'm back on the throne—because I will make it back—I need to ask our seamstress to create something like that for me. Or two. I know Elle would lose her mind to have something like that.

My heart squeezes in my chest as I think about her. My friend. My sister. If she were here now, she'd be the first to jump at the opportunity to slay witches.

"Let's do it, then." I turn back to face the forest and raise my voice. "I am the High Queen of the Woodland Kingdom, Queen of the Deer, and Protector of the Forest. You have destroyed what is Mother-created and Mother-blessed. You have slaughtered innocent animals and dese-crated their homes. This is your chance to leave now or forever be silenced."

The cackling stops, replaced by an eerie silence. For a moment, I question my choices. But then I remember the male beside me, and my friends behind me.

Dark figures emerge from the forest and stand in between the trees. I spread my hands and summon my magic, feeling it warm my very bones as it rises to the surface. It spreads through me like a living thing, desperate to be released.

And then all hell breaks loose.

The figures surge toward us, witches and cambions and a small army of the Cursed.

I summon wind and water, flinging a wave of ice to meet them. Several witches yelp, but they don't go down. Asmo splays his hand toward two incoming witches, black auras writhing around them. His quicksand freezes them in place. Tree roots jump from the ground behind them and bind the witches' arms behind their backs. Their screams are cut short by Amaris's daggers finding home in their throats.

I summon the daggers, blood spurting as they're yanked from the witches' necks. Asmo hurls black fire at them, burning them alive as they writhe in his quicksand. I return the daggers to Amaris, the witch's blood still dripping from them.

Over her shoulder, a witch beelines for her exposed back, one hand raised with black magic swirling in her palm. She hurls it toward Amaris. I shove Amaris to the ground, but it just puts her directly in the path of the ball of magic. It collides with her vest and bounces off. *Yeah, I really need to get one of those.*

I leap over Amaris and summon my flames. They wrap around the witch like an old friend. She dies screaming. Another one jumps from a nearby tree, landing on her hands and feet. I don't let her get up. I use my other hand to aim a ball of fire at her, catching her perfectly and turning her to ash.

Amaris sprints toward a Cursed bear that's reaching its paw toward Asmo's back. She splays her hand and the bear shifts its course, swiping toward a nearby witch instead. The witch screams in anger, then hurls a burst of black magic at Amaris. She chuckles as she dodges it.

"I've been waiting for my revenge for years," she says. A grin spreads across her face as she leaps into the air and slashes. Her dagger draws a gruesome split down the witch's face, from eye to chin.

Basil jumps into the air and shifts into his owl form, his feathers the color of smoke. He soars behind me and I turn as he embeds his talons into a witch's ears and yanks, wrenching her head from her body.

Holy shit.

Feet away, Asmo is locked in combat with another witch, dodging blows of black magic and swipes from her deadly nails. The witch's back is turned to me, so I pounce, shoving white-hot flames into her and incinerating her from the inside out.

Her body turns limp and I fall with her, my knees striking the ground. Asmo hauls me up with a frown on his face. "I was having fun."

I roll my eyes. He grabs my arm and forces me behind him. I whirl, just in time to see him throw up a shield. Writhing balls of black magic explode against it.

Basil cuts through the sky, talons slicing the witch's extended arms. She bats him away, but he dodges and soars directly toward her. And sinks his talons into her eyes. She falls to her knees with a scream, blood the color of the night sky gushing through her fingers as she grasps her face.

Holly's roots snap the witch's hands down to her sides and crawl over her lap, forcing her to the ground.

I survey the clearing. Ivan and Etta go up against two witches, back-to-back. Holly's roots, sharp as spears, punch through the ground at the witches' feet. Asmo fires black flames at a small group of cambions that sprint toward us.

I don't see any other witches or any other impending attack.

The witch trapped by Holly's roots looks to the sky with blackened, bleeding eyes. I walk to her and kneel. "I warned you, witch." My voice is a whisper, but it shuts her screaming up all the same.

"You'll never win," she hisses at me. "The Sister has yet to come. She'll wipe you off the face of your kingdom for the lives you've taken from her."

"Maybe so," I say as I place my hands over her mouth. She snaps her jaw open and closed, teeth seeking purchase into my skin, but they don't land. I lean down and whisper in her ear, "Tell her I said hi when you go back to Hell." I shove my flames into her mouth.

When I rise, everyone is dusting themselves off or wiping blood and guts from their weapons. Amaris's white hair is covered in sprays of black and red blood. I imagine mine looks no different.

Basil lets out a holler—in celebration, *fuck you*, or a combination of both, I'm not sure.

I glance around, but find no more cambions, witches, or anything that reeks of black magic. A squirrel hops toward me and places a paw on my scuffed boot before bowing its head. A chipmunk follows suit, then a rabbit. When I lift my head, rabbits, badgers, hedgehogs, raccoons, and foxes stare back at me. Several deer emerge from behind the trees and watch us carefully.

They step aside to allow a line of bears to pass, the corpses of the undead in their mouths. They lumber toward me and drop Cora's abominations at my feet. Limp, hollow-eyed children stare back at me, great drabar lay unmoving, and skeletal remains of Cursed animals lay broken.

I summon fire and set the pile of bodies alight. They burn and begin their journey back to the Mother, where they belong. "May their souls rest in peace." My voice is a whisper against the smoke.

The smell of death—of burning hair and rotten flesh and putrid guts—has me breathing through my mouth, but we stay until the fire dies. The sound of the crackling flames giving way to the silent night air is a relief. No more witches haunt this forest.

Asmo pulls me to him, his hand snaking around my waist. A sudden rush of exhaustion slams into me at his touch, and I fight to remain standing. I resist the urge to groan as I think about the number of steps that stand between me and my bed. Asmo turns to me and scoops me in his arms, as if he knew exactly what I was feeling.

"How did you know?" I ask, fighting the urge to shut my eyes.

"Perks of the bond, princess."

"How, though?"

He hesitates, but squeezes me tighter. "You'll feel it someday." It's the last thing I hear before my eyes close and sleep takes me.

CHAPTER 39
MARIK

ELLE SITS ON THE TERRACE, legs tucked beneath her and a knitted blanket wrapped tightly around her slender frame. I've spent the entire morning watching her from the balcony, hidden from view. She's been sitting there for hours, her only movement that of her eyes as they track the comings and goings of the guards. Her hair blows in the frigid wind and she makes no attempt to tame it.

A knock comes from inside, pulling me from my watch. The fire in the bedroom's hearth died long ago, but the warmth of the room sends a shock to my system. I yank the door open.

It's fucking Vicente.

"What?" I demand.

He shifts on his feet. "Sir—"

"Your Highness," I growl in correction.

His gaze shifts downward as his cheeks turn pink. "Your Highness, I thought you should know there was another message written on the castle stairs."

I clench my jaw. If I'm being honest, I don't care about the ominous, blood-written messages anymore. I close the door, but Vicente puts his hand up, stopping the door before it can shut.

"Apologies, sir," he says nervously, "Her Highness requested your presence."

My jaw clenches so hard that I swear I just cracked a tooth. "Why didn't you lead with that?"

Vicente, again, lowers his gaze to the floor like a child being chastised. "I apologize."

I close my eyes for just a moment, then snap them back open as I force myself to play the character I've been playing for Cora. It gets harder every day. "Well? Where is she?"

"The formal living room, sir."

The relief at his words is a palpable thing. Her location is a small mercy, one that doesn't send me further into the pit of despair that I keep sinking into, that pulls me further and further into its depths with every stroke of my tongue, every pump of my finger, every thrust of my—

Vicente clears his throat. "She did ask me to inform you of the urgency, sir."

I fling open the door and shove past him before storming down the hallway. Cora is, in fact, in the grand living room. She sits on the velvet couch, pale skin aglow in the light of the blazing fireplace, her arms sprawled across the back of the couch. Through the deep slit in her black gown, her long, slender legs are crossed. She stares at the flames with a calculating gaze that sets me on edge.

"What is it?" I ask as I walk toward her. It comes out sharper than I intended, but she doesn't turn to look at me as she responds.

"The ball will be in a few days' time."

I place my hands behind my back and clench them into fists. This is what she called me here for?

"Lovely," I say, trying my best to inject some semblance of happiness into my tone.

Again, she either doesn't care, doesn't notice, or I pulled it off. "Mae escaped," she says.

That gets my attention. I freeze and consider my words carefully. Previously, the news would have devastated me. I worked so hard to manipulate her. But now, the fallen queen is my best shot at getting Elle out of here and in safe hands.

But I have a part to play. I channel the fury I felt the day I found Asmo broken and bleeding on the floor of the throne room. The day I realized my brother was someone who could be broken, and how far my father had to go to do it. "How?"

One of her bony fingers taps along the back of the couch. "Someone incapacitated the guards by her cell and helped her escape."

Based on the hatred in his glare the last time I saw him, my first thought is Koa, but I don't say that. If Koa is helping Mae, that means he's on my side. I nearly choke on the thought. At the realization that I switched sides. Because I did, didn't I? Elle's side is now mine, and the witch in front of me is now my enemy. I'm so fucked.

"Are there any leads?"

"It had to have been that bitch of a princess," she spits. "I warned them what would happen to their children if they didn't fall in line."

That bitch of a princess must mean Cassia. I inhale, then slowly exhale. "We've talked about this," I say, my voice measured. "If you murder their children, you will never have their support."

She stands, black flames dancing in her eyes as they turn to meet mine. "I care not about their support anymore. I've given them plenty of chances, but the ball will be their last one. If they don't support the witches after that, they'll all be killed."

"What about Elle?"

She freezes. Her gaze narrows. "What of her?"

"We cannot continue to parade her as Mae. What is your plan for that?"

"We can and we will continue to use her as Mae."

Every muscle in my body is tightening, but I roll my shoulders back to ease the tension. "I have already warned you of the risks of using black magic for so long," I counter, trying my damndest to sound bored.

She sits back on the sofa, relaxing against the plush velvet backing. "I don't care if she is a shell of a thing. We will use her until she believes she is Mae. And that is that. You know that for this to work, the people have to believe Mae is on the throne." She cocks her head in thought, then says, "I suppose you could find someone else to use as her shell, but you'd have to kill the girl."

Previously, the thought of killing Elle filled me with apathy. But now, the words spark something in me...I rein it in, table it for now. To react would endanger Elle.

"Fine," I say with a nonchalance that feels like a betrayal.

She smiles, then beckons me closer with a finger. Tiny prickles of unease begin to crawl along my skin, like dozens of tiny spiders awakening.

"Do you grow tired of me, Marik?" Her voice is pleasant, but it fills me with horror. "You are but a young thing, and I worry that you have forgotten the bargain."

I walk toward her slowly, keeping my gaze fixed on hers. "Never," I lie.

She raises a dark brow. "Never is a long time."

The concept of time has never been something I truly considered, other than in vague concepts. But now, I'm disgusted with myself to realize that I would rather spend an eternity in hell with Cora than let her use Elle any longer. I kneel before the witch, bony knees landing on the hardwood floors. "It's true."

"Good." She removes a hand from the back of the couch and grips my jaw, jagged black nails biting into my cheeks. "I would hate to see this pretty face in the fire."

I stare at her, willing myself to look at her lovingly, to hide the hatred that I truly feel for her. Her grip along my jaw eases and she shoves me away from her. "Leave me. I have a ball to plan."

As much as I want to skitter away like the coward I am, I know she wants me to grovel for her. This is the time to show her how much I want her, how much I still love and need her. I slide a finger up her exposed thigh, leaving a trail of goosebumps in the wake of my touch.

Her legs part for me and I continue up her inner thighs, tracing the dark veins as they thrum beneath her pale skin. I used to love these veins, the way they shone through her translucent skin. I would spend hours staring at them and tracing each one. All my life, I felt so different from the other princes and princesses. So different from Asmo, even.

When I met Cora, I felt seen. Like she was made from the same darkness as I was, sick and twisted and filled with everything that is wrong. When I learned who she truly was, it felt like a gift from the heavens. Like we were fated to be together and rule.

But now, as I stare at her, I realize that I was right and wrong. She was a gift, but it didn't come from the heavens. She came from Hell.

And I think I made a blood deal with the devil.

When I get back to the balcony, Elle is gone. I storm from my room and reach for the bond that links us. It's still there. As much as I want to peer into her mind, I don't. Now that I know what it truly is, it feels like a violation. I let my feet guide me, following the invisible tether to my mate.

Leaves crunch as I cut through the dead forest. A light breeze drifts past me, stirring barren branches. The sound of trickling water grows stronger. Just ahead, the backs of two black uniforms come into view. I pass the guards, who mutter something that I don't care about. I could ask them where Elle is, but I can sense she's close, so I save my breath.

Finally, I see her.

And the sight of her makes me want to rip the throats from the guards.

She lays in a shallow creek, her white nightgown clinging to her sallow skin. A knife sticks from her arm, blood trickling and flowing into the water. She stares at the sky, eyes barely open. Empty and dull.

I turn, slow and controlled. The guard on the left—surprise, it's the same gnat I threatened the last time—straightens.

"Your Highness, what's wrong?"

I gesture to Elle. "You're supposed to be protecting her," I hiss.

"All due respect, Your Highness," the guard says, "our duty is to ensure she stays alive." His gaze shifts nervously to her. "And she is alive."

I take a step toward him, and they both back up. I throw a hand out, freezing them both in place. "Did you forget our conversation?" I ask the one on the left.

His pupils are blown wide open, and he shakes his head vigorously. "N-no, Your Highness, but—"

I dart toward him, gripping his meaty neck in my hand. "And what did I say?" My voice is low, barely audible. But I know he can hear every word. He trembles in my hand. Good.

His mouth opens, but I slam it shut with the butt of my palm.

"Agh!"

"I'll remind you. I told you," I say through gritted teeth, "that the next time you disobeyed me, you could ask your maker where I got my flames." The scent of urine assaults me, and I chuckle. "Pathetic."

His screams are garbled as my flames lick every inch of his skin, a writhing kiss of death. The smell of his flesh burning has my nose crinkling.

The second guard stares at me, now trembling. "I t—I tried to tell him, Y-Your Highness," he stammers.

I don't respond. Not with words, at least. I dart forward and sink my fangs into his neck, forcing venom into the bite. He drops to the moss-covered ground with a satisfying thump. I leave him and walk to the creek. Even with all the commotion, Elle still stares lifelessly toward the gray sky. I stand over her, but her gaze drifts through me.

"Get up," I command.

She doesn't respond.

I lean down and yank the knife from her arm. Blood pours from the wound, mixing with the clear water, like smoke twisting in the air. The wound begins to heal itself, but slower than I had anticipated. I remove my shirt and tie it around her arm. It turns crimson.

"Get up," I repeat.

"Make me." Her voice is raspy, as if she hasn't spoken in ages.

On instinct, I reach for the bond, for the compulsion it allows me, but I stop short. It feels wrong. "No."

She doesn't respond, just continues to lie there staring through me. I kneel, the icy water soaking into my pants as I hover over her.

"Get up," I growl.

Again, no response.

I lean down and cup the back of her head, forcing her to look at me. "Would you stop your fucking wallowing and *get up*?"

That seems to do the trick. Her eyes snap into focus, and finally, she looks at me. But it's still empty, devoid of the fire that makes her *her*.

"Put the knife back in," she says.

The knife lays in the creek, glinting with the reflection of the sun. "What are you even doing?" I ask. "What is the point of this?"

She huffs a quiet laugh. "If I left it in long enough, I'd bleed out. Eventually."

I focus on the soft curve of her neck, on the way her hair looks like a living flame as it dances in the current, on the way the pebbles bite into my kneecap. Anything to avoid thinking about when I tried to do the same.

"Listen to me," I whisper, but my tongue feels too thick at the reminder of a time from long ago. "I'm trying to help you. I can't get you out of here right now, but I'm trying. Now, get up."

The next thing I know, I'm the one lying in the river. Elle hovers above me, the knife resting against my throat. Water streams from her soaked hair and nightgown, pouring onto me like raindrops.

"You're such a fucking liar," she spits at me. "You're trying to manipulate me, just like you manipulated Mae."

She has a point. I dip my head in understanding. "I've had a change of heart." Well, more like *My heart changed.*

She throws her head back and laughs incredulously. "Fuck your heart." She yanks the knife from my neck and stabs it into the center of my chest.

White, hot pain erupts. My vision blurs, and even though I'm laying down, the world somehow tilts. I let loose a string of curse words that Father surely would have punished me for. Showing any reaction after physical pain always resulted in his wrath.

When I can finally draw a full breath, I feel for the knife and wrench it from my chest. It goes flying. I blink and the darkness that was closing in slowly recedes. I stand, the back of my pants now soaking wet, while the front of my chest drips with blood. I rub the spot where she stabbed and hiss. She really stabbed me, for fuck's sake.

And now, she's gone.

It doesn't take me long to find her. She's bent over, searching through the pockets of the dead guard that I didn't burn to a crisp. I step on a branch, and she whirls toward me. Then takes off.

I catch up to her in a few strides, wrapping my arm around her midsection and pulling her against me. She flails, and it's like holding onto a wet cat, for the Mother's sake. I haul her back to the lifeless body and the charred remains of the other guard.

See, I'm trying to help you, I hiss into her mind.

Fury comes back down the bond. She rages against me, bare feet and frail hands pounding against my shins and chest. "What is wrong with you?" she shouts into my chest.

I take every hit. I deserve it. I wish she'd stab me again and again. I wish it could kill me. It doesn't take long for her to tire herself out. The hits come slower and slower, until she stills in my arms.

"If I put you down, will you run?" I whisper.

She doesn't respond. I set her down in front of a wide, ancient tree trunk, then cage her in with both arms. She stares back at me with pure hatred. I wish I had the freedom to look at anyone other than myself like that.

"I swear on my wretched life, I am trying to find a way to get you out of here that doesn't end with you in a grave," I say, trying desperately to convince her that I'm telling the truth.

She glares at me as she processes my words. After approximately five seconds of staring at me with an intensity that feels like it penetrates my very bones, she tilts her head in curiosity. Good. Maybe she believes me. My shoulders relax. Barely.

"Why?" she asks.

That wasn't what I was expecting her to say. I don't really have a good reason to give her, other than the truth. *Because you're actually my mate? Because I made a huge, terrible mistake?* I clear my throat. "What does it matter?"

She scoffs. "*Why,* Marik? You tried to kill Mae. You killed the High Family. You've been forcing me to do your will for months. What's with the sudden change of heart? I refuse to believe you suddenly grew one."

I run a hand through my damp hair in frustration. "All I can say is that I'm trying to get you out and I need you to..." I fumble, knowing asking her to trust me won't go over well. "I just need you to just believe me that I'm trying to get you out."

She stares up at me through long eyelashes, amber eyes still full of unchecked fury, but now tinged with the gleam of skepticism, of curiosity. My heart flips in my chest.

"It won't save you from Hell," she says apathetically.

I chuckle. I already know that. "Do you care about my dalliances with the underworld, little fawn?" She stomps on my foot in response. It might have hurt more if she hadn't stabbed me in the fucking heart just minutes ago. "Always violence with you."

"You deserve it."

Yes, I do. I deserve to burn for what I did to Mae and her family. I deserve to burn for all the sickening, miserable, foul things I've done to get here.

"In a few days, there will be a ball. If we can slip away, I can funnel you out of here."

"Why can't you funnel me out of here now?" she asks, looking around pointedly at the privacy we have.

I shake my head. "There are too many guards, too many little spies for Cora all around this place."

She narrows her gaze. "What's your plan, then?"

"I don't know yet, but I'll figure it out. Do you trust me?"

The question hangs between us.

"Not at all," she says.

Silence blossoms between us once more.

"Have dinner with me tonight," I blurt. She stares at me like I've grown antlers. "You need to eat if this is going to work."

Elle claps her hands together and smiles, but it's faux-saccharine and full of loathing. "Do I get to choose this time? Or are you going to take control of my body and make me walk and talk like your little puppet?"

My cheeks warm as shame floods me for the first time in a long, long time. "It's your choice," I manage to whisper.

"Oh, wonderful. I would rather choke on every piece of food for the rest of my life than eat dinner with you," she fires back.

I shrug, the act of nonchalance one that I'm well versed in.

"What are you going to do about them?" she asks, hand gesturing flippantly to the dead guards.

Great question. "I'll handle it." I look down at her, at her hair, still soaking wet, at the goosebumps that line every inch of her skin. Her sodden clothes cling to every curve. I tear my gaze away. "You need to get inside."

She scoffs. "It's so funny that you all of a sudden act like you care. It doesn't matter what you say, High King," she spits. "There is no heart that beats in your chest."

If that's true, then why does it beat in tandem with yours?

CHAPTER 40
MAE

"How many times am I going to fail at this before we accept I can't do this?" I ask through gritted teeth.

"Depends on how many times you're going to make disparaging comments about yourself," Asmo retorts as I pace back and forth in the training room.

I huff a sigh. "We've been at this for almost an hour and I'm no closer to shifting."

"Then you're doing something wrong," he says maddeningly calmly, as if I'm not about to pull my hair out.

I come to a stop, crossing my arms and facing him. "Or you're teaching me wrong," I say with a glare. "Or, like I said, *I can't shift.*"

His jaw clenches, his first and only sign of annoyance. "You can funnel, so you can shift. But if you keep believing you can't shift, then you won't. I told you, you have to imagine yourself in your shifted body and will it."

"I don't even know what my animal form is," I fire back for the fifth time today. We've been having different versions of the same argument for the last hour.

"You don't have to know," he says, also for the fifth time.

"It's probably like...a mouse," I say as I throw my hands up.

One corner of his mouth twitches upward. He strides toward me. "It would be the most beautiful mouse I've ever seen." He pulls me to him, and the tightness in my chest recedes. "But, again, you know that's not true." He reaches for my antlers. My back arches at his soft caress, nerve endings lighting at his touch. My buzz dims as I remember the last male who touched me in this way. Marik.

"Your antlers are an obvious indicator of your animal form." His hand moves to my hair, gently stroking the white strands, the buzzing returning, humming pleasantly in my belly. "And you know that hair color is another good sign of what your form will look like."

"That's the problem," I grumble. "I've never seen a white deer."

Asmo's fingers snake to the back of my head, gripping the roots and tugging. That buzzing in my belly turns into something feral, my annoyance now long forgotten, replaced with something else entirely. His dark eyes bore into mine. "Have you forgotten who you are? The First Deer Queen's granddaughter? Direct descendant of Wrena? Why would you think just because you haven't seen something, that means it can't happen? The Mother created you. Why do you keep forgetting that?"

Because I grew up thinking I was weak and nobody. Because I've never believed in myself. Because sometimes my skin crawls and I can't turn it off unless I harm myself. Because there's something wrong with me.

"It just feels..." I look to the ceiling as I search for the right word. Wrong. Impossible. Insane. "I'm just me."

He tugs on the roots of my hair again, forcing my gaze back to his. "You were created by the Mother to save our kingdom. To be the light that protects all of us from the darkness. This is what you were born to do. You can do it. So, I need you to start believing that you can."

"But what if I can't?" What if I can't ward off the darkness that is Marik and Cora? What if I'm not enough? The thought is a whisper, one that I can't stop from escaping. One I normally tamp down and hold onto, shielding it from the rest of the world.

He brings my hand to his lips, presses them against my inner wrist. To the space where his fang pricked the vein that thrums below. Where our blood mixed when we became one. "You can. And you will. And it's that simple."

I want to fight back. I want to tell him there's so much more to it than that. But maybe he has a point. If I don't start believing in myself, who will? Maybe that's where I need to start. With myself.

I rise and press my lips to his, soft against mine. "Thank you," I whisper against him. "For telling me I'm enough."

"You're more. In fact, if you were the only thing I saved in this wretched kingdom, I'd be fine with that. Now," he says, arm tightening around my waist, "Shift."

He releases me, and it takes me all of one second to wish I was back in his arms, which are now crossed. He gives me a pointed glare. Fine. I begin to pace the room again, thinking about what the hell a white deer even looks like, when the training room doors crash open.

"Sorry to interrupt, Your Highnesses, but a scout just returned with some urgent news," Basil says from the doorway.

A young male, snow-white hair matching my own, stands next to Basil. His clothes are rumpled and his hair is greasy. He looks like he hasn't bathed in days. Based on his large front teeth and oversized ears, I'm assuming a rabbit hybrid. His gaze flits nervously between Asmo and me.

Asmo shifts in front of me. "What is it?" The question is a command, the Prince of Darkness on full display.

I step around him and offer the rabbit hybrid a warm smile. "What's your name?"

"Ewan, Your Highness," he says nervously. "I just got back from the High Castle and came straight here."

"What's going on, Ewan?"

He looks to Asmo once, then back to me. "It appears they are preparing for a ball, Your Highness. I found castle staff running about with decorations and such. Some also made comments in passing about a ball."

"Who's they?" Asmo demands.

Ewan grips his hands together tightly. "The—The false king, sir."

Marik and Cora are throwing a ball? Why?

"Do you know when?" I ask.

Ewan nods eagerly. "Yes'm. I overheard two guards complaining about their women being too busy with the preparations. Said 'Only three days to set up for a ball. She's mad,'" he says with an exaggerated deep voice.

"Do you know why?"

He shakes his head. "Sorry."

I wave the apology away. "While you were there, did you see a red-haired female with antlers?" I ask, dampening the hope in my voice.

He hesitates. "Y-yes, Your Highness..."

His response puts me on guard. I steel myself but ask, "And? Is she okay?"

"She is alive, Your Highness. But she seems very...sad."

The weight on my shoulders returns. What have they done to her? What have I done to her? I've never seen Elle sad. Happy, angry, frustrated, excited...but never sad. What have they subjected her to? A memory of the osseris pressed against me. The scrape of its—Marik's—claws. I shudder.

That creature is her mate.

We need to get her out. Now.

Asmo turns to me, and I can see the gears turning in his head. "A ball would be a good opportunity to attack," he whispers.

He's right. "We need to meet with everyone," I say, turning back to Basil. "Canis and Ursidae, too."

"Shouldn't we at least discuss the plan with Etta before we meet with them?" he asks.

"No," Asmo says, "We only have a few days until this ball. This might be the only time we have. We don't have the time to iron out details here, then do the same with the other Houses.

"Gather the Herd and send a message to Canis," I order. "We'll all meet at Ursidae."

I n under an hour, we're all seated around a wooden circular table. Although the table is huge, there are far too many of us. Houses Ursidae, Canis, and the Herd all sit crammed together. Asmo's leg rests against mine, solid and warm.

"So," I say, "I think it would be wise to strike during the ball."

Torben leans back in his chair. "You think it would be...wise...to attack when they most likely have heightened security, a heavy witch presence, and innocent civilians present?" His tone is dubious at best, but mostly insulting.

My ability to keep calm is an accomplishment of its own.

"Yes, Torben, I do." I turn to the rest of the group. "Think about it. They're not going to be expecting it. They don't even know that we have the Fae or the Lower House members behind us, nor do they know that we've been in communication with the other Houses."

"Unless it somehow got out that you slaughtered all the witches here," Barrett says with a grimace. He tosses me an apologetic look.

"You're right," I agree. In hindsight, maybe that wasn't the smartest move, but it gave a family—a court—hope, and I don't regret it. "But I think that's a risk we take. Even if they know we've been in communication and we visited your court, they still don't know that we have the Lower Houses or the Fae behind us. Those numbers alone are big enough to make a difference in battle."

"And how do you propose to keep the civilians safe?" Queen Sasha asks.

The question hangs in the air as we all silently consider the best option. The first to speak, to everyone's surprise, is Princess Eden.

"Are the Lower House hybrids able to shield themselves?" Her question is directed to Etta, voice timid, hands wringing in her lap.

"Most of them, yes," Etta responds.

"Are they powerful enough to shield others?" Eden asks.

Etta looks at Basil, who answers, "Some of them."

"What if we disguised Lower House hybrids as guests? They would need to be placed strategically throughout the crowd. They could also help direct the citizens away from the battle."

The idea is solid. "That could work, Eden," I say. "Every citizen is invited to the ball, so they could just walk right in."

She blushes and shrinks back into her seat.

"All of the High Houses are invited, so us getting in won't be a problem. But how are you going to sneak yourselves in?" Torben asks.

I smile. "We have the answer to that."

Asmo explains the dark magic spell to change our appearance. Torben looks disgusted at the idea of using it, but Princess Lola leans forward in her seat and listens with rapt attention, eyes gleaming. Princesses Arella and Eden look at their parents skeptically.

"I'm not downplaying the use of black magic," I say hesitantly, "but we need to use every tool at our disposal. Glamours are too easily broken. It's our only option."

"This is the fate of the kingdom." Asmo's reminder is quiet, but it strikes everyone like a fist to the gut. We have to use every advantage we have, even if that advantage makes my skin crawl. If we don't, the kingdom will fall. And if the Mother's dream is true, Her creation itself will fall next, and the oceans will turn to blood.

"What is the objective here?" Etta asks, pulling me away from the memory of the dream. Asmo quirks an eyebrow. "Is our plan to slaughter everyone? Kill the witches and everyone who agrees with them?"

Asmo defers to me. If he were to respond, I think the answer would be an unequivocal *yes* to killing everyone who wronged us. But that's not who I want to be.

"You said there was a witch who helped you escape? That she was working with Koa, right?" Etta asks. I nod. "What if there are more like her?"

This is something I've been considering. To slaughter everyone who's sided with Marik and Cora is foolish and cruel. It makes us worse than them. At least they gave everyone a chance to agree with them before they started executing anyone who disagreed.

"As much as I'd like to see every single one of them dead," Asmo says, "I think a well-planned rescue mission is the better option. We should still have Lower House hybrids in the crowd to protect citizens should things get out of hand, but attacking shouldn't be the priority. At least not right now."

I nod in agreement. "Elle is the priority."

"Getting to her is going to be challenging," Asmo admits. Ivan glares at him from across the room. Asmo throws a hand up. "I'm just being realistic. She's going to be heavily secured. It's likely going to result in people getting hurt. Are we okay with that risk?"

My heart beats in my chest, once, twice. "No, but without her, we can't defeat Cora, and more people will die. This is just one of the costs of war."

My words reverberate through my chest, through the air, lighting every inch of bone and skin and fiber of magic that courses through me.

This is war.

Amaris's voice is quiet, but it slices through the air like a dagger. "Let us not forget, she is also a Fae princess. We must bring her home."

Asmo clears his throat and turns to Torben and Conall. "Are your people prepared to fight?"

Conall lifts his chin, ice-blue eyes meeting Asmo's pools of night. "They are, Your Highness." Torben echoes Conall's words with a singular, firm nod. His jaw is locked, affect somber. Artis reaches for her husband, gripping his hand in solidarity.

People are going to die. I am sending people to their deaths.

Asmo's voice interrupts my thoughts, derailing them before they have a chance to take hold. "I know our intent is not to attack, but we need to be prepared for every scenario. Although the witches are beatable, we need to begin training everyone on how to beat them. It's one thing to fight, but it's another to fight efficiently," Asmo says. "And we can't forget that Cora will be there."

We spend the next several hours carefully discussing every consideration for how to pull off this rescue mission while minimizing the risk of harm to civilians. Although I could slit Minerva's and Vasuki's throats for what they did to Asmo and the way they raised him, I can't help but admit that his background was invaluable today.

He is a warrior, through and through.

Which means Marik is, too.

"Why are swords so *heavy*?" I grunt as I swing the blade toward August. He deflects it with a singular flick of his wrist, as if his own sword weighs nothing.

"These are pure iron, princess," Asmo calls from the other side of the training center. "What made you think they'd be light?"

I ignore the question and swing the blade again, only to be deflected. Again.

"Why don't you use wind to help?" Barrett turns from the collection of weaponry affixed to the dirt wall.

During our war-planning meeting, we decided the High Princes should train everyone how to fight together. There will be groups of Lower House hybrids, Ursine hybrids, Canis hybrids, and Fae strategically placed in every training group to learn how to fight as a singular unit. August will be spending the afternoon teaching groups how to attack witches and their creatures, while Barrett and Amaris will be spending their time teaching groups how to fight together.

"What do you mean?" I ask.

"Use your wind to help move the sword," Barrett says with a shrug.

August scratches his head. "I thought the whole point of this was to teach her how to fight without magic?"

Asmo walks to the wall of weapons and snags a crossbow, a dagger, and a smaller sword from the wall. The image of him with all manner of pointy things makes my mouth dry.

"Then that's not the right weapon for her," he says. "She doesn't have the muscle for that." I want to object, but I know he's right. "We're fighting in a matter of days. Teach her with other tools." He floats the three weapons in front of me.

The crossbow looks too difficult to learn and the dagger involves getting closer than I'd like. I pluck the sword from the air.

Asmo smiles at the choice. "The shortsword."

I grip it in one hand, its weight a nonissue after handling the last sword. I swing my arm and it cuts through the air with a *whoosh*.

"Alright, Your Highness," August says. "Back to work."

Every moment over the next several days is spent preparing for Elle's rescue mission. Asmo comes to bed exhausted every night, collapsing onto the mattress and falling asleep within minutes.

In a surprising turn of events, I've been teaching Holly and Cally the basics of self-defense and combat. Luckily, Etta knows how to fight and has been helping them practice. I walked through everything Elle taught me, my heart aching at her absence.

Despite my terrible teaching skills, they both pick up on everything far quicker than I ever did. Holly, Cally, and I work together the most, both of them slowly morphing from awkward blade wielders to something more like blade slingers. Etta usually ends up claiming some reason to leave after about an hour of practice, citing some errand or task that needs completing. And Cally, Mother bless her, would rather sit on a bench with a good book than spend time dodging and striking.

But I see the way Etta's eyes turn heavy and full of longing as she watches Holly's vines snap around my ankles, the way my wind and fire whip through the room like another weapon. I don't miss the way her shoulders fall as she leaves the training center, the way the sheer relief of no longer having to pretend falls over her the moment she steps out.

Holly darts toward me, her own shortsword barely missing my forehead. Exactly what I intended. I duck and slide my feet out, catching hers. She goes down with a curse, but she doesn't get back up. She sits there, staring up at me, eyes heavy and posture slumped like the weight of the world is resting on her slender shoulders.

I know when a girl is beat, so I drop to the floor beside her. A sigh escapes my mouth as I lean against the wall. Across the training center, Asmo paces behind a group of hybrids locked in battle against one another, hands clasped behind his back as he carefully assesses each group, nodding in approval or offering murmurs of feedback as he passes by.

"He's going to be a good High King," Holly whispers beside me. I know she's right. Asmo was born to lead. I lift my head in agreement as I stare at him, at the way he seems to glide through the air, as if it parts for him.

After a few more rounds of drills, the princes end their group trainings. Hybrids rack weapons, thank the princes, and exit the training center. Barrett walks over to me, wide frame blocking out the light above as he nears. "How are you feeling about tomorrow?"

"Good," I say, even though I feel like vomiting all over the dirt floor when I think about it.

The last time I faced Cora...the last time I saw Marik...

Dreadful bells toll in my memories, a flash of crimson blood coating the hardwood floor. Screams of terror and cries of pain cut through the air like untold reminders of not a wedding, but a funeral.

Facing the witches was nerve-wracking, but the idea of seeing Marik again, of seeing what he's done to Elle, of seeing the only mother I ever knew...

Fear and anxiety are twin blades, aimed right for my throat.

CHAPTER 41

ELLE

Ruby and Nora arrive at my wing unannounced, their relentless banging on the door luring me from the staring contest I was having with the ceiling of my bedroom. When I open the door, Ruby's mouth falls open in surprise, either from the state of me—currently in days-old clothes, greasy hair, and a general sour smell emanating from being tangled in tear- and sweat-soaked bedsheets—or from the sight of me, not Mae.

This is the first time I've seen Ruby and Nora since the wedding. I wave them in, then try to slam the door in the Serpent guards' faces that follow closely behind them, but no luck.

Nora wraps me in her arms. She smells like five different flowers all at once, and a headache begins to bloom. I don't let go. I was never a hugger, usually offering my own mother some backwards version of one to satisfy her. But I haven't been touched like this in months. I return it, content to hold and be held. She pulls away too soon.

Ruby clears her throat, gaze flitting around the room. "We're here to prepare you for the ball," she says, casting nervous glances to the guards that surround us and watch us like hawks.

Questions rise like bile—*How much do you know? Are you safe? Where have you been?*—but I swallow them. I don't say anything as I lead them—and the hawkish guards—to the bathroom, nor do I apologize for the state of it. Dirty clothes are everywhere, but I've learned I no longer care. I don't have the energy to.

I lower myself into the makeup chair, and Nora reaches for the matted mess of my hair. My ends hang stiff and dry from her hand. "Oh, Elle..."

I open my mouth to respond, although I'm not sure what I was planning to say. *Why bother when they're probably going to kill me soon?* I know Marik said he was going to get me out, but I don't trust him for a second. Even if my net didn't snag when he said it. Whatever my response was going to be, it's cut off by the sound of a door banging open.

I know it's Marik.

Think of the devil and he will appear.

To nobody's surprise, he wears his usual uniform of all-black. His entire body is rigid with irritation. Good. He turns to Nora and Ruby. "You were supposed to wait for me to enter."

Something in the back of my mind twitches at his words. Liar.

"Apologies, Your Highness," Ruby says meekly, eyes downcast. "We were told we were allowed in."

Marik's gaze snaps to the guards. "Out," he commands.

"But, Your Highness—"

Marik's eyebrow raises infinitesimally, but it's enough. The guards scramble, eager to exit the confined space of the bathroom and away from their master.

"I requested that Ruby and Nora assist with preparing you for the ball," Marik says to me, harsh tone gone, replaced by something softer. "However, they do need to prepare you as Mae."

I'm so tired.

One last time, little fawn, Marik's voice whispers in my mind.

He hands me a blade, a bold thing to do. But I don't have the energy to use it against him. I take it from him, then dig it into my skin and whisper the words. Mae's image comes to mind swiftly, and I hate the ease with which I can become her. I feel as if I lose a little bit of myself every time.

Ruby and Nora do their best to not look fully freaked out, but they have a difficult time hiding their alarm.

"The guards will be close, but they won't bother you," Marik says, his eyes lingering on mine for a moment too long before turning and exiting the bathroom.

The duo work in silence, Nora working out the knots from my now-white hair, while Ruby pulls out bottles of liquid and powdered makeup. Nora's brush tugs at every knot. She mutters apologies with every forceful yank, while Ruby dabs different liquids on my face, her movements tender.

Normally, I'd hate it. But right now, I'm just thankful that she's in between the mirror and me, blocking the reflection. Maybe I can pretend it's really me they're getting ready.

"What are you thinking for your dress?" Ruby asks as she brushes shimmery blush along my cheekbones.

I shrug. "Pick something for me."

Her expression turns somber. Mae must have had all manner of opinions about her wardrobe. Yet another disappointing thing about me on the throne—I would rather spend my days locked in battle and drenched in sweat than wear a gown. I would happily wear a pillowcase to the ball, if only to wipe the smirks from every single person there.

Ruby returns from the closet, holding a sleeveless jade green gown made of velvet. Intricate floral embellishments spun from gold thread cascade down the skirt. "What about this?" she asks.

"Sure."

She sets the dress down with a sad smile.

"Almost done," Nora says from behind me. She managed to de-matt my hair, and it feels like my scalp is bleeding, but I'm grateful for it. She comes around to face me, perfecting the placement of each curled lock, then motions to Ruby, who walks over with the High Crown. She places it on my head, secures it around my ivory antlers, then steps aside.

"Ta-da!" Ruby says.

Mae stares back at me in the reflection of the mirror with dead eyes. I look away.

Ruby helps me into the velvet dress, every button done with care. When it's on, I collapse back into the chair.

Ruby and Nora gather their supplies and give me hugs that are over too soon. I could go entertain myself with a book until it's time for the ball, but the guards never come back, and I don't feel like being watched by them. Not yet. So, I spend the remainder of the afternoon in the bathroom. I resume my staring contest, but this time, I stare at the floor. Anything to avoid my reflection. To avoid the reminder of the way I continue to slip away.

Half an hour later, footsteps come down the hallway. I brace myself.

The door opens, and the quiet sound of dress shoes on the tile grows closer. "Are you ready?" Marik asks from behind me. It's too soft, and my skin prickles. How dare he treat me like I'm something fragile when he's the one who made me this way?

He places something cold around my neck. The necklace is back. After being free of it for so long, its weight feels suffocating. "Just for appearances," he says, his black leather loafers coming into view as he steps around the chair. He crouches down and peers up at me with eyes like starless galaxies.

The necklace, the dark mark, the leash I wear that connects me to him. I can't do it anymore. I can't.

I snap.

I launch myself from the chair. He stumbles back, and we both collide with the floor. My teeth sink into his brow. Pain blooms as they jar against the hard surface of his skull, but it feels like a victory. He curses as metal coats my tongue, my blood mixing with his.

Crimson drips from his brow, cutting through his eyelashes and streaming down the curve of his cheek, the sharp angles of his jaw, the slope of his neck. He does nothing to stop it. He just stares at me from the floor, me on top of him. He grips my forearms, leaving crescent moons embedded in my skin.

I meet his gaze, loving the way the flames ignite in my chest, the way my anger feels like a simmering hearth, stoked and ready to burn him. Underneath me, his chest heaves. His pulse thrums—rage? Fear? Or... something else? Something dark and twisted that I cower at? That I can't stomach the thought of? That makes me want to hate myself even more than I hate him?

"I hate you," I grind out.

He smiles at me with blood-drenched teeth. "I know." He pushes himself onto his elbows, his face now inches from mine. His tongue darts from his mouth and he licks the blood from his bottom lip, his teeth scraping and tugging with the movement. My skin tingles, and I fight the urge to run from whatever the hell this feeling is.

I'm the first one to back down, uncomfortable with the way his breath begins to mix with mine, the way his gaze goes from anger to something closer to hunger. I haul myself from him and stare at him on the floor, blood soaking into the collar of his pressed shirt.

"You need a new shirt," I say with a sneer, then leave him on the bathroom floor.

When he exits the bathroom, he looks as if nothing happened. The blood is gone, and his eyebrow looks good as new. He flicks his wrist at me. I don't feel anything, but when I wipe my mouth with the back of my hand, it comes away dry, not a splatter of red to be seen.

Shame.

He straightens his black blazer over his shoulders. "I'm going to ask you once more, little fawn. Are you ready?"

"Never," I hiss at him. His answering smile drips of pity, reminding me of the way he looked at Mae on the night of their wedding, right before he stabbed her in the back. "When this is over, I will rip you limb from limb."

Looking forward to it, his voice slithers in my head.

The playful tempo of the violin thrums as the violinist pushes and pulls her version of a blade across the strings, her music a weapon of her own. The sound entrances me. On second thought, maybe it's the three glasses of champagne I've downed in the last hour.

A female in all black approaches, hair slicked into a tight bun at the nape of her neck. The light of the chandelier above reflects from a delicate gold necklace at the hollow of her throat. She holds a platter of bite-sized portions of salmon, crostini, and smoked shrimp. "Salmon, Your Highness?"

I wave her away, intent on drinking myself to death tonight while nobody notices. But she lingers, jade eyes staring into mine. Freckles line her cheeks.

"I have freckles just like that," I say.

She frowns. "Yours are white, Your Highness."

Fuck. She's right. I down the glass of champagne and hold it out to her in a silent request for more. Marik swoops in behind me and snags the glass. "She's done. No more for the night."

Now I'm the one frowning.

His voice brushes against my mind. *Trust me. Please.*

I huff a sigh and turn toward the crowd. Couples dance on the floor, but their heads keep turning to the witches that are spread throughout the crowd and the guards lining the walls. Koa dances with his sister, one arm wrapped protectively around her as a witch passes by. I don't contain my eye roll. I haven't forgotten the way he stood there in silence as his father called for the executions of innocent civilians.

Marik mutters something about checking on a guest that I don't care about, and my breath catches in my throat as another figure walks toward me. Eliza Rainey.

Asmo.

I force myself to keep my relaxed posture, to keep my nerves settled, my pulse slow and drunken and lazy. Marik can't know who stands before me.

"Hello, Eliza," I say warmly. My eyes threaten to betray me, to bounce around the room to find Marik or Cora, to make sure they're not watching.

"Your Highness," she says with a smile. "What a lovely ball."

"Yes, yes, thank you. I didn't plan much of it. My husband and his... partner are mostly responsible for everything you see tonight," I say cheerfully.

A twitch of a smile pulls at the corner of her mouth. "Well, I just wanted to come and say hello, let you know I was here. My partner is with me, and we'd love to see you after the ball, if that could be arranged."

I nod slowly, combing through the words, the alcohol buzzing in my head making it more difficult. Partner? Is Mae here? Or is that just small talk?

"My friends are also here. I'd love to introduce you to them. I've just gifted them necklaces," she says with a chuckle as she fiddles with a delicate gold necklace around her neck. It's identical to the one the waitress was wearing. "And please, do your best to avoid the wine. I've heard there was a bad batch from Pernrith recently."

"Thank you for the heads up," I say as my mind reels. Asmo is here. Maybe Mae, too. With help. The waiters are their friends. Is this a rescue mission? Are they attacking? A sob threatens to burst, but I shove it down. Eliza—Asmo—gives me a final smile and turns away, stepping from the throne platform and back to the festivities below.

A male waiter approaches. He adjusts his neckline, a glimpse of gold flashing underneath. "Appetizer, Your Highness?"

"Please." I grab a bite of the salmon and a skewer of blackened shrimp and shove them both in my mouth, fighting a laugh as I remember how Mae used to worry about her manners as High Queen. I really need to sober up. I grab another helping.

Marik returns, eyeing me with something like disgust as I lick my fingers. He lowers himself into the throne next to me. "The announcements will be made soon."

I don't respond. Instead, I survey the crowd carefully. Waiters float through the crowd, champagne and red wine sloshing on thin slabs of wooden trays. One approaches a group of five witches, all of them in floor-length gowns in shades of scarlet, charcoal, or black. The waiter offers them wine. A hybrid reaches for the last remaining glass, but the waiter ignores the request and darts back through the crowd.

They poisoned the wine.

"Let's get this over with," Marik mutters. *I'm going to speak through you to make the announcement,* his voice says in my mind.

Since when do you give me a warning? I shoot back, but it's only met with silence.

My legs betray me, forcing me to rise, and my lips curl upward into a mockery of a smile. The crowd hushes as Marik and I stand in tandem. All eyes turn to us.

"People of the Woodland Kingdom, thank you for gathering here today," Mae's voice bellows from my mouth. "It is an honor to host the woodland hybrids, the humans, and the witches." The words taste like rot. "It is also my honor to present my aunt, Willa Ryley, the lost High Fae Princess of the fallen Fae Kingdom." My hand gestures to Cora as she approaches and joins me.

Her black aura is gone, eyes now back to the crystal blue of Mae's aunt. She smiles at me dotingly. I don't have to control my snarl; Marik does it for me.

"Thank you, Mae." Cora's voice is warm. "Many years ago, the Fae Kingdom fell at the hands of the witches. However," she says, grin spreading, "over the last year, I have had the opportunity to extend the olive branch. There have been many discussions of wrongdoings and reparations. With Mae's help, we have entered into an agreement with the witches, allowing them to assimilate into our kingdom, into our home. In a formal act of forgiveness, Mae and I are pleased to announce the joining of the witches as an official High House and to recognize them as citizens of the Woodland Kingdom."

Murmurs ripple through the crowd, hybrids shooting uneasy glances toward the witches. Hesitant smiles and half-ass applause are scattered throughout.

Cora's smile doesn't falter. "I understand this may come as a shock to many. The witches have been a painful subject for this kingdom for many years. It is my sincerest hope and belief that the citizens of Woodland can rise above the challenging history and begin to forgive the wrongdoings of the past."

Despite the snort I can feel forming, my mouth spreads into a grin instead, then says, "A blood oath will be completed with the delegate for the witches to make the joining official."

A witch delegate. Because Cora and Willa can't be in the same room together.

A stunning raven-haired witch walks to the stage, her golden eyes alight, her blood-red gown floating on a subtle wind behind her. She forms a shallow curtsy. I want to shove her.

"Your Majesty." Her voice is dripping in seduction, luring me in like a siren.

"Levana," I say warmly. She smiles, but her eyes are cold. Dead. "You have been given the responsibility and the honor to speak on behalf of the witches."

She holds one arm out and presses a razor-sharp nail to alabaster skin, inky blood sprouting from the wound.

"Repeat after me," Mae's voice says as Marik speaks through me. "With this oath, I swear on the blood of my people that we will uphold the rules and values of the Woodland Kingdom, that we will do no harm to its citizens. I swear that we will collectively work together with the Woodland folk to create a better kingdom, one in which we all thrive."

Her blood evaporates in the air as she repeats the words, and the magic takes hold.

"Should this oath be broken by a witch, they will be prosecuted by the High Crown, just as any of the Woodland citizens would be," my voice says.

I want to chew them and spit them at Marik.

Cora comes from behind me and offers a hug to Levana, who wraps her arms stiffly around her in response. She pulls away and turns to the crowd. "Your newest High House!" she beams. "Please, enjoy the rest of the ball. Eat, drink, and be merry. This is the beginning of a new era!"

The words clang through me. Cora laid her trap, and we all fell into it. She disappears into the crowd, and I feel like I can relax as Marik's control slips. He watches me, a sad smile on his face. I lower myself back into the High Throne and motion for a glass of champagne. He doesn't stop me.

The members of the newly appointed House of Witches begin dancing and calling for more wine, their shrill cackles ringing through the grand room.

Levana approaches the throne. Her mouth opens, but Marik stands and offers me a hand. "Darling, a word, please?" His control is nonexistent right now, so I could tell him to kindly fuck off, but I don't. It's easier not to. "Excuse us," he says kindly to Levana, but she glares at him.

Interesting.

Marik leads me from the throne, one hand on the small of my back as we descend the stairs and step onto the dance floor. Groups part to allow us to walk through. I make eye contact with two separate wait-staff, peeks of gold flashing underneath their white-collared shirts.

Marik comes to a stop in the back, right beside the band, who's currently strumming a celebratory melody. He wraps an arm around me and pulls me to him.

"Why?" I whisper.

"Is the question...Why are we dancing? Or why do I think you'd want to dance with me?" he asks, bending his head to mine.

I look away. I don't answer, just let him lead me in a dance that I don't care for in a room that I've grown to hate.

I need you to listen to me and I need you to trust me, his voice whispers into my mind.

I tense.

Promise me you will do those two things, he says.

I grunt—in agreement or disagreement, I have no clue.

I am going to get you out of here, but I need you to follow my lead.

Every word is laced with the truth, but warning bells ring in my head. What game is he playing? What is the ulterior motive for this? Why, why, why?

Liar, I fire down whatever bond links us.

He shakes his head, then smiles as he tries to recover the slip-up. *I know you know that I'm telling you the truth. Follow my lead, or you're going to get us both killed.*

He stops suddenly and cups my cheek, his cold hands sending shivers down my spine. *Look at me,* he growls.

I scowl up at him.

Well? he asks.

Fine, I say. Even if it's another trick, another betrayal, I have nothing to lose. I slip away more and more every day.

He dips his head and pauses, his lips inches from mine. My pulse skyrockets, and I'd be surprised if his Fae hearing couldn't pick up on the way my heart slams against my chest.

Please don't bite me, he sends down the bond.

You would be so lucky, I manage to fire back.

He closes the distance between us, and my heart riots. His lips are soft, and I don't know how, when everything else about him is sharp edges and fangs and the relentless ferocity of wrath and its cruelty. The kiss is achingly gentle, and some part of me stirs. Something I refuse to acknowledge. Something I will never allow myself to examine.

He pulls away, and my heart begins to calm. The champagne is not helping.

Wrap your arms around me and make this convincing. Please.

Internally, I sigh, but I do as he says. I resist the urge to run my finger along the slope of his neck as I remember the blood that coated it just hours ago. *I liked you better as I watched your blood spill,* I whisper down the bond.

One corner of his lips twists in a flash of an almost-smile. *One more time,* he says in warning, then dips his head again.

My body reacts before I can stop it, and this time I close the distance between us, pressing my lips against his. I jolt as his tongue probes at the space between my lips. But again, my body reacts, and I part my lips, grazing my tongue with his.

I tell myself that the feeling coursing through me is hatred, that my blood is on fire because I'm kissing a monster. Too soon, not soon enough, he wrenches himself away from me and pulls me from the throne room. We leave the celebration behind, my hand clasped in his.

I follow him, flames of self-loathing threatening to burn me from the inside out.

CHAPTER 42
ELLE

MARIK LEADS me down a dimly lit corridor, the sounds of drunken witches receding with every hurried step. Every few seconds, he glances back over his shoulder. I take it his witchy plaything wouldn't approve of this.

"Where are we going?" I huff. I used to spend my days running and training, but I've spent the last two months lying in bed and crying. Or the dark magic has taken an even bigger toll than I thought. My lungs heave and my feet stumble underneath me as I try not to trip over the hemline of my dress.

"I told you. I'm getting you out."

I try to toss a sound barrier around us, but my magic stutters. My stomach drops. It's been weeks since I last summoned. I'm so weak.

Sound barrier, I say down the bond.

With the flick of his wrist, the sounds of our feet pounding against the hardwood floors soften.

"Well, your plan wasn't very well thought out if you didn't even consider a sound barrier as a part of our escape," I hurl at him, but I struggle to get the insult out and control my breathing.

"Sorry, did you want to get out? Or would you prefer to go back to slowly dying in that bedroom?"

He comes to a stop and shoves me into an alcove, pressing his body against mine. I raise my hands, fully intent on shoving him away from me, but he grabs them before I can.

"Someone's coming," he whispers, his breath tickling my nose.

Muted footsteps approach, and I don't move an inch. They pass, and my blood pounds in my ears as I hold my breath. Marik pulls away and pokes his head from the alcove. "Just a guard on patrol," he says. "Let's go."

He grips my hand in his and takes off, all but dragging me behind him. We make it exactly three steps before something strikes our barrier. It disintegrates on impact. I whirl, but Marik shoves me behind him.

Cora's black aura pulses around her angrily. "And where do you two think you're going?" she hisses.

I fully expect Marik to burst into laughter, to finally reveal the game he's been playing. I flinch when he moves, but it's not toward Cora. He throws up another shield and tosses me over his shoulder, turning and running down the hall. Okay, now I believe him. This is happening. He really is trying to get me out.

Cora bobs in my view as he sprints away, but she doesn't make a move toward us. She just watches us with fascination. Marik cuts down a side hallway and she disappears, but it does nothing to lessen the way my stomach twists.

"What's the plan here, Marik?" I ask, not bothering to hide the panic in my question.

"Get you out and funnel you away from here," he grunts below me.

"*That's it*? You planned for years to get on the throne, but you couldn't come up with a half-decent strategy to get me out of here?!"

He mutters something unintelligible, but it sounds an awful lot like obscenities hurled in my direction. "There are wards on the inside of the castle that prevent funneling. I need to get you outside to funnel you out. That's the only plan. Get you outside," he huffs as he runs.

"Let me down. I can lead us out of here. It will be faster."

He slows his pace, then all but throws me from him. Without the sound of his heavy breathing and his feet slapping on the floors, I make out the sounds of...many pairs of feet running toward us.

Shit.

I take off. He easily matches my pace, trailing slightly behind me to follow my lead. He hands me a dagger, and I jump at the sight of it, ready to defend myself. But the hilt is facing me.

"Mar the mark. It will help," he says as he jogs beside me. "And take the necklace off. It's not locked."

I yank the necklace and throw it to the ground, then grab the dagger and slash at the hidden sigil on my stomach. My dress rips, but it works. I feel like my lungs can fully expand, like I'm no longer carrying a weighted rucksack over my shoulders. My steps lighten and I palm the dagger in my hand as my legs pump. I cut down another hallway, my mind racing at the quickest way to get the fuck out of here that also is the least populated. The library. It's near the throne room, so it's a risk, but it might be the best shot.

Even with the dark magic no longer weighing me down, my thighs still scream, begging me to stop. I press forward, panting, sucking deep breaths into my lungs, urging them to continue to just *hold on, please hold on, we're almost there.* The racing footsteps behind us grow louder. Closer. My heart is a pounding mess of adrenaline and fear and full-blown panic.

If I don't make it out of this, they will kill me.

I will not die. Not today.

A turn ahead looms closer. The final turn before the library doors. I round it and skid to a stop. Marik slams into me from behind.

Cora blocks the path to the library door, a group of witches behind her.

Fuck. Think, think, think.

But I can't think as she stares at me, and the sound of footsteps behind us is nearing and time is running out, ticking by so slowly, so quickly. I didn't have enough time.

I don't want to die.

A burst of fire flies past me, landing at Cora's feet. It spreads around her and the witches, flames licking and growing higher. I turn, ready to defend myself against the witches behind us. But it's a group of wait-staff. With gold necklaces.

Asmo's friends.

I don't waste a second. I turn and cut through them, sprinting back down the hall. Marik follows close behind me. The front doors are the only option now. I'd rather face a line of guards than Cora and her witches.

The sounds of shouting and glass breaking comes from behind me. I look back and stumble on my dress. Marik catches my elbow and pushes me forward.

The front doors come into view. Four guards stand in front. The only barrier between me and the outside world is four guards. That's it.

There are more footsteps behind us now. I don't turn to see if it's Cora, her witches, or Asmo's friends. I don't care. All I care about is getting past those guards, getting through those doors, and leaving this fucking castle behind.

Marik fires black flames at the guards. Two go down. They scream, but only for a moment. The remaining two watch Marik with wild panic and confusion. I take advantage, hurling the dagger toward them. It finds its mark in the guard's neck. Marik reaches the final guard, who stands like an idiot caught in between fight or flight.

He flees.

And just like that, the doors are free. My pace slows as I remember the steep set of limestone stairs on the other side that will lead me to certain death should I tumble down them. I slam my shoulder through the doors and inhale the sweet, frigid air of freedom.

"Elle!" someone cries from inside the castle, but Marik grabs my arm and pulls me down the path and away from the castle, away from the voice screaming my name, not Mae's.

Mine.

Someone who knows that I'm trapped in here.

"Marik, wait—I think—" I stutter as I almost trip over this fucking dress again, but his arms are around me and hauling me back to my feet.

"Elle!" the voice calls again as Eliza busts through the castle doors.

Asmo.

"Marik—" I gasp, but his arms are still around me and then wind starts to circle around us. *No, no, no.* I shove against him, desperate to get away and run to his brother, to safety, but he holds me too tightly and the dagger is gone and I'm too weak to fight his grip.

The funnel fades away, revealing a broken home in the middle of a forest. I collapse. My knees hit the ground, colliding with pine straw and dirt and pebbles that bite into my knees like teeth.

The first sob is one of relief—I'm so fucking relieved to be out of the castle that I once loved, that morphed into a source of pain and memories of death and blood and loss. I bury my head into the ground and scream into the dirt.

The second sob is one of anger—no, wrath—toward Marik, Cora, and everyone who helped them steal the throne. Anger toward myself for giving up, for letting them control me, for letting them win.

The third sob—more a scream than anything—is full of misery for what I've let myself become. My tears cut tracks through dirt-covered cheeks. I fist the ground as it all waxes and wanes, rolling through me in waves that come from an ocean that has no end.

I drown in it.

MARIK

Elle's breathing is a steady rhythm that grounds me as my thoughts threaten to spiral. She lies on the floor on a makeshift bed of curtains and dusty blankets, the only soft things I could find that weren't moldy. Her head rests on my jacket, her hair a bed of flames against my black blazer. It was the only thing I knew for certain wasn't covered in filth.

After Elle screamed and cried herself to sleep on the forest floor, I carried her inside. Once I knew she was sound asleep, I spent hours shaking out dust-filled curtains, chasing squirrels from dilapidated cabinets, and getting rid of the hundreds of dead—and alive—bugs that once sought shelter in this home. I spent the next hour tackling the mold that I could, burning each spore to oblivion. There was nothing I could do about the moldy furniture, other than throw stained blankets over them. No matter what I do, the musty smell won't dissipate.

Light enters through the cracked window, sun shining on Elle as it dips below the tree line. Tonight will be the test. To see if I was able to get her out safely.

I have no earthly idea where we are, but I'm assuming we're still in the Deer Court, which sets my nerves racing whenever I think about it for too long.

When I funneled us away, I panicked and couldn't think of an actual place to take us. All I could think about was that damned female sprinting toward us, reaching for my mate. And so, we somehow ended up here, in this random abandoned house with a porch that's nearly falling off and ivy that appears to be taking over every exterior surface.

I almost grabbed Elle again and funneled her back out of here, but I didn't dare touch her, not with the way she screamed with her entire body, every single muscle tensing, every vein popping at the strength of her howls.

It was physically painful not to hold her. To see her agony personified. I wanted to eviscerate myself, knowing I was the cause of it.

Her hand twitches in her sleep. I wonder if she's thinking about reaching for me, clawing my skin off. I wish she would.

The sky darkens and the moon begins to rise. I walk through the house, checking every entry point. I drag furniture in front of doors and windows. They won't keep Cora out, but the sound is all I'll need to grab Elle and go.

The house creaks and my pulse skyrockets, but it's just a gust of wind. A wind chime floats in the breeze, sending chills down my spine. This house has clearly been unoccupied for years, maybe even a decade. The wooden boards beneath my feet are warped and rotted in several spots. My foot fell through a rotten board earlier.

The night passes by uneventfully. I don't sleep; I'm too terrified to close my eyes or shut off my senses for even a second. Fear keeps me alert and wide awake, every inch of me taut as I listen for anything out of the ordinary.

Somehow, two days pass. They are the longest two days of my life, every second spent in fear of hearing shuffling feet on the forest floor, glancing at Elle, or checking the bond to make sure it's still there. I'm not sure if I'm wishing for its presence or its absence.

My stomach growls, curling inside of me as it contracts and screams at me to eat. I ignore it. Asmo and I spent nearly two weeks without food once when we were twelve. But it is a reminder of the fact that Elle most likely wasn't raised with cutthroat parents who tortured their children. I sigh and tiptoe from the room, although I'm wondering if I should start stomping around to wake her up.

The wind curls around me as I step from the dilapidated house, carrying dead leaves and the scent of pine. The porch stairs creak under my weight as I descend. I survey the forest slowly, but everything looks as it should—no sign of Cora or her witches.

I understand the way Elle broke down the moment our feet touched the forest floor. The moment she saw the house, when she realized the castle had been left behind. Relief rolls me through like a physical thing, but then I remember the reason why we're here, and the relief shifts to self-hatred. I shut it off. That is a conversation I cannot afford to have with myself right now.

I ensnare a tawny rabbit, trapping it in quicksand and piercing it with my fangs before cooking it over my flames. The smell of smoked meat wafts toward me and I salivate, but I shove the hunger down.

The musty smell of the house hits me like a wall as I enter. I turn into the living room and nearly drop the rabbit. Elle is sitting on the couch, rubbing sleep from her eyes.

"Good morning," I say, but it comes out hoarse.

She glances out the window pointedly. "It looks like afternoon." Her voice comes out worse than mine—raspy from lack of use. And probably screaming.

I hold up the rabbit. "Dinner?"

She frowns but grabs her stomach, an audible growl filling the silence and answering the question. "I guess."

I hand her the rabbit. She bites into it, wrenching a piece off with her teeth. Her wild hair, drool-crusted cheeks, and gaunt face make her look feral. I could look away, could push this feeling down and lock it away, but I don't. I watch her as she eats, as her eyes close with the first bite, at the way her long lashes land like butterflies against her too-pale skin. My heart beats traitorously in my chest.

"Where are we?" she asks around a mouthful of steaming-hot rabbit.

I clear my throat. "No clue. Likely your court, based on the trees and climate."

Her freckles dance as she chews. I want to count every single one. She swallows, and I stop myself from staring at the delicate curve of her neck. "You don't know where we are?"

"No," I admit. "I saw that female running toward you. I panicked, and we ended up here. But it seems safe enough."

She grabs another chunk of the rabbit. Her eyes meet mine, her affect now somber. "That female was your brother. He was trying to get me out, too. And you fucked it up."

If she had taken a knife to me, it would have hurt less. I would have welcomed that instead of those words. I turn from her, unwilling to break, unwilling to show her how fucking miserable I am, how disappointed I am in myself. How much those words make me want to collapse onto the floor. She would have been better off with him. She would have been happier with him. She was reaching for him and I—

"How long have I been asleep?" she asks, interrupting my thoughts. Saving me from myself.

I run a hand through my hair and gather myself, then turn to face her. She holds the rabbit to me. I wave it away. "Two days."

"Great, well, I'll be out of your hair shortly." She tries to rise from the couch, but her legs give out and she sinks back into it.

"You're not ready yet. You need to eat."

She rolls her eyes but doesn't attempt to get back up. "Fine. One more day, then you'll never see me again."

I nod curtly, then turn away from her, exhaustion slamming into me all at once. "Wake me up if you hear anything."

I collapse into the makeshift bed. The scent of Elle wraps around me, and I tumble into nothing.

CHAPTER 43
MAE

"WHAT DO YOU MEAN, *Marik took her*?" If Etta was from House Serpent, powerless or not, the question would have spewed venom.

"I said exactly what I mean. Marik took her before Asmo could get her." I unbuckle the shortsword sheath from my hip and let it drop to the ground.

Etta takes a measured step toward me. "You're telling me we traded her jailor for another? And now we have no clue where she is and no clue what he's doing to her?"

A groan works its way from the very depths of my soul. "Yep," I say tersely.

"What happened." The question isn't a question, so much as a demand.

"I would recommend watching how you speak to your queen." Asmo's voice slithers through the room.

Etta turns her cold gaze to Asmo. "I'm speaking to my sister."

Asmo takes a step toward Etta. "And my mate."

Etta doesn't back down. "My. Sister."

I open my mouth to speak for myself, but Asmo looks down at her like she's something that flaked off his boot. "Your family threw her aside until you died and the kingdom needed her. Don't speak to me about how she's *family*. You barely know her. And she is your High Queen. Treat her as such."

Etta's stance falters, but she recovers quickly. She turns away from him without another word and looks at me, but her eyes have softened.

Behind her, Asmo explains, "Elle and Marik were both running away from Cora. From what it looked like, he wasn't forcing her to do anything she didn't want to do. I called for her and she reached for me, but Marik had already begun the funnel." He shakes his head—confusion or frustration, I can't tell—and unfastens the hidden weapon holsters along his chest and thighs. "I think Marik was trying to get her out. They disappeared from the ballroom, after...kissing."

Etta's eyebrows shoot up. "Kissing?"

"If I know my brother, it was a ruse. Everything he does is calculated. It looked like he led her from the ballroom to get her alone."

Etta rubs her temples as she mulls over the news. Asmo and I finish racking our weapons in silence, the weight of tonight hanging between us heavily. Our first act as High King and Queen, a failure. The training room door opens. The rest of the rescue team enters the room, the silence feeling like a tangible thing, the only sounds those of buckles and holsters being removed and weapons being racked.

Holly and Ivan won't meet my gaze.

Escaping the witches was easier than I thought it would be, but we didn't make it out entirely unscathed. Several Lower House members were caught by bursts of dark magic, but they'll recover. We downed several witches, groups of hybrids and Fae working in tandem as units. With Marik and Elle taking out the guards to the nearest exit point, we were able to get out quickly and funnel away. It wasn't perfect, but it was better than I expected.

We got lucky this time. They weren't expecting us. They won't make that mistake again.

"Take the wounded to the healers. Let's debrief in the meeting room," I call, then storm from the training room.

"Princess," Asmo calls behind me. His hand wraps around my wrist and he whirls me to him.

Months ago, I might have pushed him away. But now, I collapse against him with an exhaustion that feels like it penetrates my bones. My soul. I've been so tired for so long. I thought we'd have a win right now. I thought Elle would be back with us. But now, we have no clue where she is and I've failed her and I've failed my kingdom again and I'm just so, so tired.

Asmo's arms are anchors that keep me from drifting into my thoughts and drowning. They hold me steady against the riptide of emotions that threaten to pull me under. Even now, the waves rise and threaten to spill in salty tears.

"We'll get her. I promise," he mumbles against my forehead.

I allow myself exactly three more deep breaths, then pull myself away, instantly missing the warmth and strength of him. He reaches for me again, intertwining his fingers with mine. He doesn't let go.

We're the first ones to arrive to the meeting room, but the others join within moments. Holly, Ivan, and Basil lean against the wall in silence while Amaris paces in front of them. Houses Canis and Ursidae sit in respective groups in quiet discussion. Etta sits by herself, spine straight, hands clasped on the table.

Asmo is the first to speak. His voice comes out calm, but firm. "This is war," he says, "Let us not forget that. There will be wins and losses. While we did not complete the objective—"

"We didn't rescue Elle," Etta interrupts.

Asmo continues like she never spoke. "We still got valuable information. We all made it out alive. Nobody was injured. We helped facilitate Elle's escape."

Amaris's voice is low as she says, "Please explain how you've managed to spin this into *helping* her when you just allowed Marik to *escape* with her?" Her tattoos begin to swirl, white lines and circles moving like a lazy hurricane. She glances down at them with a frown.

Holly clears her throat. "Marik and Elle were running, then they ran right into Cora and the witches. We were able to fight them and hold them off to allow Elle and Marik time to escape." She takes a deep breath and continues. "King Asmo is right—Nobody was gravely injured, and that is a huge success."

Ivan nods beside her, but the movement is stiff. "We were expecting casualties. Our careful planning helped keep everyone safe. That is a win."

"And Elle is out of Cora's hands," August adds.

Amaris's gaze turns as sharp as one of the many daggers still on her person. "I agree with Princess Etta. She may be away from Cora, but she's now with Cora's lover. Let us not forget she's *still* in enemy hands and worse yet, we now have no way of knowing where she is."

I wish I could sink into the floor and disappear at the reminder. I dig my nails into my palm, hating that I feel the need for pain right now to distract myself and hold it together.

Asmo's foot twitches against mine. "She is with her mate. I understand my brother is...dishonorable, but her mate is the safest place for her right now. There is no earthly way he would hurt her. His only instinct is to protect her."

"Maybe physically, but who's to say he can't hurt her emotionally?" Holly whispers. "From the scout's reports, she was barely hanging on. What will he do to her when they're alone?"

I don't let the question take hold. "Is there anything we can do to find where she is?" I ask the group.

"I'll increase the number of scouts we have on patrol, but I'm not sure how helpful that will be," Etta says. "There's a lot of land to cover and only so much time. They could be anywhere."

I turn to Asmo. "Where do you think he'd go?"

He rubs the back of his neck with a frown. "He would want to take her somewhere safe. There's one place I can think of, but it's in our court, so I don't think he would go there. Not with her, at least."

"It's worth a shot," I say.

He nods his head silently, slowly, then stands. "Let's go." He offers me his hand, and we leave the too-quiet room behind.

Outside, stars freckle the night sky, white and bright. "Where are we going?" I ask Asmo.

He tears his gaze from the sky above and looks at me, his eyes softening as he does, as if looking upon me is even greater than looking at the stars. "I'm taking you to the place I used to call home."

The entrance to Squall's End fades away. The sky grows darker, but the air grows drier, warmer. The wind dies, and Asmo turns me in his arms.

"Welcome to the City of Sand."

We stand on a cliff overlooking a small city, buildings hewn from clay and stone scattered throughout the small metropolis. The smell of sand and dirt is a far cry from the scent of pine that permeates the High Court.

In the distance, an angry ocean beats against the outcropping of tan rock. Asmo points to a building that spans the cliffside.

"The Vasuki manor."

Walls of glass overlook the vast expanse of the Sitani Sea. The manor looks intimidating, and my stomach clenches. "Do you think it's a good idea to visit right now?" I manage to ask.

He squeezes me tightly. "We're not going there. Not right now. Come on." He motions me away from the edge of the cliff. Behind us, an entrance to a cave looms, dark and ominous.

Asmo stands at the entrance, one ear tilted toward the interior. No sound comes from the cave. Just darkness that threatens to swallow us whole. He waves his hand, and tiny, controlled balls of flames vanish inside, settling along the walls and lighting the path forward. The air inside is stale, as if nobody has set foot inside for years. After several minutes of walking, the cave comes to a dead end. Asmo's shoulders drop. He turns to me with a somber expression.

"They're not here," he mutters, running a hand through his hair.

The cave is mostly empty, save for a couple of dusty blankets and a wooden box. "What is this place?"

His smile is sad. "This used to be our hiding spot as kids. We always came here to escape Mother and Father. They have no clue it exists, so I thought maybe it would be his safe space to take Elle."

Well, now I feel like a piece of shit thinking about the privileged Serpent twins in their glass house on the sea, who had to come to this empty, desolate cave to escape their parents. Although Willa—Cora—betrayed me, at least I had a safe home.

"It's..."

Asmo snorts. "Yeah, it's bare."

"Did you used to bring girls back here?" I ask, eyeing the dusty blankets.

"Is that what you're thinking about, princess? Me with other females?" He raises an eyebrow suggestively. "Because I'd love to tell you all the ways I've pictured you with other males. But, another time."

My cheeks flame. He grabs my hand with a chuckle and leads me from the cave, summoning wind to douse each lantern that flickers with his black flames. His suggestive comment replays in my head, but I don't bring it back up. It's absolutely not the time to think about me, him, and certain other High Princes. In bed. I make a mental note to bring this up later, maybe when I'm back on the throne. If I ever make it there.

"Az?" I whisper.

He squeezes my hand. "Hm?"

"What do we do if we can't find them?"

We walk in silence for several steps. "We will, princess. I promise you." Truth in every word.

"But how do you know?" I ask as we step out of the cave and back to the cliffside.

He chews his lip as he surveys the city that sprawls beneath us. "I have a trick up my sleeve..." I quirk an eyebrow. "But we'll need to go into the manor."

My stomach quivers. The manor feels intimidating. "Wh—Do you think that's safe?"

He nods. "Yes. Mother and Father will still be at the ball. I can funnel us in and out."

"What if someone sees us?"

"There are hidden passageways that we can take." He turns me toward the manor. "Look, the only lights that are on right now are the outside lanterns, and there are four guards stationed by the entrance, which means nobody's home."

I bite my cheek as I survey the Serpent manor. But he's right. The rest of the building is dark, but it won't be for long. Word will have gotten out about the ball, and this could be our only chance.

"Fine," I say.

He turns me to face him. "Are you sure? We can funnel back to Squall's End now, and I can return without you."

"No, I'm not sure. But where you go, I go."

His hand is warm against my arm as he pulls me to him. The warm air stirs around us, the cityscape below vanishing. Darkness surrounds us as Asmo funnels us into the den of vipers.

CHAPTER 44
MAE

Asmo's bedroom is the size of my entire cottage. It faces the Sitani Sea, the dark water churning below us as it crashes along the cliff. The walls are painted black, but the room still feels welcoming. Centered along the wall is a sprawling bed with an oak headboard and sheets the color of clouds. The wall facing the water is not a wall, but an invisible barrier, just like in the High Castle's library. The breeze stirs an open book on Asmo's side table.

It feels like home.

Asmo opens an interior door, revealing rows of neatly pressed jackets, shirts, and pants. A sword, made of glimmering black, hangs on the wall in a glass case. He walks to a chest of drawers and begins rifling through. He extracts a handheld mirror, its oval surface surrounded by scalloped edges, embellished snakes, and black roses.

"This will show us where Marik and Elle are," he says, shutting the drawer and placing the mirror on the bed.

"What is it?"

"It's imbued with a spell that will allow the user to see whoever they request," he explains.

I reach for it, but he darts toward me and stops my hand. "But there is a risk. He would be able to see us on whatever surface allowed us to see him. It must be used sparingly and wisely."

I place my hand back in my lap. "I've never heard of anything like this."

Asmo settles onto the bed, resting the mirror on top of the open book. "My father spelled it with dark magic. Marik and I used to use the mirror to spy on him and Mother." A ghost of a smile graces his lips, but it falls quickly.

Asmo stares at his hands as he wrings them together in his lap, his jaw working.

"What's wrong?" I ask.

"I never thought I'd have the High Queen in my bed," he jokes, but it falls flat.

I don't budge. "What is it?"

"I—I think I'm just having a hard time being back here," he says. "There are so many memories—mostly bad, but some good ones. It's hard to imagine this is how my family ended up."

If anyone can empathize with that, it's me. My entire life has been a lie, but that doesn't mean there weren't good times. It just means those memories are now tainted. I scoot toward him on the bed, resting against the headboard and leaning against him. He wraps an arm around me and pulls me closer.

"Do you want to talk about it?" I whisper.

"No." My net tugs, but I won't press him any further on this. There will be time to recount the details of our lives to one another, to heal the trauma and to soothe away the pain. But not until we're both ready.

He extricates himself and stands from the bed. "Come here," he says, walking toward the barrier that separates his room from the drop-off below. "I want to show you something."

I join him, watching as the ocean below churns, the reflection of the moon dancing on its surface. He points to something in the distance, but all I see is the endless expanse of the black ocean.

"What?" I ask.

"Watch the surface closely," he whispers, then turns his palm upward, fingers moving slowly.

The waves begin to thrash, but something writhes below. Dark, scaled figures, a mass of serpentine bodies growing with every passing second.

"What...are...those...?"

"Sea snakes," he answers, then drops his hand. In a flash, the snakes dip back below the surface. The idea of that many sea snakes hidden below the surface has my lip curling.

"How did you do that?" I ask. He must have summoned hundreds of snakes, all in a matter of seconds.

"Mother and Father used to keep us locked in our rooms for days, sometimes weeks. The only thing I had to do to entertain myself was practice my magic and watch the sea. One day, I tried to force the waves to move, but a snake answered instead," he says.

My heart breaks for him. The more I learn about the Serpent Princes, the less I blame Marik for the way he turned out. But then I remember the male Asmo became, and my sympathy disappears.

"Do you remember when you told me you were a terrible male?" His jaw clenches, but he nods, stony gaze still locked on the sea. I face him, looping my arms around his neck. "You're a good male, Asmo."

His gaze still doesn't meet mine, but his eyes turn glassy. I stroke the mating tattoo on his neck, the snake head just below his ear.

"I—I don't deserve you," he says, his voice low and thick with emotion.

My net doesn't stir, and I squeeze my eyes shut. How could he believe that? "No, you don't deserve anything that happened to you."

His hand grips the small of my back, and he pulls me flush against him. He dips his head, pressing his lips against mine with a tenderness that threatens to split my heart in two.

Did they damage your heart so terribly, Asmo? Did they kill what's mine?

He places soft kisses down my neck, my skin erupting in fire and ice with every brush of his lips. He lifts my shirt over my head and drops it to the floor. His fingers trail over the mating tattoo, to the space in between my breasts. He leans down and presses a kiss to the blackened space over my heart, and it bucks in my chest.

When will our hearts stop bleeding? Will they ever stop?

He drops to his knees, placing torturously slow kisses along the flat plane of my stomach. It twists, butterflies and dragons and fireflies taking flight.

I cup his jaw, forcing him to look up at me, and he does. Like I'm the sun, the moon, and all the stars in the sky.

"What are you doing?" I whisper.

The crook of his smile.

"Worshipping you."

The truth in his words.

He trails his kisses downward, and I squeeze my legs shut, anything to ease the throbbing. He doesn't miss the motion, his smirk only adding to the slickness between them. He stands and scoops me into his arms. He tosses me on the bed, then peels my pants off and throws them behind him haphazardly.

"You deserve to be worshipped. Every day," he says as he stares at my slick center. He lowers himself, parting my legs further, and places gentle kisses on my inner thighs. Every kiss only exacerbates the throbbing.

Finally, his tongue grazes the sensitive bundle of nerves, and my eyes roll to the back of my head. Every expert movement of his tongue takes me higher, each brush sending me one step closer to the edge as he feasts. I fist my hands into his hair and clench my thighs together as he hits the perfect spot.

"I—don't stop," I pant as the wave reaches its peak. With one more flick of his tongue, my hips buck as it crests. I smother my moans in the crook of my arm as it washes over me, my muscles relaxing as it recedes.

I open my eyes. Asmo stares at me from the edge of the bed, straining in his pants. I push myself up and reach for him, but he grabs my wrist and spins me around, securing me against him. His erection pressed against my backside makes me wet all over again, and his hand splayed against my stomach doesn't help.

"Do I get to have a turn worshipping you?" I ask, but his hand inches lower and lower. I squirm against him.

"Being able to fuck you is the closest to being worshipped I'll ever get," he says against my neck, the words making my head roll back as I lean against him.

I understand what he means. Being one with him feels like something holy.

"Then fuck me, Asmo," I whisper.

It's as if the words were a key sliding into a lock, but the lock was hiding a beast within. He bends me over, my face landing in the softness of the bed below. The sound of his pants unbuttoning, his belt hitting the floor with a thunk, the brush of his length against my backside. I press against it, desperate to feel him inside me again.

Desperate for another taste of the divine.

He rubs himself against my soaking center, teasing me from behind. "So fucking ready for me," he says, his voice low and throaty.

I wiggle my hips in a plea, and it goes answered. My back arches as he fills me, his moan almost sending me over the edge. His strokes start slow, every movement sending shooting pleasure into every nerve.

He pauses as my orgasm threatens to explode through me, but his next words have me panting all over again. "I'm going to fill you up, then fuck you again. Would you like that, princess?" Nodding is the only thing I can do, because the ability to speak has left me. "I want you dripping by the time I'm done with you."

He slams into me with a moan and stills as he empties himself into me. My body reacts instantly, my orgasm spreading like wildfire this time. I sag into the bed as it dissipates, and Asmo pulls himself out. When I turn my head, he surveys the mess he made appreciatively, his length glistening with his seed. He grabs my leg and pulls me over, twisting me onto my back.

I part my legs and he hooks his arms underneath my knees, lifting my center to his glistening hardness once more. He summons a pillow and places it underneath me, then slides into me again.

And holy heavenly fuck, he was made so perfectly for me. I want to cry out to the Mother, I want to fall to my knees and thank Her for him. I smother my moans with my hands as he rails into me with the same passion as earlier. But this time feels different. This time, he fucks me like he's paying penance for having me.

I reach for him, but his gaze is locked on where we're joined, watching every stroke as he thrusts into me. It doesn't take long for us both to climax again, and he collapses onto me, his heart pounding in his chest, in tandem with mine.

This. I would fight the entire world for this moment. I would claw through dirt and glass and fire if it meant another moment with Asmo, his heart beating against my chest as it recognizes mine.

He brushes sweat-slicked hair from my forehead, his own black locks damp. "Princess, I—" He pauses as he fumbles for the words.

I reach up and cup his face. "I know."

There isn't a word for what's between us. Love isn't enough. So all I can say is *I know,* because I know exactly what he's trying—and failing—to say. He places his hand on the mating tattoo on my chest, my heart thumping against his hand.

"Mine," he says.

"Yours," I whisper into his lips before sealing the promise with a kiss.

We lay there as our hearts return to normal and the sweat dries from our flushed skin. My eyes begin to drift shut, and I force them open. "We need to go. The ball could end at any moment."

He rises with a groan. "You're right. These things usually go until the dawn, but with what happened tonight..." He shoves his legs into his pants and tosses me my clothes. We dress quickly, and he grabs the mirror from the nightstand, tucking it into an interior pocket of his coat.

Asmo funnels us away, and my shoulders relax as we step into Squall's End again. We manage to run into Rain on the way back to my private quarters, and she assures us that she'll notify Etta and the Herd of our return.

Once inside the privacy and darkness of our own room, Asmo extracts the mirror and sits on the bed. He extends his fangs, pricking his wrist and drawing a bright drop of red blood. He smears it on the scalloped edges and grips it with both hands. "Show me Marik."

The mirror goes from a smooth, reflective surface to a foggy image of...a living room. Marik sits on a pile of blankets, watching Elle sleeping beside him on the floor. I do a double-take at the tenderness in his eyes.

Holy shit. It has to be true, then. He never looked at me that way. The only person who's ever looked at me that way is Asmo. My mate.

Asmo doesn't seem to notice, gaze flicking all over the mirror as he tracks every detail.

Marik rises, Elle shifting as he walks from the room. The mirror darkens, then shifts to a new view, still foggy. Marik walks down a hall-way. He disappears, then the image changes again, and he walks onto a front porch, then down a set of stairs into a forest, the soaring trees as familiar to me as the back of my hand. His footsteps are quiet, but the sounds surrounding him are not. Songbirds tweeting, owls hooting, and the rustling of animals traveling over the forest floor are the only things I need to hear.

They're still in the Deer Court.

It only takes three days to find them. Etta and Basil spread the word to all their scouts and dispatched extras to scour the forests in the Deer Court. A squirrel shifter races into Squall's End one frosty morn-ing. One second, a squirrel is flying down the hallway; the next, Etta and Basil are sprinting in the opposite direction, brown-haired male in tow. They pass Asmo and me on our way to the training room.

"What's going on?" Asmo demands.

Etta rushes to me, her eyes shining. She grabs my forearms. "She's safe."

There can only be one person she's talking about. Our sister. Elle.

Etta's smile is shaky, like she can't believe Elle's okay. Like she's relieved. It surprises me. She hasn't seemed to show any interest in her long-lost sister. Come to think of it, she hasn't shown much interest in getting to know me either since I've been at Squall's End. But her palpable relief at finding Elle tells me maybe there's more to Etta than meets the eye.

"Where?" I ask. "Where is she?"

Etta releases my arms and joins Basil's side once more. The scout stands behind them, shifting on his feet and stealing glances of Asmo and me when we're not looking.

"An abandoned house. You were right," Basil says. "Deer Court."

I reach for Asmo's hand. "Let's go."

She crosses her arms, her mouth an angry slash. "We need to assemble a team. You can't go alone."

I turn to the shifter. "Who's at the house?"

"Just the two of them, Your Highness. The girl and the traitor," he says, casting a nervous glance at Asmo, then promptly looking at his feet.

"Good. Take us there, please," I say.

The shifter looks to Etta, seemingly for her permission.

"We don't have time for this," Asmo mutters. "As your H—"

I jab him with my elbow to shut him up. "What's your name?"

"Joel, Your Highness."

I smile, hoping I'm coming across as sweet, yet slightly intimidating, if there ever was such a combination. "Joel, it is imperative that we get there as quickly as possible. Would you mind funneling us to them?" I turn my gaze to Etta. "Once we are there, Joel can funnel back. If we do not return within...fifteen minutes, send Joel back with reinforcements. How does that work?"

Etta's jaw ticks, but she nods. "Fine."

I motion toward the direction of Squall's End's only entry and exit point. "After you, Joel." He throws one last nervous glance back to Etta, then sets off down the hall.

Outside, the sun is starting to dip behind the trees. We were right not to wait—a rescue mission in the dark would have been idiotic. Joel places his hands on my forearm—right after shooting another nervous look at Asmo—and then one on Asmo's forearm.

The forest is eerily silent as we step from the funnel. I turn to look back and thank Joel, but he's already gone. Asmo and I stand back-to-back as we take in the surroundings. Bare trees tower above, leaves fallen to the ground long ago left to rot on the forest floor. The air is fresh, a soft breeze passing through the trees. A tiny tornado of dead leaves flits past, leaves spinning in the funnel.

Like the forest, the house is also dying, wood rot spreading along the gray siding, moss and ivy creeping up its sides, taking back what belongs to them. The front porch sags and holes pepper the stairs while window shutters hang crooked.

But a light flickers from a window on the first floor.

And then a flame appears.

A flame of crimson pierced by two bone-white antlers. As quickly as it appeared, it disappears. And then the front door is thrown open, and Elle is running, she's sprinting, she's crying and I can't see anything anymore because I'm crying, too. She crashes into me and I wrap my arms around a frame that has grown too bony, too sharp, too different from the version of her from before.

But she's here.

Two sisters. Together again.

Over her shoulder, Marik descends the staircase. His movements are slow and awkward. I close my eyes. Elle pulls back and wipes her tears away with the heels of her palms.

"Holy shit," she says. "I can't believe you're here."

I can't help it. I laugh through my tears. "Me either." I study every inch of her exposed skin, but there aren't any visible wounds. Her dress is slashed, right in the center of her stomach, revealing the echo of a hidden sigil. But otherwise, she's unharmed. "You're okay?"

She gives me some combination of a shake and a nod. I know what that means. Physically, she's fine. Emotionally, mentally...Of course she's not okay.

The sound of fist striking flesh registers, followed by the smell of blood.

Asmo has Marik on the ground. Blood spurts from Marik's nose—which currently hangs at a crooked angle—and flows down his neck. Marik doesn't make any attempt to defend himself. His hands lay palm down on the floor, limp and unmoving. His head jerks to the side as Asmo's fist strikes his cheek. Asmo pulls back again, and Elle lurches away from me. She reaches for him, but his fist catches her in the jaw, and she falls to the ground with a curse.

Asmo turns, eyes wide in pure panic. "Shit," he swears as he reaches for her, but Marik shoves Asmo away.

He pushes himself to his feet and rushes to Elle. He bends down, blood dripping from his crooked nose. "Elle," he whispers, hands reaching for her, landing on skin so pale it's nearly translucent. Even from here, I can tell Marik's touch is gentle. She looks up at him, eyes softening for a whisper of a second, before pushing him away.

"I'm fine," she says as she rises to her feet. She rubs her jaw, at the pink mark that's now blossomed.

Asmo stands and assesses her. "I'm so sorry, Elle. I didn't mean to."

She waves the apology away. "Good to see you, too, Asmo," she says with a smirk.

Something warm unfurls in my chest. I have no idea what Elle has been through. I'm assuming it was some version of hell. Whatever it was, it wasn't enough to erase her. Not all of it, at least.

She pulls Asmo in for a hug. He wraps tentative arms around her. Marik watches them with a sad expression.

"If there are no more punches to be thrown," I say, "We need to get back." Elle looks at me quizzically. "You'll see. It's safe."

She walks toward me and grabs my hand, then reaches for Asmo's. "Let's go." Her voice is steel, as if she's preparing herself for whatever is thrown at her next.

"Er—Elle," I say, "Marik has to come with us."

He stands watching us, face still dripping with blood from a gash on his cheek and what I'm assuming is a broken nose. Elle refuses to look at him.

She shakes her head firmly, her gaze locked on something over my shoulder. "No. Come on, let's go."

I close my eyes. I would love to say *You're right. Let's leave him!* But I can't. We can't. I breathe through my hatred for him and for the Mother and for everything that's led us here. "We need him."

She drops my hand and stares at me with hardened eyes.

I soften mine. "I know," I say gently, "But it's the only way. There's so much you don't know. But we need him if we have a chance at winning this thing. At beating Cora."

Her jaw flexes. "Fine." She turns that angry gaze to Marik, to the mate she knows nothing about. "Let's go."

He follows her orders, hangs his head. I can't help but wonder if he knows already. Elle grabs my hand once more. I reach for Marik's arm, everything in me revolting at the touch.

Asmo funnels us away.

But something is wrong.

The kiss of the chilly night air is absent, replaced by smothering heat instead.

Squall's End is on fire.

CHAPTER 45
MAE

Despite being swathed in angry flames, the entrance to Squall's End remains standing. Thick smoke smothers my lungs, and I cover my mouth and nose with my shirt. Sweat beads along my forehead, and my eyes water at the blazing heat. The fire crackles, but the tree stands tall.

"Fuck," Asmo mutters. He looks to Marik. "Help me."

"Wh—" Marik starts, but Asmo turns and sand pours from his hands, quieting the flames. Marik joins him, the two of them working together to smother the fire. I watch them, chewing my lip the whole time, my thoughts racing.

Etta is in there. I just got back my sister. I can't lose the other. I can't lose my friends. Cally, Holly, Ivan.

The fire dies easily, the raging flames now sleeping embers. But smoke still pours from the entrance. Squall's End is still burning.

"What is going on?" Marik demands. Blood no longer drips from his nose, but is now caked on his face, his neck, the collar of his shirt.

I want to yell at him that he doesn't get to ask questions. "I don't know," I snap instead.

We were just here. We were just talking to Basil and Etta. Screaming comes from the inside of the tunnel city. I dart forward, but Asmo blocks me with his arm.

"We need to think through this before we dive in there," he barks.

"What is there to think through? There are people in there!" I hiss.

"It's a tree?" Elle asks, confusion evident in her tone.

I turn back to her. "This is the entrance to the home we've been staying in. It wasn't...It's not supposed to be on fire. Something is wrong," I explain hurriedly. "We have to help them." I turn to Marik. "Can I trust you to protect her?"

Elle's eyes widen at the question. "What the fuck, Mae? No, you can't."

I place my hands on her shoulders. "It will all make sense when I get a chance to explain everything. You *can* trust him."

The words make me sick.

She stares back at me, horror, betrayal, sorrow, all flashing through those amber eyes, the same eyes that look back at me in the mirror. "Wh—I don't understand."

"I know you don't. Marik, please tell her you'll protect her so she knows you're not lying." Every word is hurried. We don't have time for this. Every second that's wasted is a second I could be saving my court. My friends.

He hesitates but meets her gaze. "I promise I will protect you. I won't...I won't betray you. Your wellbeing is all I care about."

Truths.

I know Elle feels them, too. She stares back at me, anger still burning in her eyes.

"Elle," I interrupt. "I know what he's done. But for the sake of those people in there, I need you to trust me." She grits her teeth, but nods. Thank the Mother. "Are you well enough to fight?"

Marik begins to answer for her, but she steps in front of him to cut him off. "Yes."

We don't have time for this. Elle is an adult. Marik is powerful and will watch out for her.

"What's the plan?" I turn back to Asmo.

"I don't know," he admits as he rubs his jaw. "I don't know if this is a rescue mission or a battle. Or both. If this fire was set intentionally, we need to be ready to fight. If you see a discarded weapon, grab it. Be ready for anything." More screams cut through the air. "Ready?" Asmo stares at me.

Yes. No. I'm terrified. But I meet his eyes, loving the way they soften for me but harden for everyone else.

He gives me one final look, then turns toward the entryway to Squall's End. The three of us follow him, through the smoke and into chaos.

Because chaos it is. And it threatens to bring me to my knees.

Drabars fly through the air, thick, black membranous wings rippling through the smoke, sharp talons slicing and felling hybrids as they make contact. Undead animals and children sprint through the space, leaping on backs and sinking teeth into soft skin. Witches fire black magic at groups of hybrids, who fire back as they defend their home. The home they've spent decades building and hiding from everyone. The home that we stumbled upon, that these hybrids offered to us, to keep us safe...It's all under attack. We brought this to them.

I'm so fucking tired of this.

Fire, wind, ice, water, earth...It all comes rushing to me.

A cambion sprints toward me. I strike it down with a flick of my wrist, its body engulfed in white flames. A drabar flies toward me. I fire another burst of white flames at it. It drops, body charred and smoking on the ground.

A witch spots us, black cape billowing behind her as she strides toward us. Asmo chuckles. He raises his hands. Loose dirt rises, then rushes straight toward the witch in a concentrated funnel. A squirrel hybrid leaps out of the way with a yelp. The witch's smug expression turns to panic. She turns and runs, but Asmo shoves the funnel of dirt down her throat.

Another witch sprints for me. I throw out a wave of white flames. She dodges them with a leap. I summon wind and force the flames upward. She screeches as they find her and take purchase. I funnel more flames, more heat, more more more. Her ashes fall to the floor, mixing with the dirt. The four of us clear the entryway within minutes.

A female hybrid runs to us, dirt and sweat marring flushed cheeks. A group of hybrids follow behind her, half of them in fighting leathers, the other half still in sleeping clothes.

"What happened?" Asmo demands.

The female shakes her head. "They took us by surprise. Somehow, they knew of the entry point. All of a sudden, witches and their demons from Hell started pouring in and attacking."

Fuck. "Is Cora here?" I ask.

Her eyebrows scrunch together. "Who?"

"Witch in charge. White eyes," I explain.

She looks to the group behind her. Everyone shakes their heads. "We've been busy fighting, so it's possible she slipped in without any of us noticing. Bunch of them managed to get past us."

This doesn't sound good. The last time we fought Cora, it ended with Elle and me nearly dead. And she didn't have any witches or the Cursed.

But this time, Cora thinks she's trapping us in. If she is here, and we can surprise her...It might be the advantage we need.

"Leave. Now," I command the group of hybrids. "Get out and live."

The female plants her feet and the group shake their heads. "Respectfully, Your Highness, but no," the female says. "This is our home. Let us fight."

Asmo grunts in what I assume is approval.

"Fine. We stay as a group. Numbers work the best against them. We fight together." I look to Marik and Elle. "You two, protect the rear."

They give curt nods and head to the back. Both of them still wear their outfits from the ball, but Elle's gown is ripped and tattered, fraying at the hem. Marik's nose is still crooked and his cheek is still swollen from Asmo's fist.

We move as one through the halls of Squall's End. Fire, wind, ice, and blades all felling the dark creatures. We pass Lower House hybrids and Fae fighting in duos, but members of Houses Ursidae and Canis are nowhere to be found. And neither are the witches.

Where are they?

Slash, fire, freeze, slash, on repeat until we come to a stop outside of the healing center. The doors are shut, but it doesn't stop the sounds of battle from within. Screams of anguish, of terror, of anger. Swords clashing and things combusting.

I run to the doors and yank the handle, but they don't budge. I hurl fire at them, but it dies the moment it makes contact. "What the fuck?"

"There must be a protective barrier around it," Asmo says as he inspects the doors.

Marik joins his brother and places a hand on the door. "Dark magic barrier. See the way it glints?" He glances to Asmo, who nods in confirmation.

Shit. This must be where Cora and the witches are. And the rest of the hybrids, who are now trapped.

"How do we break it? We have to get to them, Az," I say, desperation lacing my tone.

He shakes his head, but Marik answers. "The only way to break it would be to destroy or damage the mark. It's likely carved into the wood on the other side, but the barrier blocks it."

My face falls. "So, you're saying there's no way to do that from this side?"

Marik shakes his head. "The only way to get in there would be to blast away a section of the wall."

I gasp. "Or portal through it! Like we did for the dungeons."

Asmo grins at my stroke of brilliance. "I can't believe I forgot about that. You're right."

"I don't know how to do exactly what they did, but I was able to—"

Screams and gasps of pain. But they don't come from the other side of the door. They come from behind us.

Cora stands with a smirk on her face, surrounded by eight witches. Each one holds a hybrid captive, razor-sharp nails pressed to their necks. The hybrids stare at us, the whites in their eyes huge and gleaming with terror. They claw at the hands on their throats, but it's no use. The witches hold them with iron grips.

Behind Cora, Luca stares at me with a self-satisfied smirk.

"You," I hiss. "What have you done?"

He doesn't say a word. Coward. I'll burn him alive for this.

Cora smiles, and it splits her face into something ancient and dreadful. "I've come for what's mine." Her white eyes pan from me, landing on Marik.

Motherfuck. As much as I would love to throw Marik back to Cora and kick her the fuck out of Squall's End, I need him. *We* need him if we have a chance of beating her.

"You did all of this for a male? How embarrassing," I say.

She quirks an eyebrow. "Well, he *is* quite talented with his tongue." Her grin is malicious.

Ew. My lip curls in disgust. "Unfortunately, you can't have him."

Her smile slips, and her attention turns to Marik. "Do you let her boss you around now?"

He doesn't respond. From my peripheral, I can tell the way he stands rigid as he faces her. His hands are balled into fists. He looks nervous, uncomfortable, and I hope he hates himself right now. I hope he's going through every decision he made and regretting every single one. I hope the weight of his regret smothers him, leaves him gasping for every breath just to survive.

"Come now, Marik. I know you can't stand her." Those bone-white eyes turn back to me. "You should have heard all of the awful things he said about you dear," she tuts. "The way he mocked you and how you pined after his brother. Pathetic, I think was his most frequent adjective he used about you."

It's not so much her words that stoke fire, but more so the way she speaks to me like she feels sorry for me. I don't bite.

Her head twitches back to Marik. "What's your choice? Are you going to come back home? Or do these people need to die? Just like the wedding guests?"

"What are you talking about?" Marik asks. "They were released. You gave me your word."

She snorts. "I lied. Surely you can't think I'd be that dumb to let them go after they knew the truth?"

My blood turns to ice. Everyone. Dead. Innocent people, their only crime wanting to see me get married. Cally...If Asmo hadn't gotten Cally out...

"Enough of this, Marik. Come." Cora's voice is harsh as she speaks to him. Like a dog.

"No."

The ground shakes. Dirt falls from the ceiling as Cora faces Marik. Her black aura sputters out, then flares.

Fuck this. I summon twin daggers from a witch's belt. I snatch them from the air and imbue them with my flames. Rage courses through me as I surge toward two witches and sink the hilts into their necks. They drop, and the two freed hybrids dash to the other side of the room.

Asmo fires blazing paths of black flames to two more witches, downing them, but not killing them. They douse the flames with their cloaks and reach for their captives, but Marik finally jumps into the action and hurls fire at them. They hiss and drop to the floor to dodge the blast, and the hybrids escape.

Cora's nostrils flare as she watches Marik. But she doesn't watch for long. She hurls a burst of black magic at him and Elle. Marik grabs Elle and they narrowly avoid the blast. It collides with the walls, oily black patches spreading and slowly corroding them. I remember the way her magic burned my shield like acid.

"Help!" one of the hybrids pants. Asmo and I sprint for the remaining four witches and their hostages, but we're too late. They drag their nails across their neck. Blood pours down their chests. William's face flashes through my mind. I will not lose another.

With the hostages now on the ground, I fire white flames at the witches' heads. Bile rises as the scent of flesh catching fire now fills the air. All four witches burn, while Cora's black aura forms a protective shield around her. I want to scream and rage at her and pour more fire into it, but I shift my attention to the four hybrids bleeding on the floor instead.

But I'm just one person, just two hands, and I can't help them all at once. I can't I can't I can't and I swore no more, but they are now on a list that was already too long. William and the executed and the wedding guests and now these four at my feet. Tears well at the helplessness, the frustration, the entire fucking situation of this whole thing, and I let them fall uselessly, so fucking uselessly. I wipe them away in a hurry and shake my head, shake the thoughts away to focus. But I don't know what the fuck to do.

I place my hands on their necks, but that still leaves two more dying. Elle flies toward me and covers their wounds, blood seeping between her fingers.

"I don't know what to do," I say.

She looks back at me through tear-lined eyes and shakes her head.

Mother, please, I beg. But the hybrids beneath me still, as they lose their fights with death.

Behind me, Marik yells, "No!"

And then Asmo bellows, and my world tilts, and every nerve ending in my body lights in pain. A dagger is embedded in Asmo's chest. His face is white, lips pressed together tightly as he fists the handle and rips it from his chest. He clamps a hand over the wound, blood seeping between his fingers. He gives me a shaky nod.

A figure sprints down the hall, away from us. Luca. I smother the urge to chase him and rip his lungs from his body. I run to Asmo. "I'm fine," he says, and the bond in my chest warms. I run a shaky hand through my hair and tell myself everything's okay.

But then Elle screams.

I stand and turn, ready to fight Hell for the people I love.

My knees buckle.

Cora holds Elle by the throat.

CHAPTER 46
ELLE

CORA GRIPS the back of my head, her fingers tangled in the roots of my hair. My eyes are wild as I look from Mae to Marik, praying that they have some plan to get me out of this.

"If this is who you choose, then she's mine now," Cora snarls in Marik's direction. Her nails dig into my scalp. I squeeze my eyes shut, desperate not to make a sound. I refuse to give her that. "We had a deal, remember?"

Marik holds his hands up, palms facing us. As if she can be reasoned with.

"What is this, Marik? What is she to you? She's a nobody," Cora spits.

Marik glances from Cora, back to me. His eyes are frenzied, panicked. He doesn't know what to do. Any attack on Cora will surely kill me. There's no reason for her to keep me alive.

She's right. I am just a nobody. My parents are nobodies, just a seamstress and a carpenter. Just a nobody girl from a nothing town.

My hand twitches, ready to blindly fire at this cunt who holds me hostage. But she binds them behind my back. Hot breath tickles my ear as she whispers, "I will cut your hands off if they move again. Or I'll just kill you. Do you understand?"

"Fuck. You," I grind out.

The pressure on my scalp eases. But then, a lick of pain shoots up my spine as she digs her iron-sharp nails into my antlers, nail piercing bone. A scream crawls up my throat and cuts through the air.

"Cora!" Marik's voice booms over my scream. "Enough. She has nothing to do with this."

Her nails dig deeper and my vision blurs. The room flashes to black and I try so, so hard to grasp onto consciousness. But it flickers with every wave of pain.

"Liar," Cora spits. Her hand on my antlers retreats, and I fight the bile that rises at the lingering pain. Any relief I had is temporary, because her hand now grips my throat. I gasp at the feeling of her nails embedded in my neck. Warm blood trickles down, between my breasts, dipping below the collar of my dress. My heart rate doubles and I urge it to slow, to stop pumping blood faster.

Marik's eyes darken as they track the blood. Mae and Asmo stand frozen in place as they watch the scene unfold.

Cora cackles, and the hair on the back of my neck raises. "I see..." she mutters. "Does she know? When were you going to tell her, Marik?"

My mind races at her questions. Do I know what?

Do I know what? I fire at Marik.

He ignores me.

"Take me," Marik says, taking slow, measured steps toward me. "Take me, Cora. I know I messed up. Let me make it up to you."

Cora's nails dig deeper. My back arches in pain. I don't know when I started crying, but tears stream down my face in silent pleas.

Marik drops to his knees. "Please, Cora. Take me instead. I beg you."

Why? Why are you doing this for me?

"How sweet," Cora's voice drips with apathy. But her hands rip from my neck and she tosses me to the side like trash. Asmo dashes toward me and pulls me to my feet, back to Mae. She stares at my neck, at the five different holes still streaming with blood.

When I look back, Marik is in Cora's arms. They embrace, and my stomach roils. Cora's hands wrap around his waist, slender hands clinging to him.

Her next words are a whisper, yet they clang through me all the same.

"What makes you think I still want you?"

Marik's body convulses as Cora shoots lightning into his back. He drops to the ground with a thud. The male who seemed so untouchable, so unbeatable, so full of evil and hate and wrath, is...he's too quiet, too limp, too...

Something in my chest cracks. Something is wrong, wrong, wrong, *wrong*. I grab my chest, clawing at it, at the way my own body feels like it's dying, like something is terribly, terribly wrong.

And then Mae is gone. She is a whirlwind of ice and fire and wind and earth as she slams into Cora with a scream that I swear could crack the earth open. The remaining hybrids drag the injured to the sides of the room, out of the way of the carnage. They don't attempt to get Marik, who lays lifeless on the floor, feet away from Cora.

Asmo is frozen, his eyes glassy as he watches his brother. Is there something deep inside of him that wishes he would stir, too?

Mae hurls white fire, but Cora easily deflects it. She hurls ice, but Cora melts it with a flick of her wrist. Every single movement is easily blocked. Mae might be powerful, but she's no match for the First Witch.

A writhing ball of black magic catches Mae on the arm and she yelps in pain. It snaps Asmo and me back into focus. We join Mae, each of us firing shot after shot at Cora. I pour every single ounce of magic into sending her back to whatever hell she crawled from.

But she's too strong. And it's just the three of us. And I can barely summon what I used to.

Mae faces her, pale and posture slumped, swaying on her feet. My neck wounds keep healing, then tearing open, fresh blood mixing with dried blood.

Cora stares at us with a pitiful smile. "I admire your tenacity, sweetheart. But you can't defeat me."

"Then I'll die trying," Mae spits.

Cora says something else, but I'm too distracted to hear. Behind her, Marik shifts on the floor, and the ache in my chest lessens. His skin is sallow and sweat gleams along his forehead. He smears blood from the cut on his cheek, now open and bloody once again. He draws something in the dirt with his hand.

He looks at me one more time, his dark eyes gleaming with something that I can't grasp. He wraps his hand around Cora's ankle. She whirls and tries to yank herself free. But she's too late. A portal opens beneath him, black nothingness reflecting through into oblivion. He drags her into the portal with him. And closes it shut behind him.

I stare at the ground where the portal was. Where Marik was. I refuse to blink. I refuse to believe it was that simple. But the seconds turn into minutes. And Cora doesn't return.

A whisper, a brushing against my mind.

Little fawn.

The thing in my chest cracks again.

Mae stares at the now-closed portal, the only sign it was ever there a circle of disturbed dirt. She goes to the hybrids, places a flat palm on their chests, then looks to the barricaded doors. "We need to get inside those doors. There should be healers inside."

She stands and sways on her feet. Asmo steadies her, placing a hand on the small of her back. "I'm fine," she says, walking to the wall of dirt beside the doors. She lays her hands flat on its surface and goes quiet as she concentrates.

I watch her, frozen in place. My brain has stopped working, *little fawn* on repeat in my mind.

A tiny hole appears in the wall. The hole grows wider, wider, wider, until finally—the healing center.

It's a wreckage. Bodies litter the floor, dead and alive, splintered wood from the healing tables and medical instruments scattered among them. In the distance, someone flits around the room arranging makeshift cots, while August carries hybrids to them.

Someone rushes to the opening in the wall.

That's when Mae collapses.

CHAPTER 47
MAE

MY BACK IS PRESSED against something soft, not the unyielding or gritty surface of the floor, but the cushiony give of a bed or a cot. Nobody is screaming or crying, so that's another good sign. The air is stale, but it's not smoke, and the smell of medicinal herbs and salve is strong.

"Hello, princess."

My eyes fly open.

Asmo stands before me, a half-smile on his face. His face is smeared with dirt, his hair covered in dried sweat and blood, and he looks exhausted. He looks perfect.

I burst into tears.

He pulls me into his arms, his fingers gripping me too hard, not hard enough. "Shh, it's okay. We're all okay," he mutters into my hair. And I am. I know I'm okay. I'm breathing. My mate is in front of me. We're okay.

"How long have I been out?" I mumble into his solid, unyielding chest. The one he was just stabbed in. "Wait, you were stabbed. Are you okay?"

He lets me go, and I fight the protest that forms on my lips. I prop myself up on the cot and look around. We're in a private space, a thin sheet separating us from the rest of the healing center. It's bare in here—just a cot, some sterile instruments, and a glass jar of something clear.

"I'm fine." He leans back in the chair and pulls his shirt up. I ignore the way it sends butterflies straight to my core. A dark blemish mars his chest, just above the snake's head. "Luca. He was trying to get to you. He threw the dagger toward you, with your back turned. Couldn't even face you. He didn't expect me to step in its path. He must have used a dagger imbued with dark magic. Explains why it did so much damage."

I quirk an eyebrow. If I was stabbed by a dagger, imbued or not, I'm assuming I'd be dead. "Are you not usually impacted by knives to the chest that way?"

"Not usually, no." He drops his shirt and looks at the floor.

Alright, then. A question for another time. "How long have I been out?" I ask again.

He looks back to me. "Couple hours. The healer thinks you hit your physical and magical limits."

I guess fighting the First Witch will do that to you. "Is everyone else okay? Cally? Ivan? Holly?"

"Everyone we know is alive. Etta is injured, but she'll be fine..." He grimaces. "A few people died. But you saved two of the hybrids that we thought the witches had killed."

I blink. They were dead. I felt their hearts stop. "What? How?"

He shakes his head. "The current theory is...your tears."

I stare at him, waiting for him to say *Just kidding!* He doesn't. "What?"

He shakes his head and huffs a laugh. "I know. That's the only thing we can work out. The two that were revived were the ones that you and Elle both cried on. That's the only commonality. And if you're direct descendants of Wrena's line...Her tears broke the curse on your grandfather."

I shake my head in disbelief. "That sounds..." *Impossible? Insane? Like something that's not supposed to happen?* "I take it Marik didn't come back?"

He shakes his head, the movement slow and heavy. I wish I could shoulder some of its weight. "How are you feeling about...him?" In all of this, I never once thought to ask him about his feelings toward his brother. His twin brother. The person he knows better than anyone.

He closes his eyes. "I'm okay. It was the least he could do. He's responsible for all of this," he grumbles.

"He's your brother," I whisper.

He shifts in his chair, avoids my gaze. "It's...I don't want to talk about this right now."

My instinct is to push, to demand, to pull the feelings out of him. But what good would that do? We'll have a lifetime to talk about all of the tiny cuts and the huge gashes that have left us hurting and scarred. We'll have a lifetime to heal each other.

"Okay. What about Elle? Is she okay?"

His expression turns grave, and my heart threatens to burst from my chest. "She's fine. She's just not exactly...speaking right now."

"What do you mean?"

He shrugs. "She refuses to talk to anyone. I think you need to talk to her."

"Take me to her." Once, the demand would have resulted in a raised eyebrow or a scoff, but now, Asmo scoops me into his arms. Hybrids dart out of the way when they see us coming. Some bow their heads.

The walls of Squall's End are black, charred from the flames that sought to ravage the underground city. Several hallways are blocked off, rocks and dirt blocking the way from the ceilings caving in. We pass the mess hall, but the doors are warped and stained with black. The smell of smoke still lingers.

"You saved them today," Asmo mutters as we pass another couple with bowed heads. "Everyone was trapped in the healing center. We think Cora meant for everyone to be locked inside while it burned. Without you...Squall's End and everyone inside would be dead."

My heart drops to my stomach. Etta, August, Barrett, Cally...My friends would have burned alive. Innocent hybrids would have died in a war they didn't ask for. "Without us," I manage to say. "You saved them, too."

Asmo carries me outside, the moon high in the sky. I inhale, fresh air and the scent of snow and pine filling my lungs. I didn't realize how suffocating it felt in Squall's End until now. "Where is she?" I ask.

He doesn't respond, just funnels us away. The dark night is made darker as we materialize into a forest, the trees blocking the light from the moon above. I cling tighter to Asmo, but he carries me to the abandoned house. It's hard to believe it was only hours ago that we were here.

The house reeks of stale air and mouse droppings and mildew. Asmo sets me down and points to the stairs. "I'll be down here if you need me," he whispers, then squeezes my hand before walking toward the worn couch.

The hallway upstairs is dark, but a soft light comes from the second bedroom on the right. Elle sits in a makeshift bed of rumpled quilts and worn sheets. A candle flickers in a brass holder on the floor. A large window is centered on the wall, a crack nearly splitting it in two. She hugs her knees to her chest, the train of her bloody and rumpled dress lying on the floor beside her. Her stare is vacant and fixed to the empty wall.

I lower myself to the floor and sit beside her. The silence between us is thick. I have no idea what to say to her. My sister.

My throat feels like it grows thicker as my thoughts get jumbled, as my brain struggles to form a singular sentence. How do you tell someone they're your sister? Their twin? How do you tell someone they're a High Princess?

How do you tell someone that the person who just killed himself was their mate?

"Elle," I manage to say. But she doesn't answer. She stares at the wall, rigid and silent. "Talk to me. Please," I add softly.

Her mouth opens, but no words come. Not at first, at least. A tear cuts through her dirt-lined cheeks. She swipes it away angrily, then splays her hand against her chest, above her heart. "Something is wrong. I feel...My chest feels strained." She squeezes her eyes shut and shakes her head. "No, that's not the right word. I don't...I can't think of the right word for it, but it feels...Something's not right."

I can't even imagine. When I saw the dagger sticking out of Asmo's chest, it felt like the world imploded for a moment. But he was fine. And Marik isn't. Marik is gone.

"Elle, there's something you need to know," I whisper. I steel myself, then clear my throat. "Marik..." I close my eyes and take a deep breath. "Marik is your mate. That's why something feels wrong. You just..." I can't finish the sentence. *You just lost your mate.* Even thinking it makes my heart buck inside my chest.

Elle turns to me, her thick brows scrunched together. "No, he's not. That can't be it." She shakes her head once and says, "Besides, mates aren't a thing anymore." But her gaze grows unfocused as she stares at something over my shoulder. I turn, but there's nothing there.

"There's more," I begin again, "The Mother visited me one night, before the wedding. She left me a book that told me of Wrena's tale. About a week ago, She visited me again." Elle stares at me, a blank expression on her face. "She shared a memory of my mother...of *our* mother."

Her expression sharpens, zeroing in on me in a heartbeat. "What?"

I nod slowly. "We're twins." I force a smile to my lips—one that I know doesn't reach my eyes—and say, "Surprise."

"Silas was my...He was my dad? No, that can't be. My mother...my father..." she mutters with a shake of her head. "That doesn't make any sense."

I tell her the details of the dream. From her expression, I can tell her thoughts are churning, trying to fit every puzzle piece together as I lay them down for her. She doesn't interrupt me again. When I finish, she says, "Levana. Why is that name so familiar?"

"She was the witch that Cora had as the representative at the ball. She's on our side. She helped rescue me."

Elle quirks an eyebrow. "Rescue you?"

I wave a hand at her. "Yeah, I got captured, but not a big deal. At least, it's not worth discussing right now."

She shakes her head quickly and asks, "What does this have to do with Marik?"

I tell her the details of the other dream from the Mother—the one telling how to defeat Cora. "I can only assume she showed me that because we're the other set of twins. Marik is *not* my mate. If he was, he never would have done what he did. So that means...he has to be yours," I say with a grimace. She squeezes her eyes shut. Another tear breaks free. "I know, Elle. I'm so sorry. This is so much to take in."

"I think you're right, though." Her voice is a whisper. "That would explain everything. He saved me. He got me out of the castle. He kept telling me he was going to save me, but I didn't believe him. I thought it was just another one of his games. I think he knows it, too. He—I would catch him staring at me sometimes. And he started to be kind to me when he easily could have been...his usual self." She breaks off and buries her head into her hands. "I can't believe I'm even saying this right now," she groans. "He's a monster, Mae. I don't want this."

A part of me wonders if she does, though. It sounds like she's trying to justify these tiny moments of intimacy, as if he wasn't responsible for orchestrating her capture. He could have gotten her out at any point.

"Well," I say, "It seems as if he made the decision for you. His sacrifice saved us all. Cora's gone."

Elle looks up at me from her hands. "I don't think they're gone," she whispers.

I still. This whole time, I've been thinking that battle was the end. I've been cautiously optimistic that we won the war. The prophecy stated we needed all four of us to unite and all four of us stood against Cora in Squall's End. Marik literally dragged her through a black hole.

But there's no way it would be that easy. What if Marik is still on Cora's side and they orchestrated this entire thing? How idiotic have we been to think he could have changed his allegiances?

I don't say any of that. "What makes you say that?" I ask.

She clutches her chest again. "I can feel him, somehow. It's strained, so maybe he's far away. I can't explain how. All I know is that I can still feel him. After he disappeared through the portal, he spoke to me. He—"

"Sorry, what?"

She shakes her head. "I thought it was because of this stupid necklace he used to control me, but it must have been this bond. I don't know what the necklace did, but it strengthened whatever is between us."

"Can you speak to him now?" I ask, although I'm not sure what I want the answer to be. I have no idea if Marik is on our side anymore.

Elle shakes her head. "No. I keep trying, but he doesn't say anything back. I can still feel him, though, but it feels like he's watching from afar. He's still there. I know that, at least. I just don't know where."

I sigh. We had the key to defeating Cora in our hands for approximately one hour, then it all went to shit.

"Where the hell could he be?" I mutter.

Elle shakes her head. "I don't know. Do you think Asmo would know?"

The mirror. "Maybe."

She leans back against the wall and tilts her head to the ceiling. "I cannot fucking believe this," she groans.

I stare at her profile and want to kick myself for not realizing who she was before now. Although we are opposites, we were cut from the same cloth. Her warm freckles are a stark contrast to my white, but they spread along our cheeks the same way. Her straight, slender, button-nose is nearly identical to mine. Our eyes are the exact same shade of amber, framed by long lashes.

I'm not sure what possesses me, but I blurt, "Elle isn't your real name."

She turns to me, eyes less dark than before. Less sad. "What is it, then?"

"Ellysia," I say, for the first time. I've repeated our names in my head, turned them over and studied them. I haven't told Asmo, or anyone else, my true name. It didn't feel right. But now, it does. "Mine's Maerellis."

She nods appreciatively. "Ellysia," she whispers slowly, announcing each syllable intentionally. "Sisters." She looks up at me, the flickering candle setting her smile in a warm glow. She leans into me. "You being my sister makes so much sense. You felt so familiar to me that first day I met you. I just thought it was because you were easy to talk to." She sighs. "Well, what do we do now, High Queen?"

I snort. "You should've been High Queen. I always thought that of you, by the way. That it should've been you."

She pulls away from me, eyes wide. "I don't want it."

I hold a hand up. "I know. I'm not saying that. When we first met, I just thought you would've been the better fit. You were so confident, and I felt like I was so lost."

Her smile is sad. "You grew into it. So quickly. I was so proud of you. I'm still proud of you."

I lean back into her, resting my head on her shoulder. "Are you okay?" My voice is a whisper.

She inhales. Her exhale is shaky. "I will be."

"Do you want to talk about it?"

"No. Not without copious amounts of wine," she says lightly, but I know that answer for what it is—a deflection of pain that lingers just beneath the surface.

"Whenever you're ready."

I stand and offer my hand to her. She eyes it for a moment, as if the thought of taking it, of standing, of walking out of this abandoned house and facing whatever comes next is too much. But she grabs it and I haul her up. I've grown weaker in the last few months from lack of food and exercise, but Elle has grown infinitely more so. Pulling her up is too easy.

The train of her dress snags on an exposed nail and rips. She snatches it and pulls it away. "Damned thing."

I huff a laugh. "We'll get you back to Squall's End and you can grab a change of clothes."

Downstairs, Asmo leans back on the couch, staring out the window into the dark forest. "Speaking of Squall's End—"

"Could you hear everything we said?" I cut him off.

He stands, brushing dust from his pants. As if that will make a difference in his appearance when every inch of him is coated in blood, sweat, and dirt. "I tuned most of it out," he answers with a wave of his hand before turning toward the door.

"What about Squall's End?" I ask.

"It was destroyed, princess," he says soberly.

Although I expected this—the blackened hallways and charred remains of what little furniture remained were a good indicator—a shudder sweeps through me all the same. The Lower House members were ousted from our society. That was their home. And they sacrificed it for a war they had no responsibility in creating. "Where are we supposed to go?"

"Amaris has offered her court and given us permission to funnel directly there."

"Who's Amaris?" Elle asks.

I grimace. "The Fae delegate."

Elle tenses beside me. "The Fae?"

I nod. "There is so much you don't know, but yes. They're on our side and they've agreed to help us. I promise I'll explain everything when there's time."

She gives me a terse nod, and we leave the abandoned house. I hope it's the last time any of us have to see it.

CHAPTER 48
MAE

THICK SLABS of stone and soaring white columns materialize around us. Ivy curls around the columns and the white stone railing that overlooks the sprawling city below. In the distance, a tree nearly as tall as the castle itself sits on an island, its roots crawling over spongy moss and disappearing into the water below. The air is sticky with humidity, but smells of flowers, rain, and earth.

Amaris's white hair is pulled back into a braid that begins at her roots, and her tattoos glimmer like stars, white and luminous. "Welcome to the Fae Kingdom," she says warmly.

"It's gorgeous," I say.

She smiles proudly. "I'll have to give you the tour someday."

"I'm counting on it."

She leads us to a room with a domed ceiling, a mosaic of gnarled branches and sprawling ivy and pink roses. Beams of light break through, landing on a massive circular, wooden table, where the Herd sits—Holly, Etta, Ivan, Basil, Elle, Cally, and Asmo. My knees threaten to give when I see Cally. Barrett and August also join us, soot in their hair and on their clothes. Holly and Etta sit closer together today, only inches apart.

A Fae male with golden hair sits in between an empty seat and August. The golden threads of his hair complement his violet eyes.

Amaris settles into the empty seat. "Your Highness, please meet the interim king, Aero of the Wind."

He stands and forms a bow. When he rises, his eyes have softened. "I go by Roe, if you please, Your Majesty."

I dip my head in acknowledgement. "Pleasure to meet you, Roe. Thank you for agreeing to host us." If he hadn't, our only other meeting options would have been the ruins of Squall's End or the abandoned house in the woods.

He smiles and returns to his seat, whispering something to Amaris. After Cally gives me a hug that threatens to crack my bones, I sit beside my mate and look to my court and my allies. Elle leans against the wall, awkward and looking like she's been dragged through every inch of hell with her torn dress and her wild hair.

Several of us, me included, are still dressed in the waiters' uniforms from the ball. Roe is the only one who looks somewhat prepared for an official meeting, dressed in an all-white tunic and pants.

I straighten and push my shoulders back. "I'm so thankful to see everyone here, safe and sound. We got lucky," I say, and I regret the choice of words as soon as they're out. Basil bobs his head, but he won't look at me. His shoulders are slumped, and the slash of his usual smile is gone. He looks defeated. His home is gone. But we were lucky. Incredibly so. He almost lost so much more than his home. His life. His friends' lives.

I take a deep breath. "It's time to end this. Cora and Marik are gone, but I have reason to believe they're not dead. We need to find Marik if we have any chance of truly defeating Cora. But while she's gone, I think we should attack the castle."

I turn to Basil, who watches me with an emptiness that adds to the weight on my shoulders. "Basil, if the Lower House members assist us, I would be grateful. However, they have helped us enough and sacrificed too much already. Our deal is met. Any further assistance would be appreciated, but it's not needed to fulfill the bargain."

He bows his head in response, and I'm too scared to ask if that's an agreement to help or a respectful decline.

"We will fight with you," August says. He stands tall, hands clasped behind his back and chest puffed.

Beside him, Barrett says, "As will Ursidae."

"You have the Fae beside you," Roe says from his chair.

"Our help is yours," Basil says.

Nausea curdles in my stomach. I swallow. "We attack at first light."

Turns out, portaling an entire army takes more time than I anticipated, but we manage to get everyone to the High Castle. The castle is still about a mile away. We could have portaled closer but didn't want to risk alerting anyone to our presence. The woods are deadly quiet around us as we near, everyone inside sound barriers as we trek toward the castle.

It makes my heart hurt. The forest used to be so lively, full of birds chirping, and squirrels jumping from branches, and deer bounding through. But now, it's desolate. Dark clouds hang overhead, low and thick with the promise of rain.

I can only pray that Cora is far, far away. Elle says she doesn't think Marik is near, so we're hoping that wherever he is, he's keeping Cora occupied.

We come to a stop at the base of the stairs that lead to the castle, our barriers keeping us hidden. I turn to the army we've managed to cobble together and project my voice.

"Today, we fight for our kingdom. We fight for our lives. We fight for the animals and the children. We fight for those who cannot protect themselves against the sharp teeth of the cambions and the Cursed, who can't defend themselves against the tide of black magic. We fight for what is right." I pause, the words reminding me of a guard who once said something similar. My chest tightens.

The values of our court are what keep the kingdom...good. And that's worth protecting.

William.

"Someone once told me that goodness is worth protecting," I add. "So today, we fight for goodness."

The crowd roars inside the sound barrier, but my stomach churns. My choices were responsible for William's death. Who else will die today, because of me?

Hybrids stare back at me, a mixture of wide eyes, of clenched jaws, of nervous energy. Those who don't have the ability to summon fire wield fireswords, a last-minute addition to the armory, created by one of the Fae. Asmo, Elle, August, Barrett, and I spent all night imbuing our fire magic into them, creating swords with an eternal flame, perfect for felling witches.

Roe, outfitted in a suit of white armor, steps forward. "To my people, revenge is ours. We will take back a piece of our history and stop the witches from destroying another kingdom. They die today."

The Fae warriors raise swords that most likely fought the witches the last time, their bellows of anger sending my blood humming.

We march.

Asmo, August, and Barrett break the sound barriers the moment we breach the stairs. The doors open of their own accord, welcoming us into the castle, as if begging for rescue. The guards are taken by surprise, knives through their necks before they can draw their swords.

August leads a section of our army and ascends the stairs to the second level, while the rest of us disperse throughout the castle. Asmo and I stick firmly in the middle, protected, but ready to help if needed.

The throne is empty, much to my relief. I was half-expecting Cora to be waiting there, but the only thing that waits for me here are haunted memories and silence.

My stomach churns as we pass through the empty hallways. Something's not right. I was expecting the entire castle to be crawling with witches. Even if we attacked while they were asleep, they should have been up and out by now. Where are they?

I flash Asmo a look, and the expression on his face tells me he's thinking the same thing. Up ahead, a Canis hybrid does a double-take as he passes by a window. "Your Highnesses," he calls, eyes locked on whatever is outside.

"What is it?" Asmo orders.

"You should come take a look."

I steel myself for whatever awaits me outside. But it's worse than I imagined.

Outside, the grassy field is full of lines of black-leather witches, undead creatures surrounding them. Behind the witches, two figures sit atop two massive, Cursed grizzly bears, their fur matted and teeth rotting.

Cora.

Her onyx hair flutters in the wind, her aura writhing around her.

How did she know?

Seated beside her is an ethereal-looking female. Her hair is the color of charcoal, sleek and straight. Her riding leathers are jet black, not a lick of color to be seen. She, too, has a black aura around her.

"Who is that?" I whisper.

"Thera," a voice calls from the end of the hallway. From behind us. I whirl.

Levana stands in the center of the hallway, her raven hair pulled into a tight braid that hangs over one shoulder. Her golden eyes watch us carefully. Asmo shifts me behind him.

"The creator of the witches and Goddess of the Underworld. Your goddess's sister," Levana explains.

The Sister is coming.

"End this, Mae," Levana says—no, commands. "Thera will destroy this kingdom if Cora isn't destroyed first."

I push Asmo aside. "How?"

Levana shakes her head. "Cora is at her most powerful right now because of the amount of witches she has. If you take that away, you can buy some time. Focus your energy there," she says, now addressing the hybrids. "The only ways to kill a creature made of dark magic are beheading, fire, and ice. That includes the witches."

I knew ice worked on the cambions and the Cursed, but not the witches.

"What of Thera?" I ask.

"She can't interfere. To do so would be a direct violation of the treaty. Ignore her. For now, at least. Focus on the witches. That's the key to winning this."

The treaty? I glance at Asmo, but he doesn't meet my gaze.

"Why are you doing this?" Asmo's voice is gruff.

Levana looks to me. "The witches will take until every inch of the kingdom is blackened and turned to rot. They do not belong in this kingdom. They belong in the underworld."

"Are you not a witch?" I ask.

Her golden eyes turn luminescent. A chill spreads through me. "I am something other. As I was a friend to the Fae Court and to your mother, I am also a friend to you."

All truth, as bizarre as it is.

"Your aura..." Basil says, head tilted as he stares at Levana. "It's not black."

"She's telling the truth," I whisper to Asmo.

He turns to Basil. "Go get the rest of the hybrids. Reconvene at the front. We'll march as one," Asmo orders.

Basil gives Levana a final look, then shifts into his owl form and soars back down the hallway. Last night, Asmo shared the dark mark with all the shifters that would keep them clothed.

"You should know I'm not the only one," Levena says. "There are others that are friendly to the High Crown."

"How many of you are there?" Asmo asks Levana as he walks toward her.

"Not many," she admits. "At least not here. We're spread throughout the kingdom right now, trying to do damage control in the other courts." She motions to a red ribbon tied around her wrist. "This is how you can find us."

"Thank you," I say.

She turns to me, glowing eyes looking me up and down. "I tried to tell the red-haired one. I tried to tell her she wasn't alone, that there were two pairs of mates, two sets of twins."

The words make no sense to me, but I don't have time to puzzle over them. Basil's owl form glides through the air, then shifts into his human form. "They're coming." The hybrids stir at his words. It's almost time.

Asmo grabs my hand and leads me away from the group. He spots a hidden alcove and pulls me inside, pressing me against the wall and cupping my cheeks. I wrap my arms around his neck and memorize the feel of his lips against mine.

This is it. This is going to be the biggest battle we've had so far. But we're going into this one together. He pulls away, and the light green of his eyes captivates me. The first time I saw these eyes, I couldn't look away. Even now, I can't seem to turn away from them.

His hand travels down to my chest, to the mating tattoo, to my beating heart. "Mine." His voice is low, gruff, full of emotion.

I lean toward him, rising on my toes. "Yours," I murmur against his lips.

Someone clears their throat behind us. I pull away and peer over Asmo's shoulders. August's icy blue eyes stare back at me, eyebrows raised. "Pardon the interruption, but we do have a battle to attend to whenever you two are done."

Asmo presses a final kiss to the inside of my wrist, then he turns back to the small army. Hybrids stand shoulder-to-shoulder down the wide hallways. My mate stands tall and proud, his chest puffed and face solemn. He is a leader through and through. He was born to fill this role. He was born to sit on a throne.

"We've gained some intel about the witches' and Curseds' weaknesses," Asmo's voice bellows. "Ice will also kill them. If you can't summon enough to freeze them outright, use it to slow them and then behead them. There are friendly witches in the crowd that you are not to harm. They are wearing red ribbons. Kill everyone else. Do you understand? Do not attack Cora. Focus your energy on the witches. They die today." He pauses, lifts his chin. "We take back the kingdom today."

Murmurs of agreement begin to ripple through the crowd. August watches Asmo appreciatively. Elle stands beside August, jaw clenched tightly. This is the fight for our birthright. For the one piece of our father that remains.

Outside, a crack of thunder booms, and the wind stirs. Witches sneer as we approach. Our army is larger, but they are stronger. Even from across the battlefield, Cora watches me as I take my place behind my army.

The wind dies, and Cora speaks. Her voice is projected, surrounding us as if carried by the wind.

"I have something that belongs to you." She shifts her gaze to Elle. "Or maybe to you."

Elle's spine stiffens. I don't know why the fuck we thought it would be a good idea for her to be here. She just escaped this place, this witch. But she insisted on being here. On fighting.

The Cursed bears move, revealing a third undead grizzly bear.

A body hangs from its maw.

It lumbers forward, the army of witches parting for it as it cuts through the crowd.

"If you want him so badly, you can have him," Cora calls as the bear passes the first line of witches, then opens its mouth. The body hits the ground with a heavy thump.

Horror crawls up my throat. I grab Elle before she can sprint toward the male that lies motionless on the ground.

Marik.

CHAPTER 49
ELLE

I DIDN'T KNOW my vision could turn red. Black, yes. Blissful unconsciousness and sleep are welcome friends.

But red, no.

Yet, when the Cursed drops my mate from its mouth, red is all I see. The crimson stain on his shirt, the dried blood that covers his nose, his mouth, the dozens of wounds that pepper his torso.

My heart slows in my chest as I stare at him, as if it's trying to match the nearly nonexistent beat of his.

He can't be dead. The bond is still there, writhing and angry and vicious inside of me.

Blood pounds through my veins, echoing in my ears, as I stare at him. As rage fuels me.

Rage at Cora, for what she's done to my mate. Rage at the Mother, for making him my mate. For turning him into something cold and cruel before I had the chance to know who he was before the world hardened him. Rage at Her for the life he was forced to live, to the little boy who wasn't given a chance to know kindness and love before hate began to grow in his heart. Rage at myself for not being able to turn away from him even now, when he deserves this fate.

Bright, hot, crimson rage settles over me as I fix my gaze to the First Witch.

I scream.

CHAPTER 50
MAE

ELLE'S SCREAM makes the hair on the back of my neck stand. It's filled with agony and anger and desperation.

It is the perfect war cry.

We charge, meeting Cursed and cambions and witches with swords and fire and a love for this kingdom that they'll never have. We falter and stumble. The first line of Cursed fall quickly, putting our army directly in the path of the witches. And they're walking toward us, hands already writhing with dark magic.

Marik's body lays unmoving in the middle of the two armies.

A hand clamps around my shoulder. "Your Highness," Basil pants. "He's alive. His aura is still there."

With the way Marik looks, I wouldn't be surprised if his aura barely clung to him. I don't ask Basil, though. Not with Elle nearby. "We need to get him," I say to Asmo.

He frowns. "What if it's a trap?"

I tug on the end of my braid as I think through the options. As much as I would love to leave him in the middle of two armies to be trampled on, we need him if we have any chance of defeating Cora. I spin around and charge toward Roe. "Change of plans," I order. "Enact phase one now."

He nods curtly and turns to his soldiers. "Now!" he barks.

A portion of the Fae holster their weapons and splay their hands. The witches begin to shriek as they fight off hallucinations of their worst nightmares, clawing and swinging swords at creatures—or whatever is enough to make a witch scream—that aren't there. Some of them accidentally strike other witches, only adding to the chaos.

I sprint back to Asmo. "I just bought us some time. Let's go."

"Cover me." He shifts into his serpent form and slithers through the hybrids. I sprint after him and summon a shield, tossing it over him as he nearly knocks a hybrid from their feet as he passes. Thankfully, most of the witches are too distracted to notice us as we approach them. My shield is attacked, the acidic sting of black magic eating away at it. Another hit comes, but it holds firm.

Asmo reaches Marik and scoops him into his jaw. He turns back to me, and my shield is attacked again. I grit my teeth and strengthen it, but when I turn, a witch blocks our path. I duck as a wave of black comes toward us.

It never reaches my shield.

"Go!" a voice calls, and Asmo slithers past the witch, now dead, Amaris yanking her fire-imbued daggers from the witch's neck. She stands her ground, watching as we retreat behind the front lines once more.

Asmo drops Marik, and Elle rushes toward him. She leans over him, says his name, then resorts to beating on his chest and screaming at him. But he doesn't stir.

Asmo shifts back into his hybrid form. He glances at me, worry on his features. I don't know what to do either. I don't know how to handle this. What would I want someone to do if my mate was laying lifeless in front of me? What would I *need* someone to do for me?

I crouch beside her. "Elle," I say softly. "I know this isn't what you want to hear, but we have to join this fight. Or they will take him again."

She whips her head to me, teeth bared at my words. But then her face falls, and she buries it in her hands. "I fucking hate him, Mae."

My chest squeezes. I could have easily ended up with Marik as my mate. "I know. We'll figure it out together," I say, because I don't know what else to say.

She wipes a tear from her cheek and shoves herself from the ground. Her red hair is a bright contrast to the black fighting leathers she wears, whisps pulled loose from her braid and flying in the wind.

The battle is in full swing now. Screams, bellows, elemental magic, and black magic fly. Fae warriors fall from portals in the sky with swords drawn, landing on unsuspecting witches and felling them. Cursed hawks and vultures take flight, deformed talons reaching for exposed necks as they swoop down. I incinerate them before they can even get close. Ash falls, coating my hair and landing on my lips like morbid snowflakes.

Beside me, Asmo surveys our army.

"How did she know we were coming?" I ask him. "I can't figure it out."

He shakes his head. "I'm not sure. It's been bothering me, too. The only thing I can think of is the mirror. Cora is essentially made from black magic, so she has access to the same spells we do. Maybe that's how she got around Luca's blood oath." The mention of the traitorous weasel has my blood boiling all over again. "My theory is that after she learned you were still alive, she found a way to watch you."

I groan. I'm not sure why we didn't consider that. I make a mental note to figure out how to block that whenever we get back on the throne. There's got to be something.

Asmo continues to watch the battle as it rages on, firing black flames intermittently or providing shields to protect hybrids as needed. So far, all I've managed to do is char some undead birds. I need to get higher. I need a better vantage point.

Elle is re-braiding her hair for the fifth time, a habit that I also tend to do when I'm anxious. She's used to being involved in the action, too. Neither of us knows what to do back here. The plan was to keep Asmo, Elle, and me at the very back. Not only are we the High Family, but we're also the key to winning this thing. If we die, the war is lost.

But the urge to *do something* is overwhelming.

I turn, desperate to find something to stand on. But there's nothing. August and Barrett shout orders over the mayhem of the battlefield, directing their assigned groups.

Barrett. I sprint to him. "I need you to shift so I can sit on you and see. I can't see anything down here, so I can't help."

"Do it," August orders.

Barrett shifts into his grizzly form, and I have to crane my neck to tell him to sink down. He's huge, and if I didn't know him, I would be terrified. On all four feet, he towers over me. He lowers himself as much as he can, and I climb onto his back. I grip his soft, brown fur and hold tight as he rises. He stands at his full height, and although the ground is a shocking distance beneath me, I breathe a sigh of relief at what I see.

We're advancing on them.

We're actually doing this. Beheaded witches lay limp on the ground, ashy piles of undead animals and witches are trampled through as our line advances. Our ranks have thinned, but not by much. The Fae's hallucinations gave us a slight advantage. Two hybrids take on a witch in all-black leathers. The witch is supernaturally fast, but we trained for this. All the work we've been putting in is making a difference.

The witch spins, slashing out with razor-sharp claws. The rabbit hybrid dodges as their partner slashes at the witch's ankles. The witch rears back as the hybrid drags his fire-imbued scabbard across her neck. She drops to the ground. A cambion races toward the duo, but they down it with a singular burst of ice.

A scream pulls my attention away. A Canis hybrid goes down, overwhelmed by two witches. I watch in horror and frustration. The hybrid is too far away for me to help. Anything I fire will likely result in someone else getting hit.

An enormous black bear sprints toward the hybrid. It swipes its paw at the back of the closest witch. The witch shrieks and fires, striking the bear and sending it staggering. The hybrid, still on the ground, hurls a ball of flames at the witch, striking her in the back. She drops to her knees, and it's all the hybrid needs to sink their sword into her neck.

Small, measured wins. This is how you win a battle.

I look back to the two witches leading this army. No, the witch and the goddess. The undead bears remain where they were, milky eyes staring vacantly at the battle before them.

But Cora and Thera are gone.

I scan the crowd, but there's no sign of them. Asmo is still on the ground beside me, calling out orders and surveying the battle scene in front of us. Elle watches Marik's unmoving body with something like fear and disgust.

I lean down. "Did you see where Cora went?" I ask Barrett.

He shakes his massive head once.

The sky darkens, the clouds growing thicker and blackening. Just like my wedding night. I rub the mark over my heart as I remember Cora's storm clouds and their lightning. I wave my arms at Asmo, but he's too busy shouting orders to notice me. I bang on Barrett's shoulder. "Let me down!"

He obliges and I hop from his back. I hurry back to Asmo. "Did you see where Cora and Thera went?"

His frowns. "No." He turns his gaze to the undead bears and his frown deepens. "You didn't see them from up there?"

I shake my head. "You don't think she just went home, do you?" I smile nervously.

Asmo's smile is full of pity.

A drop of water lands on my forehead in warning. The sky opens, and rain begins to pour in thick sheets. Lightning strikes overhead. My heart rate quickens.

Asmo steps closer to me. "This is intentional," he murmurs into my ear. "Don't let her rattle you."

But it's hard not to. It's hard not to think about all that was stolen from me the last time this happened. And now, despite being a queen without a throne, I have so much more to lose this time around. I have a mate. I have two sisters. I have a family of sorts, a family that I created. And it would kill me to lose them.

This time, there is so much more on the line.

Rain pelts my skin, streaming down my face and into my eyes. The salty taste of sweat and rain stings a cut on my lip I didn't even know I had. A powerful gust of wind sends hybrids stumbling, cutting a path right through our army.

Cora stands at the other end, her raven hair and aura writhing all around her.

"Remember the objective!" Asmo yells. "Go!" His hair is plastered to his forehead. He shoves it back, water spraying with the motion. He unstraps an obsidian dagger from the holster around his hips and fists it in his left hand, splaying his right hand. "I've been waiting for this moment." His voice promises death.

He strides toward her. My heart slams into my chest as they stare each other down, the battle raging around them.

She gives him a wicked grin.

He attacks.

His flames writhe as they reach for her, but she deflects them with a flick of her wrist. A bolt of lightning flies toward him. He ducks, but I throw up a shield to absorb the bolt and prevent it from striking anyone else. It shatters but does its job. Nobody was hurt, at least not by that bolt.

More lightning bolts land haphazardly, striking witches and hybrids without mercy. Asmo and Cora are locked in a whirlwind, a tornado of magic and fury as they attack and block and dodge. Asmo is a force to even be able to meet her blows. But he is just one person.

I know this battle won't end unless I help send Cora back to whatever hellhole she crawled out of. I sprint toward them, sending a controlled burst of wildfire toward Cora. The flames struggle against the downpour, but I summon more fire as the rain attempts to extinguish them.

Cora eyes the incoming wall of fire, and another gust of her wind forces the flames toward Asmo. I yank the magic back, and the flames die. Okay then. Asmo slashes at her with his shadow sword, forcing her to jump away from each invisible blow. How she can sense it, I don't know.

As she tries to dodge Asmo, I send another burst of wind and fire racing toward her. I grit my teeth and use my other hand to grow ivy. I've grown branches, but never ivy. It comes easier but feels wilder. I pull it back before it can close around her ankles, then urge my flames faster.

Asmo presses her, blow after blow after blow. All Cora can do is dodge. He slices a lock of her hair, and she hisses. He delivers another blow, and just as Cora tries to leap out of the way, I snap the ivy over her ankles and surge my fire. She trips and falls into it with a scream.

The flames lick and scorch her pale skin. She leaps into the air, away from the flames, and sends another bolt of lightning toward Asmo. He dodges, and I'm forced to cushion the blow before it can strike August this time.

A midnight black wolf sprints toward Cora's back. I protect him with a barrier and release it as he crashes into her, teeth sinking into her neck. She whirls, but he doesn't let go. She grips his thick coat with one hand. I summon wind and force them apart before she can call her lightning. The wound in her neck has already healed, but blood runs down her neck, her raven hair sticking to it.

A portal forms above Cora, and Amaris falls from the sky, two obsidian daggers gripped in her hands and aimed for Cora's skull. A drabar swoops from the air and knocks Amaris out of the way. She lands with a hiss and fires the dagger at the drabar with an angry bellow. The dagger finds its purchase and it crashes to the ground, landing on a hybrid and witch locked in battle.

I start toward them to save the hybrid, but another witch is there, a flash of red around her wrist. She drags the hybrid out and leaves the other witch trapped.

A bolt of ice flies past me, narrowly avoiding my shoulder, and I jerk away. August joins the fight now, firing bolts of ice at Cora with rapid speed. She throws a hand out, throwing his strikes off course, but one of them sinks into her gut. She screams as she grips the massive icicle with two skeletal hands.

Before she can pull it from her stomach, Asmo pounces on her and hammers sand down her throat. She flings her hands out. They land on Asmo's chest, and she shoves him away from her. Lightning cracks, but it doesn't come from the sky.

My chest cleaves.

My heart stutters in my chest. And stops. No, not my heart. The bond inside of me. I scream as his body hits the floor, limp and lifeless. I fall, knees colliding with the dirt with a force that sends my teeth clattering. My vision shatters into something other—something like the very depths of the Icebound Sea and the darkest parts of the night sky— black and empty and desolate, and somehow, I know I'm alone. Agony roars through me.

I fist the dirt, and stagger to my feet.

I can't look. I can't look at the male on the ground. I can't look at his chest to see if it rises. I know it won't.

A chill spreads through me, some otherworldly feeling of magic and power and a rage that feels like it might set me on fire. One that might burn me and then consume the rest of the world.

Roots burst through the ground and snap around Cora's feet. She flicks her wrist, and they fall away. Her lips curl into a cruel smile. "I told you, girl. You're no match for me."

I use everything I used the last time—wind, fire, earth. She dodges everything, as expected.

I form a ring of fire around her, blocking her in, watching as she smiles. She and I both know she can get out of this. But she doesn't expect me to funnel into the fire with her. I land directly behind her and reach for her face, for the bone-white eyes and the cruel smile. A gust of wind tries to knock me off course, but I command it down. A bolt of lightning tries to strike me, but I command it gone.

I am of the Mother. I was made by Her to defeat Cora.

I don't need Marik, or Elle, or Asmo.

It was always Cora and me. It always has been. I don't need anyone to help me destroy her. She raised me. She made me who I am.

And I will be the one who ends her.

I grip her face in my hands, fingers splayed over her cheeks and digging into the corners of her eyes. Ivy and roots shoot up her legs. They climb her torso, and she writhes, but I am fueled by a mix of sorrow and an ancient, all-consuming rage that threatens to tear me in half.

I grit my teeth and command *more*. The ivy transforms into ropes of fire, and Cora bellows as they mottle her skin. A bolt of lightning lands beside me, but it is an element, and I am the master of the elements.

I am the Queen of the Forest, of the trees and the flora and the fauna and the storms that ravage them. I was created by Mother Nature. I am born of all things that make this world, and therefore, I am the master of all that is born of this world.

The skin that knits Cora's chest together is paper-thin. I descend into the tissue, caressing the muscle and brushing against the bones that protect her rotten heart. She reaches for me, and a vine encased in fire snaps her hand back down. I wrap my hand around her heart.

I smile. And pull.

Her heart is black, but it beats just like anyone else's. It turns to ash in my hands. I pull the magic from the circle of fire that pulses around me and step away from Cora, coming to face her. The female who raised me stands before me, held up by branches and vines. Her chest gapes, and her mouth is frozen in a scream.

I set her ablaze, watching as her flesh burns. The smoke from her body rises, curling in the wind and the rain. I turn away.

August, Barrett, and Amaris watch me carefully as I walk toward Asmo, who still lays limp on the ground. Someone reaches for me, but I shove them away and summon a shield as I walk toward my mate.

My chest has cracked in two, and I scream for the bond, but it doesn't answer. I need to take him away from this fucking place and get him out of here. There has to be something, some way to save him.

When Elle was nearly dead from the cambions, the stag arrived just when I needed him. But the stag isn't here now. Only me.

I didn't need anyone else to kill Cora, and I don't need anyone else to save my mate.

I squeeze my eye shut and imagine I'm running through the forest—twigs snapping, birds chirping, leaves rustling, and crisp air brushing against my skin. I picture jumping over fallen legs and bounding over babbling creeks. I think about walking through the throne room, watching me on the throne, as if I were the stag.

A shudder runs through me, and my senses sharpen. Every yell, every strike, every weapon drawn is louder, clearer.

I shifted.

But it's useless if I can't get Asmo on my back. I circle him, nudging him with my snout. My throat tightens at how lifeless he is. Heavy footsteps pound toward me, and I flinch.

Elle. "Let me help you."

I lower myself and try not to focus on how she has to drag him. She drapes him over my back. He's heavy, but I can carry him, something I would never have been able to do in my hybrid form.

I don't waste any time. I take off. I don't know where to go that's safe, so I just run, trampling through the forest and down the mountain. I pass barren trees, their trunks thick and ancient, and finally, I understand that *this* must be what regret truly feels like—the dead, crushing weight of my mate on my back.

Please, I beg to no one, anyone. *Please. Please.* Please.

The forest is still silent, not a single animal to be seen or heard—just me, praying to whoever deigns to listen.

Then, I hear it. The rushing sound of the river.

It cuts through the mountain, running beneath the castle. A perfect place to hide. I trudge along the riverbank, the gray water looking cold as ice. The sunlight fades as I carry Asmo deeper.

When the light has nearly disappeared, I lay him on the bank of the river and shift back to my hybrid form. Asmo lays horrifyingly still. My hands shake as I cup his face, willing him to smirk, to frown. *Anything, please,* I beg again.

But his face looks like it's carved from marble. Pale, cold, still marble.

"Asmo," I whisper. He doesn't stir. "Asmo!" I shove him, I beat on his chest, I shake him. But he doesn't move.

I refuse to accept this. This cannot be what the Mother intended. This cannot be the cost for ridding the world of Cora. I have given too much. I have lived this fucking life, and I have played their fucking games and I refuse to believe that anyone would ask this much of me.

I scream and cry and beg for the Mother to help me, but She is silent.

And so is Asmo.

"Hello, Mae," a voice whispers, so light it could've been the wind. A jolt bolts through me and hope blooms in my chest. I whip my head up and stare at Asmo's lips, but they remain frozen and blue.

My blood turns to ice. I turn, shifting my body to cover Asmo's.

A dark figure stands on the riverbank, eerily still.

I wipe my tear-stained eyes and squint. The figure steps forward.

Thera. If the Mother's eyes are like the ocean, Thera's are like the night sky. Black pits with glistening stars, a whirling galaxy for an iris.

"What do you want?" I hiss. "*What else do you want?*"

She frowns, then speaks. Her voice is like the swing of a blade before it finds its mark, swift and light and filled with the promise of all that is terrible. "Your tears can no longer save him, Child of the Mother. He is too far gone." She pauses, filling the cave with the sound of the river as it rushes past. My chest rises and falls, but mine is the only one. "But I can."

"Who are you?" I whisper.

Her eyes crinkle, and galaxies shift. "I am Thera. I am the Sister. I am death. But in death, there is rebirth. And I am your mate's only option."

"What is the cost?"

She quirks her head. The movement is too quick to be natural. "You will owe me a debt. To be called upon at my convenience."

Any sane person would throw this offer into the river left untouched. But I know what Asmo would do. I will suffer through whatever needs to be done to have my mate back. I will damn myself if that is what it takes to see his chest rise again. If it means one more kiss, one more "princess," one more moment staring into his eyes.

I will do anything.

"Deal."

She smiles, and the galaxies shift to black holes. With a flick of her finger, the palm of my hand slices open. I hiss and cradle it against my chest. Bright, hot blood spills. She dashes to me and yanks my hand to her, staring at the crimson now pooling in my palm.

She lifts it to her mouth, and drinks.

It is done, her ancient, cold, horrifying voice echoes inside my head. Horror crawls like tiny spiders along every inch down my spine. I just made a deal with the Goddess of the Underworld.

As suddenly as she appeared, she vanishes.

And Asmo's chest moves.

CHAPTER 51
MAE

ASMO GROANS, and I burst into tears. The thump of his heart against my cheek is the sweetest sound I've ever heard, but I can't bring myself to look at him. I'm terrified he's not the male I remember. Terrified I just signed away his soul. Terrified he's some Cursed version of my mate.

His hand cups the back of my head. "Princess." The "ss" is slithery and I'm brought back to the very first time I met him. I let loose another sob.

Please, please, please.

"It's okay. It's okay. We're okay." His voice is warm and comforting and feels like home.

His shirt grows damp from my tears. He shifts beneath me, propping himself on his elbows. I force myself to look up at him, and something in my chest warms as I find those fern-green eyes. I reach for the mating tattoo on my chest, for the way I know he's still there, still a part of me. He wouldn't leave me. Not the male whose eyes soften when they fall upon mine, who would rather look at me than the stars.

I curl my fingers in his hair, still damp from the rain and gritty with dirt from the riverbed. "Az," I whisper. Even with that one syllable, my voice breaks.

"Princess." One corner of his mouth quirks upward, and I threaten to break again.

I press my lips to his, tasting sweat and dirt and everything that makes him real. Alive.

"Mine," I whisper.

He doesn't repeat the sentiment. He just smiles against my lips. That's all I need.

"Where are we?"

"The river that runs through the mountain," I answer.

He blinks. "How did we get here?"

"You...Cora hurt you," I say. "I shifted and managed to get you here."

"Well, I guess that explains why you're naked."

I look down, at my fully nude body sprawled all over him. A laugh threatens to spill, but then I remember Thera finding me on top of him. And what came after. *What have I done?*

Asmo glances down, assessing himself. He moves his arms, then pats his stomach, his legs. "I feel fine...But it must have been bad if I don't remember it. What happened?"

"You jumped on Cora and...She pushed you away, but she used her lightning." *And then your body hit the ground and my chest cracked and you*—I squeeze my eyes shut. "And you didn't get back up."

He pushes himself into a seated position and pulls his shirt up. Unlike my interaction with Cora's lightning, there isn't a single mark on Asmo. It looks like it never even happened.

"How am I alive, princess?" His voice is deep, commanding. He knows. And yet, something in me screams to keep the truth from Asmo. For the second time, I wonder what he would have done. He would've made the deal and lied about it so I wouldn't worry.

I force a smile. "My tears, remember?" I wipe them from my cheeks. "I don't know how or why, but they can heal."

He shakes his head in disbelief. "You're..."

"Made by the Mother," I whisper.

"I was going to say you were something else." His lips press into a grimace. "I'm sorry. I acted recklessly." He peels his shirt off and hands it to me.

I pull it over my head, thankful that it falls to my mid-thighs. I wave the apology away. It doesn't feel deserved. Not after I just lied to him about why he's alive. Not after I might have just thrown our future away by promising a favor to the Goddess of Hell.

"We need to get back to the battle," I say as I rise.

He pushes himself to standing and tries his best to brush mud and dirt from his pants, but it barely makes a difference. "What was going on when you left?"

"I killed Cora."

He turns his head to me. "You did what?"

I fight to contain the smile. It's a sick and twisted joy that comes from killing another person, but she wasn't even a person. People have have hearts, souls, a conscious. Well, I guess technically she had a heart.

Asmo nods appreciatively. "Alright, then. That's a conversation for later. What else?"

"When I left, everyone was still fighting the witches and the Cursed."

"Let's go then. We have a kingdom to secure."

We walk back in silence, hands clasped, both of us on high alert for any sign of witches or Cursed, or anything else Cora managed to drag up with her from below. But there is nothing. Nothing crafted from dark magic, at least.

Deer have begun to venture through the trees once more. A rabbit hops past us. The rain has stopped and the clouds have begun to disperse.

I don't hear any screaming, which means the battle has either been won...or lost.

Back at the battleground, Barrett and August stand before a group of witches. They sit on the ground, hands bound behind by their backs, hissing and spitting at the two High Princes. On the other side of the field, Elle and Basil help wounded hybrids walk to an area filled with makeshift cots. Healers tend to stab wounds, burns, and the like. I smile when I see Brynn, the healer who helped my cambion burn, among them.

Witches lie bloodied and limp on the floor, their heads burned or missing altogether. Hybrids and Fae drag them into a pile. Ivan has begun creating a separate area for fallen hybrids, resting their bodies with care side by side.

Once, I kissed August on this field. I watched young hybrids chase each other as their parents smiled at them. I met my mate here.

Now, it's a graveyard.

"We need to get those witches into the dungeons," Asmo says, pulling me from the memories of my coronation day.

Throw the witches into the dungeons, dispose of the dead ones, hold funerals for the deceased hybrids, heal the wounded, figure out what the hell is going on with Marik, save the world, redeem a favor for the Goddess of Hell—

Asmo steps in front of me and tilts my face upward. "Hey," he says softly.

I blink and focus on him, shoving my racing thoughts to the side. "Sorry," I say. "Witches. Dungeon. Yes."

He stares at me, eyebrows drawn together. "I know this is a lot. It's okay to not be okay right now. But stay strong for everyone. You can lose it later."

I clench my jaw. He's right. *Add "lose it later" to the list.*

He rolls his shoulders back and strides toward everyone. I imitate him, hoping to show everyone that I'm confident, that I know what the fuck I'm doing, that I'm not a fraud. All the emotions from the first week of being High Queen resurface—the anxiety, the insecurity, the feelings of being an imposter. I just won back my kingdom. My home.

But all I can think about is the unknown fate I just doomed myself to.

"Mae!" a voice calls. I turn. Elle, her hair threatening to come undone as she sprints toward me. She pulls me into a fierce hug. I cling to her. My sister. "You're okay." She pulls back and stares at Asmo. "You're alive."

He cocks his head. "Yes?"

She shakes her head. "No, I just...I thought you were dead."

"Happy to disappoint, then." His smile is razor sharp, his teeth dazzlingly white.

"Your Highness," Ivan calls as he walks toward us. But his gaze is fixed on Asmo. "We need to transfer the prisoners and get the wounded inside."

Asmo and Ivan walk away, Asmo's hands clasped behind his back as Ivan details what should happen next.

Elle stands beside me, our shoulders brushing as we watch the two get farther away. "How is he alive?" she whispers.

"I don't know," I admit. It's the truth. I have no fucking clue what happened or what I did. "What happened after we left?"

She moves to stand before me. "When you killed Cora, the Cursed just...fell." She points to the battlefield, where animal corpses lay amongst the mud and trodden grass.

Add "burn the Cursed" to the list.

"We were able to turn all our efforts to the witches," Elle continues. "Some of them surrendered, but many of them fought to the death." She looks at me, a smile threatening to break loose. "It's over, Mae. We beat her."

My eyes close and I inhale, deep and true. We beat Cora. We saved the kingdom. I know I should be happy—and I am—but my stomach twists again. *What have I done? What will Thera ask of me?* "How are you feeling? About...Marik?" I ask.

"Oh, that," she says, her smile fading. She looks at the ground, mouth twisting as she stares at her feet. "He's..." she hesitates. "Alive but...not. He's breathing, but he won't move or open his eyes."

"How are you feeling about that?" I ask.

She shrugs and, again, looks down, seemingly intent on studying the pattern of the laces in her boots.

I don't press. "Okay," I say with a sigh. "Then we need to get him to a healer."

She nods slowly. "Get everyone else checked first. Marik should be the last. He did this, after all."

I nod once. "If that is what you wish."

Her gaze finds mine. "I wish for none of this."

The library is dark and silent, a far cry from what it used to be. In a way, this place helped transform me. I've always found solace in books, comfort in others' stories, in the way the characters handle trials and tribulations, in who they become. Tales of dragons, princesses, love, and loss have shaped me over the years.

But this library has helped shape my own journey—my first day at the castle, sipping coffee with Elle, laying here with Koa, Asmo breaking my heart. Now, I've gained everything, lost everything, and fought tooth and nail to get it back. Maybe even bartered my soul. But I have no regrets. Not yet, at least.

If I had fought for this kingdom, only to have to sit on a throne by myself, I would've burned it all over again.

"Do you plan to stare into the darkness all evening?" Asmo drawls from behind me. I smile, but it falls almost instantly. It was too close. "Brynn is wrapping up with the injured."

I sigh. "Let's go see Marik."

Marik was moved to the spare bedroom in my wing. He lies on the bed, black shirt and trousers torn by the Cursed's teeth, dirt crusted along his jaw, and hair matted and stiff with what I'm assuming is blood and saliva. Elle sits on a plush chair, her head in her hands. She lifts it as we walk in. Purple shadows line her eyes.

She probably hasn't slept in at least a day. It's hard to remember that the ball was only last night. I sway on my feet at the reminder, but Asmo's hand steadies me.

"Anything?" I ask.

Elle shakes her head. "He's alive. I don't understand it. His wounds from the Cursed bear have even healed themselves."

"Let's see what Brynn has to say," Asmo says.

She nods and leans back in her chair, foot bouncing on the ground.

"I plan to speak with the Herd after this," I say to Elle. "You're welcome to stay here though, if you'd prefer."

She shakes her head again. "I'd rather not sit and stare at the male who ruined my life."

Okay, then. "Of course," I say. A soft knock on the door. Ivan cracks it open. "Brynn," I say warmly. "I'm happy to see you."

She forms a deep bow, then smiles at me. "You have no idea how happy we are to see you, Your Highness." She turns to Asmo. "And you, Prince Asmo."

He opens his mouth, but I shoot him a look. We'll make the announcement later. He shuts his mouth and smiles politely.

I motion toward Marik. "We have no idea what has happened to him, and we would love a healer's perspective."

Brynn begins her silent assessment, hands hovering over every extremity, lips pursed in concentration. Her hand passes over his chest and her eyes widen for a flash, but she schools her features quickly.

Elle leans forward. "What is it?"

Brynn shakes her head. "Nothing." Elle shoots her a glare and Brynn adds, "There is a connection." She looks nervously to me. The mating bond.

Fuck. I didn't think about this. "We are aware. Please, Brynn, this stays between us."

She nods in agreement and continues her assessment. After another minute, she removes her hands and straightens. She clasps them in front of her as she addresses me. "He is alive, but he is...elsewhere. His body is here, but his soul is not."

My stomach hollows. "What does that mean?" The soul is always connected to the body. When the body dies, so does the soul. Both sink back into the earth and begin the journey to the heavens. Until weeks ago, I never even considered the possibility that a soul could journey downward, to the hells. There is so much I don't know.

She shakes her head. "I don't know, Your Highness. I've never dealt in matters such as this. I'm sorry, but I'm not sure what I can do to help."

"Thank you, Brynn," Asmo says curtly behind me.

She gives us a final bow before skittering past us and shutting the door softly behind her.

"What does that even mean?" I groan.

Elle's head is back in her hands, her nails digging into pale skin.

Asmo paces the space of the room, jaw working. His hands clench into fists before he shoves them into his pockets. "I don't know. But I think I have an idea for how to find out."

"Wh—"

Another knock on the door before it clicks open. "Your Highness," Ivan's voice comes. "The witch is requesting an audience."

I cock my head. "The witch? Are they not all in the dungeons?"

"The lead witch. Levana."

Ah. The witch ally.

"Tell her we will meet with her at sundown. In fact, we will meet with all of you at sundown. My mate needs rest," Asmo says firmly. Before I can protest, he ushers everyone from the room.

With everyone gone, I feel like I can breathe. I sink onto the couch and rest my face in my hands as I fill my lungs. The couch shifts below me, and a hand rubs my back. I lean into Asmo and feel my eyes drift shut.

"Come on," he says, scooping me into his arms. He leads me to the spare bedroom and rests me on the plush bed. I begin to argue, to tell him we have things to do, people to rescue, plans to make. But it dies on my lips as I sink into the soft give of the pillows.

Asmo places a kiss on my forehead. "Sleep, princess." He shuts the door behind him. I close my eyes, the calm of sleep settling over me swiftly.

I shift to get more comfortable, and the grit of dirt on the sheets sends a flush of irritation through me instead. There is an ungodly amount of grime and dirt and sweat and blood crusted on every part of my body.

With a groan, I haul myself from bed and exit the bedroom. "I'm gonna take a shower, if you want to join," I call, but it goes unanswered. "Az?"

No response.

The wing is empty. No sign of Asmo anywhere.

I open the door that leads to the rest of the castle. A small group of guards—Fae and hybrid—turn to me.

"Where did Asmo go?" I ask.

A squirrel hybrid tilts his head. "He hasn't left, Your Highness."

I freeze. Maybe I missed him in the wing? I thank the guards and turn back inside, calling for Asmo and searching everywhere, but he's gone. The wards make it impossible to funnel out of here. But he escaped the dungeons, so there must be a way.

Maybe he left a note, some sort of explanation. But the kitchen counters are bare, and there's no note anywhere. His jacket lies on the couch, and I reach for it, turning pockets inside out as I search for any clue.

The handheld mirror clatters out. *Why is he carrying this around?*

I grab a dagger and draw blood, smearing it over the mirror. "Show me Asmo."

The reflection shows walls of red clay, of packed sand...Squall's End? No. The tunnel from Asmo's childhood. The cave where he and Marik used to escape to.

Asmo stoops and flings open the chest. Dust flies as it creaks open, revealing an assortment of blankets, novels, parchment, pens, and other seemingly random items. He pulls out a stick, a candle, and two small... rocks or dice, I can't tell. He sets the unlit candle on the ground and uses the stick to draw a circle around the candle.

I set the mirror down, grab my jacket and shove my shoes on. If Asmo can funnel out of here, I must be able to. I concentrate, willing myself to be at the cave's entrance. I imagine myself stepping through, imagine my foot landing on the red clay of the cliffside. I feel the wind picking up, but it struggles. I grit my teeth and *push*.

It flickers, and I stumble onto the cliffside. I throw a sound barrier up and enter the cave, my stomach twisting as I follow the path. Something feels wrong.

Asmo sits in front of the circle, his back to me. The candle in the center of the circle blazes, orange flames burning several feet in the air. I'm six feet away, and I can feel the heat that radiates from the flame.

Darkness hangs in the air like a blanket made of ink—thick and tangible—but the candle remains burning bright.

"Osseris," a deep, otherworldly voice whispers behind me, hot breath tickling my ear, sending shivers down my spine. My stomach hollows. The sound does not come from behind me, but echoes throughout the cave.

No.

"Where is my brother." It is not a question, but an order.

The voice is ancient and filled with a hollow rattle. "The prince is in the Woodland Kingdom."

Asmo scowls. "His body is, but his soul is not."

"You know where he is, High King."

"Tell me," Asmo commands.

The voice inhales. The air in the cave whooshes toward the circle. A chill crawls through me. "Your brother is in a grave in the place where you were born to rule, Asmodeus."

Asmo hisses a curse. Like the osseris confirmed his suspicions. *What is he hiding from me?*

I drop the sound barrier and step forward. "Where?"

The osseris turns slowly, fixing its eyes on me. Eyes made of galaxies, black holes, vortexes swirling into nothing. "Ah, she speaks."

Asmo whirls to me, his mouth falling open, then slamming shut. His face drains of color.

"Congratulations on your bond," the osseris says, the corners of its mouth pulling into a cruel grin. "Bold of you to reveal it to me."

I keep my gaze on this thing, despite the way my flesh crawls as its eyes swirl and rove over my body. "Where is Marik?"

"He is in his rightful place. Where he was born to rule, just as your mate was. And now that you've accepted the bond, as are you."

A bead of sweat rolls down my spine, but I feel cold. "*Where?*" I command.

It gives me a knowing smile and the swirling vortexes in his eyes still. Its teeth are made of sharp, rotting bones. "Hell."

CHAPTER 52
MAE

ASMO EXTINGUISHES the flame and the connection with the osseris dies. He stands, staring at me like I'm a scared animal that might run away.

Who are you?

Every instinct in my body is telling me to flee. "What is this, Asmo?" I demand, fighting the way my voice shakes—fury, fear, horror, I don't know.

His eyes don't move from mine. "What he said was true—"

I cut him off. "I know. Don't waste time trying to lie. Tell me the *truth.*"

"Years ago, Thera came to visit me in my dreams, just like the Mother visited you. She told me a tale, just like the one the Mother told you. She told me I had a mate, and that we were born to rule together." His gaze cuts to the candle, where the osseris just was, then back to me. "She also told me that Marik and I were created to rule Hell."

My pulse slams in my throat, which now feels too thick and my skin itches and my feet beg to run far, far away.

"You asked me once why I was even participating in your courting. My parents urged me, but so did Thera. I said no, and I told Marik to say no. But I guess Cora and Thera got to him. He agreed. I came to your court to keep an eye on him. He had changed in the years prior, but I didn't realize how much." He takes a deep breath. "Mae, I...I didn't expect *this*—" he waves his hands in the air "—to happen. I didn't know Marik would do what he did."

Truth, truth, truth. All of it is the truth. "So, you...you knew? You knew about Cora? This whole time?" My voice breaks. I don't care.

He winces, but he nods. "Kind of. I knew some things about the prophecy. My parents have been spewing this bullshit for years. Cora was not a new face to me. She had been working with my parents. But I didn't know she was pretending to be your aunt, and I didn't know that Marik killed the royal family. I had my suspicions, but...I was looking into it." He rubs the back of his neck, drops his hands to his sides. "I had no clue who she truly was, Mae. I promise. I had no clue that any of this would happen."

"Why didn't you tell me? Any of this?" I whisper.

His face falls. "Because I knew there was a chance you'd reject the bond if you knew who—what—I truly was."

Heat flushes through my body and I ball my hands into fists, clenching the fire that rises. "That should have been my decision to make."

"Mae, if you had rejected the bond, we wouldn't have been able to defeat Cora."

"*That should have been my decision to make.*"

He grips his hair. "See? What the fuck was I supposed to do? Sacrifice your *choice* or take the chance that you'd reject it and destroy the kingdom?"

His words feel like a slap to the face. He feels like a stranger to me. "You think I would have thrown away the fate of the kingdom because I was pissed at you? I swore an oath to protect this kingdom. You should have *talked to me*. I'm your *mate*. Or is that some lie, too?"

His chest heaves as he stares at me with wild eyes. I've never seen him like this. "I have meant every word I've ever said to you," he bites out.

"Because you know I can detect your lies! It's all the unsaid, Asmo. Now answer the question. Am I actually your mate? Or was it a lie?"

He places his hand to his chest. "It was never a lie. I am your mate. You are mine. That will never change."

If it's the truth, why does my chest feel like it's about to explode? Why does my heart feel like it was just twisted and drained? Is it because I thought I escaped a monster, only to find out the haven I thought I had was actually the lair of another nightmare instead?

"So, what now?" I spit at him. "What's next in your little plan that only you know? Or are you secretly fucking Thera, too? Is that what the Serpent Princes like to do? Seduce poor, unsuspecting Mae, while they're fucking some ancient deity behind my back?"

He closes his eyes. His jaw clenches. "No, Mae. I'm not. Like I said, I wanted nothing to do with this. But fate had a different plan for me."

I snort. "You let some goddess dictate how you live your life. You're a fucking coward."

He breathes through his nose. "I deserve that."

"I'm going back to the castle. You can come or stay here and rot. But if you come, you will pretend like nothing has happened. We have to figure out what comes next. I still have a kingdom to rule."

I don't wait for him. I funnel back to my wing, trying to untense my muscles as the clay walls fade and the familiar living room materializes. I storm out the doors, desperate to avoid being caught here alone with Asmo.

Ivan is in his office, reviewing weathered parchment as he paces the cramped quarters. "Your Highness," he says with a smile.

Even though my world just crumbled, again, I can't help the smile. It feels full circle to see Ivan in this space again. "Ivan," I say warmly. "I'm really sorry for the change, but would you mind gathering everyone, including Levana, to meet in the throne room? I'd like to discuss what comes next."

He sets the parchment down. "Of course."

"Thank you." I turn and leave, walking through still empty hallways.

My footsteps echo through the throne room as I walk toward my rightful place, its branches and berries as familiar to me as the back of my hand. The High Crown floats above the throne and I summon it, plucking it from the air and placing it around my antlers. Like before, I cast a subtle glow around my features.

Despite the blood- and sweat-stained leathers I still wear, I feel like a High Queen again.

The doors part open and I turn, ready to compliment Ivan on his speed. But it's not him.

It's the stag.

His warm brown eyes stare at me as he walks toward me. Mother, I could fall to my knees and weep right now. For a moment, I can pretend I'm in the past, when everything was normal. When I was prancing the halls with Elle, when William was still beside me, before I found out that Willa and Marik weren't who they claimed to be. Before I learned I had a mate, who turned out to be like his brother—a liar and a manipulator. Oh, and a Prince of Hell, apparently.

I reach for the stag. He huffs a warm breath into the palm of my hand. "Hello, you," I whisper.

He blinks in response and presses his muzzle into my hand. I fight tears, shoving them aside and straightening my spine. We walk to the dais together, and I perch on the throne of branches and berries. The stag takes his usual spot, right beside my feet.

It feels surreal to be back. The throne room is a different version of itself—the ancient hardwood floors replaced by cool, white marble. Black veins trickle through the marble, reminding me of Cora.

I inhale. Maybe I'll keep the marble in reminder of all that I've overcome to get back here.

The doors open again. Asmo strides in, black hair perfectly in place and eyes cool as he stares at me. He's silent as he strides to the throne. He doesn't place the crown on his head.

He turns to me, his expression pained. "Mae, I—"

Ivan strides into the throne room, and Asmo's mask of indifference slides back over his features. It takes everything in me to not crawl away in horror. He is as practiced in this as Marik is.

I was—I am—such a fool.

The rest of the Herd comes next, including Etta, Basil, and Amaris. I force myself to look at each of them, to distract myself with memorizing their features, to ignore the anger that simmers below the surface.

Holly walks beside Elle, who twists her fingers together. Barrett and August walk together, hair mussed and cheeks gaunt. Levana follows all of them, head down.

"Thank you for meeting with us on short notice. I know we agreed to meet in the morning, and I'm sure you all are exhausted," I say as warmly as I can muster. "However, it didn't feel right to rest while the fate of the kingdom hangs precariously."

Murmurs of agreement sound, and August gives me an encouraging nod. I ignore the way that small gesture makes me feel. Like home. My throat burns, and I swallow the thick lump in my throat.

Ivan clears his throat, hands clasped together. "I would recommend ordering an increase in guard patrol and burning the witches' bodies immediately."

Asmo leans forward. I ignore the urge to turn toward him. "Are the witches in the dungeons?" he asks. Ivan gives him a firm nod. "Good. Ensure there are always extra guards there."

Barrett clears his throat. Wisps of hair hang from his bun, framing his rugged face. "I would recommend a higher-ranking official watching, too," he says.

I lean back in the throne with a sigh. "I agree, but I only trust us, and we all need to sleep."

"I can sleep down there," Barrett offers.

"Me, too," August adds.

I shake my head. "You don't have to. I'm sure there's another way."

"If there is, I'm too tired to think of it," August admits. A still-healing cut marks his bicep, red and angry.

"Go home," I order the both of them. "Send someone you trust from your courts in your place."

They nod graciously.

I squeeze my knuckles as I think through what should come next. I wish I could just ask Asmo, but I'm feeling too stubborn and embarrassed and prideful to do so. "Hunt the witches in the remaining courts," I say. "They can either surrender and be placed in our dungeons to await their fate, or they can be sent back to Hell. Round up anyone harboring witches and toss them in the dungeons to await a trial." I take a deep breath as I give my next order. "Bring in Houses Serpent and Panthera for the same."

August and Barrett wince at the order, but they don't object.

Levana's voice projects from the back. Like everyone else, she is covered in filth and her shoulders slump from exhaustion. "This battle is won, but the war is not over. Not yet."

Amaris narrows her gaze, watching her with some mix of suspicion and interest.

I quirk my head. "What do you mean? Cora has been defeated."

"Make no mistake, great progress was made tonight, Your Highness. But Thera will return to Hell and more witches and Cursed will be made. There is no telling what other creatures she will create. This will not end, not as long as she is still allowed to exist."

A chill spreads through me, harsh and all-consuming. She's right, whatever it means. The dream didn't say anything about Cora. Just the Sister. *Fuck. Why did I assume defeating Cora would be the end of this?*

She takes a deep breath and looks at me. "Do you trust everyone here?"

I falter as I think of Asmo, but I say, "Yes."

She nods. "You and your mates," she says as she looks to Elle, "are the keys to defeating Thera. I've been alive a long time, long enough to have known your mother. I have been aware of the prophecy for as long as it has been around. The only way this ends is with you four uniting and vanquishing her."

Truth.

"But Marik..." Elle says.

"His soul is in Hell," Asmo says.

I straighten in my chair. I wasn't expecting this information to be shared, but okay then.

"I thought that might be the case," Levana says gravely. "There is a way to get him back, but it will require someone going to get him. He cannot make the journey back alone."

"Then we will bring him back," I say with finality.

What other choice is there? Even if Marik went to Hell voluntarily, I would pull him out of there kicking and screaming. This must end. And I have the power to end it.

If what the osseris said is true, I'm the High Queen of Hell now.

EPILOGUE
MARIK

THE FIRST BREATH I take is pointless. Dirt fills my mouth and nose, and panic flares. I swallow it and force myself to stop breathing. I was trained for this. Mother and Father made sure of it.

Father's words come back in a rush. *This body isn't real. They can't kill you here.*

But that doesn't mean I can't feel the pain of it. Of my lungs suffocating but never asphyxiating.

I punch upward, feeling the kiss of scorching air against my fists. I grab whatever I can and pull, fingernails cracking as I haul myself from the shallow grave.

My face hits the air next. I gasp, inhaling air roiling with heat. The only kind of heat one place can provide.

The one place I swore I'd never come back to.

I bellow. The ground shakes. The sky alights—in welcome or in protest.

I push myself to my feet and begin the trek back to a throne I abandoned long ago.

THE END

Continue reading for *TLDQ* bonus chapters from Asmo's POV.

CHAPTER 13
ASMO

"Tʜᴀᴛ ᴡᴀs ᴀ ꜰᴜᴄᴋɪɴɢ ᴅɪsᴀsᴛᴇʀ."

The frigid air bites against my skin as I exit the castle. Despite the High Castle being nowhere north, the temperatures here get too cold for my liking. Even on the coldest days of winter, it never gets this cold in the City of Sand.

"What did you expect?" Marik asks. "You have a penchant for these sorts of things."

I grunt. He might have a point.

"What happened when you two spoke privately?" he asks, shoving his hands in his pockets and hunching forward. My brother was never one for the cold, either.

Loose pebbles skitter as I step from the main path, back to the guest cottage. When Ivan first showed us our lodgings, I almost funneled right back home, to its concrete buildings and clean angles. Its sunbaked rocks and warm sand.

Marik clears his throat. A reminder of the question.

"I told her the truth."

"Which is...?"

"That I don't want to be here."

Marik's sigh is impressive, somehow full of disappointment and humor. He must have inherited that from Father. The sigh that always morphed into a smile whenever we failed, whenever we cried, whenever we screamed. Whenever it meant he'd just get to enact whatever hell he had created upon us again.

"Az...Just pretend," he whispers.

Just pretend. Pretending was never my strong suit. Marik, on the other hand, was always better at it. Pretending when he wasn't about to break down. But I could always tell.

"There's no point to it," I grumble. "You know it, Mar. I'm to be the Serpent King, not the fucking High King. I have to. There is no other choice." But that's a lie. If I really wanted, I could become the High King and Marik could lead our court.

But that would mean Marik would inherit the throne below. And he's not strong enough for that.

It is a blessing and a curse. But mostly a curse. Actually, it's entirely a curse.

The cottage door swings open. I shut it behind us and flip the deadbolt.

"Leave it unlocked," Marik says, "for the others."

"They'll figure it out," I say with a shrug before trudging upstairs. The room I selected is the largest. According to the Chief Advisor—or whatever he calls himself—this was the original Deer King and Queen's cottage. They lived here as the castle was being built. I chose their old bedroom. If I'm not going to the High King, I can at least sleep comfortably while I'm here.

Across the hall, Marik's door shuts. I think I hear a muffled "Night," but I don't respond. None of this is his fault, but sometimes I resent him.

I climb into bed and stare out the window, watching the crescent moon overhead, dark clouds drifting by lazily.

White, hot pain bursts in my chest.

I reach for the dagger that's surely embedded in my ribs, but there's nothing there. Just the pounding of my heart.

What the fuck?

I summon my flames, but my magic feels slow and groggy. The room is empty, and my chest is clean. Bloodless.

A flash of white hair, soaked, and tinged with blood.

My heart twists in my chest again. I double over, and clench down on a scream.

Another flash of an image. A mouth wide open, teeth bared, a silent scream.

The Princess.

I stumble to the door and out into the hallway. Marik's door opens after the third thump, and I all but fall inside.

"What the hell?"

"Get to—" Tears streaming, fists balled, a head slamming into stone. "Castle," I manage to say through gritted teeth.

"*What?*"

"Now. Mae. Something. Wrong," I gasp.

Marik stares at me with the most fucking annoying look of confusion on his face. "Wh—How do you know?"

I shove him out of the bedroom. "*GO!*"

"At least let me get a shirt," he says, slinking past me in the doorframe and plucking a black shirt from the floor.

Another flash—crimson and anguish. It feels like my heart is about to twist itself into two.

"Please, Marik. Hurry," I say, trying not to panic at the way my voice sounds, at the amount of panic that I feel. Not for myself, but for her.

Because something is terribly, terribly wrong.

⬦

A knock on my door, then the click of it opening. The pain in my chest subsided nearly an hour ago. I counted every second in an effort to *not* think about what this means.

"She's fine," Marik's voice says, voice barely above a whisper.

I nod, but I don't look at him. I keep my gaze locked on the ceiling.

"How did you know?" he asks.

I turn away from him.

I go back to counting, trying not to think about why I care how much blood was in her hair.

CHAPTER 22
ASMO

The tug came in the middle of the night, in the middle of my search for Marik. It was minor enough but quickly grew into something uncomfortable. I rubbed the spot over my heart, but that didn't help. It got worse. I took my hand off. And it still got worse. But it still was nothing like the first night I felt it.

Now, the forest is eerily silent. So different from home, always filled with the roar of the sea or the distant sounds of city life. Then again, maybe the forest is always this silent. But something tells me tonight is different. Something tells me the deer and rabbits and squirrels are gone. Hiding.

Because something is wrong.

My dagger is fisted in one hand, my other hand splayed, the shadow sword only a thought away.

I'm not sure what I'm listening for or who I'm looking for. Marik or the queen—maybe both.

Maybe they're together. Maybe I'll stumble upon them locked in an embrace, her back pressed against a tree.

I shake my head. No. She wouldn't.

Her scream echoes through the night, and my blood roars. Panic turns into a living thing in my chest, crawling over my skin.

She yells something, and I forget the plan. There is no point in being silent and searching if she dies.

There is no point to anything, if she is who I think she is.

There is no more point to everything I've worked for in my life. To being king of my court. To keeping Marik out of hell and out of Thera's grasp. If he doesn't take the throne below, I'll have to. But if I'm right, that means I'd be leaving something above.

Mae screams again. "HELP!"

My careful trek through the forest turns into a sprint.

A cambion is tugging her into the woods. She's shoving and planting her feet and flailing, but those things are too strong for her to fight off with sheer strength.

The whites of her eyes are glassy. I can smell her fear.

The cambion is speaking to her in its true voice. Its demonic voice. It's no longer trying to play.

My vision turns red, and its head goes flying. I want to curse at myself for using the shadow sword from so far. I could have killed her.

She whirls, but she doesn't see me still in the shadows. She's trying to peel the dead cambion's fingers from her forearm, but her hands are shaking too much.

I emerge from the shadows, head swiveling, but no other cambions or dark creatures come for us. "Mae!" I whisper-shout. "Are you okay?"

She's silent, and I feel like my chest might explode if she doesn't answer within the next five seconds.

Her cheeks are so soft against my hands, always rough and calloused. I force her gaze to mine, her amber eyes full of unshed tears. "Are you okay?"

She gives me a shaky nod, and I force myself to step away from her. There is no damn reason I should be fighting myself to not pull her into my arms.

She looks fine. Unharmed. Except for the burn that I know is underneath the cambion's hand.

"Get it off me," she croaks, holding her shaking arm out to me.

I peel the cambion's fingers back, revealing pink, bubbling skin underneath.

Mae sways on her feet. "What the fuck was that?" Her voice is low but no longer shaking.

"What did it say to you?" She shakes her head. I tilt her chin up and force her to look at me again. She's still blinking back tears. "Mae, this is important. Think. What did it say to you?"

Her throat bobs. "It said my High King was waiting for me."

"Fuck." I run a hand through my hair and turn back toward the forest. Still, nothing else emerges from the shadows.

"What does that mean? Asmo, what's going on?"

"Marik's missing," I snap. "That must be what it meant." What the hell is Marik doing? Captured by a cambion?

"It was trying to take me into the woods." She freezes. "Do you think he's in there? What about Koa?"

"What? What are you talking about?"

"I left Koa in the library. We have to go back."

Her voice is panicked, and I want to tell her that Koa is a big boy, but I don't. And for that, I really should be given a monetary reward or something. I wave my hand in dismissal. "He can take care of himself. I have to find my brother."

My fingers dance along the edge of the blade of my dagger. The burn on Mae's arm is bright pink and beginning to blister. Yet, she's acting like it's not hurting at all. She must be in shock. "Listen to me," I say. "Go back into the castle. Go into your wing, and do not open the door for anyone. I'll come get you when it's safe."

Why I even offer to return for her, I don't know. I need her to stay away from me, not find reasons to be near her.

She plants her feet and glares up at me. "What are you talking about? I'm coming with you to get Marik."

I blink. Is she forgetting who she is? "Damnit, Mae. No. You're the High Queen. I can't put you in danger like that."

"Shut up, Asmo. I'm coming. Tell me what I need to know."

Something stirs, deep within me. Like a sleeping snake has awoken from the challenge in her voice. With a shake of my head, I shove it as far down as I can. "Fine. Listen to me closely. That thing was a cambion. They're designed to lure you into a dangerous location before they torture you. They feed on fear. Do not trust what you see. Trust me and stay by me. Do not let any of those things touch you. They mute your magic. Do whatever you need to do to kill it or incapacitate it to keep it from touching you."

If a cambion somehow got its hands on Marik, he might be in a lot of trouble. But we've been trained to deal with these things. Was he just distracted? Was he not suspecting it? Did it sneak up on him?

I hand Mae my dagger. What the fuck is The Herd doing letting her walk around without a weapon? And how in the hells did Koa not wake up when she walked out? "Use your magic first. Use this as a last resort. They usually travel alone, but if Marik was taken, I'm assuming there's more of them."

She grabs the dagger and holds it with the weakest grip I've ever seen. Okay, maybe that's why nobody's letting her walk around without a weapon.

"How did you kill that one from so far away?" she asks.

"Magic."

"Oh, duh," she says with a delicious roll of her eyes.

Fuck. I'm in trouble.

"Come on," I say, heading down the path through the trees. My head is on a swivel, waiting for anything to pop out. Waiting for something to grab the queen behind me. My senses are on alert, but Mae's hearing is probably better than mine. I stop and turn to her. "What do you hear?" She stares at me blankly. "You're a deer. I'm a snake. Your hearing is better than mine. Do you hear Marik? Do you hear anything?"

She tilts her head, then motions down the path. "I hear voices, but I can't tell what they're saying."

"Probably more than one, then," I say, turning away from her and setting back down the path.

"Asmo," Mae whispers behind me. I grit my teeth. My name on her lips should not be making me feel this way, Mother damn it.

When I turn, she's pointing into the forest. I put myself in between her and the direction she motioned toward. Whatever she heard, I'm not risking it snatching her. A groan comes from about ten feet away.

Damnit, Marik.

I step from the trail, Mae close behind me. I can feel her. Too fucking close.

Marik is in a clearing, his arms tied behind him around a tree trunk. Blood drips from a cut on his temple. He's unconscious. Warning bells toll. Marik and I have taken on dozens of cambions before. We know how to get out of situations exactly like this.

Something is wrong. I just don't know what yet.

A branch cracks behind me and Mae tries to pass me. I throw my arm out and give her an exasperated look. She mouths an apology and I know I'll be thinking about the way her lips moved all night.

"Pretty, pretty High Queen, come to rescue her High King," a high-pitched voice whispers, echoing through the trees.

"Can she save him? Will she dare?" another voice comes from the opposite direction.

Fear radiates from Mae like a beacon. I pull her to me, setting her in front of me and caging her in with my arms. I lean down, the scent of a flower I can't recognize wrapping around me, and whisper, "There are only two. Go free Marik, and I'll protect you. They'll come for you as soon as you're away from me, but I need to see them so I can kill them."

She looks up at me, and it takes all my willpower for my gaze to not drift to her lips. Motherfuck.

"Go. I've got you, Mae," I manage to say.

She stares at me for another beat of my heart and then leaves my arms. A high-pitched scream cuts through the silence of the night, and a cambion sprints toward her, reaching for her.

I hurl my dagger. It lands true. Right in the undead boy's temple.

Mae stumbles to Marik and begins working on the ropes that tie him to the tree.

Another cambion sprints from the trees, and I hurl a ball of fire toward it. But it dodges. Mae turns, and of course, makes eye contact with the cambion.

"Fuck's sake," I mutter, summoning my shadow sword and severing its head from its body.

"You didn't tell me not to look at it!" Mae whisper-shouts.

I ignore her and motion toward Marik. "Hurry up. We need to go."

She saws at the ropes and the tension gives. "He's passed out. Can you carry him?"

Of course I can carry him. He's my brother. I've carried him through the barren wastelands below, just as he's carried me through the blackened coals that Father had us walk over. I toss him over my shoulder. "Let's go."

Elle and Luca are waiting at the front doors of the castle. They lead us inside, to the grand formal living room, and I toss Marik onto the couch. He's still limp, but I know he's fine. We've had so much worse. I just don't know how the hell a cambion knocked him out. There's got to be more.

But a cambion on the grounds...I've only ever seen them in the basement of our manor. And in the underworld. They are not something that most know about. They are nightmares, stories told to scare children. But they, like most nightmares, are real.

"Luca," I say. "It was a cambion."

The deer hybrid stiffens. "You're certain?"

I nod. "Three of them."

Luca demands that Mae tell him what happened, as if she's someone to be ordered around. And damnit, she does it. The burn on her forearm is still bright and angry.

A healer arrives and Elle points to Marik. I want to yell at everyone here. I step in front of my brother. "Mae has a burn on her arm. Can you look at that first?"

Mae scowls. "No. I'm okay. Look at Marik first, please."

I shoot her a look, but she matches it. Fine. If she wants to be stubborn and walk around with a hand-shaped burn on her forearm, she can be my damn guest. I move out of the way from the healer's path and stand beside Mae again. I should've stood by the wall. I need to stop listening to my instinct to be close to her.

That is only going to strengthen this need inside of me. Or maybe it will make it go away. That's what I'll tell myself. Giving in will make it go away faster. It will satisfy the itch I always get when I'm interested in a woman. I get curious, I satisfy my curiosity, and then I move on.

That's all that needs to happen here.

The fact that it's the High Queen shouldn't make a difference.

"He'll be fine," the healer says. "He was just knocked out. It's better to wait until he wakes naturally, which should be soon."

"What of the cut on his forehead?" I ask. *How did he get it?* I want to demand. Marik is a good fighter. How did someone land something on him?

"I would imagine he was knocked out, then taken to wherever he was kept. I'm assuming his head probably bumped against something in the process. Although it looks bad, it's superficial. I can heal it, though, if you'd like."

Maybe he was overwhelmed by cambions and then something else knocked him out. I dip my head. "Thank you."

She heals the cut and asks Mae to take a look at her arm. I tilt my head, ready for Mae to deny the healer. But to my relief, she doesn't.

I guide her to the couch, giving into the urge to place my hand on the small of her back. I sit beside her, my leg pressing against hers. Every instinct in my body is telling me to pull my leg away. Every instinct in my body is daring me to keep it there. I don't move.

"Prince," the healer says, "Would you mind going to get a bowl of cool water? Not too cold, but not warm or hot. I have the other materials with me, but the burn needs to soak in cool water before I can dress it."

I rise. I know exactly the temperature the queen needs. I'll never forget my first time. I was young. Six, maybe. It was days after Cora first waltzed into our doors. My hand balls into a fist whenever I think about her. When I think about how our lives changed after that.

I have no doubts that Father would have forced us to train without her. That he would have been ruthless in teaching us to become men. But Cora made it worse.

Cora showed Father there was another world for the taking.

That we had to become the monsters below to be their masters.

We were so young.

It's been at least a year since I last saw that bitch. I hope she's chained in some hole in the ground.

When I return with the bowl, I place it on the table in front of Mae and sit beside her. The healer gives her instructions to place the burn in the water. Her spine bends as her hand slips into the water.

"You okay?"

"It feels a little better. Still hurts, but not as much." She tilts her chin toward Marik. "You worried about him?"

Yes, I'm worried about him. I'm always worried about him. But not because he's passed out on the couch. "Nah. He'll be fine. It's not the first time we've seen these things."

I want to suck the words back in as soon as they're out. Cambions are not a Woodland animal. But Mae doesn't catch on.

"I've never heard of them," she says, "I didn't even know creatures like that existed in our world."

"They don't. Not really. They used to, centuries ago, but we killed them all." And then Mother and Father welcomed them back. "They're created and controlled by witches using dark magic."

"How did you know about them?" she asks.

Mother, she is so fucking innocent.

"Part of my training." Cambions, osseri, drabar, wraiths, Cursed, witches, mairdre, and a whole host of other things that would have her terrified to close her eyes at night.

"Thank you, Asmo. You came for me. I was so scared." Her voice is a whisper, and I harden my heart against it.

"You would have been fine," I say shortly. Because she would have. She would have figured it out. If she is who I think she is, she's a fighter. And a powerful one at that.

"I've never been in a situation like that. I thought I was going to die. I've been very blessed growing up the way that I did. When that...when that thing turned, and I saw her eyes, I tried to get away, but she wouldn't let go. And the terror I felt...I've never felt that. I froze. All I could think to do was scream. I don't want to think about what would have happened if you didn't hear me and come." Her eyes turn glassy again, unshed tears pooling at the bottoms and threatening to spill across her white freckles.

And that's all it takes for my heart to soften again. *Even if I hadn't heard you, I would have felt you.* I cup her cheek in my head and stare into eyes crafted of honey. "It's okay to be scared, Mae. It's okay to be terrified. It's what you do when you're scared that counts, and you were brave in the face of fear. You helped me save my brother. I should be thanking you, princess."

She doesn't scowl at the nickname, even though it's an insult. It's meant to prick at her. Instead, a tear escapes, and before I can think better of it, I swipe it away.

"Sorry," she says, blinking furiously. "I cry when I get frustrated, and I feel frustrated that I couldn't protect myself."

I scoff. "You can train for that. That's the easy part. The hard part is moving forward when you're terrified. You can't train for that. That's in here." I tap the space over her heart. "That's not something you can teach. You'll be fine, Mae."

"Thanks, Asmo," she says, and I swear she leans into my hand on her cheek.

Fuck. I can't help my smile. "Quit thanking me."

"Mae!" someone shouts across the room.

I yank my hand away. Ivan and Koa stroll toward us. That fucking pussycat of a party boy.

"I'm fine," Mae says placatingly, "I promise. Asmo saved me."

Damn right I did. Good for nothing—

"Thanks, man. I'm sorry to hear about your brother. He'll be okay?" Koa has the nerve to speak to me.

I stand and face him. "He'll be fine. Where were you?" My voice is low, but I know he hears every word.

"Excuse me?" he asks.

"Didn't this happen on *your* date? Where *were* you?"

"Asmo, he was passed out. It was the middle of the night when I left. This isn't his fault," Mae says cautiously.

"It doesn't matter," I snap at her. "He never should have fallen asleep with you. The fact that he could sleep deeply enough without waking up when you moved is enough to tell me that he's not the one for you."

"Asmo," she says quietly, and it feels like a warning and a threat and I hate myself for how much I love it. "I am fully capable of deciding that for myself."

But she's not. If she chooses him, then she's not fully capable of deciding anything. If she chooses anyone but me, then she's wrong.

I take a step toward her. She doesn't back down. "Does it not bother you that he didn't wake up when you left? That he had no clue you were gone? You're supposed to be the most precious thing to him, the only important thing to him. Yet he didn't stir when you left the safety of his side?" Fire, black and hot and writhing, burns through me.

"Hey, man—" Koa starts, but he shuts up when I whirl back to him.

Mae's hand closes around my forearm. I turn back, and the anger subsides. As much as she pushes me, I won't—I can't—I take a breath.

"I am a smart and capable female. If I want your opinion on how I should feel about something or someone, I will ask you. Until then, that is enough." Her voice is quiet, but firm.

I run a hand through my hair. I don't feel like fighting her on this. She's not mine to fight for. *Yes, she is.* "Fine. Whatever." Before I leave, I pause at the doorway and turn back to her. "I'll see you tomorrow, Mae."

ACKNOWLEDGMENTS

Are you kidding me? Another book down?

It's actually crazy how much goes into writing a book.

First, always, I want to thank my husband. The number of weekends he's spent sitting with me in silence while I edit is...far too many to count. Thank you for always supporting me and pushing me to do better. Thank you for making me laugh every day. My favorite thing about us is how much time we spend giggling. I love you.

Rachel and Jordan. Thank you so, so much for your constant support. You both have been incredible to bounce ideas off of. Okay, and fine, you've both been incredible friends.

To my alpha and beta readers. R.G. Wesley, again—the best alpha reader. Thank you for your corrective feedback. You continue to make me a stronger writer with every round. I yearn for your compliments, as rare as they are. (By the way, reader, if you made it this far—go read *The Strange Hour*).

To my beta readers—Nita, Amelia, Samantha, Jasmine, Caitlin, Anna, and Lizzy. Your feedback was instrumental in getting this book shaped up to what it is today.

To my editor—Pocket Edits. You are incredible!

Thank you to everyone who listened to me talk about *TLDQ* and had to suffer through a second round of ravings for *TFSK*.

And always, thank you to the reader. Thank you for sticking with Mae and her journey. Thank you for sticking with me in mine.

If the mental health aspect of his book resonated with you, please know you are not alone. It gets better, I promise. But if you ever need someone to help you until it does, don't suffer in silence. Reach out to a friend, a stranger, or even a hotline. It gets better, I promise. <3

Also by the Author

The Lost Deer Queen
The False Serpent King

9 798999 362001